EYES OF TOMORROW

BOOK NINE
OF THE DUCHY OF TERRA

EYES OF TOMORROW

BOOK NINE
OF THE DUCHY OF TERRA

GLYNN STEWART

FAOLAN'S PEN
PUBLISHING
faolanspen.com

This edition published in 2021 by:

Faolan's Pen Publishing Inc.

22 King St. S, Suite 300

Waterloo, Ontario

N2J 1N8 Canada

ISBN-13: 978-1-989674-12-3 (print)

A record of this book is available from Library and Archives Canada.

Printed in the United States of America

1 2 3 4 5 6 7 8 9 10

First edition

First printing: April 2021

Illustration © 2021 Tom Edwards

TomEdwardsDesign.com

Faolan's Pen Publishing logo is a trademark of Faolan's Pen Publishing Inc.

Read more books from Glynn Stewart at faolanspen.com

CHAPTER ONE

THERE ARE NO PLEASANT FINAL DUTIES OF A STARSHIP'S Captain. The best-case scenario was surrendering command to another. The worst-case scenarios were far more permanent.

"Scan complete," a borrowed technician told Captain Morgan Casimir. "There are no life signs aboard *Defiance*."

"What resolution did we run at?" the blonde officer asked. Morgan was in her mid-thirties, her promotions accelerated by a combination of war and her stepmother, the Duchess of Terra.

She'd spent most of her adult life aboard warships of one kind or another. First as part of the Duchy of Terra Militia, and then, after the first war she'd served in, as an officer of the A!Tol Imperium that ruled humanity.

The *!* was a glottal stop, humanity's pale attempt at the beak snap of their conquerors-slash-uplifters. The "A-tuck-Tol" were space-going squids—large and intimidating creatures like the technician she'd borrowed from Squadron Lord Tan!Stalla.

"Resolution was set at one-point-three kilograms," the tentacled technician told Morgan, the translators both of them wore handling the unit conversion. "The ship's working animals would have been detected."

"Good," Morgan agreed with a nod. She'd been surprised to realize how common having a dozen or so animals—dogs and cats aboard a human-crewed warship like *Defiance*—was aboard a warship.

Pests, however, appeared to be a universal factor.

The A!Tol technician was silent, turning back to her consoles aboard the shuttle orbiting Morgan's cruiser. The once-elegant starship was a broken wreck. Her flared wings were missing. Her spine was broken.

Morgan's command wouldn't have been reparable even if they were closer to home...and Tan!Stalla's fleet was positioned next to the Astoroko Nebula, on the far side of the Laian Republic from the A!Tol Imperium.

The Republic were allies, but Morgan had found *something* in the heart of Astoroko. Until someone else was in position to secure the Nebula, Tan!Stalla's thirty-two capital ships were the only shield the galaxy had against that threat.

And Morgan was wasting time.

"Fire in the hole," she whispered, tapping a command on her personal tablet.

Eight one-gigaton antimatter charges detonated simultaneously. Placed inside *Defiance*'s compressed-matter armor, the scuttling charges incinerated her interior systems instantly. The almost-unbreakable armor plates, robbed of their supports, scattered into space a few moments later.

And with that, Morgan's command was gone. With *Defiance*'s death, Morgan no longer had a duty station. Given the fleet of insane bioships she'd discovered inside the Astoroko Nebula, though, she doubted she was going to get time to cool her heels.

"Take us back to *Jean Villeneuve*," she ordered. "I have an appointment with the Squadron Lord."

JEAN VILLENEUVE WAS NAMED for Morgan's honorary uncle, the French Admiral who had commanded Earth's defense *against* the A!Tol—and then commanded a mixed Militia-Imperial force to defend the system against two later attacks before his death.

Given everything Jean Villeneuve had been, Morgan agreed with the decision to make his namesake part of the five percent of the Imperial Fleet that had mixed-race crews. Squadron Lord Tan!Stalla was an A!Tol—the Tan! marked her as a relative of the Empress—but even her command staff had members of three races in it.

Her chief of staff, for example, was Ivida. Prott was short for his race, with darker red skin than most, but he had the unmoving facial features and double-joint limbs of his people.

Prott was the one responsible for leading Morgan to meet Tan!Stalla as she returned from scuttling her ship. He seemed to understand roughly where Morgan was mentally and didn't attempt to engage her in conversation as he led the way through the superbattleship.

Finally, the Ivida stepped aside, ushering Morgan into Tan!Stalla's office. She took a regulation four steps into the room and crisply saluted the Squadron Lord.

Tan!Stalla's office was odd-looking to human eyes. Even for A!Tol, it seemed unusual to Morgan. There were sprayer systems set up along the walls, constantly misting the space with water. When Morgan had served as Tan!Stalla's executive officer, her office hadn't had those.

The A!Tol's old office had shared the massive array of screens and controllers that covered one wall, allowing the Squadron Lord to survey every aspect of her fleet as she managed systems with her sixteen manipulator tentacles.

"Captain Morgan Casimir, reporting, sir," Morgan said crisply.

"Have a seat, Morgan," Tan!Stalla replied. A manipulator quirked and a chair emerged from a wall, trundling over to Morgan on powered wheels. "I've reviewed your report and we've discussed this, but..."

The A!Tol shivered, her skin darkening. The species wore their emotions on their skin, the colors shifting with their moods.

A tentacle flickered at the display.

"Your opinion on our ability to maintain containment, Captain," the Squadron Lord asked calmly. "Sixteen *Galileo*-class superbattleships and sixteen *Bellerophon*-C-class battleships against what you saw."

Morgan looked at the screens, picking out the warships of Tan!Stalla's command. A surprisingly large amount of Imperial warship design had taken place in Sol over the last thirty years, with the Imperium using technology they'd begged, borrowed, and stolen from across the galaxy to rapidly upgrade their military.

Ton for ton, the *Galileo*s could stand against any other fleet in the galaxy, and the *Bellerophon*-Cs weren't far behind them...but...

"Our best guess is that there were at least fifty Alavan mothership shells still present in the nebula," Morgan noted quietly. "Each of those was at least one thousand kilometers in diameter...and appeared to have been *completely* subsumed by an Infinite bioform."

That was what the creatures had called themselves. The Infinite.

"Scans suggested the presence of somewhere in excess of ten thousand other bioforms of various sizes," she continued. "We did not have time to resolve distinctions between bioforms other than the apparent main form in the eye of the nebula, but all of the bioforms demonstrated an unknown reactionless engine and the ability to organically produce plasma weaponry comparable to our plasma lances."

She shook her head.

"The largest had the ability to produce targeted microsingularities at high percentages of lightspeed," she finished. "The threat parameter of the overall Infinite fleet is difficult to judge, and there is an open question of how many bioforms they will be able to equip with hyperdrives, but..."

"Our chances are low," Tan!Stalla concluded.

"I will need to run more numbers based on our scan data, sir," Morgan admitted. "But my expectation would be that even one of the bioforms wearing an Alavan compressed-matter-armor shell could take on this entire fleet."

"You will need to run those numbers," the Squadron Lord agreed. "We have data from the Laians on what one of their mobile shipyards *should* be carrying, but..."

"Do we know what *this* one was carrying?" Morgan questioned in the silence Tan!Stalla left.

Builder of Tomorrows was the Laian mobile shipyard in question, an FTL-capable space station designed to repair the Laian Republic's two-hundred-megaton war-dreadnoughts on the move. Accompanied by a mixed force of Laian and Wendira capital ships, its owners had been trying to provoke a war between those two Core Powers.

Their plan had been to use the war as cover to find a semi-mythical fleet of ships belonging to the long-dead Alavan Precursors. They'd succeeded in finding that fleet...and might have just doomed *everyone*.

"Not with certainty," the Squadron Lord admitted. "You will have access to all of the data we possess. I need some idea of what's coming at me, Captain, and that will be your task."

"My task, sir?" Morgan asked.

"I have a full staff, but they have not encountered these Infinite," Tan!Stalla told her. "I am adding you to my staff as a special advisor on this threat. I recommend you pull together a team of tactical and engineering specialists.

"I want you to go over everything you learned and put together a threat assessment. A realistic one, even if I expect that to be utterly terrifying.

"We know very little about what we have found—but without knowing more, all we can do is stand guard where we know the conspirators entered the nebula and hope the *idiots* managed to wipe their navigation databases."

Tan!Stalla's skin was a gray-black color that Morgan had seen before—but only during the darkest hours of the first campaign they'd fought together.

"Give me answers, Captain Casimir," she ordered. "And let us hope that your friend Rin Dunst is successful in convincing our Laian allies to take the threat seriously."

CHAPTER TWO

PROFESSOR RIN DUNST WAS QUITE CERTAIN THAT HE HAD almost no business being in the meeting he was in. The stockily built dark-haired academic was a xenoarchaeologist, a student of the fifty-millennia-dead Precursors who had called themselves the Alava.

His expertise had drawn him into far too many strange situations for him to say *anything* was unexpected, but he would never have expected to be present as the fate of two Core Powers was decided.

The Core Powers were the oldest and most technologically advanced species of the galaxy, all resident closer to the galaxy's center than the Arm Powers like the A!Tol Imperium. The Laian Republic was the Imperium's closest Core Power neighbor—and the Wendira Grand Hive was their age-old enemy.

"The presence of these bioforms is concerning," Princess Oxtashah of the Grand Hive stated. She was a Wendira Royal, a four-winged being almost two and a half meters tall with scales and wings of iridescent gold and purple. "They were a threat to the Alava fifty thousand years ago, and we are mere children against Those Who Came Before.

"But." A clawed arm waved at the other sentients in the room. "The Infinite did not kill thousands of my people's children."

"As we have provided more-than-sufficient proof, the deaths and violence here in the Dead Zone were caused by a rogue faction of *both* of your states," First Fleet Lord Tan!Shallegh said grimly, his skin the dark gray of a determined A!Tol.

Tan!Shallegh was Rin's boss today, the supreme commander of the Imperial Grand Fleet. Technically, they were there as allies to the Republic. But since it was the Imperium's officers—in the form of Rin Dunst and Captain Morgan Casimir—who had dug out the conspiracy and found the Infinite, the Fleet Lord was playing moderator today.

"Princess Oxtashah, we stand amidst a hundred dead worlds," the Laian member of the talks said quietly. Tidirok was the Eleventh Voice of the Republic—the eleventh-highest-ranking member of their entire military. The scarab-beetle-esque sentient spoke for the Grand Parliament just as thoroughly as Oxtashah spoke for her Queens.

"Your people and mine murdered these worlds," Tidirok continued. "We burnt stars and shattered systems in our anger and our hate. *Billions* died in the graveyard we stand amidst. Billions.

"We both came here with claims and righteous anger," he said. "But all I have left are fear and fatigue. Your people, manipulated by these conspirators, killed thousands of mine. My people, equally manipulated, killed thousands of yours.

"We have both reviewed Fleet Lord Tan!Shallegh's evidence. We were fooled. Do you doubt this?"

"Whether I believe it is irrelevant," Oxtashah replied, her wings folding in to reduce her size. "What is relevant is that the Queens sent me here to demand satisfaction for those deaths. This new threat is concerning but remains quiescent so far."

Rin wished he were as certain of that as the Wendira Royal. He'd left Captain Casimir behind, hoping the Imperial officer could find her reinforcements, and fled here to warn these people.

"We have had minimal contact from Captain Casimir and Lord

Tan!Stalla," he interjected. It *probably* wasn't his place to speak, but Tan!Shallegh had brought him there. He doubted the A!Tol had expected him to stay quiet.

"We cannot assume a *lack* of news means the Infinite remain contained," he pointed out. "They now possess a Laian mobile shipyard. We have no idea how long it will take them to adapt our hyperspace technology to their biology."

"I hope," Tidirok noted, "that even my traitors were wise enough to destroy *Builder of Tomorrows* before she fell into the Infinite's hands."

"We cannot count on that," Tan!Shallegh replied. "Since Dr. Dunst already revealed the situation in the Kosha region, I feel justified in saying our analysis suggested that the Mother had *already* reverse-engineered a biotech hyperdrive. She simply didn't have the power to open a portal to move her own immense body."

"But the Mother was a *sun eater*," he noted. "She was as large as the stars she consumed. The Infinite are not. I imagine it will not take them long to construct hyper-portal emitters—and even less time for them to mount the Laian technology on cyborg versions of themselves."

"They have already consumed and subsumed the hulls of an Alavan war fleet," Rin pointed out. "Those motherships were larger than anything our current technology could move through hyperspace: thousand-kilometer spheres of hyper-compressed matter. Even if all the Infinite retain from those ships is their *armor*, those shells make them dangerous to us."

"The Republic has accepted the threat," Tidirok said grimly. "I have communicated with the other Voices of the Republic. We are deploying other ships to reinforce Squadron Lord Tan!Stalla...but so long as a Wendira armada threatens our borders, *my* fleet must remain facing the Dead Zone."

Oxtashah snorted.

"You blame me for your lack of action?" she demanded. "But it is your own traitors who have delivered the key to escaping their trap into the Infinite's hands. Why, then, do you expect *us* to help *you*?"

When Rin had first delivered the news of the Infinite, Oxtashah had seemed sufficiently, well, *afraid* to allow him some hope. Now she'd clearly communicated with her Queens and received updated orders. He couldn't read Wendira body language, but he had to wonder if she was truly as determined to cause trouble as her translated words suggested.

"The Republic has learned not to trust your Queens without confirmed commitments and action," Tidirok told her. "I am prepared to forego *our* righteous demands for recognition and satisfaction for our dead if you do the same.

"As you have said, we are children before the might of Those Who Came Before. If we stand together, perhaps we can protect our people. But if we continue to glare at each other across the Dead Zone, we make ourselves vulnerable to an enemy even *gods* could not defeat."

Oxtashah closed her jewel-like eyes, bowing her head and allowing her antennae to droop.

"The Queens do not fully believe in this tale of conspiracy you have spun," she admitted. "They accept the existence and threat of the Infinite, but they—*we*—believe this conspiracy is an attempt by the Republic to deflect the responsibility for your actions onto an imaginary third party.

"We"—she didn't mistake the pronoun this time—"believe this is a crisis entirely of the Republic's making, and while we recognize the threat on our borders, we are not prepared to ignore the recent actions of the Republic's fleet."

"Are you mad?" Tidirok asked.

"You must be, if you think we will allow the Republic to brush aside our murdered children and call us to help you deal with the monster you have unleashed."

Oxtashah hadn't yet opened her eyes. She wasn't being *nearly* as effectively diplomatic as Rin suspected her Queens would like.

She was, unless he missed his guess, doing everything she could short of *begging* Tidirok to agree to her Queens' price.

The Eleventh Voice of the Republic was unmoved. He gazed levelly at the larger Wendira Royal and was silent.

"Are you all lost to reason?" Tan!Shallegh demanded, his skin a burnt-orange color of anger and fear. "There are single bioforms in the scans from *Defiance* that outmass your entire fleets, and you are arguing over responsibility?"

"My Queens do not believe we are responsible for protecting the Laians against their own folly," Oxtashah said. "*We* did not deliver a mobile shipyard into the hands of these Infinite. While we recognize the threat, we are not yet convinced it is directed at us."

Her eyes were still closed.

"We recognize the threat," she repeated, "so we are prepared to *assist* the Republic in this matter *if* our most recent grievances are laid to rest. This is the will of the Queens and, as such, is beyond my contestation."

That was as close as Oxtashah was going to get to admitting that she had no say in this, Rin figured. She'd been overruled.

"I will speak with the Parliament," Tidirok finally said. "But I suspect your demands will fall on closed ears, Princess Oxtashah. There were as many Wendira in the conspiracy that brought us here as Laians, after all."

Rin wasn't sure of that—but it wasn't like he'd stolen the conspirators' personnel files while he'd been acquiring the data he'd used to find the Infinite.

It wasn't lost on him that *all* of this was his fault, either.

CHAPTER THREE

MORGAN WASN'T ENTIRELY SURPRISED TO FIND COMMANDER Bethany Rogers waiting for her when she found her new "office." The young redhead had been her executive officer aboard *Defiance* and was just as at loose ends as Morgan was.

"Captain Casimir," Rogers greeted her with a salute. "I'd say I was about to go looking for you...but in all honesty, I just found our new department myself."

Morgan grimaced.

"Not much of a department," she told her subordinate. "You're assigned to me? I haven't had a chance to check the personnel list."

"Seems like the Squadron Lord didn't want to break up the team and only had so many people to spare," Rogers confirmed. "We've got Lesser Commander Nguyen, too, but she's currently in sickbay. Stress breakdown."

Morgan didn't see any reason to *stop* frowning over that. Mental health issues were dangerous. She had her own appointments scheduled, but she'd also been kidnapped and used as a hostage at five years old.

She'd had a *long* time to learn how to be mentally resilient. Most people didn't have that...*privilege*. Lesser Commander Thu Nguyen had been the woman running *Defiance*'s guns and defenses. It wouldn't take much for her to blame herself for everything that had happened.

Morgan certainly blamed *herself* for it, so she could see how it happened.

"I'll check in with the doctors later," she told Rogers. "I imagine Thu isn't the only one of *Defiance*'s crew in need of support."

She gestured to the door they stood outside.

"Any idea what we've got?"

"It's a conference room and a couple million marks of processing equipment," Rogers told her. "Four of Tan!Stalla's operations staff to start with—and you've got a blank check to pull in our old people from *Defiance*."

"Not even an office," Morgan said, but she was smiling as she said it. *Jean Villeneuve* might be immense—two-point-five kilometers long and over twenty megatons of mass—but every scrap of her was already spoken for, especially with her serving as a flagship.

"I'm surprised they even found us this much," she admitted. "All right. Time to go work out how to politely explain to everybody just *what* we poked with a stick."

THE CONFERENCE ROOM was larger than Morgan had expected, but it had clearly never been designed for its current use. The long table intended to hold dozens of officers had been pushed against one wall.

The table's holographic projectors were showing a map of the Eye of the Astoroko Nebula, a natural pattern of half a dozen newborn blue stars that made a giant mess of local hyperspace. At the center of them was a stellar object most easily described as a gas giant —though it was likely a not-yet-ignited star.

That gas giant had been the anchor the Alavan fleet had used for its final jump to evade their Infinite pursuers, and was now home to the Infinite fleet. More displays around the room focused on particular sections of the familiar rogue planet, identifying regions and objects that Morgan's people had flagged as either Infinite or potential Infinite.

"Officer present," one of the four analysts present in the room rumbled. The speaker was a massive Rekiki, one of the largest of the race Morgan had ever met and with an unusual jet-black color. The Rekiki were lizard-like hexapods with their front third turned upright for tool-manipulation—much like the centaurs of Greek myth mixed with a crocodile, with long snouts that added to the crocodile impression.

None of the other three officers in the room were human either. A blue-feathered Yin, a bipedal race with a human-enough build to draw human eyes but black eyes and a sharp beak, rose and saluted crisply.

The third officer was smaller, the smooth, gray-skinned form of a Pibo. With few visible features, Pibo strongly resembled Earth myths of the Grays—a resemblance no one had yet explained, so far as Morgan knew.

The last was actually the largest of the analysts, large enough that they must have struggled to get into the room. Built like nothing so much as a four-legged barrel with arms on the sides, this particular Anbrai was a bright yellow that contrasted sharply with their black Imperial uniform.

"At ease," Morgan ordered. "Report. And introduce yourselves, for that matter." She held out a hand, palm-upward. "It's been a nasty few cycles and I'm not as caught up as I'd like."

"Lesser Commander Shotilik of House Rayana," the Rekiki introduced herself immediately. Only Noble Rekiki would automatically introduce themselves by their House, which meant that Shotilik was literally a natural herd leader, with hormones that would make other Rekiki inclined to follow her.

"These are Speakers Took, Ito, and Kadark," Shotilik continued, gesturing to the Yin, the Pibo and the Anbrai in turn. Each saluted.

"And where were you each poached from?" Morgan asked dryly.

"I'm an engineering officer from *Jean Villeneuve's* tech detachment," Kadark rumbled. "I have some experience working with xenoarchaeologists and xeno-technology intelligence analysis in a prior posting."

"That's going to be handy," she told him. "Though *tech* isn't quite what we're looking at."

"So we're seeing," Ito said. Their voice was very different from any Pibo Morgan had heard before, and she studied the small officer intently for a second. It was hard to tell—Pibo were relatively featureless and all much the same shade, but *almost* every Pibo Morgan had ever met had been neuter. Ito, however, was female, with a noticeably sharper pitch to her voice.

"I was in Commander Ashmore's operations group," Ito continued. "The Commander is Squadron Lord Tan!Stalla's operations officer."

"Thank you," Morgan told the Pibo woman. She hadn't actually known that, which was a damning sign for how not-caught-up she actually was.

"The Lesser Commander and I are both from *Jean Villeneuve's* tactical department," Took said swiftly, the Yin woman covering her breasts with crossed arms as she studied the two humans. "Commander MacWilliam suggested that this would be good for our careers."

"If we live, probably," Morgan agreed with false cheer. "If we don't, well. Do planet-sized living starships have careers?"

That chilled the mood in the conference room.

"Tell me what you've got so far," she told them. "I can see *Defiance's* data all over the screens, but that doesn't *explain* anything."

There was a long pause.

"I think we're still processing it all," Ito admitted. She tapped a command, zooming in one wall on the planet and on the immense creature that had lifted itself out to capture *Defiance*. "I mean, what even *is* this thing?"

"A sentient bioform well over one hundred thousand kilometers long, capable of engaging hostiles with plasma bursts, kinetic hits, and focused near-*c* singularity fire," Morgan told her crisply.

"And it is the *second*-largest such bioform we have ever encountered," she continued. "Do you have the data on the Great Mother?"

The room was silent and Morgan sighed.

"Rogers? I don't suppose you have it to hand? If these officers weren't cleared for that, they are now. On *my* authority."

She wasn't sure she had that authority. She did not care.

Rogers stepped over to one of the computers and started tapping commands.

"*Villeneuve*'s computers have it all," she told Morgan. "Just need to authorize and... Here we go."

One of the walls gave way to the image of the Great Mother.

"*That*, officers, is what the Alava created when they stole Infinite code and clones and created their own bioform," Morgan said quietly. "Just over two solar masses. Two-point-three million kilometers from tip to tail.

"It was a stellarvore, in a way I don't believe the Infinite are," she continued. "The Great Mother, the Great Womb, the sun eater... Its servants called it a bunch of things, but it was smart enough to talk a bunch of Imperial scientists into worshipping it.

"The Alava broke the Mother, I suspect," she told them. "She would not have thought or acted the same way as the Infinite and had Alavan *additions*. But biologically, she was fundamentally the same."

"Plains of fire and water," Shotilik whispered. "What do we... How do we..."

"First, I suspect we need a taxonomy," Morgan told them all. "Right now, the sheer scale and oddity of what we're looking at is making it difficult for us to do any analysis.

"We don't expect bioships. We don't expect singularity weapons. We don't expect to encounter creatures that lived fifty thousand years ago and fought the Alava. We need to get past all of that.

"I think we start by classifying. At the low end, we have the Servants, the small bioships the Mother provided her Imperial worshippers. At the high end, we have the Mother...and we have that."

Morgan gestured back at the creature that had lifted out of the super-Jovian at the heart of the Astoroko Nebula.

"The Queen," she murmured. "I don't think that's necessarily the mother of them all, but it definitely seemed to be *in charge.*"

The five officers in the room with her seemed to shake themselves as one.

"Size makes the most sense, I think?" Kadark suggested. "An exponential categorization, and then we break down oddities within each category."

"That makes sense to me," Morgan agreed. "Category One being the original Servants we encountered, so...roughly hundred-meter bioforms?"

"And then each exponent is another category," Ito agreed. "Category Two is kilometer-long ships. All the way up to..." The Pibo gestured helplessly at the screens. "Up to Category Eight, where we can probably put in everything over *a hundred thousand kilometers long.*"

"I think...I *hope*...we only need to worry about two of those," Morgan said. "And one of them is dead."

There was a long silence in the room as everyone looked at the image of the Great Mother.

"*How?*" Took finally asked.

"We fired a starkiller into the sun it was eating," Morgan said flatly. "And part of our job, officers, is to find a *better* solution than that to the Infinite."

AFTER TWO HOURS of going through the scans, the good news was that there were fewer Category Seven bioforms than Morgan had figured after her initial panicked flight. There were "only" eight bioforms that fell between ten thousand kilometers and a hundred thousand kilometers in length, and only one of those was more than twenty thousand.

Even the largest bioforms were still fascinatingly similar to the Servants Morgan had encountered in the Kosha sector. They had the same basic sperm-like shape, scaled up by half a dozen orders of magnitude. What limited spectrographic analysis they could do from *Defiance*'s data suggested they were basically the same material: an organic carbon-silicon amalgam in a crystalline form previously unknown to Imperial materials science.

Large and small bioforms alike could generate organic bursts of plasma, superheated jets of fusing plasma traveling at near-light-speed. That was where the similarities ended, though.

The Servants had used the same organic plasma to propel themselves, and it had been their only weapon systems. A small portion of the Mother's Category Two and Category Three bioforms, the largest she'd created, had been equipped with the same gravitational-hyperspatial interface momentum engine used by the Imperium—the interface drive.

The *Infinite*, on the other hand, used some kind of reactionless engine completely unknown to the Imperium. It seemed to lack the near-instantaneous acceleration and vector changes of the interface drive, but it *also* appeared to lack its hard maximum velocities.

And while they also used plasma bursts as weapons, the Category Seven bioforms had access to the weapon that had wrecked Morgan's command. Each of the C-7s had at least three projectors capable of firing near-c microsingularities, artificially generated black holes that had torn *Defiance* apart.

Eight Category Sevens was bad enough.

"I make it somewhere between two and three hundred," Shotilik finally concluded. "Anyone got it closer?"

"I can definitely identify two hundred and twenty-two Category Six bioforms," Ito said precisely. "Most of those appear to have been in what *Defiance*'s crew initially assumed to be an asteroid belt."

"We don't generally figure five-thousand-kilometer chunks of ice are going to wake up and start firing black holes at us," Rogers replied. "And, to be fair, we were distracted by both the Laian cruiser we were fighting and the fact that we'd just found the Alavan fleet."

"I suggest we classify the Infinite wearing Alavan shells slightly differently," Morgan told them. "I suspect the armor on those will change the threat level significantly—and we *know* that Alavan tele-porter-based weaponry can still function.

"The Taljzi had several forts online with the damn things, even putting aside the system at PG-Two," she reminded them. *That* had technically been a very confused refueling system... One that had wiped out an entire battle fleet of the most powerful warships known to exist.

"We need to expect that we're going to run into those in the Infi-nite's hands," she said with a sigh. "If we're *lucky*, they'll only show up in the Alavan spheres."

"Those are all at least one thousand kilometers in diameter," Kadark noted. "I'm including them in my Category Six list, though they're on the small end. Mark them separately as Category Six-A?"

"Agreed."

Morgan looked at the listings taking place and shivered.

"Once we're done with this, we're going to need to go back over every single scrap of footage from *Defiance*," she told them. "Because we need to *know* what each category of bioform threw at us. I know Category Seven and Category Six forms had singularity launchers.

"If every Category Five form has one too? This whole mess could be even worse than I thought."

CHAPTER FOUR

"I am leaving."

The translated words weren't truly a surprise to Rin Dunst, just a disappointment. The A!Tol on the video feed had brought him to Tan!Shallegh's flagship on her personal stealth ship, but she'd *stayed* on her ship.

Ki!Tana was extremely old, even for an A!Tol, and the price she paid for near-immortality was that she couldn't be around males of her species. Or females. Or, really, her species in general at this point.

"I wish you could stay," Rin told the big A!Tol. Ki!Tana had been a reassuring presence throughout this whole mess.

"Our...associates will require reassurance that all we say is true," Ki!Tana told him, referencing the shadowy organization that had recruited Rin and Morgan Casimir to find the people starting a war out there.

Rin doubted those associates had suspected any of what they'd actually found out there.

"Can you convince them to talk sense into their governments?" he asked. "The Wendira are being...difficult."

"The Queens have told Oxtashah there is a price for their cooperation," Ki!Tana said grimly, her skin dark gray. "I will bend the waters toward those who must hear. But there are no guarantees in this, my friend."

"Will you meet with Morgan?" Rin asked.

"There is no time," she replied. "I have old friends among the Laians, as well as our associates. I will head into Republic space to start and I will do what I can. You must do what you can here."

"I'm barely sure I even belong in those talks," Rin admitted. "And it's not like there's massive fleets here to send."

The gathering he'd interrupted had been intended to stave off a potential war along the Wendira-Laian border. Including Ki!Tana's *Dark Eyes*, there were only four ships there: a Wendira star hive, a Laian war-dreadnought, and an A!Tol superbattleship.

"But the people here have authority over those fleets," Ki!Tana told him. "The Laian and Imperial fleets along the Dead Zone are eleven cycles from Tan!Stalla. The Wendira fleet is sixteen. The next-nearest Laian significant deployment is *twenty-three*."

An A!Tol cycle was twenty-three hours and twenty minutes. Not quite a full day, but close enough that most senior Terrans had learned to switch between the two almost effortlessly—and Rin Dunst was a senior *Imperial* academic.

He'd spent most of his adult life away from Earth and other humans. He thought in Imperial time.

"I will do what I can," he promised Ki!Tana. "Morgan is in trouble if I don't, not that I need that extra motivation." He shivered. "I can't help but feel that the Infinite are going to *eat* us all if we don't stop them."

"That certainly seems to be their intent," the A!Tol agreed. "I will move the waters only I can swim. I leave you to move the waters you are already in. We will meet again in time, I hope."

"Gods speed you, Ki!Tana."

"And may the waters be warm where you swim, Rin Dunst."

TAN!SHALLEGH'S office aboard the superbattleship *Va!Tola* was sumptuous and well decorated. One wall was covered in a massive screen, subdivided into the usual array of windows of an A!Tol multitasking. The other two were filled with shelves holding art.

All of the artworks, Rin knew, were originals—commissioned from up-and-coming artists on the worlds Tan!Shallegh had brought into the Imperium, including Earth. The being the office belonged to had the wealth and power to have Picasso's or Michelangelo's original work removed from Earth for his pleasure, but instead he'd chosen to *support* Earth culture instead of steal it.

"Your companion once again flees without ever showing their face," Tan!Shallegh observed as Rin took a seat, gesturing to a screen showing *Dark Eyes* rapidly departing.

"You...understand her situation," Rin said carefully.

"I know exactly who Ki!Tana is," Tan!Shallegh agreed. A flush of red amusement flickered across his skin. "*Exactly*, Professor. A confidence I am not permitted to share, even if she has."

Rin looked at the Fleet Lord in confusion. There was some meaning there, he was certain, but he didn't have the context to pick it up. As a historian and an archaeologist, the feeling was familiar.

"You asked for me, Fleet Lord?" he finally said.

"Yes. We just received the first formal update from Squadron Lord Tan!Stalla," Tan!Shallegh told him.

He and Tan!Stalla were related—the Tan! meant they were both closely related to the Empress. What, exactly, that relationship entailed was beyond Rin. He had a decent understanding of what A!Tol family relationships looked like, but the Tan! were notorious about keeping a lot of those details off of public networks.

"I believed you would wish to see it," the Fleet Lord continued, tapping a command with a manipulator tentacle.

The multiple different windows on the wallscreen faded to black, providing a backdrop for the holographic image of a female A!Tol in the black harness of the Imperial uniform.

"Fleet Lord Tan!Shallegh," Tan!Stalla greeted them. The hyperfold communicators they used for portable FTL communications were faster than light, but they weren't instantaneous. Instant communication was only available to those at the massive, immobile starcom stations in major systems.

Still, this message had been sent barely eighteen hours earlier from the time stamp.

"This is an update to our earlier reports," Tan!Stalla continued. "We have, as reported, made rendezvous with *Defiance*. Unfortunately, Captain Casimir's command was beyond any possible repair-at-space.

"*Defiance* has been scuttled to protect her technology, and we have taken up a position on the course the traitors used to enter the Astoroko Nebula." A flash of purple crossed her skin as she fluttered her manipulators in a shrug.

"I lack the numbers to maintain a real blockade of the Nebula and must hope that the Infinite exit on the route used by their new captives." She paused. "We have no idea what the final fate of the conspirators was, but I must assume that *Builder of Tomorrows* is in Infinite hands.

"Captain Casimir has been assessing the threat level with a team pulled from my staff and hers. They have a preliminary report that I have attached to this transmission, but it is concerning. These are dark waters we swim in, and I fear for the survival of my command and the completion of our mission.

"Containment remains the best option against this threat, but I do not feel that my task force is sufficient to achieve that mission," Tan!Stalla admitted. "Reinforcements from any source are required by the swiftest currents."

She paused, her tentacles twitching.

"I believe, based on what we know so far, that the first wave of Infinite excursions will be scouting missions. They will be smaller ships and small in number. I have units in hyperspace, scanning for anomalies at all times, and hope to be able to intercept those scouting expeditions.

"That will keep the Infinite blind for a time, but true containment will require vastly more forces than I have to hand. You will
understand once you have reviewed Captain Casimir's report."

Tan!Stalla flashed the dark green of determination.

"We will hold as long as we can," she promised. "But every ship I
am sent will increase the chances we can hold for long *enough*."

The A!Tol's image froze, fading out to be replaced by Morgan
Casimir. Rin took a moment to just drink in the sight of his lover,
clearly alive. The slim blonde woman was perfectly turned out in her
black uniform.

Her eyes and her hair told the truth to him. Her hair was pulled
back in a ponytail, not the more complex short braid she favored, and
her eyes were just...tired.

"We have now spent roughly two full cycles working through all
of our scan data on the Infinite in the Eye of the Astoroko Nebula,"
she began, her voice precise. "We have established an identification
taxonomy with, currently, ten separate items.

"The base categorization is by size, beginning at Category One:
bioforms of up to one hundred meters, and rising exponentially.
Thankfully, we currently have only identified two Category Eight
bioforms: the Great Mother we encountered near Kosha and what we
are designating the Infinite Queen."

A holographic simulation of the monstrous beast Rin remembered from the Eye appeared above Casimir's left shoulder.

"All categories of Infinite bioforms follow roughly the same
overall structure as the Servants encountered at Kosha," Casimir
continued. "The Servants themselves represent a subcategory, as
they used organic plasma thrusters where all true Infinite bioforms
use an unknown form of reactionless acceleration."

New images appeared as she spoke, highlighting the Servants of
the Great Mother.

"For comparison with what we are looking at here, the Servants
are Categories One-S, Two-S, and Three-S. The Great Mother does
not appear to have created bioforms above Category Three.

"This, combined with our understanding of how she was made, leads me to the conclusion that the sun eater and her Servants may not be a useful data source on the Infinite...but they are what we have.

"The key secondary category currently identified among the Infinite bioforms is Category Six-A," she noted, a spherical image replacing the Servants in front of her. "While the other bioforms share a roughly spermatoid shape, the Six-As are bound into a spherical form by their defining characteristic: each of them has taken over the shell of an Alavan mothership.

"We have confirmed forty-six of these units," she said grimly. "Given the strength of the Alavan fleet we know the Infinite pursued into the Astoroko Nebula, we believe there may be more.

"The units will be significantly more survivable than the rest of the bioforms and may even be in possession of Alavan-style teleporter weapons," Casimir concluded. "The rest appear to be mostly armed with plasma cannons, with the Category Six and larger bioforms possessing a microsingularity weapon that defies our current ability to explain."

Tan!Shallegh's skin was dark with fear when Rin glanced at him.

"Currently, our best estimate is that there are eight Category Sevens and roughly two hundred and fifty Category Sixes," Casimir noted quietly. "We saw forty-six Six-As and approximately five hundred Category Fives.

"Category Four, with bioforms between ten and one hundred kilometers in size, is where we encounter units that are likely comparable in threat level to most capital ships of the Core Powers," she continued grimly. "Estimated strength is just over two thousand. Numbers in the smaller Categories could not be meaningfully assessed."

"Two thousand capital-ship equivalents and eight hundred more powerful than any Core capital ship," Tan!Shallegh estimated aloud. "What did we wake up?"

"I don't know, sir," Rin admitted.

Casimir was still speaking, and both of them turned their attention back to the transmission.

"The only good news I can offer is that none of the identified bioforms are capable of any form of FTL travel," she told them. "They are, as things currently stand, utterly trapped in the Astoroko Nebula.

"However, once in possession of hyperdrive technology, it is extremely likely that they will be able to create their own version of it. This *will* take them time, however..."

Captain Morgan Casimir visibly swallowed, then squarely faced the pickups.

"Based on the Category Six-As, I believe that the Infinite are more than willing to incorporate hard tech into their bioforms," she admitted. "I estimate that we will see a small number of cyborg-style vessels equipped directly with Laian hyper-portal emitters in the near future.

"Their numbers should remain low so long as the Infinite do not come into possession of significant amounts of the raw materials necessary to build more emitters. Most especially, exotic matter."

She shrugged.

"If we can restrict their access to exotic matter and exotic-matter-production facilities, that could limit their ability to provide FTL capability to their forces. On the other hand, I hesitate to suggest that a species capable of generating black holes on command lacks the ability to produce exotic matter for their own needs.

"The Laian hyper-portal emitter system is similar to most others I've seen," she noted. "Even putting aside exotic matter, it requires elements not easily found at the heart of a nebula. *Builder of Tomorrows*, of course, carries significant supplies of those elements—and is herself made of more. Since the Infinite will have little interest in building Laian-style ships, I suspect every portion of the traitor fleet that entered the Astoroko Nebula will be broken down to build hyperdrives.

"We are working now on estimating how many portal emitters that might enable them to build while they are...growing their own."

She shook her head.

"It will be a very vague calculation, even once it's done, but it will give us an upper limit. I do not expect that limit to apply for long. Based off what we know of the Great Mother, I would estimate it will take no more than one long-cycle for the Infinite to have significant numbers of biotech hyperdrives.

"And that is assuming the Infinite are *only* as capable as the Mother."

Casimir exhaled.

"Further detailed technical reports are attached to this, but the fundamental assessment is this: we are facing a force with a greater weight of firepower than *any* individual Core Power. They are limited in range due to the lack of smart or FTL weaponry, and in interstellar mobility due to the lack of hyperdrives.

"Thanks to their possession of *Builder of Tomorrows*, they will unquestionably work to fix the latter. Having engaged multiple modern ships in combat successfully, I suspect they will *also* work to fix the former.

"Keeping them contained inside the Astoroko Nebula will limit their ability to do both. If they break out and acquire significant resources at this point, I believe..." Casimir paused, and swallowed hard.

"It is the consensus of my analysis team that if the Infinite break out and come into possession of *any* average star system at this point in time, we will be facing an existential threat to not merely the Laian Republic or the Wendira Grand Hive...but to galactic civilization itself."

CHAPTER FIVE

THERE WAS A PERSONAL MESSAGE FOR RIN IN THE DUMP OF files from Tan!Stalla's task force as well. He took the time before Tan!Shallegh presented everything to the Wendira and the Laians to seclude himself in his quarters to watch it.

He didn't have a *lot* of time, but he wanted to see Morgan.

She looked sufficiently identical in the video she'd sent him that he suspected it had been recorded within minutes of the official report. This message *wasn't* official, however, so she was spending less effort to conceal her exhaustion.

"Hey, Rin," she said softly. "I'm sorry I didn't manage to send anything sooner. I hit the ground running here and... Well, I've barely slept. I'm recording this for you, then I have a message for Victoria, then I'm going to fall over."

Victoria Antonova was Morgan's girlfriend, the long-term partner she'd already had when Rin had met her. The recognition of their long separations had led them to have an officially open relationship —and Victoria was actually married to a third woman, while being *very* firm that she was still Morgan's partner as well.

Rin had been Morgan's technically-secondary-but-physically-present partner for a while now, but he still couldn't pretend he understood the full complexities of the situation. He understood enough of what applied to *him* to be happy, which was more than enough.

"I hope…" She sighed. "I hope you're doing okay. I haven't heard anything from *you*, either," she pointed out. "I'm getting everything filtered through the formal reports that Tan!Stalla is getting, but it sounds like things aren't going quite the way we'd hoped.

"I know you and Ki!Tana made it safely, and for that I thank whoever is listening." She smiled tiredly at him. "There's a lot of things to say, and I'm never sure what's most important. But I'm also going to bury some work in here."

Rin chuckled. He'd figured. He and Morgan had met dealing with the Great Mother, and *work* had always been at the heart of their connection, even as their personal relationship had grown.

"You know more about the Great Mother than anyone there," she reminded him. "You're the only person to have studied all the Alavan iconography and suchlike we have on it, too. You know more about that thing than any of us, and I think that's relevant right now.

"But the differences between the Infinite and the Mother might be more important. I don't know enough… I don't have enough data here to guess what those are beyond the basic technical distinctions.

"That the Mother didn't birth bioforms with reactionless drives and singularity guns tells me she was missing *something*. You… I don't know, but you could probably say if that was intentional or not."

There was a long pause, which Rin used to consider the suggestion.

"I'm glad you're safe," she repeated. "My understanding is that Tan!Shallegh wants you as his advisor, so I won't see you soon. Hopefully before too long, but hopefully for good reasons."

She forced a smile, but he could *tell* it was forced.

"Sorry, I…meant to have more to say, but I'm wiped." She blew the recorders a kiss. "I need to record for Victoria before I collapse. Talk soon."

The image faded away, leaving Rin with both a heart-aching sense of longing...and a mind whirring with possible interpretations of the data they had on the Great Mother's birth.

———

HIS BRAIN WAS STILL WHIRRING as Tan!Shallegh played a condensed version of Morgan's report for Tidirok and Oxtashah.

"We have time," Tidirok finally noted. "That is good news. We have ships coming up from the core fleets as we speak."

"Forgive me, Eleventh Voice, but my understanding is that the entire Laian Republic fleet only numbers about six hundred war-dreadnoughts, correct?" Tan!Shallegh said. "One hundred twenty billion tons of capital ships?"

Tidirok's eyes flickered toward Oxtashah.

"Something like that," he conceded grimly.

Rin suspected Tan!Shallegh was being intentionally vague.

"There are *single bioforms* in the Astoroko Nebula that outmass your entire fleet, armed with weapons that can fire black holes at your ships," Tan!Shallegh noted. "How do you plan on containing that once the Infinite *do* have hyperdrives?"

"Carefully," Tidirok replied. "And with friends. It would be *easier* if I was not also watching the border for the Wendira."

And that was why everyone was still *there*. The Wendira used hundred-million-ton star hives, supercarriers stuffed full of close-range starfighters piloted by short-lived Drones, instead of the war-dreadnoughts—but Rin's understanding was that the hundred-and-twenty-billion-ton number was probably about right for them, too.

"I have made the Queens' position clear," Oxtashah said calmly. "Once the Republic takes responsibility for the actions of its officers along the Dead Zone and provides appropriate recompense, then we will be prepared to consider discussions around a shared containment protocol.

"As you yourself said, we have time. The A!Tol data suggests one of their long-cycles before the creatures will be able to leave the Nebula in force."

"That is extremely optimistic," Rin interrupted, his thoughts around Morgan's words having clicked together into a final point. "That estimate is based on the known capabilities of the Great Mother, the sun eater.

"But you have to understand what the Great Mother *was*."

Oxtashah's wings flicked wide in irritation, but Tidirok held up a claw.

"Princess Oxtashah, Professor Dunst is the A!Tol Imperium's foremost expert on Those Who Came Before," he noted. "More, he is the *only* expert on this creature. Please, Professor."

He gestured for Rin to continue.

"The Great Mother was a product of a rogue Alavan faction," Rin said quietly. "They had samples and potentially even live specimens of the Infinite, and they were attempting to co-opt Infinite biotechnology for their own purposes.

"We saw two major instances of this: the cloning facility the Taljzi used to turn a few dozen transports of refugees into an expansionist empire that threatened both the original Kanzi nation and the Imperium, and the Great Mother itself.

"The cloner was an interesting example. It predates the Mother and was based on a brute-force duplication of Infinite biotech. While the cell structure is the same—it's clearly based on cloned Infinite organs—it was both a sophisticated and a crude adaptation at the same time.

"It was also, without question, completely non-sentient," he said. "At its full extent, after several hundred years of the Taljzi feeding it every scrap of organic matter they could acquire, it could be argued it was a Category Five bioform. But because it was based on cloned *organs*, not cloned entities, it did not think. It simply duplicated whatever was fed into it—and did so far more perfectly than any cloning technology available to our current galactic civilization.

"In the cloner at Arjtal, we see what that rogue Alavan faction was trying to perfect: Infinite biotech *without* Infinite minds."

Rin now had everyone's attention, a situation he was used to...but not at *quite* this level of political power. He concealed a swallow, realizing that his next words could change the course of the next few months...and could decide whether the Infinite were actually contained or not.

No pressure at all.

"They created the entity we now call the Great Mother as a local self-sustaining defense node," he told them. "The creature's purpose was to draw on the mass and energy of a star to assemble a fleet that would protect a system against low-grade threats.

"I suspect that the ships it originally could make were more in line with Alavan warships than the ones it made to face us," Rin noted. "Certainly, the Servants would have been almost useless against an Alavan mothership.

"But the key thing to realize is that the Great Mother was born with a *computer* for a brain," he said. "We can see it in the iconography and images we have from the Alavan structures in the region. They were impressed with themselves for managing it, but the Mother was never intended to be independently intelligent.

"She had a control center, manned by an Alavan crew, roughly the size of a Wendira star shield," he told them. His audience would be more familiar with the ten-megaton warships the Wendira used as star hive escorts than they would be with A!Tol battleships.

"Like all other Alavan technology, that control center died when their systems broke," Rin concluded. He didn't know if his audience was aware of exactly how that had happened—*he'd* heard the Mesharom story of a dangerous experiment to modify the laws of physics to accelerate their ships.

An experiment gone very wrong, to the point where all Alavan computers stopped working—including the ones they'd installed in their own heads.

"Without its control center, the Mother had no mind of its own," he told them quietly. "It still fed on the star, however, and it eventually got bigger. A *lot* bigger—enough bigger for the intentionally shriveled leftover of its brain to become sentient in its own right.

"The Great Mother was not raised by Infinite. By their standards, she was basically a lobotomized child," he noted. "I would guess that she basically recreated the concept of the Servants from fragments of her pre-sentience memories.

"The Infinite did not come to awareness alone in the dark," Rin told his audience. "They were never lobotomized or damaged or built to be a *tool*. They will be smarter and more capable than the Mother was.

"And, as we pointed out, all evidence was that the Mother created organic hyper-portal emitters within six months," he concluded. "If you assume it will take the Queen that long, you are risking a *lot*.

"You are assuming that the peak specimen of a species will have the same abilities as that species's lobotomized giants."

He shook his head.

"Whatever time you expect the Infinite will take to be ready, they will be ready faster," he said quietly. "We cannot judge the Infinite by the bastardization of their cloned flesh the Alava built."

The room was silent.

"I see," Oxtashah said quietly. "I... My Queens are stubborn. I will speak with them. But I also sense an answer that I think we might have all missed."

"Highness?" Rin asked.

"If that is what the Alava did to the Infinite, no wonder the two were at war."

CHAPTER SIX

BEING IN COMMAND OF A SPECIAL ANALYSIS TEAM LEFT Morgan's position on the flag bridge in a certain degree of question. She wasn't part of the Operations department, so she didn't have a station there. She wasn't part of Communications or Logistics or...

Fortunately, the Imperium designed their flag bridges with some flexibility. Morgan's job was to provide advice and context to their encounters with the Infinite, which meant she needed to be available to the Squadron Lord when things went down.

"It's confirmed," Commander Nitik, the Ivida woman who headed up Tan!Stalla's communications team, announced. "A task group of war-dreadnoughts is being detached from the First Defense Fleet."

"The Wendira finally saw sense, did they?" the A!Tol task force commander said with a flush of purple relief.

"Reading between the lines, they're still swimming around the point, but they've given the Laians enough assurances that the Voices are ordering ships our way," Nitik replied. "Ten war-dreadnoughts and fifty cruisers are due to arrive in ten cycles."

Morgan concealed a sigh of relief. Their task force was half made up of *Galileo*-class superbattleships, which punched well above their weight even by Core Power standards, but a war-dreadnought was ten times bigger than the Imperium's best capital ships.

Well, *active* capital ships. Morgan's father ran the Duchy of Terra's military shipyards, the home of much of the A!Tol Imperium's experimentation. She was well aware of the new leviathan-type warships—but none of those fifty-plus-megaton behemoths were scheduled to enter service in the next long-cycle.

And the Laians already had hundreds of two-hundred-megaton behemoths. *Jean Villeneuve* and her sisters might outrange the Laian warships, but nothing the Imperium had could take a hit like a war-dreadnought.

"More ships from their core fleets are due five cycles after that," Commander Ashmore pointed out. "Fifteen cycles and we'll have thirty war-dreadnoughts here."

"At that point, I might start to relax," Morgan said dryly. "*Maybe.* Thirty war spheres would make me happier."

"Assuming they were on our side."

Morgan wasn't sure exactly which one of Ashmore's subordinates had muttered that, but she couldn't disagree. The Taljzi—a xenocidal offshoot of the Imperium's long-running enemies, the Kanzi Theocracy—had represented the threat they had because of Alavan technology.

That had brought the galaxy's Elders, the Mesharom, out to investigate. Forty of their war spheres—each the size and mass of a *hundred* war-dreadnoughts, at least—had arrived to "help."

Of course, the Mesharom had then realized the Imperium was experimenting with a slew of technologies based on scans of Mesharom and Alavan ships. The argument that had followed had stayed nonviolent. Barely.

The Mesharom had then swept off on their own and into a trap that had wiped out a fleet that could have single-handedly conquered any Core Power Morgan cared to name. Their involuntary sacrifice had spared the Imperium from walking into the same trap, but the

Mesharom had basically disappeared from the galactic scene afterward.

Condescending and reclusive as the big caterpillars were, Morgan would have given anything to see them back right now.

"No one has seen the Mesharom in a while," Tan!Stalla reminded her people calmly. "We can and we will deal with this situation ourselves. So long as we can keep the Infinite in the Astoroko Nebula, their threat is limited.

"The more hulls we have, the better for that—and I'm not going to swim away from handing responsibility for these dark waters over to a Laian officer!"

"HYPERSPACE ANOMALY DETECTED."

Three words. Just three words that sent Morgan's heart dropping into her stomach. A video link kept the flag deck and the bridge permanently linked together. At that particular moment, *Jean Villeneuve*'s Captain was on duty—but Squadron Lord Tan!Stalla wasn't.

Morgan was, in fact, currently the senior officer on the flag deck. The flag deck didn't really have a watch-officer structure in the same way as a regular bridge, so that hadn't occurred to her until those three words echoed over the link.

"Any details?" Captain Germain Arnaud asked calmly. Not only had the Imperium picked a human officer to command the ship named for Morgan's honorary French uncle, they'd picked a *French* man.

"Negative," the superbattleship's sensor officer reported. "I'm looking at the relay from the destroyer, and it's a vague contact at best. *Not* an interface drive...but something moving."

Even the destroyers in hyperspace were too far out to pick out a hyper portal opening in the eye of the nebula. Everyone had assumed, Morgan realized, that the Infinite would be just as detectable as their own ships.

"Do we have a vector?" Arnaud asked, his tone still calm and precise.

"Reverse of *Builder of Tomorrows*'s, it looks like," someone reported. "No clarity on numbers or...anything."

"Understood."

Morgan glanced around the flag bridge and realized the other officers were doing the same. Tan!Stalla was out of communication for the next few minutes—even alien admirals showered, or some equivalent thereof, after all.

"Ashmore, who are the destroyers on standby?" she asked the operations officer. She had enough seniority to give orders to the flag deck staff, at least.

"*Winding Road*, *Jambalaya*, *Kitorath*," Ashmore replied crisply. "Plus, *Starsong* just portaled back in with that report."

"All right." Morgan inhaled. She might be exceeding her authority, but *someone* had to act—both she and Arnaud could justify it, but *she* was the one on the flag deck who knew the Squadron Lord was out of contact.

"Nitik, orders to all four of those destroyers," she told the com officer. "They are to enter hyperspace and approach to closer contact with the anomaly. We need more detailed vector analysis and, if we can manage it, numbers.

"They are *not* to approach within the visibility bubble."

Hyperspace made a giant mess of sensors of every type. A hyperspatial anomaly scanner could pick up another ship passing through the chaos, but that was all. To see with any regular scanners required two ships to be within a light-second of each other.

A range at which Morgan was grimly certain the Infinite's plasma cannons would obliterate the destroyers she was sending out.

"Sending the orders now," Nitik confirmed. She wasn't questioning Morgan's authority to take action.

"And let's make sure Squadron Lord Tan!Stalla is advised the moment she's available," Morgan said dryly. "I'll send out scouts myself, but if the Infinite are coming...she needs to know the enemy are here."

TAN!STALLA was back on the flag bridge long before the destroyers returned, the A!Tol flag officer flickering tentacles in acknowledgement of her staff as she approached the stool that served as her seat.

She didn't seat herself, instead remaining standing in front of the big display as her manipulator tentacles fluttered with a level of concern Morgan had rarely seen on her superior before.

"They are not going to exit hyperspace near us," she finally told her staff aloud. "There is no one else along the vector we are seeing, which means it is almost certainly the Infinite."

The two thoughts were disconnected, but Morgan saw the Squadron Lord's point.

"Your orders, sir?" Ashmore asked. His voice was *almost* level, but Morgan was the only person who fully *heard* him. There were no other humans on the bridge but the two of them, and everyone else was getting the operations officer's question through their translator earbuds. They wouldn't catch the slight tremor of fear in his voice.

"We will wait for the scouts to return," Tan!Stalla ordered. "But while we wait, the task force will clear for hyperspatial engagement."

"Understood," Ashmore confirmed.

Morgan concealed her grimace and began to pull up her analyses again. None of their reinforcements were there, which meant the Imperial task force was alone—and an Imperial task force gave up their two most powerful weapons in hyperspace.

Their long-range missiles worked by jumping into hyperspace to travel the distance to their target. The hyperspace missiles were fired through portals fully contained inside the warship, which made them useless outside of normal space.

Their main energy weapons were the hyperfold cannons, which

used the same transmission system as their hyperfold communicators to send massive pulses of energy across several light-seconds. Those, too, couldn't function in hyperspace.

"We don't know if they have an anomaly-scanner equivalent," she told Tan!Stalla as she pulled out their tactical data on the Infinite. "Their plasma bursts maintain integrity to about ten light-seconds and should do the same in hyperspace, but they're going to be at least partially blind."

"That's the first positive thought I've had all day," Tan!Stalla said. "How blind is 'partially blind,' Staff Captain Casimir?"

The A!Tol words for "Captain" as a rank and "Captain" as the commander of a ship were different. English didn't have that distinction, however, so the translator turned the rank of any non-ship-commander Captain aboard a starship to Staff Captain.

It was awkward, but there were a lot of awkwardnesses tucked away in the Imperium's astonishingly sophisticated translators.

"This first wave is almost certainly using Laian hyper emitters," Morgan told her superior. "They are quite possibly using Laian hyperspatial anomaly scanners as well—likely on the same ships.

"But they won't know what the data means as well as we do, which gives us a chance."

"Hyper portal," Ashmore reported. "*Jambalaya* and *Starsong* are back, sir."

"Let's get their report," Tan!Stalla ordered. "And confirm where the *other* two destroyers are before we take the fleet into hyperspace."

CHAPTER SEVEN

"The rising wind is that *any* movement in hyperspace appears to trigger some level of anomaly," Commander Voyun reported. The Yin officer was rigid-spined as he faced the pickups. He had to know his report was going to every senior officer of the fleet.

"The falling wind is that those anomalies are far weaker than those left by an interface drive," he continued. "We believe we have some resolution on the target flock, but the aggregate was only detectable due to the total mass."

Morgan had been afraid of that. She wasn't sure what logic the Infinite would use to pick the ships they cyborged up with hyper emitters and suchlike, but *she* would have put them on the biggest ships she could find—the Category Six-As, if that was possible.

"We estimate we are looking at between two hundred and three hundred individual contacts," Voyun continued—and the bottom dropped out of all of Morgan's theories.

"They should only have a dozen hyperdrives," she muttered. "*How?*"

"The largest contacts are, we believe, Category Four bioforms, with the majority being Category Three," he noted. "They are maintaining a steady velocity of approximately twenty percent of lightspeed along the course *Builder of Tomorrows* took into the Nebula.

"Without approaching within the clearer air of the visibility bubble, we could not learn any further details. *Winding Road* and *Kitorath* remained in hyperspace to maintain a lock on the enemy course."

"Understood. Forward your data to the analysis team," Tan!Stalla ordered. "Thank you, Commander."

The channel closed and Morgan watched new downloads flicker across her screen. She doubted she'd get more at first glance than Voyun had already provided, and she kept her attention on the Squadron Lord.

"Your estimate, Staff Captain?" Tan!Stalla asked Morgan.

"I'm not sure, sir," Morgan admitted grimly. "We expected approximately a dozen units cyborged with hyper-portal emitters moving forward to scout on their own, but..."

Hyper-portal emitters.

She sighed.

"I think we forget that not every ship needs its own hyperdrive," she told Tan!Stalla. Hyper-portal emitters were sufficiently easy to manufacture that no galactic power would dream of sending ships into hyperspace without them—but you *could* pass through someone else's portal.

"I would *guess*," she said carefully, "that we're looking at ten to fourteen bioforms with hyper-portal emitters, as we expected. Those units opened portals for larger bioforms to join them in hyperspace as escorts.

"Most likely, the emitter-equipped bioforms are also the ones with anomaly scanners," Morgan noted. "Which...presents an opportunity, I think, sir."

"We can't detect exotic matter outside the visibility bubble,"

Ashmore objected. "I see the logic, sirs, but without any ability to differentiate between targets except by gross mass...I'm not sure strategic targeting is even *possible*."

"It wouldn't be," Tan!Stalla agreed. "But we *do* have sensor drones, Commander Ashmore. We would not normally deploy them in hyperspace, as they are likely to be destroyed before they enter the visibility bubble.

"I do not think that the Infinite have sufficient understanding of hyperspatial warfare to realize the necessity. The elimination of the current generation of hyper-capable bioforms would render the rest of this force irrelevant."

The flag bridge was very quiet.

"Casimir, Ashmore. Work together with Arnaud's people to prepare a spread of sensor probes for hyperspace deployment. You won't have very long," Tan!Stalla warned grimly.

"Orders to the task force," she continued. "All ships will enter hyperspace and prepare to engage the enemy."

JEAN VILLENEUVE SHIVERED around Morgan as the superbattleship plunged into hyperspace. Fifteen of her sisters followed her, the massive *Galileo*-class ships spreading out into a four-by-four wall in the gray void.

A second set of sixteen ships followed them through, the *Bellerophon*-C class battleships expanding the wall into a fat cross as they moved onto the superbattleships' flanks.

Forty-eight heavy cruisers—all hyperspace missile–equipped *Thunderstorms*—formed up in front of the capital ships. It was a powerful force, but Morgan was painfully aware of the odds they were up against.

"Anomaly localized and on the tactical plot," Ashmore reported. "We are at one light-hour hyperspatial distance. Infinite force velocity has not changed; continuing on their vector at twenty percent of lightspeed."

"Bring us onto an opposing course and up to point-five *c*," Tan!Stalla ordered. "At ten million kilometers, the fleet will reverse course, match their velocity and hold the range."

Morgan nodded to herself. Her best estimate was that the effective range of even the singularity cannon was *maybe* three million kilometers—ten light-seconds. The interface-drive missiles in their magazines had a velocity of point-eight-five *c* and a sixty-second flight time—over *five times* that range.

Of course, their *hyperspace* missiles had a range measured in *light-minutes*, but they weren't available in this environment. The main battle line of the A!Tol fleet was heavily optimized for normal space engagement.

"All ships have the course locked in. We are advancing," Ashmore reported.

"Probe spread is set to launch at maximum missile range," Morgan reported a few moments later. "We are co-opting all of *Jean Villeneuve*'s launchers for the spread, one hundred and twenty probes.

"They'll have a two-minute flight time, and we need to hope that the Infinite force doesn't maneuver significantly in that flight time," she noted. "The probes don't have anomaly scanners."

They *did* have sensor probes with anomaly scanners, but those craft didn't have much *else*. Those drones were meant to be left in hyperspace as long-range observers, their data recorded and collected later.

Morgan could have used them to guide the rest of the probes, but even at fifty light-seconds, she figured she could control the spread well enough to put them inside a target six hundred thousand kilometers across.

"They *shouldn't* be able to maneuver that much," Morgan concluded aloud.

"Good." Tan!Stalla fell silent. She was still standing by her seat, studying the tactical display showing the fleet around them. All of their ships were within the visibility bubble of *Jean Villeneuve*, allowing them clean communications and sight.

Relayed sensors from the rest of the ships meant that their true visibility bubble was larger than it otherwise would be. Against a missile-equipped enemy, they'd deploy their defensive drones to spread it even farther.

The Infinite didn't have missiles or interface drives. In theory, the Imperials had more than enough of a range and maneuverability advantage to make this a *winnable* fight.

In practice, Morgan's team had finished their analysis of the mass of the anomaly heading their way. They couldn't definitively break it down by types or armament, not in hyperspace and not with their limited data on the Infinite...but there were over half a *trillion* tons of bioforms headed their way.

Versus the roughly seven hundred million tons of Tan!Stalla's task force.

"DRONES ARE DEFINITELY inside the Infinite's effective range," Morgan reported as her robotic minions approached the enemy. "They either don't see them at all or aren't registering them as a threat."

"Both are possible," Ashmore pointed out. "If they're using unfamiliar scanners that they've somehow plugged into their nervous systems...calibration's got to be a giant pain."

Morgan winced at the thought of wiring sensors into her brain—calibrating the systems the Infinite were bolting onto their bioforms was probably *a pain* in more ways than one.

"Visibility bubble in ten seconds," she reported. Truthfully, her probes were already on the other side of the Infinite and blazing into the nebula, but lightspeed delay was still a thing for anomaly scanners.

Her drones were programmed to turn around and come *back* once they were twenty light-seconds clear on the far side. She could track the probes, but she wouldn't have *any* data until at least one of them made it back into her com range.

"Visibility bubble," Morgan reported grimly. Alerts flashed across her screen as the long-range scanners made their assessment of her drones' fate.

"Infinite engaged the probes zero-point-five-six seconds after they entered the visibility zone," she told Tan!Stalla. "We lost twenty-nine before they left the visibility zone. Some of the Infinite are continuing to engage, which suggests they do have anomaly scanners.

"They just weren't sure what to make of the signatures of our probes."

She watched as more of her probes disappeared, grunting as the plasma fire appeared to cease around six light-seconds. "Forty-two probes destroyed, all told," she said. "Seventy-eight continuing on course. Six will detour back to us at maximum speed and should arrive in approximately ninety seconds.

"The rest will make another pass of the swarm in just over a minute."

"Understood," Tan!Stalla said calmly.

At that point, the Imperial force would be making Tan!Stalla's flip. They'd hold the range and pound the Infinite with missiles the bioships couldn't reply to.

The problem Morgan was concerned about was that the Infinite had fought her old ship. They'd fought the traitors with *Builder of Tomorrows* and they'd, presumably, won that battle as well as the one against *Defiance*.

The Infinite had to be aware of how short their weapons' range fell against those of their new enemies. Morgan had to anticipate what the aliens would pull out of their hat, and she was feeling frustratingly unclairvoyant.

"Sir," she said slowly, looking at the data rippling across her screen. They still couldn't localize the exotic matter in the Infinite swarm, but an entirely different thought had caught her mind.

"I recommend deployment of the Buckler platforms," she told Tan!Stalla. "We know they've mounted Laian hyper-portal emitters and apparently Laian hyperspatial anomaly scanners on cyborg units.

"I can't, now that I stop to think about it, come up with *any* reason they couldn't do the same with missile launchers."

The flag deck was silent, and Tan!Stalla snapped her beak in frustration.

"Darkest waters," she cursed. "All ships, deploy Bucklers *now.*"

"New anomalies!" Ashmore barked. "Range is thirty-five light-seconds and we have missile anomalies. Estimate one thousand incoming."

"Well, at least they underestimate us," the Squadron Lord said drily. "Buckler deployment time, please?"

"Forty-five seconds to first wave," Ashmore reported. He swallowed. "Seven seconds after missile arrival."

"Laian missiles," Tan!Stalla noted. "No faster than ours, but smarter and with better electronic warfare systems. Correct?"

"Can't say at this range," Morgan admitted. "But that's most likely, yes."

"Let's see if the missiles' brains make up for the Infinite's lack of knowledge," the flag officer replied. "All ships, adjust ninety degrees to starboard, increase velocity to point-six *c.*"

A ship with an interface drive could go from rest to point-six *c* in under ten seconds. Adjusting velocities once active took a bit longer, but not much. Morgan didn't pretend to understand the physics— something about multidimensional surfaces being used to create three-dimensional velocity vectors—but she knew what it did.

The Infinite weren't as informed. If Morgan had fired their salvo, she'd have spread out the angles, shotgunning missiles across space and relying on the weapons' maneuverability to bring them together in the end.

The swarm had fired them in one large bunch, aimed at the center of where they'd seen the anomaly of Tan!Stalla's fleet. Like the probes Morgan had sent at the Infinite, the missiles were blind outside the visibility bubble.

Missile hit chances in hyperspace *sucked*, but an enemy who knew the game would make sure at least some of the missiles made it close enough that their brains could find a target.

The Infinite didn't know how. Not yet. Their sudden vector change left the missiles to hurtle harmlessly off into deep space.

"Staff Captain Casimir. Do you have targets for me?" Tan!Stalla snapped.

Morgan was checking as the Squadron Lord asked. The first drone had just returned, and she was running through the data from the robotic spacecraft at a hundred to one acceleration. All she saw was gray void...and then there was something more.

"Not sure yet. Feeding full data from the drones to all ships," Morgan reported. "We need to ID the portal ships."

The first thing she realized was that they'd made at least *one* miscalculation. The lead bioform was *not* a Category Four. Eight hundred and fifty kilometers long and four hundred wide, it was unquestionably a Category Five—which meant that it *might* have singularity cannons.

They were pretty sure the Category Fours didn't have the black hole projectors. They were *not* as certain about the Category Fives. They might be about to find out.

"We have a Category Five," she reported aloud. "It does *not* appear to carry hyper emitters; I am not reading material quantities of exotic matter." She paused. "That might also answer the question of whether the Cat-Fives—or, at least, *this* Cat-Five—have singularity cannons."

New contacts were resolving even as she spoke. The probes had passed through the visibility bubble at seventy percent of the speed of light. She only had a bit less than three seconds of scan data until the second wave of probes reported in.

"I need targets, Staff Captain," Tan!Stalla pointed out. "Before they shoot at us again."

Morgan's team was running the data, and she double-checked the analysis herself at the Squadron Lord's request. It wasn't nearly what she'd like.

"We know what *doesn't* have hyper emitters," she admitted. "But we haven't narrowed down our exact targets. We'll have our second data set in a few moments; that should help."

"All right." There was a pause as Tan!Stalla made up her mind, then she gestured for Nitik to get her a channel.

"All ships, target priority is the Category Five bioform until further notice. Fire at will."

Hundreds of new icons appeared on the screen as the task force launched their own missiles—but Morgan's attention was riveted on the second salvo the Infinite had launched.

They didn't have the full hang of it yet, but they were learning a *lot* faster than she liked. The first salvo had been inside a point-one-degree cone at most. These were spread across a three-degree cone.

The Infinite had likely already learned that radio coms didn't work in hyperspace either. A lot of those missiles would be lost...but this time, some of them might actually make it into the visibility bubble of the task force.

"I have a vector change on the anomaly," Ashmore snapped. "They are now accelerating toward us. One-point-five percent of lightspeed per second."

At some point, the Imperium and their allies were going to get their hands on an Infinite to dissect, Morgan knew. If they could work out just what the ancient aliens were using for acceleration, that might change a lot of things.

It wasn't as fast to accelerate as the interface drive—but she'd already seen that it didn't have the same *maximums* as the interface drive.

"Any idea what our missiles are going to do to the Cat-Five, Casimir?" Tan!Stalla asked.

"They have no shields, but the bioforms we encountered at Kosha were heavily armored," Morgan told her. "They weren't up to compressed-matter levels, but it's entirely possible these guys *are*.

"They did, after all, fight the Alava—and the Alava were much better at creating compressed-matter plates than anyone we know."

"So, it'll hurt, but the big sparkshark is going to keep coming," Tan!Stalla said grimly.

Morgan wasn't entirely certain just *what* a sparkshark was—probably something native to A!To, the A!Tol homeworld, with an English name assigned to evoke the right image. The Squadron Lord's intent came through regardless.

"Most likely, sir."

"Please find me those portal ships," Tan!Stalla told her. "Because we have about forty seconds until they are moving *faster* than we are and start closing the range."

Morgan nodded and dove back into the data with her team. There were signs of implanted mechanical hardware on a lot of the smaller bioforms, but the exotic matter was the key. It was a fundamental component of the hyper-portal emitters—and the synchronization between emitters required to create a portal almost guaranteed that they had to have *enough* of them on one ship to open a portal.

"The portal they opened had to be big enough for the Cat-Five," she told Rogers. "That gives us a *minimum* amount of exotic matter. How much?"

Her former XO whistled quietly through her teeth. "Four-hundred-kilometer-diameter portal requires fifty emitters of the size the Laians use, so....umm...one hundred fifty negative kilograms."

"And we're seeing just over twelve hundred negative kilograms total?" Morgan asked. "So, six portal ships?"

"And they can't be the Cat-Ones," Rogers agreed. "They're just not big enough. If they didn't bolt them onto the big guys, then I'm guessing they're on Category Twos—cruiser equivalents."

"If we narrow it down to that, can you flag our most-likelies?" Morgan asked

"On it."

"Missiles inbound," echoed a report from Arnaud's bridge. "Three salvos in space. Estimate fifty missiles of the first will enter the Buckler perimeter."

"If we can't handle fifty missiles, we all need to go back to school," Tan!Stalla replied. "Keep up the evasive maneuvers. I do *not* want that Category Five within plasma range of this fleet!"

The range was dropping. Not quickly—not yet—but the Infinite had enough acceleration to keep up with the task force's evasive maneuvers.

Even as Morgan joined her team in going through the data on the midsized Infinite bioforms, part of her mind was doing the math on the closing speeds.

The faster they found the portal ships, the better—because Morgan Casimir wasn't sure they could stay out of the Infinite's range for long!

"THERE," Morgan exclaimed as the last pieces of her analysis fell into place. "Rogers, double-check that. I've got a three-hundred-meter Category Two that's reading negative mass numbers at the right level.

"Check my numbers."

The negative mass of exotic matter was relatively straightforward to detect with any of the sensors available to the Imperium—but with *so many* contacts in a relatively short period of time, picking out that signature from everything else going on was a pain.

"Running the data," Rogers replied. "Got it. Sixteen percent metal by mass, almost ten percent more than the rest of the Twos. One hundred sixty kilograms negative mass. That's our portal ship and probably our anomaly-sensor platform."

"Take the pattern, ID the others," Morgan ordered. She ran one last set of analyses, an almost-automatic matching of the drone sensor data to the hyperspace anomalies, then turned to rest of the flag bridge.

"Squadron Lord, we have a target," she reported. "Using the signature to ID the others, but we definitely have a line on one of the portal ships. Passing it to Operations."

"Got it," Ashmore reported. "Transferring to all ships."

He paused.

"I hope this one is less tough than the big guy," he said. "Because I *think* the Cat-Five is falling back, but we've put *thousands* of missiles into the bastard."

"It's one-tenth a percent of the Cat-Five's size," Morgan pointed out. "It should be a *lot* less tough."

"The good news is they've stopped shooting missiles at us and they didn't manage anything with them," Tan!Stalla noted. "The bad news is that we have about five minutes before we're in plasma-lance range...and probably the Infinite's plasma range.

"So, make sure all of the tactical departments have those targets, Ashmore. We are not playing with these people in plasma range."

Morgan held her tongue as she checked the math. Even if they took out every portal unit, there were still dozens of Infinite bioforms closing on the fleet. The Category Three units were a bigger threat than the Category Twos.

If the portal ships were the only ones with anomaly scanners, they had a chance after taking them. But that was a big *if*.

"Multiple hits from the first salvo on the portal ship," Ashmore reported. "Anomaly is...gone. The bioform might still be with us, but she's not moving anymore."

New icons popped up on Morgan's display before anyone could ask, and she tapped a command.

"Sending you the targets for the other portal ships," Morgan told him. "We think there's only five left, but we're flagging ten, as target identification isn't perfect."

"We didn't need the entire fleet's missiles to kill the last one," Tan!Stalla noted. "Split our fire, get them *all*. Then we can assess the rest of the fleet."

Morgan realized a new marker had added itself to the main tactical display. There were no features or geography to hyperspace, so all that was on that display were the maneuver cones of the Imperial task group and the closing Infinite bioforms.

The new marker was a countdown, tracking the minutes until the Infinite units entered their estimated range of their ships. There were only three and a half minutes left.

"Fleet navigation will stand by for my orders," Tan!Stalla noted. "*Running* doesn't seem to be working, but I have an alternative plan.

"But kill me those portal ships, please."

Thirty-two capital ships and forty-eight cruisers of the A!Tol Imperial Navy fired a *lot* of missiles, even limited to the systems that worked in hyperspace. The Infinite lacked the maneuverability of interface-drive ships, making them easier targets in hyperspace.

"We got four of them," Ashmore reported as the Imperial missiles struck home. "Still six targets on the board, but next salvo is already inbound."

Morgan checked the timer. They had time. In theory...but she wasn't sure what happened *after* the portal ships were gone. There was still a *fleet* of ships sixty to a hundred *kilometers* across, heading their way.

"All targets down, all targets *down*," Ashmore barked. "Casimir, what's our chances?"

"Ninety-five percent we got them all," Morgan replied. "It's *possible* we mis-IDed one, but there's no way to tell now."

"Then we take the chance," Tan!Stalla ordered. "*Villeneuve* Navigation, confirm: we have exited the Astoroko Nebula's hyperspace shadow, correct?"

"Yes, sir," one of Arnaud's officers replied. "We estimate we are least a light-month outside the nebula."

"Good. All ships will open portals and transition to regular space in half a thousandth-cycle," Tan!Stalla ordered. "This collection is trapped in hyperspace. I am *not* risking this fleet to deal with them now!"

CHAPTER EIGHT

The countdown timer on the screen was down to its last half-minute when the portals flared to life in front of the Imperial warships. The destroyers, almost irrelevant in the missile exchange that had just occurred and *definitely* irrelevant in a plasma exchange, went first.

Then the heavy cruisers. Then the battleships. Morgan suspected half of the flag bridge was holding their breath as a group when *Jean Villeneuve* finally flashed through her own portal and plummeted back into the void of deep space.

"Watch for portals," Tan!Stalla ordered. "If we estimated wrong, this could get messy fast."

Morgan went right back to holding her breath. The team that might have got things wrong was *hers*—if they'd missed even a single portal ship, the entire Infinite strike force might come out of hyperspace on their head.

On the other hand, in normal space with hyperspace missiles and hyperfold guns, they'd potentially be able to wipe out any remaining portal ships and flee back into hyperspace again. They just wouldn't do so without paying for it.

"No portals on the screens," Ashmore reported. "Anomaly scanners suggest that the enemy may be slowing into position around us. Hard to tell just yet."

The irony of anomaly scanners was that they could still track FTL ships from normal space—but they tracked that data with a regular lightspeed delay. That had been useful for Earth, prior to joining the Imperium, when an array of scanner satellites had allowed them to locate Imperial worlds before they ever knew what they were looking at.

Right now, they'd be able to detect the Infinite fleet coming back toward them...but they wouldn't know until the enemy was right on top of them, separated only by an impenetrable barrier of reality.

"Keep an eye on them; hold the fleet at battle stations," Tan!Stalla ordered. "Nitik, get a hyperfold pulse to the main fleet ready. Dump everything we've got. The Laians need to know there's a fleet wandering loose in hyperspace in the region as their reinforcements approach.

"Even if the Infinite are blind now, our allies will need to be careful."

Morgan was already going over the data of the last thousandth-cycle or so they'd been in hyperspace, and she shook her head as the Squadron Lord spoke.

"They're not blinded, sadly," she reported. "We definitely got the portal ships, but they were still tracking us after the portal units went down. I'd guess several of the larger units also had anomaly scanners."

"It was worth a hope," Tan!Stalla replied with a flush of purple disappointment. "But those are the waters I anticipated. If they truly had been blind, we could have stuck in hyperspace and bled them until we ran out of missiles.

"Maybe even risked a plasma engagement. But..."

She fluttered her tentacles.

"Prott?" Tan!Stalla turned to her chief of staff. "Once we stand down from battle stations, I'll need a coordinated meeting with all of the Captains. We got out of this bloodlessly, but we're also trapped in normal space for the moment.

"Let's learn what we can from the experience. Getting *out* of here is going to be an entirely different storm."

A TWENTIETH-CYCLE—A bit over an hour—later, it was clear that the Infinite didn't have any portal ships left. It was also clear that they knew *exactly* where the Imperial fleet had gone back into normal space, their anomalies leaving measurable wakes as they flickered around Tan!Stalla's fleet.

The virtual meeting had a grim tone, one that Morgan shared. They'd achieved their mission and kept the Infinite contained, but now they, too, were trapped.

"Captain Arnaud, I know we've all mathed the swim out," Tan!Stalla said after the last officer linked into the massive conference. "Lay out the waters as your team has calculated."

"Comme vous voudrez," Arnaud replied.

His blip of French brought a momentary smile to Morgan's face. Everyone else's translators would have rendered "as you wish," but hers was programmed with her understanding of French—and the phrase reminded her of *Defiance*'s Marine CO, an intentionally prissy but overwhelmingly competent officer who'd insisted on scattering French through his English when dealing with his human subordinates.

"My navigators have run up a full course," *Jean Villeneuve*'s Captain continued. "The problem is inevitable, of course. They are in hyperspace. We are not. Assuming a minimum safe margin of distance between us and the Infinite of one light-cycle in hyperspace..."

He shook his head.

"We estimate a minimum of one month—thirty cycles—

underway at full cruising velocity," he concluded. "Hyperspace densities are always in flux, so even that may not be enough."

"And farther is better," Tan!Stalla noted, turning her attention to the hundred–plus faces in the conference. "Staff Captain Casimir, your assessment of our ability to engage the Infinite at close range."

Morgan wanted to grimace as everyone's gazes turned to her.

"In hyperspace, we are limited to plasma lances, proton beams, and interface-drive missiles," she reminded them all. "We've already fired off thirty-two percent of our sublight missile magazines.

"Based off our sensor data and our encounters in Kosha, it is a safe assumption that Infinite plasma weaponry is more powerful than our own," she said. "Without shields or high metal concentrations for the plasma lances' magnetic tubes to latch on to, we do not believe we have a range advantage over them. Lightspeed is lightspeed, after all."

The conference was almost perfectly silent, and she shrugged.

"Most likely, the Category Five bioform is capable of generating plasma pulses that can vaporize a *Galileo*-class superbattleship in a single hit," she told them. "The Category Fours can likely vaporize a cruiser—*if* they hit. Hyperspace is an awful targeting environment for any system.

"Unless they have something else we haven't predicted, their tachyon scanners won't work in hyperspace any better than ours do. We won't have instantaneous targeting—but neither will they.

"On the other hand, their firepower is utterly overwhelming at close range. I do not believe that this fleet would survive to clear the Infinite swarm's plasma range if we were to transit into hyperspace in our current relative locations."

If she was being entirely honest, she didn't believe the fleet would survive past the first ten seconds. A close-range engagement with the Infinite was *suicide*.

"So, what do we do?" Squadron Lord Exex asked. The Catach sterile was a chitin-armored mammal that resembled a cross between a human, a fox, and an insect. "If we cannot outrun and we cannot engage them, do we simply wait?"

"Our first wave of Laian reinforcements is due in less than eight cycles," Tan!Stalla noted. "We have not yet established contact with them via the hyperfold-starcom network, but we will be able to inform them of the situation.

"I hope to be able to have an actual conversation with Fifty-Sixth Pincer Korodaun, but that is uncertain at the moment," the Squadron Lord said.

To have that conversation, Korodaun and her fleet would need to exit hyperspace to allow them to directly connect via hyperfold com. Right now, their messages were being relayed to the nearest starcom and *then* sent to the Laian fleet.

"Even without direct planning, ten war-dreadnoughts is a far more equitable matchup with the enemy advance force than ours," Tan!Stalla continued. "Especially given that we *will* be aware once the battle is opened."

"Would we be wiser waiting for the second wave of reinforcements?" Arnaud asked, the Flag Captain raising Morgan's own thoughts.

"Most likely, yes," Tan!Stalla agreed. "And if I am able to have a conversation with the Fifty-Sixth Pincer, I will make that recommendation. *Twenty* war-dreadnoughts is better than ten. Thirty is better still.

"But I remind everyone that our objective was to *contain* the Infinite inside the Astoroko Nebula. The destruction of their first wave of portal ships achieves that goal. There is now an Infinite swarm trapped in hyperspace blockading *us*, but that force cannot enter normal space.

"They will be destroyed or they will starve in hyperspace," the A!Tol flag officer said grimly. "We have bought time for our Lain reinforcements to arrive. More ships will come in over time and we will secure the nebula."

"When do we move against the Infinite?" Division Lord S!Ra asked. The A!Tol commanded one of the escorting squadrons of cruisers.

"Not soon," Tan!Stalla replied. "Review the analysis Staff Captain Casimir's team did, Division Lord," she instructed. "Even range-limited by their use of ballistic near-*c* weaponry, the Infinite main cluster represents an astonishing threat level.

"Once the Laians are on the same page and have implemented a successful blockade of the Astoroko Nebula, plans can begin to be made to neutralize the overall threat." Tan!Stalla's tentacles shivered.

"I do not believe those waters will be cleared without more blood than any of us wish to spend," the Squadron Lord concluded. "But those decisions will be made at higher levels. Our task was to contain the Infinite until the Laians arrived.

"Unless something strange happens in the next fifteen cycles, we appear to have succeeded."

Morgan shivered. She couldn't disagree with her superior...but those were dangerous words.

CHAPTER NINE

"WE'VE TRADED CONTAINING THEM FOR CONTAINING US," Morgan's image admitted to Rin. "That's not the official word, but it's roughly where we are. They can't get out, but they've got a pretty solid plug in hyperspace keeping *us* right here.

"My team is busy trying to guess how quickly they're going to get their own hyper-portal system working," she continued. "We've got a few ugly little facts out of our close scan of the fleet that came at us, though, that I wanted to share with you.

"They *all* have some level of exotic matter in them. I'm guessing it's a critical part of what makes them tick—potentially even part of how they traveled FTL during Alavan times. Unfortunately, if they can produce exotic matter, very little of our tech is truly beyond them."

Rin didn't know about *that*, but he wasn't a technical specialist. He was a xenoarchaeologist and, outside the Alava, most xenoarchaeology sites didn't deal with hyper-advanced technology.

"Sorry to fill up our personal call with work," Morgan said after a few moments' silence. "It's filling my every waking thought, and Victoria isn't cleared for this."

She sighed.

"I did get your message," she noted. "I have to agree that it's dangerous to apply the Mother's abilities to the Infinite. We *know* they have to be more capable than she was in many ways. On the other hand, she was a hell of a lot bigger than even the Queen.

"Some stuff had to benefit from that." She snorted. "And work again. Sorry. I'd like to plan for what to do when we get back to Earth, but...I have no idea when this will be over.

"When it is, you and I are going home and spending time with Victoria and Shelly," she told him. "Well, maybe not Shelly. That's up to her."

Rin chuckled. He wasn't entirely sure how, exactly, Shelly—Victoria's wife—fit into his own relationship with Morgan, but he'd traded a few friendly messages with Victoria. Polycules were almost as hard to keep track of as departmental politics, even if there were fewer people involved.

Morgan blew him a kiss.

"I'm going to go get some rest," she admitted. "But if there's any fires you can light to get more ships headed our way, I'm pretty sure I can find a way to make it worth your while. Night, Rin."

She gave him an exaggerated wink and then her image froze.

Rin sighed and closed the video. He didn't know what levers he had. Most of the ones he could think of were better pulled by Ki!Tana or Tan!Shallegh, but he was at least *there*. His role seemed to basically be "advisor to the Fleet Lord," which at least put him in the room where things happened.

The truth, though, was that not much *was* happening—regardless of whether Rin Dunst said anything.

———

DESPITE QUESTIONING HIS VALUE, Rin joined Tan!Shallegh again. Every day since he'd arrived aboard *Va!Tola*, he'd joined the

A!Tol Fleet Lord in the armored and secured conference chamber deep in the superbattleship's bowels.

There, they met with Princess Oxtashah and Eleventh Voice Tidirok. There, they listened to the two insect-like aliens beat their heads against the same points of conflict again. And again. And again.

Rin had been there for over a month now. Tan!Shallegh had been there longer. The original need for the conference was clearly fulfilled—the two nations weren't shooting at each other.

Now the conference was about the Infinite...but the Wendira continued to hold their position that the Laians had to compensate them for their losses to the provocateurs who'd tried to start a war.

Of course, they weren't willing to compensate the *Laians* for the Republic's losses from the Wendira part of those provocateurs. It was a simple point, one around which the two sides had been circling for weeks, and Rin Dunst was a student of history.

These kinds of deadlocks didn't break without an outside force. He just wasn't sure what that force was going to *be*.

"Have you reviewed the reports I forwarded you both about Squadron Lord Tan!Stalla's encounter with the Infinite?" Tan!Shallegh asked once the formal niceties were done. "We now have a more detailed combat engagement than *Defiance*'s near-destruction."

"We do," Oxtashah agreed. "I must admit, I find these creatures far from as intimidating as you seem to. They are large, perhaps, but they failed to inflict any damage at all on the A!Tol force. Your ships are not Core Power vessels, and they survived the encounter unscathed."

"And are now trapped in an empty stretch of void far from any warmth or shore," Tan!Shallegh replied. "If they were to reenter hyperspace, they would be obliterated. The limitations of the Infinite's range were expected, and Squadron Lord Tan!Stalla used them perfectly.

"It is what the Infinite had that we did *not* expect that concerns me."

"They appear to be very efficient scavengers," Tidirok observed. "Thirty-four cycles to study, adapt and integrate stolen hyper emitters into their own biology. Plus missiles. I will admit I did not expect either so quickly."

"These beings terrified the Alava," Rin said quietly. "We are reasonably sure *this* group of Infinite defeated the Alavan sector fleet the conspirators were hunting and sent its survivors fleeing into the Astoroko Nebula to hide.

"Like Alavan technology, much of their old weaponry is likely nonfunctional. But they have had fifty thousand years to work through that problem."

"You are still trying to convince me that this danger is sufficient for us to lay aside our dead," Oxtashah pointed out. "I am *not* convinced. My Queens have made their demands clear."

"And the Grand Parliament has made their counteroffer," Tidirok snapped. "We will compensate the Grand Hive for their losses if the Grand Hive compensates the Republic for ours."

Rin figured that actually *was* a good compromise—though he also suspected any remotely honest accounting would result in something close to a wash. The provocateurs had been targeting both sides relatively evenly.

"The presence of a Laian mobile shipyard amongst the provocateurs suggests to us that the royal's share of the blame lies with the Republic," Oxtashah snapped. "We are not responsible for what happened along this border."

"Enough," Tan!Shallegh told them, his skin flashing dark in despair. "There is no purpose in swimming the waters again and again every single day. We must look to the reefs ahead before we all fall."

Somehow, that was enough to bring both of them to a momentary quiet, and Rin sighed into it.

"You've already both committed not to attack each other until this is resolved," he pointed out. "That means the fleet available to

Oxtashah is not necessarily needed sitting at the border, glaring at us all.

"I know I'm not one of the diplomats or military officers here, but may I make a suggestion?"

"An academic's perspective might be useful," Tidirok said. "Princess?"

"You are here to speak of the Alava and the Infinite, not of our politics," Oxtashah said coldly, but her wings flickered in agreement. "But as the Fleet Lord suggests, we circle the same pile for suns on end. Speak, Professor."

Rin concealed a mental cringe as he realized what kind of *pile* the Wendira metaphor referred to, but he faced the three senior aliens levelly.

"You are not yet prepared to work together," he told them. This wasn't news to anyone. "But you aren't going to stab each other in the back yet, either. The Eleventh Voice has already relied on this to send ships to support Squadron Lord Tan!Stalla.

"But the Laians and the Imperials can only blockade the portion of the Astoroko Nebula in the Dead Zone or in Republic space," he noted. "They don't even have the hulls to do that effectively—as I understand it, they are only blockading the route the provocateurs used to enter the Nebula and hoping they can intercept if the Infinite leave along an unexpected vector.

"But there is a section of the Nebula that is in Wendira territory, where the Laians would hesitate to send ships even if they *did* detect the hyperspace anomaly of the Infinite."

He shrugged.

"The Laians have already drawn down their forces here. I suggest that Princess Oxtashah does the same and sends the ships in question to block the other exits from the Nebula.

"You do not need to ally with the Republic to secure your own borders against the threat we have found. We are all best served if the Infinite remain trapped in the Astoroko."

And if the Infinite left the nebula into Wendira space, Princess Oxtashah would quickly be the one begging for Laian help. Unless, of course, the Infinite were *far* less of a threat than anyone anticipated.

"That...is a reasonable suggestion," Oxtashah said slowly. "I will consult with the Commandants. I make no promises. I am a diplomat. I do not command the Dead Zone Fleet. But I believe we can spare a few carriers to secure our own borders."

"We will all benefit, I think," Tan!Shallegh replied. "If you are prepared to share their patrol patterns with my people, I will commit to making certain we have all vectors covered without informing the Republic of their location."

Rin suspected that Tidirok wanted to object to that plan—but it wasn't really that the Imperium didn't trust their allies. It was that they *all* knew the Wendira and the Laians had spent the last several hundred years killing each other in numbers that made any sense of scale impossible.

And all of it mostly because a Laian looked like a Wendira Worker caste with no wings.

CHAPTER TEN

WATCHES IN THE ENDLESS VOID WERE A QUIET THING. *JEAN Villeneuve* and her companions were dozens of light-years from anything other than the Astoroko Nebula. Their reinforcements weren't due for cycles yet, and their enemy hadn't demonstrated any ability to threaten them through the hyper barrier.

The flag deck didn't have formal watches the way a ship's bridge did, but there was still a schedule to make sure at least one senior officer of the flag staff was on the deck if the Squadron Lord wasn't.

Tonight, that officer was Morgan Casimir. She was trying to keep an eye on everything going on on the flag deck, which was overwhelming for any soul. Practice was teaching her what she *needed* to watch, which made the whole endeavor good training.

She could follow the sensor data more easily than some of the other reports feeding to the fleet's command center, which meant she was giving the tactical plot the smallest portion of her attention—and she almost missed it when things changed.

"Wait," she murmured. "Speaker Atraxis, can you double-check the anomaly scanner for me? I'm seeing something odd."

Atraxis, an Ivida officer in Ashmore's Operations department, leapt to obey. He pulled the anomaly scanners up on his own screen as Morgan brought them up on the main holographic tank at the center of the flag deck.

"They're leaving," Atraxis said quietly, confirming what was now obvious on the larger display.

Anomaly tracks for a moving ship were strangely stretched, an artifact of a faster-than-light travel signature that arrived at light-speed, but the pattern was clear. The entire Infinite force that had been lurking "next" to them in hyperspace was moving away.

"I make their course for the Astoroko," Morgan said. "You see the same?"

"I do, sir," Atraxis confirmed. "Should I confirm with *Villeneuve* Tactical?"

"Please, Speaker," she told him. "Let's make certain what we're looking at—then I'll brief the Squadron Lord. If the Infinite are going away, that's a relief for everyone."

She still watched the tracks stretch across her display. It was hard to judge the speed—or *anything*, really—of the anomaly from regular space, but they could get an estimate. The Infinite swarm was up to about a third of the speed of light in hyperspace—and hundreds of times it in regular-space pseudovelocity.

"What changed?" Morgan murmured. "I was expecting you to stick around until the Laians kicked you off. *We* didn't do anything, and the bugs are still five days out."

She shivered. It *looked* like good news...which meant that she didn't trust it at all.

THE MIST UNITS IN TAN!STALLA'S office were running at full power as Morgan reported to her former Captain. Humidity was always high in the A!Tol portions of Imperial ships, but this much water was new to Morgan.

"Sir," she greeted the Squadron Lord with a crisp salute...that squelched slightly as her hand touched her damp chest.

"Take a seat, Staff Captain," Tan!Stalla ordered. "I saw the report from the sensor teams. It looks like good news.

"So, what do you think is *actually* going on?" she asked.

"I have no idea," Morgan admitted truthfully. "We can't guarantee that the Infinite are operating on any set of principles we understand, sir. If it were one of *our* forces, though..."

She trailed off but Tan!Stalla gestured for her to continue.

"Finish your thought, Casimir," the Squadron Lord ordered. "No one knows anything. Your guesses are as valuable as anyone else's."

"They either had a strict timeline they were supposed to return on all along, or they got a recall message," Morgan guessed with a shrug. "Either seems...iffy, given that they have no ability to open a hyper portal.

"On the other hand, they could have *kept* a set of portal emitters at the Eye, in which case they might be able to get everything except the Category Five back into regular space there."

Tan!Stalla snapped her beak in thought.

"*I* would have held on to at least one set of spare emitters," she admitted. "That wouldn't help them send out new fleets, not without the ability to create portals at the target, but it could let them bring their bioforms 'home' in this kind of situation."

"We're assuming the Infinite attaches value to the individual bioforms," Morgan warned. "We don't know that. The Great Mother certainly didn't seem to—but that doesn't prove anything. She was... not Infinite. Not culturally, so to speak."

"That's an important distinction," Tan!Stalla agreed. "The Tosumi, Ivida and Pibo are not A!Tol physically, but...culturally, most of their culture is A!Tol-derived. That is why they are the Imperial Races."

Those three were the species the A!Tol had annexed and uplifted before they learned how to do so *without* wrecking the preexisting cultures. Morgan's understanding was that Imperial integration was still considered a work in progress, with humanity—the current 'latest acquisition'—being held up a sign of their progress and success.

"Where the Taljzi were biologically Kanzi but not culturally Kanzi anymore," Morgan suggested. "Their separation from the main body of their species and their reliance on the Alavan cloner made them something very different."

"And the Great Mother had no exposure to the Infinite, as I understand it," Tan!Stalla said. "So, we are better judging the Infinite by their actions than by her. Their *actions* so far do not provide a definitive answer, but they *suggest* that they place a value on at least the larger bioforms."

"Ease of replacement may also be a factor," Morgan said. "So long as they are trapped in Astoroko, we don't know if they can create new bioforms at *all*—and I suspect the larger bioforms take hundreds of long-cycles to reach that scale."

"Or thousands," Tan!Stalla murmured, tapping a command that adjusted a sprayer to point more directly at her. "A hundred thousand long-cycles in the dark, Staff Captain. It is possible, perhaps even likely, that most of the larger bioforms saw the war against the Alava."

That thought sent a chill down Morgan's neck.

"God, Rin would *love* to talk to them," she murmured. "So far, our only conversation was them demanding our hyperdrive and then shooting at us."

"We may find a way to communicate yet," Tan!Stalla said hopefully. "We have crossed language and culture barriers before. Not always well, but we have done it." She snapped her beak. "The Laians and Wendira would be better off, in some ways, if they *hadn't* managed to get their video formats to talk to each other."

"I'm not certain everything between them can be blamed on visuals, sir," Morgan said. "But...it's hard to make peace with someone you can't talk to."

"This is true." Tan!Stalla shifted...and there was a cracking noise Morgan had never heard from an A!Tol before.

"Sir, are you okay?" she asked.

The A!Tol was flickering black streaks of pain.

"No," she admitted slowly. "Give me a moment, please."

Tan!Stalla reached inside her desk and produced a strange, gun-like device. It took Morgan a moment to recognize it as a modified liquid-bandage applicator. She didn't see where Tan!Stalla used it, but the A!Tol was still flickering black in pain as she laid the applicator down.

"Not all A!Tol age gracefully," Tan!Stalla finally told her drily. "My girlfriend convinced me to get the sprayers"—she gestured at the misting units around the room—"but my body has decided to remind me that A!Tol are barely meant to be *amphibious*, let alone land-dwellers."

The black darkened for a moment, then began to fade toward a dark purple of bitter amusement.

"All A!Tol must rest in water to avoid skin issues," Tan!Stalla noted. "And we keep the areas we live in as humid as possible. For some of us, however, our ability to survive in drier air fades over time. Va!Sara Syndrome, it's called."

She shivered her tentacles.

"I was already showing signs when I commanded *Jean Villeneuve* with you as my XO," Tan!Stalla admitted. "But I am a stubborn fool at times. When I returned home to spend time with my love, she saw the difference—*she* is a doctor, a far wiser soul than I."

"And she insisted on this?" Morgan gestured at the mist-sprayers.

"They help," Tan!Stalla agreed. "And it helps that my girlfriend *is* a doctor and can issue a medical order the Fleet will recognize. All waves know the Fleet treats Va!Sara Syndrome as best as we can, though. !Lot could have just insisted I see a Fleet doctor...but she wanted to be certain."

"It sounds like she cares deeply for you," Morgan noted. *Girlfriend*, she knew, was the translator picking a *close-enough* word, since English didn't really have the language for the gradations of A!Tol romantic relationships.

Given that A!Tol reproduction was invariably fatal to the mother, an issue corrected by vast amounts of technology these days, it was hardly a surprise that same-sex relationships were actually more common than reproductive partnerships among the squid-like aliens.

"She does. And she is eternally patient with one who is rarely home," Tan!Stalla said with a flush of red pleasure that broke some of the pain. "And she would insist that if I am having skin cracking issues, I should see the ship's doctor."

Morgan smiled.

"And she would be correct, I believe," she told her superior. "The Infinite, for whatever reason, have left us be for now. We are safe for the moment—which makes this the best time to make sure our Squadron Lord is in top form when the enemy returns!"

CHAPTER ELEVEN

HYPERSPACE HAD BEEN QUIET FOR SEVERAL DAYS WHEN THE portal appeared. By the time the anomaly of the ships' travel through hyperspace caught up with their exit portal, Morgan had already identified the war-dreadnoughts from the sensor data she was reviewing.

"Multiple war-dreadnought signatures," Ashmore reported. That was his job, after all. Morgan's was to keep Tan!Stalla advised of what they figured the Infinite were doing.

So far, she didn't *think* she'd stepped on Ashmore's toes too badly.

"*Villeneuve* Tactical makes it ten dreadnoughts, plus cruisers," the operations officer continued, glancing toward where Tan!Stalla waited at the center of the flag deck. "Fifty-plus contacts."

"That should be Fifty-Sixth Pincer Korodaun," the Squadron Lord observed. "Commander Nitik, channel to the Pincer's flag, please."

The war-dreadnoughts were barely a light-minute away. It was a matter of maybe thirty seconds to get a hyperfold com link established between the two flagships, filling the holographic tank at the center of *Jean Villeneuve*'s flag deck with the image of the inverted step pyramid of her Laian equivalent.

Centered in the hologram was a Laian officer who practically *gleamed* in the lights of her flagship, iridescent greens and oranges glittering under the lights as the bejeweled carapace of a female Laian shifted to allow Korodaun to see her counterpart.

"Squadron Lord Tan!Stalla," Korodaun greeted them, using a mandible snap to emulate the beak snap. Most Laians left that to the translator, which Morgan took as a positive sign. "I appreciate your continual updates on the status of the Infinite's forward deployment.

"My approach would have needed to be very different if they had still lurked in the shallows here."

"It will serve no one if we follow different currents against this enemy, Pincer," Tan!Stalla replied. "Your arrival is appreciated. We were starting to feel a bit lonely out here."

"It is a lonely chunk of nowhere," Korodaun agreed. "I have left several of my cruisers in hyperspace to maintain a long-distance watch, but I think we will need to consider our strategy now that we have augmented our forces here.

"May I invite you aboard *Scion's Sword* for further discussions?"

"Of course," Tan!Stalla said instantly. "This is a *Republic* chunk of void, after all, and I am delighted to turn operational command of the blockade over to you."

Korodaun's command also outmassed the Imperial task force by over three to one—and not that long before, a *single* war-dreadnought would have been capable of destroying an entire Imperial Fleet.

Times changed, though, and the Imperium had cheated.

"Of course, Squadron Lord," Korodaun said. "I estimate we will make rendezvous in fifteen minutes. I look forward to seeing you and any officers you feel necessary for our conversation then."

"PROTT, CASIMIR," Tan!Stalla snapped the moment the channel closed. "With me. We'll need Marines. Honor guard only."

"I'll arrange it," Ashmore promised. "They'll meet you in the shuttle bay."

Fifteen minutes was more than enough time. Probably.

Morgan and the Ivida chief of staff fell in around Tan!Stalla as the Squadron Lord exited the flag deck.

"Is surrendering command a good idea, sir?" Prott asked. "I know we decided it in advance, but I worry. We have not seen a recognition of the depth of the waters yet from the Laians."

"Korodaun appears to understand," Tan!Stalla replied. "But even if she didn't, we have no choice. As I told her, this is Laian space—or, at least, the portion of the Dead Zone they still claim.

"We have no real authority here, and she has more firepower than we do. By any reasonable logic, this is her command, and we are now the supporting allies we were always supposed to be."

"Besides, aren't there more Laian ships on the way?" Morgan said. "Another twenty war-dreadnoughts at least."

"Over the next ten cycles, yes. Our Grand Fleet is remaining with the main Laian Dead Zone defense force, the First Defense Fleet, until the storms stop thundering at each other."

"I had higher hopes for the Wendira, but I guess I don't know them well," Morgan admitted.

Prott clicked his tongue in a soft chuckle. His people's faces didn't move, but she still felt his bitter amusement.

"None of us do and we hesitate to take the Laians' opinion at surface value," he said. "But it seems that this kind of game is normal for them. The Queens do not comprehend that anything can threaten them."

"Even Oxtashah has done her duty as a Royal caste," Tan!Stalla reminded them. "She is mother to ten *thousand* children. No Royal caste who has not done the same would be permitted to leave the Queens' reach.

"They guard their bloodlines and their power obsessively. Even the Mesharom never truly convinced the Queens that they were a threat."

Morgan shivered.

"I saw a Mesharom battle fleet," she murmured. Ten war spheres could outmass the entire Wendira military—and the Mesharom had possessed over a hundred of the planetoid warships before the Taljzi campaigns. "Ignoring *that* takes...imagination."

Tan!Stalla flashed blue and red in amused acceptance, snapping her beak in surprise laughter.

"Yes, it does take a certain ability to twist the waters of reality," she conceded. "The Laians, for their arrogance and their flaws, are at least more realistic about the galaxy they live in. That, I think, is why we have managed to make allies of them."

A shuttle was already waiting for them as they stepped into the shuttle bay, a squad of Marines falling into place around it. To Morgan's surprise, the Marines were all human—and led by her former Marine CO, Battalion Commander Pierre Vichy.

"Aren't you a little senior for a platoon command?" she murmured as they stepped up to the tall dark-haired Frenchman.

"Oui," he agreed. "But flashy medals and insignia are a necessity for honor-guard duty, and everyone believed mine would be most... readily available and ready to go.

"Pour quelque raison." He grinned.

"Are we ready, Battalion Commander?" Tan!Stalla asked.

"The shuttle is fueled and prepped," he confirmed with a crisp salute. "I have an honor guard of twenty Marines ready to go in dress uniforms. No weapons."

"Good, good." Tan!Stalla paused, studying the sleek lines of the Imperial assault shuttle. "Then let us get to the waters. Duty awaits."

JEAN VILLENEUVE MASSED twenty-one million tons. She was twenty-five-hundred meters from bow to stern, with flared arch-like wings that stretched to a full kilometer in width and height. She was the largest warship the A!Tol Imperium had yet deployed.

And against *Scion's Sword* and her sisters, she looked like a toy. *Scion's Sword* was nine kilometers in length and three wide, a long beetle-like dome that resembled her builders' carapaces. Just under ten times *Villeneuve*'s mass, she carried roughly fifteen times as many interface-drive missiles, proton beams, and hyperfold cannons.

Her sensors were keener and her missiles were smarter than the Imperial ship's—but ton for ton, her armor and shields were actually weaker, and she lacked any equivalent to the faster-than-light weaponry of the Imperium's hyperspace missiles.

When Morgan had been a child, a single war-dreadnought had been enough to threaten the entire Imperium. Now the ship she was approaching was no match for a squadron of well-handled Imperial ships that matched her mass.

Time marched on and the galaxy changed. The Laians, once enemies, were now friends. The Imperium, once irrelevant to the Core Powers, was now rapidly approaching membership in their ranks.

"The Category Five we saw would tear them apart at close range," Prott murmured as they approached their destination. "The sheer scale of the Infinite's larger bioforms renders anything we bring..."

"Underweight," Morgan finished the thought after Prott was silent for a few seconds. "Any Category Four could take down *Scion's Sword* if they made it into range."

"That's the big *if*, isn't it?" Tan!Stalla told them. "Maneuverability and range are our advantages over the Infinite. Size is their edge over us. Do we have any idea, yet, how much firepower they can even put out at close range?"

"Not really," Morgan admitted. "My team has been going over the data from the probes we passed through their formation, but only the lighter ships engaged there."

She shrugged.

"We're still deriving most of our assessment of their armament from the Servants," she said. "But projecting from that...well, the Category Five probably couldn't one-shot a war-dreadnought unless they hit with *everything*."

The shuttle was silent and she heard Prott click his tongue.

"But it would win the fight against a war-dreadnought," the chief of staff concluded.

"It would win the fight against all *ten*, if it could bring them to plasma range," Morgan said. "As Tan!Stalla noted, if they get in range of us, we are doomed."

CHAPTER TWELVE

A WAVE OF ALMOST SUPERHEATED DRY AIR SWEPT INTO THE shuttle as the ramp slid open. The air aboard a Laian ship was breathable to all of the members of Tan!Stalla's staff, but the dryness almost instantly hurt Morgan's throat.

It also left her a bit concerned about the Squadron Lord and her Va!Sara Syndrome, but Tan!Stalla forged forward without hesitation. Since Morgan's only real concern was the A!Tol, she followed.

At least some of the heat and dryness quickly turned out to be an artifact of their own shuttle arrival, though the shuttle bay was still brighter, drier and hotter than any Imperial ship except *maybe* one with a pure Ivida crew.

Vichy's Marines had already led the way, forming a double file that matched up with their Laian counterparts like they'd practiced it. Morgan followed her CO through the files of Marines and Laian soldiers toward their destination.

Korodaun glittered even more brightly in person than she had over the camera, the iridescent colors of her carapace shining under the shuttle bay's lights. There were other Laian females in the room, but she was still the most brightly colored of them.

Morgan had to wonder if there was some kind of cue or meaning to the Pincer's coloration. She knew that Laians had a severe sex imbalance, with their distribution skewing toward the sperm-donor end. She'd grown up with a monogamous Laian couple as friends of the family—and had realized that most Laians regarded that relationship as strange at best, deviant at worst.

"Squadron Lord Tan!Stalla," Korodaun greeted Tan!Stalla. "Welcome aboard *Scion's Sword*."

"Thank you, Pincer of the Republic," the A!Tol replied. "This is my chief of staff, Staff Captain Prott, and my special analyst for the Infinite, Staff Captain Casimir."

Morgan folded her hands together in a way that was mildly uncomfortable and bowed over them, reciting a few long-practiced phrases that her tongue *barely* managed to wrap itself around.

Korodaun's mandibles widened in surprise and she chittered delighted amusement. Then she bowed her head in return.

"May the sun shine upon your home and crops as well," she recited, the translator turning her Laian into English. "I haven't heard that greeting in some time, Captain Casimir. It is archaic, but your dedication is to be admired."

Morgan wasn't surprised it was archaic. She'd learned it from the Laian Exiles on Earth, the descendants of the *losers* of the civil war that had turned the Laian Ascendancy—a barely limited constitutional monarchy, as she understood it—into the Laian *Republic*—a representative democracy with an unlimited franchise.

A civil war that had been hundreds of years earlier.

Morgan also suspected that Korodaun could guess where Morgan had picked up the greeting, but that only made her *more* amused.

"Come, Squadron Lord, Staff Captains," the Laian officer told them. "We have much to discuss."

THE CONFERENCE ROOM that Korodaun led them to was notably cooler, dimmer, and damper than the rest of the ship. A diligent Laian junior officer urged Tan!Stalla, Prott and Morgan to a specific side of the table as well—a side that turned out to be even *more* humid.

A!Tol were *terrible* at concealing their emotions, and whorls of blue and red relief flashed across Tan!Stalla's skin as she settled onto the stool set out for her.

The chairs around the table were each shaped to the species of the individual they were meant for, which impressed Morgan. She wasn't sure at what point Korodaun's people had known what species Tan!Stalla was bringing with her, but even her and Prott's chairs were slightly different, accounting for the extra joint in the Ivida's legs.

Against the backdrop of the deep earthy-red walls—Morgan realized they were actually baked clay, with three-dimensional mosaics worked into the several-centimeter-thick wall covering—the moisture and the various specialty chairs, the plain black wooden table was almost weirdly prosaic.

It wouldn't have looked out of place as a conference table on Earth, let alone on any of the multiracial warships Morgan had served on.

"Squadron Lord, you have already engaged this enemy," Korodaun noted once everyone had taken a seat. "Without losses, which is impressive, given what I've seen of our scans. Would your team share the light of your impressions?"

"Casimir?" Tan!Stalla gestured to Morgan, who nodded and leaned forward.

"I was in command of the ship that found them," Morgan told Korodaun, in case the Pincer hadn't been told that. "We were looking for the Alavan fleet, and we weren't expecting to find the people that killed them."

They had *also* been running away from the conspirators who'd tried to start a new war between the Laians and the Wendira, but that was a different story.

"Our encounter was short, but they very nearly destroyed my ship," she noted. "We had to scuttle *Defiance* due to her damage, in fact. The main weapon system we encountered in the Astoroko Nebula was c-fractional microsingularities, a weapon we did not see in the force we met in hyperspace.

"That force engaged us with stolen Laian missiles and plasma cannons. They were extremely ineffective in their use of the missiles, but they were learning."

"An intelligent enemy, then," Korodaun concluded. "To be presumed, I suppose, when they are themselves starships. You survived a fleet engagement with them as well. Tan!Stalla?"

"We kept out of their range and relied on their inability to properly use the missiles they'd stolen in hyperspace," the Squadron Lord noted. "I don't believe we could rely on the same weaknesses in a normal space engagement, and they will quickly learn to make up their shortcomings in a hyperspatial engagement.

"We did, however, identify and destroy every bioform carrying a stolen Laian hyper emitter," Tan!Stalla said. "That should buy us time. We have to assume, however, that they will find a solution now that they have seen hyper portals in action under their control."

"I agree," Korodaun replied. "Do you have any intelligence, Squadron Lord, to shed sunlight on where they may be headed when they leave? I agree with the logic of your current positioning, but they have already been beaten here once."

"Unfortunately, I believe you have all the intelligence we have," Tan!Stalla said. "I agree that they are likely to attempt to divert around us in hyperspace, which could be a problem."

"Currently, I have a swarm of ten cruisers in hyperspace creating a sensor screen," the Laian officer told them. "They are spreading out as we speak. The plan is for them to drop into regular space and send their detection reports by hyperfold, allowing the main fleet to enter hyperspace and intercept any breakout attempt.

"As I receive more units from the main fleets, that sensor swarm will expand and we may even split our fleet into nodal forces," Korodaun continued. "Interception is possible and we will do all we can to maintain containment.

"You have sensor data to identify the portal bioforms?"

"We do," Morgan said. "But the next wave of portal ships will likely be using a purely Infinite biotech portal emitter. They will not match the signature."

"No, of course not," Korodaun agreed with a wave of her pincer. "But it will give us a starting point. Your methodology of trapping them in hyperspace will be useful, I think. I will inform my subordinates to begin refreshing their crews' training in hyperspace combat.

"We have sufficient weapons to challenge them there, but we must prepare for them to update their missiles and missile tactics, as you say," she concluded. "Containment *will* be maintained."

Morgan appreciated both the Pincer's determination and her apparent willingness to listen to the Arm Power officers.

"Our biggest vulnerability is their straight-line speed," Morgan told the Laian officer. "Their acceleration is lower than ours, but they can get up to velocities where even our missiles can't catch them."

"That will probably be the hardest part to make sure our people account for," Korodaun replied, glancing at the other Laian officers in the room. None of them had been introduced—or had even said a word once Tan!Stalla was seated.

"We are all accustomed to operating in an environment where the rules of maneuver are fully illuminated," she continued. "No power in the galaxy has used anything except the interface drive in millennia.

"Yet the system used by these Infinite, as you say, has its own advantages over the interface drive. We must adapt. If we do *not* adapt, the Republic is in danger. As is your Imperium."

"That is the largest danger of the Infinite, I fear," Tan!Stalla said. "We do not understand them. We do not know their technology. We do not know their minds. They fired upon *Defiance* without warning, their only communication to demand that Captain Casimir turn over her hyperdrive.

"They do not fight as we expect, and they may not even plan or act as we expect," the Squadron Lord continued grimly. "And we do not truly know how long we have before they have adapted to all of our technology.

"They have access, after all, to one of your mobile shipyards —*plus* whatever was left of a mixed Laian-Wendira fleet. We cannot afford to underestimate them."

"They fought Those Who Came Before," Korodaun said calmly. "If they challenged *gods*, Squadron Lord, we who remain must prepare as if we must battle gods.

"So we will. And while I do not assume we can be victorious where Those Who Came Before failed, I *do* believe that we can keep the Infinite contained. A few more cycles and we will have thirty war-dreadnoughts to bar their way.

"Twenty cycles, thirty? We will have a *hundred* war-dread-noughts. Plus, I hope, more ships from *your* fleet and assistance from our old enemies. We *can* contain these creatures—and then, I hope, find a way to deal with them."

CHAPTER THIRTEEN

It was a small adjustment of positions, in the grand scheme of things. The A!Tol superbattleships moved less than a million kilometers, shuttling away from the Astoroko Nebula at minimum power, their battleships and cruisers and destroyers falling in around them.

Replacing them, ten war-dreadnoughts of the Laian Republic moved up, accompanied by forty attack cruisers. The dance had been carefully choreographed—not because the careful planning was truly *needed* but because they had the time and it reduced risk.

When it was over, there was no question which of the two fleets would face the Infinite first. Two billion tons of Republic capital ships waited in the void, a thin line of metal and flesh against the monsters hiding in the dark.

There was an audible sigh of relief on *Jean Villeneuve*'s flag deck, the sensation of thirty sentients from five species releasing their tension. Morgan hadn't even realized how much strain was wrapped into the air of that room until it was released.

"Pincer Korodaun assumes operational command," Tan!Stalla said loudly and firmly. "Note it for the record, Prott."

"This mess is their problem now," the Ivida agreed cheerfully. "We just have to help."

"*Just*," Ashmore muttered, barely loud enough for Morgan to hear him from barely a meter away.

"We have time now, people," Tan!Stalla told them all. "Stand the fleet down to the lowest alert. Get what rest you all can. In a cycle, we'll bring the fleet back to ready status and begin exercises based on the data Staff Captain Casimir and her team have assembled.

"We expect significant Laian reinforcements before the Infinite are able to move again," the Squadron Lord reminded them. "Nonetheless, we will remain here until relieved by the Grand Fleet. We have our own responsibilities to follow.

"Now stand down," she ordered. "Prott has already called the third watch up to take your stations. Rest, people."

REST DID NOT NECESSARILY MEAN *sleep*. If nothing else, Morgan was going to have to prep the exercises everyone else would be going through in less than twenty-four hours.

Still, she made sure to take a break, retreating to her quarters and pouring herself a glass of wine. She carefully closed her work messages for the moment—she'd look at those on the other side of the wine and eight hours of sleep—but a new-message icon popped up.

The digital file had come a long way. First, it had been sent up to the starcom station in Earth orbit. Then, it had been transmitted to a "transfer station" for messages near the A!Tol-Laian border, where it had been moved from an Imperial starcom station to a Laian one.

Then it had been sent to the nearest starcom base to their current location, a military facility intended to support the defense of the Dead Zone, and transmitted into the hyperfold relay network. A dozen hyperfold relays had carried it from there to *Jean Villeneuve*—and now Morgan Casimir looked at a blinking alert telling her she had a message from her stepmother.

Taking a sip of her wine, Morgan tried to remember the last time she'd sent the Duchess of Terra—or even her *father*—a message. It hadn't been since losing *Defiance*, that was for certain.

Ignoring a twinge of guilt, Morgan started the message.

It was *both* of her parents. Elon Casimir sat next to his wife on the couch in the penthouse apartment Morgan had grown up in. From the stories Annette Bond had told her children, she'd never been a fan of the luxury of the apartment, but it had already been bought—along with the floor beneath it, converted to security barracks—before anyone really asked *her* opinion.

"Captain Casimir," Annette Bond greeted her stepdaughter. She didn't salute, but she still gave the woman she'd raised the respect of the rank Morgan had earned. "If I'm reading all of the reports right, it might be as much as five or six days before you get this, but I hope you're well when you do."

"Even if we learned that you'd lost your ship from Tan!Shallegh," Elon Casimir added drily.

"Be nice, Elon," the gracefully aging Duchess told her younger husband with a smile. "*You've* never commanded a starship or been involved in fleet command. I have. Morgan is busy, believe me."

"Officially, we know nothing about what's going on out there," the Ducal Consort told his daughter. "If the Imperium isn't briefing the Dukes, that tells me a lot all on its own."

"They've told us that they don't expect the Wendira and Laians to start shooting," Bond corrected. "But the full details of what you found are still classified at the highest levels."

Morgan chuckled and took another drink of wine. That was as close as her stepmother was going to come to admitting that the pair of them knew *everything*. They might not have been briefed as Dukes —the rulers of the Imperium's various semi-autonomous racial home-worlds—but they were also the primary shareholders of the Imperium's fifth-largest shipyard.

And Annette Bond was A!Shall's *friend*, one the Empress found useful as a sounding board, Morgan suspected.

"I've told Victoria what I can," Bond continued. "I imagine you have as well. She...gets it. I'm sure you knew that, but it can't hurt to be reiterated. She *does* command one of my orbital forts, after all."

Morgan's parents were almost embarrassingly supportive of her... somewhat complex relationships and love life. The only time they'd drawn a line was when they'd found out she'd slept with one of the Ducal apartment security guards.

That had gone down like a lead balloon. Morgan, at eighteen, had suddenly received an *extremely detailed* further explanation of the concept of *conflict of interest*.

"I do wish we'd heard that you'd lost your ship from you," Elon Casimir said quietly. "That's not meant to guilt-trip you, Morgan. As Annette said, I don't fully get how busy you are. But...I do know that's a hard path to walk, and it's one that's always walked alone.

"We love you and we want to have your back, in anything and everything."

Morgan found herself blinking away tears...and not just in gratitude at her parents' love.

"Duty is a harsh mistress, Morgan," her mother reminded her. "But you're not alone in facing it. Never. Not while you have us, not while you have your sisters—not while you have Victoria and Rin, either.

"Or Tan!Shallegh, for that matter. The old squid will have your back, you know that, right?"

"I do," Morgan muttered, wondering where all of the tears were coming from.

Over a hundred of her crew had died aboard *Defiance*. Seven times that many had come back with her and been scattered through Tan!Stalla's fleet, but she'd lost a hundred souls—and killed some of them herself when she'd ordered a power core ejected to save the ship.

She had to pause the message for a moment, letting the tears flow freely as she finished her wine. There was no one there to see, and she had, for the first time since firing the scuttling charges, a moment to herself without tasks to complete.

Peace wouldn't last. The creatures they'd found at the Eye of the Astoroko Nebula weren't going to leave her peace, any more than they'd spared her crew. But right now, she had a quiet moment along with the holographic images of her parents.

Morgan Casimir knew how to handle nightmares and how to handle grief. And sometimes, the best way to remember your dead was to simply let yourself cry.

Her parents would understand if it took her a while to finish their message.

CHAPTER FOURTEEN

"So, the exercise for the fleets," Shotilik rumbled as Morgan and her team gathered in their conference room again. "Do we assume the worst, the best or somewhere in between?"

Morgan snorted and tapped a command, dropping a *smaller* Category Seven bioform into the hologram above the table they surrounded.

"I was trying to forget those existed," Rogers said drily. "Fifteen thousand kilometers. Multiple singularity cannons. Probably multiple plasma cannons. Anything else I need to mention?"

"Missiles, hyperdrives, anomaly scanners," Morgan reeled off. "We know they have tachyon scanners and the full gamut of everything we use for realspace scanning, so we assume the next wave has everything we use for hyperspace scanning."

"Everything the Laians had on *Builder of Tomorrows*," Ito said, the Pibo woman dropping a list of key components next to the giant bioform's hologram. "Whether the Laian systems grafted onto bioforms or their own biotech equivalent, we can assume they have point-eight-five missiles, hyperfold cannons, hyperfold coms, tachyon scanners..."

Took shivered, the blue-feathered Yin woman considering the list.

"They couldn't have adopted all those winds in a few dozen cycles, could they?" she asked.

"We have to assume they could," Morgan replied. "Hence Ito's point. We *know* they have copies of the Laian versions of all of these —and we also have to assume, at this point, that they have full access to *Builder's* computer systems.

"Maps. Tech databases. The works. The maps are Pincer Korodaun's problem," she said with relief. "But the tech databases are our problem. So, for those exercises we're giving them tomorrow, I want us to mock up a dash-X category modifier, for ships fully modernized with the Laian weapon systems."

"So, missiles, IDMs... Shields?"

"Shields and interface drives," Morgan agreed. "Using whichever of their reactionless or our interface drive seems more efficient at a given moment. A Category Four-X will have *everything*, people."

"Any other category modifiers we should be thinking of?" Shotilik asked thoughtfully.

"Dash-H, for units like the ones we saw in the last attack," Took suggested. "Standard bioforms with hyper emitters."

"We'll use dash-H for hyper-equipped units and dash-M for IDM-equipped units," Morgan told them. "But for the *simulations*, the only thing we throw at people is dash-X. Worst-possible-case scenario."

"Makes sense," Rogers agreed. "If we train to fight the worst possible scenario, the reality can't help but be better, right?"

"I'm not taking that bet," Took said flatly. "If I did, I'd pull out all my feathers from stress. I'm going to have to pull launcher and magazine estimates by mass. They've got to be lower than Laian numbers, right? If they're basically bolting the Laian system, one way or another, onto existing forms?"

"Run me two sets of numbers, Took," Morgan ordered. "First, the one that we'll probably use for training purposes, is where they've updated themselves with an equivalent launcher-to-mass ratio as Laian war-dreadnoughts.

"Second, your best guess of what they'll look like if they're adding a Laian launcher-and-magazine assembly to an existing bioform, but trying to get up to a number of launchers that can seriously challenge us at range.

"That'll be the one we use for intelligence and operational assessments," Morgan concluded. "Run it conservative but realistic. We don't want to terrify people outside of training scenarios, but we don't want to underestimate these creatures, either."

"I'm on it," Took confirmed.

Morgan pivoted to Kadark.

"Kadark, you were Engineering, right?" she asked the big Anbrai.

"Yes, sir," he confirmed.

"I want you to tear into whatever we have on the Laian mobile shipyards," she told him. "I need to know just what *Builder* probably carried—but more importantly, what she can *do*. If she can update and modify war-dreadnoughts, she can probably at least do implants and modifications on Category One, Two and Three bioforms. I want an idea of how much she might have done to them in terms of implants and grafts."

"On it," he confirmed.

Morgan turned to Ito, Rogers and Shotilik and considered them.

"Ito, Rogers, I want you two to start putting together our scenarios for the training," she told the Pibo and her former XO. "Use the numbers from Took once she has them, but you'll need to come up with guesses for shields as well. We're almost certainly going to be staying out of ranges where plasma and hyperfold cannons matter for now, but if they start having shields to eat our missiles, it's going to change the math."

"And their use of plasma for missile defense is going to get better as well," Rogers suggested. "It wasn't that long ago that even the Imperium relied on shields alone to handle missiles, but we've already seen them shoot ours down."

"Agreed," Morgan said.

Finally, she turned her assessing gaze on Shotilik, the second-senior member of her team after Rogers.

"Tactical, right?" she asked the Rekiki.

"Yes, sir," Shotilik agreed.

"You and I get the most fun job," Morgan told her. "We're going to go through the Infinite's resources and the numbers everybody else puts together, and *we* play OPFOR. We're going to assess their resources and try to extrapolate their goals and objectives.

"Everyone else's job is to assess what the Infinite *have*. *We* get to try to guess just what the Queen will *do* with those resources."

THE SIMULATED CATEGORY Five-X blazed across the hologram at eighty percent of the speed of light. Eight hundred kilometers across, it seemed to spray missiles like a sprinter spraying sweat. The tiny icons scattering in front of the behemoth represented Laian war-dreadnoughts, the largest warships available to the defenders.

The dreadnoughts' missile fire was almost invisible against the tsunami the Infinite bioform unleashed, but their defenses rallied in trained synchronicity. Plasma-cannon-armed equivalents to the Imperium's Buckler drones opened fire at two light-seconds against the portion of the missiles that reached their target in hyperspace, and they dodged away, taking advantage of every bit of maneuverability their interface drives gave them.

It was...not enough.

Morgan watched grimly as their simulation ground to its inevitable conclusion. Shotilik hadn't even used the bioform's interface drive to match the Laians' maneuverability. The Rekiki had simply taken the Infinite forward and smashed the dreadnoughts to pieces with overwhelming missile fire.

"So, I'm hoping that is *not* our conservative estimate of the Infinite's missile armaments," she observed as the last war-dreadnought—controlled by Rogers this time—blew apart.

"It isn't," Ito confirmed, the Pibo looking tired. "That's Laian war-dreadnought ratios—six launchers per megaton. But on an eight-hundred-kilometer bioform...that's *millions* of missile launchers, sir."

"Millions," Morgan echoed, looking back at the simulation. "And the more conservative estimate?"

"Their ratio appears to be ten to one for length versus average height and width," Ito said. "So, an eight-hundred-kilometer-long unit is two hundred kilometers wide and high at its largest point, average of eighty kilometers. Volume of over twenty *million* cubic *kilometers*."

"They're limited by surface area, but..." Morgan wasn't even sure how she'd meant to finish that sentence.

"My conservative estimate is that a Category Five-X bioform that has been fully updated with Laian tech will have a hundred thousand missile launchers at the minimum end," Ito told them all. "That's a unit that is a *mere* hundred and twenty, say, kilometers long. At the high end, the eight-hundred-kilometer bioform we used here... A minimum of a million."

"I'm not sure I can even wrap my brain around those numbers," Morgan admitted, understanding why Ito sounded tired. "That's entire *fleets*' worth of firepower in a single bioform."

"The Category Three-X ships look more like regular warships," the Pibo said. "But a top-end Category Three bioform is already larger than a Laian war-dreadnought. So, my *conservative* estimate is that a C-Four-X unit is going to carry a minimum of two thousand missile launchers."

Morgan nodded, throwing the three smallest categories up in the hologram to replace the Category Five. The One-Xs were...well, from her team's analysis, they'd made for decent destroyers, but they were still almost irrelevant in the clash of titans she was facing. The Two-Xs were bigger, but still smaller than even the cruisers the blockade would bring to the fight.

The Three-Xs were real warships, ranging in size from as small as the Laian attack cruisers and *Thunderstorm*s of the blockade fleet to as large as the Laian war-dreadnoughts. Ton for ton, they were projecting that the X versions of the bioforms would be more lightly armed and defended than their technological equivalents, but they were just plain *bigger*.

They'd detected two thousand Category Fours, each more powerful than any ship present in the blocking fleet. The breakout force had brought at least a dozen Category Fours to go with their single Category Five.

"Do we have a *winnable* exercise to present the fleet?" Morgan asked. "I want them to recognize how dangerous an X-Category bioform is going to be. We need the worst-case-scenario models in the exercises—but we also need to present a scenario the blockading fleet can *win*. At least at first, anyway."

"We've got something," Rogers promised. "I'm not sure how *winnable* it will be, and I'm not sure it's realistic at all, but we've got a scenario based around them bringing a fleet of Category Twos and Threes, refitted to the X standard with shields, missiles and hyperdrives.

"I suspect we're underestimating how large a force they'll bring," the young redheaded officer admitted, "but it will give everyone a starting point."

"That's all we can do without more data," Morgan admitted. "We need people to realize how bad this can be, but we also need to set the scenarios to allow us to find ways we can win."

She looked at the hologram that had been showing the simulated Category Five-X and shook her head.

"Assuming we *can* win," she half-whispered.

CHAPTER FIFTEEN

The Squadron Lord's staff was silent when Morgan completed her briefing. She wasn't sure if the silence was good or bad —though the only bad silence would be them disbelieving her.

"What level of upgrades do you expect them to deploy in short order?" Tan!Stalla finally asked.

"That's probably our only good news," Morgan said. "Using *Builder of Tomorrows*, they can update any of the Category Three or smaller bioforms with grafted Laian technology, but a single mobile yard can only do so much work so quickly.

"They are also limited by the resources available to them. I would guess that we are probably looking at between two and four Category Three bioforms equipped with shields and missile launchers every five cycles," she told them.

"We do not have the data to estimate around when they will have a biotech version of any of these systems or how quickly they will be able to integrate biotech systems into their existing units," she continued. "*If* it turns out that they can only integrate shields and missiles into newly born bioforms, then we will continue to have a large advantage, as only the smallest units should be able to match our range."

"And if they can remap the flesh of their existing bioforms?" Prott asked.

"It depends on what the process looks like, but in that case, we are probably fucked," Morgan said bluntly. "Potentially, we could see a full revamp of *all* of the Infinite bioforms to an equivalent of our Class X categorization within a long-cycle.

"At that point, containment may well be impossible."

The room was silent again.

"We have time," Tan!Stalla reminded everyone. "We will distribute this analysis as widely as we can," she noted. "And request reinforcements from all possible allies. The Kanzi, for example, should be able to spare a fleet or two from their civil war now."

"Their civil war has been over for five long-cycles," Ashmore muttered, the operations officer sounding disgruntled. "They've just been dragging it out for politics."

"And if we disagreed with the reforms the High Priestess was implementing, the Imperium might draw more offense at that," Tan!Stalla agreed. "But I will take anyone who can lend me a twenty-megaton superbattleship with hyperfold cannons right now."

The Kanzi Theocracy hadn't cheated nearly as well as the Imperium over the last thirty years of tech development. Most of their focus recently, Morgan knew, had been on using their civil war as an excuse to dissolve their age-old institution of enslaving every non-Kanzi biped they encountered.

Morgan didn't know where that reform was going to end, but she was a lot more willing to talk to the Kanzi fighting *for* that reform than the people fighting *against* it.

And as Tan!Stalla had noted, the Imperium had traded hyperfold cannons to the Kanzi as part of the deal that had seen them fight the Taljzi together. The Kanzi fleet would be worth committing to this fight.

"The Wendira and Laians both have friends among the Core Powers they can call on as well, I hope," Prott said. "I was always surprised we were the only people involved in this fight."

"That's because any Core Power signing a deal with one of the pair explicitly *excludes* fighting the other half of the pair," Ashmore told the chief of staff. "Nobody else was dumb enough to get involved in the galaxy's oldest grudge match."

"Which meant no one else was in a place to talk them down from it," Tan!Stalla countered. "We have them talking to each other, and that is worth a lot. Hopefully, Staff Captain Casimir's analysis will help bring a fina—"

Every communicator in the room chimed at once, cutting the Squadron Lord off as she stared down at the device. A deadly new silence filled the room, and then Tan!Stalla stabbed a manipulator tentacle at her com.

"Tan!Stalla."

"Sir, one of the Laian cruisers just exited hyperspace," Captain Arnaud said quickly and grimly. "They are reporting a major hyperspace anomaly exiting the nebula—and headed directly for the last position we encountered the Infinite."

"Understood. Bring the fleet to ready status; I will make contact with Pincer Korodaun shortly," Tan!Stalla replied. She closed the communicator and turned her attention back to her officers.

"To your stations, officers," she ordered. "It appears I may have been wrong about us having time."

BY THE TIME they reached the bridge, Ashmore's tactical team had the full details from the Laian cruisers uploaded into the main holotank. There weren't as *many* details as Morgan would like, but what was there wasn't good.

"We don't have a solid mass estimate, but we do have a velocity vector," Ashmore reported as the flag staff took their seats. "Contact is headed toward our current position at point-seven-five *c*."

"In the waters of time, it becomes clear that we should perhaps have moved the fleets," Tan!Stalla noted calmly. "They appear to have a solid idea of our maximum velocity as well. This should be...interesting."

She turned to Morgan.

"Casimir, your assessment?"

Morgan was running through the scenarios her people had been working on. She wasn't sure *what* she was looking at, but *someone* had to make an educated guess.

That someone was her.

"It's theoretically possible that we're looking at a second set of cyborg hyper-portal ships," she told the Squadron Lord, but she shook her head. "I don't think so, though," she admitted. "Unless they took the conspirators' fleet effectively intact, there's no way they had enough emitters to pull that off.

"I think we misestimated how long it would take them to implement a biotech version of the hyperdrive," Morgan concluded aloud. "I'm *guessing* we're still looking at a limited number of ships acting as portal creators for the rest of the force, but those ships are almost certainly pure Infinite."

She swallowed.

"Given the previous encounter, I suspect they will have also significantly upgraded their missile capacity. In their place, knowing I had a biotech hyper system available, I would have focused *Builder of Tomorrows*'s capacity on missile launchers and, potentially, shields."

"Thank you," Tan!Stalla told her. "Keep updating your analysis as we engage the Infinite, Staff Captain. Your insights may yet be the difference between victory and defeat."

Morgan swallowed again and nodded.

"Nitik, get the tactical channels interfaced with the Laians and get me a link to Pincer Korodaun," Tan!Stalla ordered. "Let's deal with this as a unified force."

Morgan's "back of the envelope" calculations suggested even that might not be enough. If the force was merely comparable to the last one but with more hyper ships, they might already be in trouble.

The Infinite, after all, had made sure they had the velocity advantage before they could be detected. Morgan *hoped* the Infinite had simply been conservative in their estimates—because if the enemy had a clear-enough idea of what the blockading force could do that they *knew* where they would be detected, the Imperials and Laians were in trouble.

"Squadron Lord Tan!Stalla," Korodaun greeted the A!Tol.

Everyone on the flag deck could hear the conversation. Morgan kept a part of her attention on it as she continued to run numbers. What the blockaders were going to do was almost as important as what the Infinite did.

"Pincer of the Republic," Tan!Stalla said. "We appear to have underestimated our enemy...and I was not weighing them lightly."

"Neither was I," Korodaun noted. "Their velocity was chosen with intent. If we do not position ourselves directly in their path, it will be difficult to engage even with missiles. They are hoping to bring us to bay, to force us to fight if we wish to maintain containment."

"These are your stars, Pincer. What is your order?"

"My orders are to contain the Infinite," the Pincer replied calmly, only a slight chitter under her words undermining her level voice. "We will advance into hyperspace and blockade the Infinite force.

"We will send in drones and attempt to repeat the identification of the hyper-portal units that Staff Captain Casimir managed against the first force," she continued. "Then we will engage the enemy at long range to gain data on how they have upgraded their missile and antimissile systems and doctrine.

"If possible, we will eliminate the hyper-portal units and withdraw in hyperspace," Korodaun concluded. "If not, we will do what damage we can and then fall back. Containment is the objective, but I will not sacrifice our ships if it cannot be achieved, Squadron Lord.

"My staff will forward you our formation plans momentarily. I trust your discretion on the deployment of Imperial units inside those plans."

CHAPTER SIXTEEN

THE ADDITION OF THE LAIAN WAR-DREADNOUGHTS CERTAINLY *felt* like it should make this encounter go differently. The ten massive capital ships outmassed the entire Imperial force and led the way in a solid block.

The Imperial capital ships formed the second line, once again in a broad cross of thirty-two capital ships. The escorts from both forces were formed into wings around the capital ships, in position to either swing forward and reinforce the missile defenses—or to swing *back* and hide behind the bigger ships' shields and armor.

"Hyper transition complete," Ashmore noted. "We have the hostile anomaly on our scanners. Estimated range, two twentieth-light-cycles. Estimated time to zero distance, two twentieth-cycles, seven thousandth-cycles."

Roughly two and a half hours, Morgan mentally translated. They were moving toward the Infinite fleet at point-six c and the Infinite fleet was moving toward them at point-seven-five c...but velocities didn't add together neatly at those kinds of speeds.

The interface drive negated temporal dilation from relativity but not *spatial* dilation. She had no idea if the reactionless drive used by the Infinite negated anything, but the Infinite certainly didn't seem bothered if their sense of time was completely screwed up.

"Laians have deployed drones to sweep the Infinite visibility bubble," Ashmore reported. "We're still trying to resolve individual contacts."

Morgan was keeping an eye on their success on that task—and it was making her nervous. The Infinite force was spread out across a sphere at least three light-seconds wide. That expanded their visibility bubble, assuming they relayed sensor information to each other, to roughly five light-seconds.

It was the same stunt that their fleet was pulling with sensor drones and spreading out their own escorts. The Bucklers and their Laian equivalents weren't out yet, but they would interface with the sensor drones to provide an extra two light-seconds of bubble—with the Bucklers at one light-second and the sensor drones at two—in which to engage incoming missiles reliably.

The issue was that if Morgan looked at the blockading fleet's anomalies, there were clear layers of anomalies that showed the different ships and positions. There were no such layers in the anomaly she was seeing of the Infinite—which suggested a sphere of full-size bioforms three light-seconds across. One that was dense enough to cause problems with identifying individual creatures.

However Morgan cut those numbers, that was a *lot* of Infinite bioforms. The only real *good* news was that the anomaly scanner had lightspeed delays in hyperspace, too. They could see where the Infinite had been two hours before and estimate where they were now, but the Infinite wouldn't see *them* until the light from their arrival reached the aliens.

And at a combined relative velocity of over ninety-three percent of lightspeed, they would very nearly be in *range* when that happened.

THE DRONES ARRIVED FIRST, their anomalies glittering snow across Morgan's displays as they descended on the Infinite swarm. Pincer Korodaun clearly believed in quantity over quality, as there were easily thousands of the robotic spacecraft zooming in on the Infinite fleet.

And if there had been any question that *this* group of Infinite knew everything Tan!Stalla had done to the last group of Infinite, it was answered the moment the probes came within a million kilometers of the outer perimeter.

From the main fleet's range, they couldn't pick out individual plasma bursts. They could barely resolve individual sensor probes, and they knew the courses those were supposed to follow—but Morgan could tell when hundreds of probes died.

The snow metaphor came back to her mind as the dusting of tiny anomalies melted away as the Infinite opened fire. The Laians had sent thousands forward...and thousands died.

"We're not going to get detailed targeting data, sir," Morgan told Tan!Stalla quietly. "They've worked out what we did last time, and they're not going to let our drones get close enough to pick up data—let alone survive to return with it."

She was reporting the obvious, but someone had to say it. What little battle plan they had had been predicated on being able to identify their targets. Now... Now they were going to be loosing their missiles effectively blind into a swarm a million kilometers across. The missiles' tiny brains would have to identify targets and calculate vectors in the final moments of their flight.

They were *designed* for that, but it was still a big ask.

"Vector-change orders from the flag," Nitik reported. "Passing them on to the rest of the fleet. We will reverse course along this vector at fifty-two light-seconds and let their velocity bring them into missile range."

"We'll stick with the Laians," Tan!Stalla confirmed. "Those orders are confirmed."

They had enough time still. Not a *lot* of time, but enough. Thirty seconds passed while the orders were distributed, then the fleet flipped in a smooth maneuver any parade ground would have been proud of.

Twelve seconds to completely reverse a velocity of point-six *c*. The interface drive had its limits, but it also had clear advantages over the enemy's drive.

The combined fleet completed the maneuver at exactly fifty-two light-seconds from the estimated position of the Infinite fleet...and waited.

Instead of rushing toward each other, the blockaders were now moving away from the Infinite. A stern chase was a long chase—except that, in this case, the pursuers had a velocity edge of twenty-seven percent of lightspeed.

Because even when they were running away, Morgan reflected, relativity was *still* going to screw with them.

"Range," Ashmore breathed, the word echoing across the silent bridge. "All ships engaging. Scatterplot Seventeen."

At least the targeting-convention name was honest. They had no detailed information on the force represented by the anomaly they saw. All they had was its vector. The reduced maneuverability of the Infinite made them more vulnerable than interface-drive ships, but one-point-five percent of lightspeed per second was still enough to throw off targeting solutions.

And the blockading fleet didn't even *have* targeting solutions.

What they *did* have was ten Laian war-dreadnoughts, each host to almost two thousand missile launchers, backed by fifty Laian cruisers, sixteen A!Tol superbattleships, sixteen A!Tol battleships, forty-eight A!Tol heavy cruisers and eight A!Tol destroyers.

If the cascade of sensor drones before had been a light dusting snowfall, the missile salvos were a *blizzard*, a solid block of icons that almost blocked the Infinite's anomaly from view. For a moment, the fleet's sheer firepower gave Morgan hope.

Hope *she*, of everyone on the bridge, knew had to be false.

"Anomaly contacts detected," Ashmore said, his voice...wooden.

Not flat. Not level. Not calm. *Wooden*, in the space beyond reasonable fear. "Estimate one million–plus missiles inbound."

One. Million.

Morgan had to verify it for herself and swallowed a moment of fear as she saw the scans. This time, the Infinite anomaly *was* blacked out. There was no way they could derive anomalies for individual missiles...and she knew, having done the analysis, that this was still a *light* missile armament for the force the Infinite had sent out.

"New vector orders from the flag," Nitik snapped. "All ships swing ninety degrees port and go to maximum sprint speed if we have it."

"Do it," Tan!Stalla barked.

Morgan felt *Jean Villeneuve* struggle beneath her. Even the point-six *c* they'd sustained to keep up with the Laians was above their rated cruise speed, but it wasn't their full emergency sprint. That was point-six-five *c*...or twenty percent of lightspeed *less* than the hurricane of missiles coming their way.

Their vector change would get them clear of the Infinite, but it wouldn't do so fast enough to evade that first overwhelming salvo—or, Morgan estimated, the two after it. They were damned.

Except...

"Wait, what are they doing?" she asked aloud as she saw the maneuvers of the Laian war-dreadnoughts.

The Laian escort cruisers were breaking off with the Imperial fleet, fleeing the battlespace at point-seven *c* alongside the *Thunderstorms* and leaving the battle line behind. The *war-dreadnoughts* were doing no such thing.

They'd closed up their phalanx and changed their velocity, all right—to head directly toward the Infinite and into the teeth of that missile hurricane at sixty percent of the speed of light.

Unlike the Imperial ships, they had no sprint mode. That was as fast as they could go, and Morgan's heart *ached* as she realized Korodaun's plan.

"Incoming transmission," Nitik reported, throwing it into the main holotank without even asking.

"We have failed," Korodaun said, her voice flat in the way only a translator with emotional overtones disabled could manage. "Squadron Lord Tan!Stalla, I leave the withdrawal to your command.

"Get my escort cruisers out. They have the speed. My dreadnoughts do not. I will attempt to maintain a communication chain via sensor probes until...the end," Korodaun noted. "We will buy what time we can for you and our people.

"Containment has failed. The Republic endures!"

THE BLOCKADING fleet was scattering along at least nine different vectors, but Morgan left that part of everything to the rest of the flag staff. Her job wasn't to make sure the fleet had a rendezvous point and made it out safely. She had to trust that Tan!Stalla and the rest of the staff could manage that.

Morgan's job was to learn as much as she could from the final charge of the Fifty-Sixth Pincer of the Laian Republic. A daisy chain of sensor drones linked the two flagships, both of them spilling out the robotic spacecraft as they moved to create a chain of relays a quarter-million kilometers apart.

She had full telemetry data from the ten war-dreadnoughts as they charged, every launcher spitting fire as they entered the teeth of the overwhelming force. They drew the missiles in on themselves and deployed hundreds—maybe even *thousands*—of automated defense drones.

They'd also kept everybody *else's* defense drones, Morgan realized, and the Infinite missiles collided with a solid wall of laser and plasma. There were enough missiles and drones on the relayed scanner data to *walk* from dreadnought to dreadnought.

Even so, the Imperial ships wouldn't have survived at the heart of that maelstrom. Two of the war-dreadnoughts died, even their immense shields and armor unable to withstand the incoming fire.

Eight survived the first salvo. Their unexpected course change allowed them to *interpenetrate* the second salvo, leaving most of another million missiles to blaze off into the featureless gray void of hyperspace.

The time also gave Morgan a chance to *look* at the sensor data on the missiles themselves. They were what she'd hoped, in as much as she had hopes around this many missiles. They were still Laian missiles, built, presumably, by *Builder of Tomorrows*.

If the yard had built this many missiles, it hadn't been doing much else. That gave the fleeing allies a small chance. On the other hand, she had no idea where the Infinite had found the materials for this many missiles.

The third salvo was more accurately targeted, and half of Korodaun's remaining dreadnoughts died, along with *all* of their defense drones. And yet...somehow, four war-dreadnoughts reached ten light-seconds.

Those ships were already broken, Morgan knew. She could see that on their telemetry. They'd been firing missiles as they came, but they had no idea if they'd hit *anything*. At ten light-seconds, though, they could finally resolve individual targets in the anomalies facing them.

That was data Morgan and her people would go over with a fine-toothed comb later, but what was important at *that* moment was that the Laian capital ships had targets for their beams.

Battered and broken as they were, the war-dreadnoughts still commanded over four *thousand* proton beams more powerful than *Jean Villeneuve*'s own equivalent weapons. At ten light-seconds, they couldn't guarantee hits with an individual shot.

But quantity has an accuracy all its own.

Contacts began to vanish. Morgan couldn't tell if the bioforms being hit were Category One or Category Eight, but they died under beams of *c*-fractional protons. For a second, maybe even two, the duel went entirely the Laians' way.

And then the Infinite returned fire. Plasma washed over the Laian ships at a focus and quantity Morgan had only seen once before—and her data feed died with Korodaun's flagship.

Jean Villeneuve's flag deck and bridge were silent when she looked up at the others around her, turning her gaze to Squadron Lord Tan!Stalla specifically.

"They're gone, sir," she told the A!Tol. "They hurt the Infinite... I don't know how bad, but they *hurt* them... But they're gone."

"She did it," Tan!Stalla replied, her voice just as soft as Morgan's. "All ships are clear of Infinite missile range on vectors that will get them to safety. Korodaun saved the blockading force, but..."

"The blockade is down," Morgan concluded.

"We have a rendezvous point and will make our course there ASAP," the Squadron Lord declared. "We *must* inform the Grand Fleet and our allies of this as quickly as we can.

"We underestimated the Infinite. We cannot afford to do so again."

CHAPTER SEVENTEEN

THE CONFERENCE ROOM AT THE HEART OF *VA!TOLA* WAS AS silent as a tomb. Quieter, for that matter—Rin had *been* in tombs that had more noise from wildlife than the conference room had from *anything*.

A frozen hologram hung above the table, stuck at the end of the recording of Pincer Korodaun's doomed—and all-too-necessary —charge.

"Further reports from Squadron Lord Tan!Stalla and Three Hundred and Eighty-Four—I mean, Three Hundred and Eighty-*Third* Pincer of the Republic Sokotal confirm that Pincer Korodaun did some level of damage to the Infinite force," Tan!Shallegh said quietly. "However, they continued on their vector without apparent interruption."

"And what was their mission?" Oxtashah demanded.

"We can't be certain, as it was necessary for the remnants of the blockade fleet to withdraw as quickly as possible," Tidirok said smoothly, before Tan!Shallegh could speak. "Most likely, they exited hyperspace somewhere outside the nebula to acquire scan data to compare against the maps acquired from our traitors."

"So, they now know what surrounds them," the Wendira Princess concluded. "And the likelihood that your reinforcements will be able to restore containment?"

"Zero," Tidirok admitted. "I've already ordered them diverted to rendezvous with the First Defense Fleet. The first ships will join my fleet in roughly twelve cycles."

He paused, then snapped his mandibles and pincers simultaneously.

"As will I. These negotiations have become a pointless waste of my time, Princess Oxtashah. We prevented a war between our peoples cycles ago, but it is clear that *your* people have no interest in making common cause against this enemy.

"I can no longer afford to be away from my fleet, arguing that a pile is gold instead of shit," the Laian said bluntly. "See to your borders, Princess, and we will see to ours. I suspect you will regret your choices."

"Ten war-dreadnoughts destroyed without even slowing the enemy," Oxtashah noted. "This changes things, Voice Tidirok. Give me...time. Three cycles. I must commune with my Queens."

"And what difference is it going to make, Princess?" the Voice demanded. "Another hundred thousand of my people are dead. I cannot afford to waste more time."

"I can not guarantee anything, Voice Tidirok," she admitted. "But I swear to you, upon the hive of my hatching and the shells of my progeny, I *will* do all I can to convince them. As I have done all along...but this changes things."

Rin concealed a snort. He'd suspected for a while that Oxtashah was more on-side with the proposed alliance against the Infinite than her Queens had been. She was a loyal servant of the Grand Hive and had followed her orders, but her true position had slipped out before.

"I cannot wait that long," Tidirok told her. "The First Defense Fleet must begin operations against the Infinite immediately if we are to have any chance of protecting the Republic's worlds.

"I must return to my fleet."

"Then I will accompany you," Oxtashah said, her wings snapping to their full spread and glittering in the conference room's lights. "If you will permit it, of course, *Zokalatan* will accompany your flagship to the First Defense Fleet as a gesture of good will."

Rin wasn't even sure Oxtashah had the authority to do that...but she also had clearly made *her* decision. The xenoarchaeologist wasn't as good at reading Laian emotion as he'd like, but he was pretty sure he was picking up Tidirok's hesitation.

"I...will allow it," the Voice finally said. "Tan!Shallegh: may I ask that your flagship escort the star hive? *Closely.*"

"If the Princess's people will permit it," Tan!Shallegh echoed, the A!Tol's skin flickering red and blue in amused agreement.

"They will," Oxtashah said grimly. "Pincer Korodaun's fate will be shared by far too many if we continue to argue like hatchlings. You have my pledge of honor, upon the hive of my hatching and the shells of my progeny, that we will do you no harm."

"I accept your honor, Princess," Tidirok conceded. "We will be underway shortly. I recommend you return to your ship and have them commence preparations."

RIN FOUND TAN!SHALLEGH in the Fleet Lord's office, all of the screens dark as the A!Tol sat there. He wouldn't even have been certain the sentient was *in* the room if the door hadn't opened to let him in, though *Va!Tola*'s systems said that's where he was.

"Fleet Lord?" he asked the darkness.

"I'm here," Tan!Shallegh told him. There was a flicker of movement, but the A!Tol was barely visible, his skin gray-black in exhausted fear. "I..."

The room fell silent and Rin Dunst let the door close behind him. He had been in the room often enough that he was able to find a seat, and he simply waited.

"You are a student of history," the Fleet Lord said in the darkness.

"Of the wars and tribulations not just of your race or even the Imperium."

"Not primarily of war, but yes," Rin agreed. "I mostly study everything we know about the Alava, and we really don't know much of their wars."

"It seems that may change," Tan!Shallegh noted. "Tell me, Dr. Dunst, does it end? Does it ever end? Or will I be drawn into the waters of one war after another, each with the fate of worlds and races on the line?"

"The Imperium has been at peace more than at war, Fleet Lord," Rin reminded the other being. "Even in your lifetime. Even in mine, and I was a *child* when you came to Earth."

Tan!Shallegh had been a Fleet Lord of the Imperium for as long as Rin Dunst had been alive. If there was any being that had deserved retirement or rest more, Rin didn't know them. He wasn't sure what the A!Tol wanted from him, though.

"Perhaps," Tan!Shallegh murmured. "It seems...worse, I'm afraid, because there have been so many wars where we feared for so much. I have done my duty, Doctor. But I think this may be the last war I have in me."

"I don't think anyone will begrudge you that, Fleet Lord," Rin said.

"You'd be surprised," Tan!Shallegh said with a flush of blue through the darkness of his skin. "It will depend, I know, upon how this war fares. My oaths and promises stand, and I will fight these Infinite.

"But I hope and pray there is some answer in your histories, Dr. Dunst, that I do not see," he admitted. "This enemy was beyond the Alava. We have studied the Alava's technology more than any others but the Mesharom, I think, and I know how far short of their power we fall.

"Can we win this?"

"The Alava broke everything, sir," Rin reminded Tan!Shallegh. "That definitely included whatever the Infinite used for FTL and likely included many of their weapons. Certainly, none of the weapons we've seen from them so far match the weapons we believe the Alava possessed."

"This is true. And perhaps even the Mesharom will join us for this war," Tan!Shallegh suggested. "The last true heirs of the Alava. If there is *anyone* who can fight these people, it's them."

Rin nodded grimly, but he remembered the reports out of the Taljzi campaigns. Thirty Mesharom war spheres had been lured into a trap by the Taljzi—a trap built of malfunctioning Alavan technology—and destroyed.

"You're assuming they've rebuilt enough of a fleet to be willing to send out anything," he told Tan!Shallegh.

"I know," the A!Tol admitted, his skin still dark in the unlit office. "Others will come, I think, but I wonder if they can possibly come fast enough to turn the course of what lies before us."

"They have to, sir," Rin said. "But even if they don't, I trust we will find a way. We always have, sir."

There was a harshly amused beak snap.

"I trust—I *believe*—that we can defeat these Infinite in the end," Tan!Shallegh admitted. "What is open to question, I fear, is how many worlds will be sacrificed first."

CHAPTER EIGHTEEN

It had been Morgan Casimir's task to estimate what the Infinite were doing and how quickly they would be able to upgrade their resources. Now, in the aftermath of defeat, it was very clear she'd got it wrong.

The days that had passed didn't make any of it easier, though they'd at least allowed her to pull together every scrap of data they had on the Infinite from Korodaun's charge. None of it was game-changing—they'd never penetrated the visibility bubble with anything except missiles, and those didn't come back to provide updates.

She was sitting alone in the conference room that served as her team's office, studying a rotating hologram of the best scan data they had of the Infinite's missiles, when someone coughed behind her.

With a swallowed sigh, Morgan turned and arched an eyebrow at Bethany Rogers as her subordinate stepped forward and wordlessly offered her a black glass bottle.

"What is this?" she asked.

"Beer," Rogers replied. "Guinness, to my surprise. I didn't expect to find anything of real value aboard even a mixed-race ship."

"I'm on duty," Morgan said.

"No, you're not," Rogers told her. "You've been off duty for three and a half hours, sir. If you *insist* on staying up and staring at a hologram, you can at least do it with a beer in your hand." She paused. "Sir."

Morgan chuckled and tapped the three-point sequence that released the bottle cap. Pocketing the cap, she raised the bottle to Rogers.

"To the Infinite, who might just wreck my career on their way to eating the galaxy."

Rogers opened her own bottle after clinking them together. "I didn't think the *smell* of beer was that much of a depressant."

"Fair. Apologies, Rogers," Morgan said. "I know better, intellectually, than to blame myself for Korodaun and her people. But I'll be damned if I don't feel like I should have done better."

"The whole team does, sir," her subordinate admitted after taking a swallow. "Which means you and I need to shut that story down and shut it down hard. If the team starts wallowing, we're fucked."

"We might be fucked anyway," Morgan replied. "I'm not sure I'd keep this team together if I was Tan!Stalla."

"Who else knows as much as we do?" Rogers asked. "Nobody, that's who. Nobody knows *anything*, sir. We've been neck-deep for longer than anyone else, and yeah, we got it wrong.

"But right now? Even getting it wrong is data." She gestured at the hologram of the missile. "Take this. What do we know about it that we didn't before the fight?"

"We know that it's a standard Laian long-range attack missile," Morgan told her. "We also have acquired a few bits of data about Laian missiles they probably don't realize we did. *Those* go back to my father and his friends inside Jupiter."

DragonWorks was the Imperium's utterly secret, arguably treaty-violating research facility where entire new generations of military tech had been developed from samples of Mesharom and Alavan systems—alongside stolen examples of other Core Power technology.

And, as Morgan suggested, it was buried *inside* Jupiter, contained in a powerful shield bubble fifty kilometers beneath the gas giant's normal surface.

"I already checked for software back doors the Laians might have built into their missiles," Rogers told her. "No remote kill switches for us, sadly."

"We do know one thing, I suppose," Morgan noted as she studied the missile. "They fired just over six *million* of the effing things at Korodaun."

And the rest of the fleet, but Korodaun's charge had distracted those missiles.

"And?"

"And that, plus the million or so missile launchers *to* fire them, represents almost ninety percent of *Builder of Tomorrows*'s production capacity since the estimated time of capture," Morgan told her subordinate. "Assuming they had another salvo in reserve, those missiles consumed every scrap of the shipyard manufacturing ability that could be even remotely used for missiles.

"That limits what else they did. We know they mounted hyper emitters on bioforms before, but if they had *that* many missiles? I *know*, with absolute certainty, that the emitters for the second fleet were not built by *Builder of Tomorrows*.

"So, either they were taken from the wreckage of the conspirators' ships, which I don't think would have given them enough, or they have their own version of a hyper-portal emitter derived from their biology."

"Which is terrifying enough," Rogers said. "But I see the positives of it. And another one, I suppose."

"Which is?" Morgan asked. She realized her beer was half-empty and she didn't consciously recall drinking any of it.

"If they used up that much of the capacity of their only modern industrial node on them...I'm going to guess that they *haven't* worked out how to do biotech interface drives and missiles."

"Yet," Morgan said drily. "But you're right. That does give us one thing to work with: *Builder of Tomorrows* can only produce about seventy thousand missiles a cycle, and *that* is assuming a ready supply of raw material."

"They'll have that soon enough," Rogers admitted. "We can't prevent them diving into empty systems now. That's probably what they were looking for."

"My guess as well," Morgan confirmed. "They came out of the Astoroko Nebula so they could get a clear view of the galaxy, including EM signatures. They'll know which systems in the Dead Zone and near the Nebula are inhabited now.

"No matter what, I suspect they'll move in on at least one system we can't watch," she agreed. "We don't have the time, data, or hulls to prevent that. If we want to restore containment, we need to guess what they're going to do *after* that."

"No small ask, sir," Rogers told her. "But I think we have a chance. At the end of the day, we can guess their needs, and that leads to their objectives."

"Yeah." Morgan drained the rest of her beer bottle. "And before you say a word, Commander, I think both of us will do that better with some rest."

"Yes, we will," Rogers agreed. "See you in the morning, sir?"

"We're expecting to have new orders from Tan!Shallegh by then," Morgan said. "Flag staff meeting. After that, though, we'll start digging into the brain and logic of a monster the size of a planet."

CHAPTER NINETEEN

By the time Morgan joined Tan!Stalla and the rest of the senior staff for the briefing in the morning, she'd slept, showered, braided her hair, and put on a fresh uniform. It felt like she was wasting time while she was doing all of it, but she felt more human and more competent with her hair braided and everything under control.

Looking around the other officers, she suspected she wasn't the first to need to force herself through a total mental reset—and there were still officers on the staff who were going to need to do something equivalent.

Tan!Stalla looked surprisingly on the ball, unlike her officers. She stood at the front of the standard conference room, inside a section that had clearly been rigged with additional humidifiers. The presentation stage was visibly misty, a countermeasure to the Squadron Lord's skin issues, and she leveled beady black eyes on her team.

"We have new orders from Fleet Lord Tan!Shallegh," she told them. "They are, I suspect, what most of us expected. We are to finish rounding up the last of Korodaun's strays and fall back to rendezvous with the First Defense Fleet."

"Sir, shouldn't we at least make some attempt to maintain containment still?" Ashmore asked, the human operations officer's freshly shaved scalp gleaming. That had apparently been *his* mental reset.

"We never had the resources to maintain containment in the face of an active offensive from the Infinite," Tan!Stalla replied. "This was not an unknown factor, Commander Ashmore. If the Infinite were able to deploy significant numbers of hyperdrives before we were able to bring the Grand Fleet and the First Defense Fleet into position— preferably with the Wendira Battle Hives in support—we were always going to be driven off.

"We did everything reasonable to maintain containment, but it is better to return as the clan than die as the tribe. We will fall back and make rendezvous with our fleet and our allies."

Tan!Stalla's bullet-shaped torso turned to allow her to survey the rest of her officers.

"We were defeated, yes," she told them. "And we retreated, yes. But we did so because to fight would have been without purpose. If we had taken every unit of this task force and every one of Koro-daun's cruisers forward with her, we would have died with her.

"She chose to save a fleet."

"Perhaps we should use it," Morgan said quietly, before she even realized she was speaking. Every eye in the room was suddenly on her.

"Staff Captain?" Tan!Stalla intoned.

"You said our orders were to bring the entirety of our force and Korodaun's cruisers back to the First Defense Fleet," Morgan said slowly, the thought taking shape in her head as she poked at it. "But who remains if we do that?"

"No one," Ashmore replied. "We pull everyone back to stand as one fleet, where we're safe."

"A ship in harbor is safe, but that is not where ships were built to be," Morgan quoted back. "I understand the intent of our orders, sir," she told Tan!Stalla, "but there is always a degree of discretion allowed to a flag officer that I suspect Tan!Shallegh is expecting us to take.

"Between our cruisers, the destroyers and the Laian cruisers, we possess over a hundred hulls," Morgan continued. "They are not able to stand against the Infinite and we wouldn't want them to try.

"But they *are* able to maintain a sensor watch over the Nebula and track where follow-up Infinite forces go. They can evade and they can run to escape any attempt by the Infinite to bring them down—but they can keep us up to date on what our enemy is doing.

"If we take *everything* back to the rendezvous, we blind everyone."

The room was silent.

"I suspect you are correct in that Tan!Shallegh might have been thinking similarly," Tan!Stalla agreed. "I had my own thoughts upon those waters as well, but the orders from the Eleventh Voice of the Republic were to recall all ships. Were the orders solely from our own chain of command, I would agree with you.

"But I also hesitate to defy our allies in our operations in their space."

"Then we ask," Nitik suggested, the communications officer's voice raspy to Morgan's ears. Ivida didn't cry like humans did, or she'd have suspected the other woman had been weeping. "Pincer Sokotal will be able to judge the desires of his military command better than we can—but these are also *their* stars we risk leaving unwatched."

"It's the Dead Zone," Ashmore murmured. "Do these stars really belong to anybody?"

"Given that the Laians and Wendira have fought at least one war through this region since they burnt it to the surface, I will not disagree with their ownership claims," Tan!Stalla replied. "But yes, Commander Nitik. I think that may be our best course.

"Staff Captain Casimir, join me in my office after the meeting. I think you will be of service as we draft the scouting plans."

PINCER SOKOTAL WAS NOTICEABLY YOUNGER than Pincer Korodaun had been—to Morgan, at least, who'd grown up with the Laian Exiles on Earth—with a smoother carapace and shorter mandibles. He also had the duller carapace coloring of a male Laian, a ruddy bronze in his case.

"Leaving units behind to scout illuminates the field for tomorrow," he said as soon as Tan!Stalla had laid out their plan. "After Pincer Korodaun's sacrifice, I will admit my thought was to preserve the nest's defenders."

He stared thoughtfully off into space.

"I am prepared to leave several of my cruisers and destroyers here to watch the Infinite," Tan!Stalla offered, "but this is Republic space and I will defer to you as to what is required."

"The offer is appreciated, Squadron Lord," Sokotal said slowly, his multifaceted eyes looking unfocused to Morgan, "but...do any of your ships possess stealth screens?"

"No," Morgan's boss said instantly.

That was *not* strictly true, according to the data Morgan had access to. A small subset of the *Thunderstorm*s were E-class ships. Unlike the D-class ship she'd commanded, the E-class didn't carry weapons of mass destruction. Instead, they were equipped with a stealth system derived from Taljzi technology.

The biggest weakness of the Taljzi system, however, was that theirs was a *tactical* stealth screen. The handful of *Thunderstorm*-Es in Tan!Stalla's task force couldn't hide in hyperspace.

"Ten of my cruisers have full stealth suites," Sokotal told them. "Do we have any evidence that the Infinite can see through our stealth systems?"

"None," Morgan replied instantly. "We have no evidence that they *can't*, either," she cautioned, "but the sensors we detected in the Eye of the Astoroko Nebula were conventional. Lidar, radar, tachyon scans... Nothing unusual, nothing that should penetrate known stealth systems."

On the other hand, using those scanners the Imperium could reliably work out where a stealth ship had been ninety seconds earlier inside a multi-light-minute range. That wasn't enough to catch a stealth ship, but it was enough to render a scouting screen *visible*.

"It will have to be enough," Sokotal decided aloud. "I will detach my stealth ships to maintain a distant watch of the Nebula. They will have strict orders not to risk engagement. As you say, we need the illumination they will provide."

"We expect the Infinite will seek to occupy an empty system for raw materials," Morgan told the Laian officer. "There are too many candidates for us to narrow down the possibilities, but their biggest weakness right now is the lack of readily available metals and other raw materials in the Nebula."

Relatively quickly, on astronomical time frames, the newborn stars that made up the Eye of the Astoroko Nebula would break away from each other. They would tear the nebula's component gases and debris clouds away with them, destroying Astoroko and becoming a dozen new-formed independent systems. Those systems would see all the nebula's immense total mass coalesce into hundreds of planets and thousands of asteroids and meteors.

Relatively quickly, in this case, was somewhere in the region of a million years. All of the materials the Infinite needed were *in* the Nebula but weren't easily available. A more ordinary star system would provide everything in neatly packaged forms.

"That gives us some time," Sokotal observed. "I don't look forward to the fleet they will construct with those resources, but one hopes our bases and systems near here are safe for now."

"They aren't close enough and they are defended," Morgan replied. "I can't see any reason why the Infinite would go for them over unprotected resources that are closer."

The Infinite had clearly recognized the shortcomings of their weapons against the allied fleets. Morgan was quite sure she didn't fully understand their production capacities and limitations, but she *was* sure they still required raw materials.

"And if we're wrong," Tan!Stalla noted, "the scouts will let us know that. That is the purpose of watching the enemy, after all."

"We will see their movements," Sokotal agreed. "It may not be as clear a vision as we wish, but we will see where they go."

CHAPTER TWENTY

RIN DUNST HAD SEEN THE LAIAN FIRST DEFENSE FLEET AND the A!Tol Imperial Grand Fleet before. It was still an awe-inspiring sight as he stood on an observation deck aboard *Va!Tola* and studied the blinking lights swarming above a super-Jovian gas giant.

The Tohrohsail System—the name translated to "Citadel of Hope"—was home to the largest Laian fleet base in the Dead Zone and a supporting colony of fifty or so million Laians. Vast refueling and repair facilities hung above the gas giant, supporting the two immense fleets gathered there.

The First Defense Fleet contained almost a fifth of the Republic's dreadnoughts. Ten of their one hundred dreadnoughts were gone now, but the ninety that remained still vastly outmassed the eighteen squadrons—two hundred and eighty-eight battleships and superbattleships—of Imperial capital ships.

As Rin understood it, the capital ships detached to try to blockade the Infinite were returning now, which would bring the Grand Fleet back up to twenty squadrons. The ten war-dreadnoughts lost against the Infinite would be replaced by reinforcements already on their way from the core anchorages of the Republic, but there were only so many reinforcements that *could* be sent.

He wasn't certain that even five hundred war-dreadnoughts could stand against what he and Morgan had found in the Astoroko Nebula...and while the Republic had more ships than that, it wasn't by much.

"Professor Dunst," a translated voice said behind him. The translators were programmed to add certain accents to their translations, lending a distinct voice to each language even after the translation into English. In this case, the speaker was Wendira.

"Princess Oxtashah," he greeted the Wendira diplomat. There were other Wendira on the ship, but he doubted they'd bother speaking to him. Oxtashah's support team had kept very much to themselves during the journey back to the Laian fleet base. "How may I help you?"

As she stepped up next to him, he found himself fighting a sudden atavistic awareness of the Wendira Royal's sheer size. She *towered* over him and could probably break him by accident. Her multi-part thorax and butterfly-like wings gave her an illusion of frailty at any distance, but at close range, his brain lost that illusion and tried to panic.

"My old foes," she said quietly, and gestured to the tiny moving stars out the window, not answering the question. "This fleet was gathered to fight my people. It is...strange to look at them and attempt to think of them as allies."

Rin was silent. He couldn't say much to that.

"I will shortly speak with the Voice and your First Fleet Lord," she told him. "I have finally convinced my Queens. Two hundred and fifty star hives and their escorts will arrive here in ten cycles.

"If we can manage a peaceful rendezvous and cooperation, we will assemble a force such as has never been seen in this galaxy before, Professor. And yet I fear for my children."

"You and the Republic have never stood side by side," Rin finally murmured. "There are few forces in the galaxy I would expect to stand against you."

"But these Infinite are not of this galaxy. They are of the galaxy that came before, the one of the Alava," Oxtashah said softly, using that name instead of "Those Who Came Before" for the first time in Rin's memory. "Against *gods*, they were victorious. Who are we to hope for victory?"

"They don't know us," Rin told her. "They don't know our nations, our peoples, our ships or our strengths. As we have to learn about them, they have to learn about us—and they fell with the Alava, Princess Oxtashah. They are closer to the Mesharom than the Alava, I think."

The Mesharom were the only survivors of the Alavan subject races. Smashed back into the Stone Age by the failure of Alavan technology, they had clawed their way back to the stars when most of even the *Core Powers* were figuring out how to control fire.

"And we have seen that Mesharom can die," Oxtashah said calmly. "Thank you, Professor. I think that is what I needed to hear."

"I'm glad to have been of help?" Rin said. He wasn't entirely sure *he'd* have found that reassuring.

"There will come a time, Professor, when we may be called upon to break strictures of oaths held for a thousand turnings of the suns," Oxtashah told him. "When the Infinite challenge all that we are and all that we hope ourselves and our children to be, we must reconsider all that has been held as decided.

"Do you understand me?"

"No," he admitted.

"Good." The Princess's wings fluttered in amusement. "I hope it does not come to that.

"You will be advised of the conference, I presume," she told him. "We will speak again soon."

She walked away, leaving Rin Dunst staring out at the massive gas giant ahead of him and softly shaking his head. He had spent his entire adult life among nonhumans, but he *still* occasionally felt weirded out by aliens.

His only reassurance was the certainty that he was often just as disconcerting to them as they were to him.

CHAPTER TWENTY-ONE

THE FINAL HYPER TRANSITION INTO THE TOHROHSAIL SYSTEM released a knot of tension in Morgan's left shoulder that she didn't realize she'd been holding. Several other humans on *Jean Villeneuve*'s flag deck gave audible sighs of relief, and she suspected that most of the other crew members were giving their species' equivalent.

Tohrohsail was safe—for now, at least. If they didn't manage to pull together something capable of slowing the Infinite quickly, even the heavily fortified fleet base might have to be yielded while the galaxy found some scrap of unity.

"We are receiving orbit instructions from *Storm Sentinel*," Nitik reported. "Grand Fleet Command is advising that orbits provided are extremely tight—we are apparently clearing space for..."

"Commander?" Tan!Stalla asked into the silence as Nitik trailed off.

"Apologies, sir," the Ivida woman said after a moment. "Grand Fleet and First Defense Fleet are clearing space in preparation for the arrival of the Wendira Eighth, Ninth, and Fifteenth Battle Hives. Current estimate is fifteen hundred Wendira capital ships, and

Tohrohsail Control doesn't want them within three hundred thousand kilometers of the Laian fleets."

Morgan whistled silently.

"I *bet* they don't," she said aloud. "That's a recipe for a messy fight. Three Battle Hives... That's at least seventy more star hives than the Laians thought were facing them across the Dead Zone."

"And suddenly I am even more grateful that we didn't get dragged into an ice-cursed stupid war," Tan!Stalla agreed. "With the Grand Fleet and First Defense Fleet combined, we'd have had the edge, but it would have been much thinner than we thought."

"Or nonexistent," Ashmore said. "A Battle Hive can be seventy star hives...or anything up to a *hundred*. War-dreadnoughts are expected to reliably fight them at even masses, but three hundred star hives would be over half again Voice Tidirok's strength.

"And the Grand Fleet isn't *that* big."

"True," Tan!Stalla said. "Let us simply be grateful that we swim in waters where that war never happened—and those star hives and their escorts are now on *our* side."

Morgan's computer chimed as new data began to pour in.

"I'm receiving intelligence updates from Grand Fleet Command," she reported. "Including scan data from the scout screen Sokotal left behind." She skimmed through the data, looking for her worst possible nightmare.

It wasn't there.

"There have been no further encounters with Infinite forces in the twelve cycles it took us to get here," she reported. "On the other hand, they have not relocated the force that killed Pincer Korodaun. They *may* have returned to the Nebula, or they might be out wandering around and seeing what they find."

"Data is what they're finding," Tan!Stalla said grimly. "They know as little about us as we do about them, Staff Captain, correct? Every cycle there is a bioform outside of the Astoroko Nebula, they learn more about the state of the galaxy and therefore make better plans."

"Thank god for lightspeed delays," Morgan muttered, looking back at her screens. "They can only learn so much."

"That is true," Tan!Stalla agreed. "Let us hope it is not enough."

"Sirs, we have new orders from *Storm Sentinel*," Nitik announced. "Fleet Lord Tan!Shallegh has requested that Squadron Lord Tan!Stalla and Captain Morgan Casimir report aboard *Va!Tola* one twentieth-cycle after we make orbit."

Morgan blinked. She'd expected ASAP orders—at least for the Squadron Lord.

"Captain Casimir's instructions are a formal transfer order," Nitik clarified after a moment. "You're being moved to *Va!Tola* under the First Fleet Lord's command, sir."

"Ah," Morgan said. That made more sense. "I think I will need to pack and speak to Commander Rogers in that case." She turned to Tan!Stalla.

"With your permission, Squadron Lord?"

"YOU DON'T SEEM SURPRISED," Morgan told Rogers after she'd updated her subordinate.

"I'm not," Rogers said. "Your family's history with Tan!Shallegh goes back as far as humanity's history with the Imperium. He *trusts* your mother beyond anyone else—and you've proven yourself worthy of similar trust in his eyes, I suspect.

"And now you've been at the center of the greatest potential crisis the Imperium has ever seen and been the one pulling together all of the data." The redhead shrugged. "No one knows more than this team, but Tan!Shallegh needs his own Infinite analysis group. He might poach some of us later, but right now, he's claiming you."

"He's the First Fleet Lord," Morgan conceded. "If he thinks I'll be more use there, that's where I'll be."

"It also is where Dr. Dunst should be, isn't it?"

Morgan snorted.

"The thought had occurred to me, but I was considering where I would be of more value to the Imperium, not where my boyfriend is," she told Rogers. "My personal desires are secondary to the Imperium's needs, Commander."

"You're still allowed to consider that a bonus, sir," her former executive officer said. "Look, sir, you're not disobeying the First Fleet Lord. The only real *question* in this case is whether you really should be bringing the rest of the analysis team with you—and that's a discussion for you to have with Tan!Shallegh.

"Right now, I'll take over the team here and we'll continue our work while you sort out what the Grand Fleet needs," Rogers told her. "The sky won't fall in the next few cycles."

"The Infinite might fall on somebody in that time," Morgan said grimly. "But we're too far away to do anything about it, anyway.

"I'll check in with the rest of the team, but I also need to pack." She chuckled. "What little I bothered to unpack. I had more space on *Defiance*."

She'd had the Captain's cabin on *Defiance*. Visiting officers' quarters aboard a superbattleship were nicer than *most* of the officers' quarters on a cruiser, but they still fell short of a Captain's cabin anywhere. Rank hath its privileges, and all that.

"Go pack," Rogers suggested. "I'll wake the team up for a quick and dirty goodbye and get the wheels rolling. We've only got, what, a tenth-cycle?"

"Trust an XO to find the efficient path," Morgan said with a chuckle. "I swear, Captains get rusty at that *far* too quickly—because our XOs are too damn good at it!"

CHAPTER TWENTY-TWO

There were no Marines or fancy escorts waiting when Morgan and Tan!Stalla disembarked from their shuttle. They'd apparently been ushered into the quietest shuttle bay anyone could find, and Morgan had a moment of panic wondering why.

Then she saw the two people waiting for them there. The first was the person she'd expected, the tentacled form of the highest-ranking officer of her own military service. The *second*, however, was a pudgily overweight and perpetually befuddled-looking academic with a stupid grin on his face.

Morgan managed to control her urge to do something ridiculously childlike and approached Tan!Shallegh and gave him a crisp salute.

"Sir, Captain Casimir reporting," she said. "I have transfer orders."

"I know what they say, Casimir," Tan!Shallegh told her with a flash of red amusement on his skin. "I did write them."

He turned to Tan!Stalla.

"Squadron Lord Tan!Stalla, Captain Casimir, welcome aboard *Va!Tola*," he told them. "I keep meaning to transfer back aboard

Sentinel, but there hasn't been time. This is how the current flows, it seems. A split command is likely a wise choice as we proceed, in any case."

Storm Sentinel was still listed as the flagship of the Grand Fleet, a somewhat older *Majesty*-class superbattleship. *Va!Tola* had been a later addition, as Morgan understood it, and the decision had been to send one of the Imperium's biggest and most advanced ships to the peace conference.

"I have scheduled a staff briefing for you, Lord Tan!Stalla," he continued. "Captain Casimir has likely seen most of the information anyway and can use the time to get herself settled in her new quarters."

A!Tol deceived poorly, even when they were doing it for their own amusement. The flickering layers of red and yellow across Tan!Shallegh's skin were a combination Morgan hadn't seen before—she'd very rarely seen the tones that meant an A!Tol was lying.

"Dr. Dunst here has kindly offered to show Captain Casimir to her quarters while you and I attend the briefing," Tan!Shallegh told Tan!Stalla. "Will that be acceptable, Captain Casimir?"

"Yes, sir," she agreed, managing to *not* glare at her informal alien "uncle." "When should I expect to report for duty, sir?"

"We have a meeting that I will need you to attend in one tenth-cycle," Tan!Shallegh told her levelly. "I can't give you more time than that, but I can give you that."

Which, despite his skin tone betraying him, was clearly as close as he was going to get to admitting that he was setting up time for her to spend with her lover.

THE QUARTERS WERE SIGNIFICANTLY NICER than she'd been expecting. They weren't generic visiting officers' quarters, Morgan realized as she dropped herself on the bed.

"Whose room am I stealing?" she asked. "It's not *yours*," she noted as she patted the bed for Rin to join her. "It's too clean."

"I am not messy," he countered—mostly truthfully.

"No, but this is basically brand-new levels of clean, not *the room has been cleaned* levels of clean," Morgan said, leaning her head on his shoulder.

"I believe this is one of the quarters set aside for the Fleet Lord's senior staff officers," Rin admitted. "I know Tan!Shallegh's staff is still split between here and *Storm Sentinel*, where they've been supporting Fleet Lord Ab."

Ab was the second-in-command of the Grand Fleet, one of the most senior non-A!Tol officers in the fleet and definitely the most senior Pibo officer in the A!Tol Imperial Navy.

"I guess I can arm-wrestle for it later," she murmured, running her fingers over Rin's face and turning him to kiss her.

"If you must," he agreed when they came up for air a moment later. "It's been a busy time."

"And we will talk about *all* of that," Morgan said. "Everything I've learned, everything you've learned, everything we both project and suspect and guess.

"But the First Fleet Lord has moved meetings and conferences to give us two hours together with no expectations, and I *really* think you should take my clothes off before we fall back into talking about work, okay?"

CHAPTER TWENTY-THREE

MORGAN WAS FEELING THE MOST RELAXED SHE HAD IN WEEKS, at least, when she joined the senior officers' briefing for the Grand Fleet. The briefing was large enough that she was completely uncertain where she was supposed to sit until an A!Tol caught her eye with a wave of a manipulator tentacle, gesturing her to a human-style seat next to them.

"Welcome to the staff, Staff Captain," the A!Tol greeted Morgan as she took the seat. "And the deep end. I'm Division Lord I!Lorak, the Fleet Lord's intelligence officer.

"From what I understand of your role, we'll be working closely together," he continued. "How clear are the waters of this meeting to you?"

Morgan looked around the big amphitheater and chuckled. There were at least eighty people present, physically or virtually, and most of them had the crossed-spears or crossed-swords insignia of Imperial "Lords"—flag-ranked officers.

"The Fleet Lord suggested other priorities for me than getting up to speed immediately," she admitted, her cheeks warming in a way that she hoped I!Lorak didn't recognize.

"I understand," he told her—but from the whirls of red amusement in the blue understanding marked on his skin, he *knew* what Tan!Shallegh had set up for her.

"This is the first all-Lords briefing that Tan!Shallegh has held since returning from the peace conference," I!Lorak told her. "You would do well to pay attention, as he is trying to clear the waters for many of our officers who have not kept up as they should.

"It is unlikely that you will be called upon to speak but not impossible," he warned her. "You are the officer who has been present at everything so far."

"And I am guessing you wrote the briefing?" Morgan suggested.

I!Lorak's skin flashed red as he snapped his beak in a chuckle.

"You see clearly," he confirmed. "I will need to weigh your waters heavily as the current advances, my friend. You know more about this enemy than anyone, I think, and that will all factor together."

"If you're the Fleet Lord's intelligence officer, will I be reporting to you, then?" Morgan asked.

"No," I!Lorak told her. "It is Tan!Shallegh's privilege to tell you exactly his plans, but I believe the waters are intended to be much the same as your service to Tan!Stalla. You will lead a special team dedicated to the Infinite, while I focus on...everything else."

A few tentacles waved in the air meaningfully—but then Tan!Shallegh moved into the center of the amphitheater, his torso dark green with determination as he rotated, surveying the entire crowd.

"Officers of the Grand Fleet, welcome," he told his audience. "While I know we've been keeping up with broadcast information, I feel that it is time to see each other in the same waters and allow questions.

"You have all been briefed on the Infinite, the strange Precursor-era bioships we have encountered in the Astoroko Nebula. They are aggressive and they are terrifyingly powerful," he said calmly.

"Our attempt to maintain containment by limiting their access to the resources necessary to produce hyper-portal emitters has been a complete failure," Tan!Shallegh continued. "The Laians now have a small scout force of stealthed cruisers watching the Infinite's movements around the Nebula, but we know there is at least one Infinite force in Laian space.

"We expect more forces to deploy from the nebula as they decide on their goals," he concluded. "Thanks to the negotiations I have been involved with for these last cycles, we expect significant reinforcements before we move to intercept the Infinite's next operation.

"We have several teams identifying potential targets, and we will be relocating closer to the nebula shortly. We are waiting on the arrival of our latest allies: three Battle Hives of the Wendira Grand Hive."

That earned the Fleet Lord assorted sounds and gestures of surprise.

"They are due to arrive within the next four cycles," he announced. "Once they and the next round of Laian reinforcements arrive, we will be relocating as a body to a not-yet-determined system near the Astoroko Nebula.

"With major Wendira, Laian and Imperial components to the allied fleet, we expect to be able to engage an Infinite force on roughly equal terms and be able to drive back or destroy their first expeditions," he told them. "We do not expect to be able to restore anything resembling *containment* of the Infinite at this point.

"All evidence suggests that hyperspatial engagement is heavily weighted in their favor, given the preponderance of hyperfold cannons on the ships of all three powers we're bringing to the fight. We will avoid any such engagement if at all possible.

"Our task is to intercept Infinite movement against inhabited systems in the region and defend them in normal space, where this fleet can make full use of our hyperspace missiles and all of us can use hyperfold cannons.

"This is not a war-winning strategy," Tan!Shallegh warned. "This is a holding strategy while further reinforcements are gathered. We have confirmed, as of today, that the Ren, the Kazov, the Oot and the Forman have all agreed to activate security agreements with the Laians and the Wendira.

"That is four more Core Powers that have committed to reinforce us," he told them. "I have also spoken with our Empress, and another ten squadrons of modern capital ships and their escorts are going to be sent to reinforce us."

Morgan couldn't help but shiver. She'd commanded one of the Imperium's newest and most advanced cruisers, a ship that served as a starkiller deployment platform. Her clearances were among the highest the Imperium had, which meant she knew *exactly* how many modern HSM-equipped capital ships the Imperium had built.

If the Grand Fleet were going to have thirty squadrons of hyperspace missile–equipped capital ships, that would be almost half of the *entire* Imperial Navy—and it would be basically *every* HSM-equipped battleship and superbattleship they had.

"We do not expect any reinforcements outside of the Laians and Wendira for approximately half a long-cycle, at least," Tan!Shallegh warned. "Ninety cycles, minimum. That is how long we will need to maintain a holding action against the Infinite in Laian space."

The room was silent, dozens of flag officers considering what that was going to entail. Finally, someone pressed a button to indicate a question.

"Yes," Tan!Shallegh said, gesturing to the Rekiki officer. Morgan didn't know the Squadron Lord in question, but she paid attention anyway.

The questions were where she suspected she was most likely to get dragged in.

"If we are bringing in Core Powers to deal with a Precursor-esque problem, has anyone contacted the Mesharom?" the Squadron Lord asked. "They were involved with the Taljzi, and that was a far lower threat level, as I understand."

"We have attempted, through both official and unofficial channels, to make contact with the Mesharom Conclave, yes," Tan!Shallegh said grimly. "We have received no response. Our messages have made it through, we believe, but the Conclave has not replied."

Unofficial channels. A twitch ran down Morgan's back as she considered those. Ki!Tana had vanished to carry copies of *Defiance*'s sensor data to their *associates*—members of the Mesharom-led not-quite-secret society that tried to keep Alavan technology under wraps.

Security treaties or no, she suddenly suspected that their associates had been instrumental in getting four Core Powers to willingly commit warships to *anything*. The great technological advancement of the Core Powers was often held up as a sign of greater *cultural* advancement...but usually only by the Core Powers themselves.

They were often xenophobic and isolationist, drawing their inspiration from the Mesharom, the oldest Core Power—and a race that didn't even like their own kind, let alone strange aliens.

"We cannot and will not rely on the Mesharom to pull us out of this fire," Tan!Shallegh told everyone. "With the fleets of six Core Powers, even we should quickly become redundant."

"Then why are we here?" another officer asked. "We came in response to a request from the Laians to stand against the Wendira. This seems outside the scope we agreed to."

"We are here because the Laians are our allies and because all evidence suggests that the Infinite present a potentially existential threat to the galaxy if allowed to expand and rebuild," the Fleet Lord replied. "We hope to be able to communicate with them, but right now the only communications we are receiving are missiles.

"We will not risk the survival of our only Core Power ally by washing our hands of the situation," he finished. "We will also not expose all of our technological secrets in their defense, either," he warned. "Not unless it becomes necessary."

Most of the *secrets* Tan!Shallegh was talking about hadn't even been assigned to his fleet, Morgan knew. The Grand Fleet had a small force of ships that could make hyperspace denser—and hence enable significantly faster FTL transit—that they were trying to keep under wraps, but most of the rest of the Imperium's secrets hadn't been sent out.

Morgan had commanded the only starkiller-equipped *Thunderstorm*-D anywhere near the Grand Fleet. The Grand Fleet had starkillers, but they were the traditional kind that was the size of a destroyer, not the stolen Mesharom design that was the size of a shuttle.

"Next question?" Tan!Shallegh asked, switching to another flag officer as Morgan settled in to learn as much as she could of the fleet's plans.

CHAPTER TWENTY-FOUR

"Sir."

Morgan saluted as she stood inside Tan!Shallegh's office. She'd last been in one of his offices aboard *Storm Sentinel,* but this one was decorated much the same. She recognized the handiwork of several of the artists that decorated his shelves, but not the works in question.

The Fleet Lord had a well-earned reputation as a patron of the arts on Earth and several other worlds. It was a small part of why humanity had taken the being who had *conquered them* to heart as much as they had.

His repeated command of fleets defending Earth from other people had probably helped, though.

"Sit, Staff Captain," Tan!Shallegh ordered. "You were seated with I!Lorak at the briefing," he continued after she had. "Did he clear some waters for you?"

"He mentioned I would lead my own team, but not much more," Morgan said. "He felt that was your privilege."

"Reasonable," the Fleet Lord agreed. "Drink, Staff Captain? I have coffee for your people here."

"Thank you, sir."

A device concealed inside the A!Tol's desk burbled away for twenty seconds, then a panel in the desk slid open and a cup of steaming coffee rose into view.

None of *Morgan's* desks had that feature, but the Fleet Lord's desk wasn't standard Navy-issue.

"My existing staff is extremely capable and I have no desire to unbalance their working relationships," Tan!Shallegh told her. "I feel that we are dealing with a problem from outside our known waters and we should have an outside perspective on that problem.

"So, yes, you are being added to my staff as a special analyst team lead on the Infinite, much as your partner has been added as a special advisor on the Infinite," he continued. "As my staff will remain divided between *Va!Tola* and *Sentinel* to provide redundancy in the command links. That frees up the Operations department space on *Va!Tola* for your team.

"You may recruit anyone you wish from the Grand Fleet," he told her. "I ask that you leave at least some of the officers of your original team with Lord Tan!Stalla, but I expect you to recruit several of them.

"If you need additional assistance in picking officers, I recommend consulting I!Lorak's advice. He is familiar with the intelligence teams of the various squadrons under my command."

"Of course, sir. Thank you, sir." Morgan paused. "We screwed up with our guess of how quickly they could develop hyper systems, sir. We could get it wrong again. We might have got the assumptions we've already made wrong."

"You might," he agreed. "In fact, you *will* inevitably get *something* wrong. That is the analysis game, Staff Captain. You provide the best information you can to me, and I make the decision based on it. Right now, I will make those decisions in company with Voice Tidirok and, shortly, Royal Commandant Ronoxosh."

"We know the Wendira commander then?" Morgan asked.

"Oxtashah has provided some information on her brother, yes," Tan!Shallegh told her. "The Royal castes are very much a family

business, of course. I assume there is a Warrior-caste Royal Commandant with the Battle Hives as well, to act as Ronoxosh's backup, but
Ronoxosh has earned his command over thirty years of service."

The A!Tol fluttered his tentacles in a shrug.

"After fathering some thirty thousand of the next generation, of
course," he noted. "The Wendira will always seem strange to me."

Morgan said nothing. A!Tol reproduction involved their young
eating their way out of their mother's body—something entirely
replaced with artificial gestation chambers now but still how their
bodies were designed.

The A!Tol had no grounds to call anyone *strange*, in her mind.

"What do you expect me to do with this team, sir?" she finally
asked.

"What you did for Tan!Stalla but with more resources," he told
her. "We now have some more data on the Infinite—if nothing else,
an estimate of the time frame it took them to develop an organic
hyperdrive.

"So, I want you to redo all of your analysis with that estimate.
Run it through the computers we've got. Give your team access to the
relevant parts of the Mesharom Archive if you must," he concluded.
"I will bear the burden for that authorization."

"Are you certain, sir?" she asked quietly. The Mesharom Archive
was a complete download of the files and library databases of a
Mesharom war sphere, acquired during the Taljzi campaigns when
Morgan herself had led a rescue mission into a fleet wrecked in a
Taljzi trap.

That the Imperium possessed the Archive was one of its most
closely guarded secrets. Even *Rin*, who had every scrap of data
regarding the Alava from the Archive stored in a computer chip
implanted at the base of his spine, did not know the origin of that
information.

"Don't tell them where the data *comes* from," Tan!Shallegh said
with a skin-flushing chuckle. "But the Alavan portions, the ones Dr.
Dunst has access to, may be useful for your team. I would rather give

them too much and hold them to higher security standards later than not give them enough to make the right judgments.

"This enemy is..." The Fleet Lord trailed off. "'They come from strange waters bearing strange weapons and we know not their intent.'"

Morgan didn't know the words, but she recognized it as a quote of some kind.

"An outside-context problem," she murmured. "That's what it was called in my training for the Duchy of Terra Militia. A threat we couldn't anticipate because we didn't have the data. The Taljzi were an outside-context problem, but the Infinite are...even more so."

"Exactly, Staff Captain. I look to you to provide the context," he told her. "I've seen the estimate of the capabilities of the X-type bioforms, Casimir. I want you to validate those estimates with a new team—and then I want you to tell me how long it's going to be before I should expect to *face* an enemy with every weapon I have mounted on a warship the size of a planet."

"I still believe, sir, that they are limited in their ability to update the larger bioforms beyond implanting hardware on the surface," Morgan noted. "That leaves the possibilities of Category One bioforms serving as symbiotic systems on the larger bioforms but *does* limit how much firepower they can truly bring to bear."

"And that, Captain Casimir, is exactly the analysis and break-down we need," he told her. "I need to know the threat level, because right now? Right now, I am assuming the threat level is functionally infinite, and I can't fight that."

The phrasing was probably even intentional, and Morgan bowed her head in acknowledgement of Tan!Shallegh's point.

"Resources, timelines, logic and tactics," she murmured. "We'll break them all down as best as we can. I should probably get started."

"Yes," the Fleet Lord agreed. "Take the coffee with you," he noted, indicating Morgan's barely touched cup. "I have a noncom arriving in a few thousandth-cycles to take you to your new office.

"Whatever you need for your team, talk to my chief of staff,

!Pana," he continued. "We will make it happen. Knowledge is the greatest weapon against all foes but the sea, Captain."

Morgan nodded her acknowledgement—but her mind finished the old A!Tol saying.

Knowledge is the greatest weapon against all foes but the sea—and the sea cannot be defeated.

THE NONCOM LEFT Morgan alone in her new working space, and she took a few moments to just absorb what she had to work with. The Fleet Operations Center wasn't a portion of an Imperial capital ship where she'd spent a lot of time before—she'd been due for a tour as a task force operations officer before she was promoted to flag rank, but she hadn't held the role yet.

The FOC supported the flag bridge by providing a separate space for the operations officer to stuff the team of analysts and technicians that backed them up. Often, it was little more than a glorified version of the conference room she'd run her Infinite team out of aboard *Jean Villeneuve*.

Ashmore had been making full use of *Villeneuve*'s FOC. Here, though, Tan!Shallegh's operations officer was aboard a different ship entirely, which left the ridiculously well-equipped space for Morgan's new special analysis team.

It was an oval room anchored on a four-meter-long holotank, currently showing the strategic map of the Dead Zone and the Astoroko Nebula. A dozen consoles were positioned in the main room, all facing toward the holotank but leaving enough space for the senior ops team to stand around the holotank and use it as a planning board.

One wall of the FOC was a massive screen, providing an additional shared working space for the entire team, and the opposite wall was home to six offices—for the ops officer and their top five officers and senior noncoms.

It was only slightly smaller than *Defiance*'s bridge had been and was designed for only two-thirds as many sentients. Right now, Morgan was the only person in the space, and she stepped up to the holotank, tapping commands to bring up the files she'd transferred over from *Jean Villeneuve.*

The Queen appeared in the center of the display, a small scale at the bottom corner marking the almost-incomprehensible size of the immense Infinite creature.

She was easily over a hundred thousand kilometers long; they never had got a solid-enough look to get a definite number. The Queen was the entity Morgan had communicated with—and she wasn't even sure if the Queen was an individual or if the Infinite shared some kind of hive mind.

The latter seemed unlikely to her, but it was a scenario she had to consider.

With a sigh, she swept the hologram away, bringing up the data they had on the force that had driven off the blockading fleet. The final estimates had been broken down on the trip to the Grand Fleet.

Not that they were reassuring.

Eleven hundred—plus/minus about fifty—bioforms had put out approximately a million missiles in each salvo. Morgan wished she could break them down by category. She had to hope that there'd been a significant number of larger bioforms in there; otherwise, her estimates of the enemies' firepower were badly off.

"They said I'd find you here," Rin's voice said from behind her. "Already gazing into the mind of the enemy?"

"The factories of the enemy, more like," she told him without turning around. "A million launchers and at least five million missiles."

She shook her head.

"According to the Laians, *Builder of Tomorrows* could have produced that, but it would have required a *lot* of raw materials, and we're not sure if they could have accessed that much, say, raw iron in the middle of the nebula."

"Outside my expertise," Rin admitted. He pulled a chair over to the holotank and plopped down on it. "You don't have to answer those questions alone, either. This space seems designed for a few more than one."

He gestured around the FOC.

"Seventeen or so," Morgan agreed. "I have a list. I need to expand it."

She shook her head.

"I just... I'm worried I'm missing something, Rin," she admitted. "And they're basing the entire deployment of fleets around my advice and analysis. There's only so comfortable I can be with that!"

"Would you trust someone else to do it?" he asked quietly.

That question shocked a sudden laugh from Morgan—especially because the answer was immediate and definitive in her head.

"No," she admitted. "I take your point."

She waved away the data on the Infinite swarm and brought back the strategic display again.

"Their main body is still here." She tapped the Eye of the Astoroko Nebula—a rosette of newborn blue stars that screwed up hyperspace around them with gravity signatures, part of why the Infinite had never been found.

"The strength we've seen there is basically unimaginable," she noted. "Even if we brought the massed battle fleets of the Core Powers into play, I'm not sure we can actually breach the Eye and destroy the Queen.

"Certainly, we can't do it with the resources we have right now. So, it's a holding play still, even if containment has failed."

"It looks like the Alava held them in this region for a while," Rin noted. "There's some odd mining sites that the Laians took me to investigate that looked like biotech. With hindsight, I'd say they were Infinite extraction sites.

"They can access resources *fast*, if that site is an example," he warned her. "But that was from Alavan times. They still dug up most of the planet over the course of a year, which suggests they were *there* for a year."

Morgan grimaced.

"Short of Alavan-style chopping planets in half to get at the core, that's still probably the fastest I've heard of someone exploiting most of a planet," she pointed out. The Infinite seemed to work on the same scale as the Alava, and that meant the current galaxy was feeling badly out of scale.

"So, what do you think their next steps are?" her boyfriend asked.

Morgan tapped a command, highlighting a crescent of stars in orange.

"There are fourteen uninhabited systems within five cycles' hyperspace flight of where we engaged the Infinite," she told him. "None have seen significant scouting from anybody, as they have no habitable planets."

Anything in that zone that *had* been habitable was gone now—and so was its *star*. The Laians and Wendira had been *very* thorough about trying to genocide each other before they'd eventually wised up.

A little, at least.

"And we're preparing based on the assumption they're tearing those systems apart for resources, I would guess?" Rin asked.

"Exactly. And my team needs to work out what they're turning those resources into," she said grimly. "We now know it took them under fifty cycles to create and deploy a hyperspace drive out of their biotech.

"I'm *hoping* they weren't doing parallel development of other systems, but that means I'm expecting about the same time period before they start deploying either biotech missiles or biotech hyperfold guns."

She shivered.

"I'm guessing missiles," she admitted. "They haven't seen hyperfold cannons since leaving the Nebula, so they'll recreate the systems they're already using and we've used against them. Their priorities may change after the first regular-space engagement."

"Wouldn't they have seen hyperfold cannons from the conspirators?" Rin asked.

"Yep, and they have samples on board *Builder of Tomorrows*," Morgan agreed. "But the big fights they've had with real fleets have been missile duels, so I suspect we'll see them bring their own missiles to the party in short order."

"Which will basically be, what, miniature bioforms?"

"Most likely," she said. She shook her head. "I need to pull that team together and sit down and have this conversation with them. Can you see if you'll be available? We're clearing them for *everything* we know about the Alava, and I'd like you to brief them."

She heard him inhale and then release a long sigh.

"That could take a while," he admitted with a chuckle. "But I think I know what'll be relevant. I'll be here when you need me, Morgan. I hope what I know can help."

"So do I," she said. "Because I'd love it if we found an easy answer to this mess—because I'm not sure I see a solution once they start moving Category Sixes and Sevens out of the nebula!"

CHAPTER TWENTY-FIVE

Despite his assorted commitments, Rin still managed to find time to steal moments in the massive superbattleship's observation domes and breathe. Dragging Morgan along on those moments was harder, but he managed it.

His reward was to watch the tightly wound blonde slightly—ever so slightly—relax a bit as she looked out at the gas giant "beneath" *Va!Tola*. The lights of the ships and the Tohrohsail Fleet Base detracted slightly from the calming appearance, but the gas giant itself was quite pretty.

"My team is ready," she said after several minutes. "I'm going to hold you to that briefing, if we have time."

"I haven't heard much news of significance," he told her. "Things are quiet for now."

"Which makes me nervous as well." She shook her head at him. "We're in position to see them move, so why *haven't* we seen them move?"

"You're supposed to be relaxing," Rin countered. He was enough of a workaholic himself to recognize that Morgan was overdoing it, but even as her lover, he only had so much clout to get the woman to relax.

"I'm also supposed to have a briefing for the combined command staff in two cycles, once the Wendira arrive," Morgan replied. "One that we're going to base our war strategy off of for the next few weeks at least."

"And you'll be better prepared to draft and give that briefing if you *rest* once in a while," Rin told her. They were alone in the observation dome at the moment, though that probably wouldn't last. Enough of the crew would swing through on a given work shift to make the privacy with the view rare and precious.

"Fair," she conceded to his point, but he could tell that she was still thinking away.

"I was hoping the planet would be more successful at distracting you than I am," Rin told her with a smile. "It is much prettier, after all."

She turned away from the big window to look at him and shook her head. Rin figured she knew he wasn't particularly bothered by his looks or weight—but it was hard to argue that the red, green and blue gas giant wasn't absolutely gorgeous.

"You do better than you give yourself credit for," she said anyway. "Even when you're being serious, not self-deprecating."

She gave him an exaggerated leer.

"And besides, what *follows* me looking at you is *very* distracting and relaxing," she murmured.

The train of thought was interrupted by the dome door opening, revealing a pair of black-armored Wendira Warrior caste. They swept the room with multi-faceted eyes, their gazes rested on Morgan and Rin for a few moments, then they withdrew.

Rin was about to wonder what had happened when Oxtashah stepped through the door the Warriors had just checked, the Wendira Royal folding her wings in closely to fit through the portal.

"Ah, Dr. Dunst, Captain Casimir," Oxtashah greeted them. "Are you also here to watch the arrival?"

"Is it time?" Morgan asked while Rin was still processing what the Wendira had said. "It's not normally so predictable."

"The first scouts arrived a few moments ago," Oxtashah said. "We needed to be certain that there was a clear section for the Battle Hives to emerge into. I believe... Yes, there."

She pointed a pincer at a section of space visible past the gas giant, well beyond where Rin figured most of the ships would be visible even as dots.

While the next steps for everything in Tohrohsail were predicated on the arrival of the Wendira ships, he hadn't actually paid that much attention to *when* the three Battle Hives were due to arrive. It made sense, of course, that Oxtashah had been.

"I believed it would be worth watching," the Wendira Princess noted. "I do not believe that fleets of my people and the Laians of such size have *ever* shared a system without a major battle.

"It is a first—and perhaps a promising one, one that speaks to a new era for both our species and those around us."

It started with a tiny blue spark. To Rin's surprise, Morgan tapped on the glass of the observation dome, and the area they were looking at suddenly expanded as concealed optics and screens zoomed in at a command sequence he hadn't known.

The tiny blue spark was just one portal, maybe a dozen kilometers across. It was joined by others. First a handful. Then dozens. Then immense portals, a thousand kilometers across, that unleashed entire star hive carrier groups.

They had enough zoom to watch the ships emerge in their delicate-seeming formations, the ten-million-ton star shields leading the way in their hundreds. The star hives themselves were the center point, smooth pyramid-like shapes multiple kilometers high, arranged into formations of fives surrounded by star shield battleships.

More lights glinted around the capital ships, smaller vessels invisible even at this scale.

"Two hundred and fifty star hives, twelve hundred star shields, and nine hundred lighter escorts," Oxtashah said softly. "Three

Battle Hives of the Wendira, to stand alongside our ancient foes against these Infinite.

"They should never have picked this fight."

Rin kept his peace. He wasn't entirely sure the Infinite, trapped as they were in the Eye, had really had a choice. As soon as someone had shown up with a potential way out, he couldn't quite blame them for trying to seize it—even if they *had* attacked the ship he was on.

He *could* blame them for the fact that every meeting after that had *also* started with the Infinite shooting at whoever they encountered. That wasn't making them any friends and was, well, why there were now over four hundred Core Power major capital ships in the Tohrohsail System.

On the other hand, Rin Dunst had seen some of Morgan's analyses. He still wasn't sure they had *enough* ships.

CHAPTER TWENTY-SIX

MORGAN'S BRIEFING HAD GONE SURPRISINGLY SMOOTHLY, laying out what they knew with certainty about the Infinite—not nearly enough—and what she thought they were going to do next—acquire resources to produce more systems and more of themselves.

She'd been expecting a larger audience. She'd ended up presenting to three people: Voice Tidirok, Fleet Lord Tan!Shallegh, and Royal Commandant Ronoxosh. They'd been seated in that order, either intentionally or instinctively putting the A!Tol between the Laian and the Wendira officers.

Ronoxosh was smaller than Oxtashah but had almost identical coloring and other features. His wings were much more clearly vestigial than hers, tiny faerie-like things half-covered by the floor-length cape he wore, closed at the neck with the golden orb insignia of his rank.

He had waited through the entire presentation in calm silence, then leaned forward as Morgan finished up.

"I have questions, if Captain Casimir can remain to answer them," he told them, his voice soft in both translation and in the untranslated musical hum of his true voice.

"I am at your disposal," Morgan replied. "Fleet Lord Tan!Shal-legh made certain I had the rest of the cycle clear."

She knew perfectly well that the First Fleet Lord did *not* have the rest of the cycle clear, though the administrators of his flag staff would rapidly fix that if the meeting continued over its schedule.

"I do not believe my questions will take that long," Oxtashah replied, the translator picking up an amused tone. "How wide is our catchment net for scouting around the Astoroko Nebula at the moment?"

"The Laian portion of it is now up to forty-six stealth ships," Morgan told him. "With long-range anomaly scanners, they are covering a section of the nebula approximately sixty-two by forty-eight degrees across."

"We have not been briefed on the positions of the Wendira star hives covering your side of the Nebula," she admitted.

Ronoxosh paused thoughtfully.

"That coverage is less than five percent of the total surface area of the Nebula," he pointed out. "Our coverage is roughly comparable on the other side. We have not yet seen Infinite movement into our space, but I wonder..."

"Sir?" Morgan queried before the other two senior officers could say anything.

"Between us, we are covering less than ten percent of their potential exits. Are these creatures clever enough to realize that and go around our screens and scouts?"

"Yes," Morgan said bluntly. "That is one of my largest concerns at this point. Unfortunately, full coverage would require thousands to tens of thousands of scout ships, all hopefully stealthed to evade detection and elimination by the Infinite.

"So far, we have successfully intercepted them by blockading the route that the conspirators used to enter the nebula. We cannot assume that they will continue to use the same route to exit the Astoroko Nebula once they have confirmed the validity of the maps they will have acquired from the conspirators."

"It seems likely, then, that the Infinite have already evaded our attempts at surveillance and are carrying out operations we may have missed?" the Wendira officer asked.

"Yes, sir," Morgan agreed. "I have no real way of projecting what they are doing that we cannot see, beyond attempting to extrapolate their likely objectives, as I have done."

"I am not objecting to your work, Captain," Ronoxosh said. "I am attempting to make certain that I and my fellow fleet commanders understand the limits of the information we have. You are projecting that their next action will be the acquisition of resources on a mass scale. However, you've also noted that you do not know where they acquired the resources necessary for the manufacture of five million missiles."

"There is potentially sufficient raw material in the Eye to support munitions manufacture on that scale for a period," Morgan countered. "But, yes, we do not have information on how much of those asteroids, et cetera, have already been converted into Infinite biomass versus were available to be used in production of Laian-style technology.

"We also cannot speak to the degree to which they are able to reconfigure their existing biomass," she warned. "We currently believe that the portal emitters they are using are newly bred Category One bioforms, potentially existing in symbiosis with larger forms as a kind of 'add-on system.'

"Until we have regular-space visuals of a hyper-capable Infinite force, it's hard to judge. In our last engagement, we did not even get drones into the visibility bubble of the swarm."

"Have we deployed hyperfold-com-equipped drones in the most likely systems for their resource extraction?" Ronoxosh asked.

"We have," Tidirok said before Morgan could answer this time. "And more drones and scout ships are on the way to expand our surveillance. As of the last round of reports from those drones, the Infinite have not been spotted in any of the systems."

"So, it is possible that the enemy has eluded us entirely with multiple forces," Ronoxosh replied. "And even if they have not, we still have no idea where Swarm Bravo went after destroying Pincer Korodaun's forces?

"Does that summarize our problem sufficiently?"

"Yes," Tidirok snapped. "Do you have a solution, Royal Commandant?"

"No," Ronoxosh admitted. "As I said, I am attempting to make certain we are all on the same tablet of the problem." He stabbed a pincer at the nebula on Morgan's presentation map.

"As Captain Casimir has laid out, there is a force in this nebula that can destroy everything we have gathered," he said bluntly. "They could have sent out multiple secondary forces we have not yet detected, and have sent out at least one force, Swarm Bravo, that we have *lost track of*."

The room was silent.

"None of this was...preventable, I do not believe," Ronoxosh said after a few moments. "But it leaves us in a strategic situation that is far more complicated than I had hoped. Short of advancing into the nebula and engaging the Infinite's primary nest—a task we lack the forces for—I'm not certain I see a most-optimal set of next steps.

"That, Royal Commandant, is the current we are here to discuss," Tan!Shallegh noted softly. "Thank you, Staff Captain Casimir. I think we should carry on the rest of this conversation in private."

CHAPTER TWENTY-SEVEN

Sнотιℓικ was the senior member of Morgan's original team that she'd brought over to *Va!Tola*. She'd also grabbed Took and Ito, leaving Rogers to assemble a new team around herself and Kadark.

Morgan had meant to leave Ito, but Rogers had insisted that the team responsible for the entire Grand Fleet was more important than the one for a single task force. The Grand Fleet had ten forces like Tan!Stalla's, after all.

The Rekiki was standing next to the holotank, her arms moving icons around as she tested an operational contingency plan, when her superior came in. Shotilik turned and saluted crisply, fist to chest, at Morgan's arrival.

"Captain Casimir," Shotilik greeted her. "Just testing scenarios."

"Which ones?" Morgan asked, pulling a seat up.

"Where I'd go for resources if I were the Infinite," her subordinate noted. "I have more data than they do, but I'd be sending my resource-extraction units to one of these three systems."

Three unnamed systems near the Astoroko Nebula blinked red.

"They're all binary star systems with significant asteroid belts and minable planets," Shotilik said. "Depending on how many hyper emitters they have and if they can split up their bioform production, they might want to move in on all three."

"Makes sense," Morgan agreed, studying the map. She poked at the system for a moment, then brought up a green veil through the area around the Astoroko Nebula, marking where the Laian scout fleet covered.

"Except that we would have seen them move on any of those three systems," she told Shotilik, taking Ronoxosh's assessment into account. "They wouldn't have waited this long to start acquiring new resources, so if we *haven't* seen them, they went somewhere we *wouldn't* have seen them."

"But we haven't seen anything from them to suggest that they can detect Laian stealth fields in hyperspace," Shotilik replied.

"I'm not sure they can," she said. "But they know where we *were*, so even if all they did was swing thirty degrees to starboard and up..."

"We'd never see them leave," the Rekiki analyst said grimly. "Preyshit. I didn't even consider that they might try to evade our scouts—they came right at us before."

"When they want to fight, they want to fight," Morgan replied. "But when they want to hunt and extract resources, they want to avoid us. Even factoring in the Wendira side, we're not even covering ten percent of the Nebula's potential exits with scanners.

"They wouldn't even need to try very hard to evade us."

"If I factor that in, it changes where they would go for resources." Shotilik shook her long head. "I'm not sure we can get any useful information with that wide a net."

"I know." Morgan buried a sigh. "We'll go over it again and again." She snorted. "And again, until we have something useful to provide the joint command."

Morgan adjusted the display to show the entire Astoroko Nebula, all twelve light-years of it. More lights dropped onto the hologram to show the inhabited systems around the Nebula. Only one side of it faced onto the Dead Zone, after all.

"I think we need to consider our vulnerabilities," she said quietly. "Where can they do the most damage if they launch an assault directly from the nebula?"

She waved her hand into the hologram and tapped a star that she vaguely remembered.

"Solost," Shotilik said before the data even appeared.

"A Laian sector capital," Morgan agreed. "Population, fourteen billion. Seventh largest shipyard in the Republic."

More data flowed out onto the screen, confirming her memories.

"Rated for parallel production of war-dreadnoughts," she concluded. "As many as fifteen, if my memory serves. They've never actually *built* them like that there, but in the hands of the Infinite..."

"I seem to recall that the Republic targeted, what, a two-hundred-dreadnought wartime production capacity?" Shotilik asked.

"Around that, though I suspect that the true number would come up short if they actually tried to activate those yards," Morgan agreed.

The shipyards were heavily subsidized to keep "war-dreadnought scale" yards operational, but the vast majority of those yards had never been *used* to build war-dreadnoughts. Even if only half of the yards actually ended up working, though, that would give the Republic a hundred-war-dreadnought shot in the arm eighteen months into any war.

It was a hell of a backup plan—one that Morgan didn't know if the Republic had activated for the current crisis yet, but one that would take a while to have an effect regardless. Two-hundred-million-ton warships did not get built quickly, even with Core Power tech.

"But Solost would be a military, economic and political disaster for the Republic if it was attacked," Morgan continued. "It's well fortified, but I think even Swarm Bravo could overrun it. *And* it's on the other end of a hyperspace current that cuts the travel time in half."

Solost was twenty-eight light-years from the nebula, hardly close by most standards, but hyperspace was a fickle terrain. It would only take seven cycles for a force traveling the current to reach the sector capital.

"That's the kind of target we need to identify," she told Shotilik. "There will be more than just Solost—there's almost certainly equivalents in Wendira space and Ren space."

The Ren were the third Core Power that bordered on the Astoroko Nebula, sitting *between* the Laians and Wendira on most of their other approach points. They were neutral between the two powers, determinedly so.

"We've been focusing on the path they have taken and not considered the paths they could take," Morgan finished. "Pull the rest of the team in, Commander.

"We've got work to do."

BY THE TIME Morgan exhaustedly dragged herself back to her quarters, her team had assembled a list of twenty-two high-value/high-vulnerability targets near to the Astoroko Nebula—targets that could be reached by the Infinite without being detected by the scouting fleets.

The definition of "high-vulnerability" made her head hurt, since it included systems with massive sublight fortifications and, in several cases, defensive flotillas of Core Power capital ships.

She ended up sitting on the foot of her bed, staring blankly into space with one boot off.

"How do you think?" she asked the air. "If I knew *that*, I could make a call, but I don't even know what you *want*."

The air wasn't able to provide answers for the distant Infinite Queen—and neither, unfortunately, was Morgan.

The Infinite had spent fifty thousand years sealed away from even the ability to *see* the rest of the galaxy. What did they want now that they were free? Conquest? Food? To convert everything into themselves?

Morgan didn't know. She could project what the Infinite would do for any one of half a dozen sets of objectives, but even if they guessed right, the projections would be wrong.

She was starting to think she hated her new job.

CHAPTER TWENTY-EIGHT

THE SUMMONS TO A MASSIVE MEETING PROBABLY SHOULDN'T have been a surprise to Rin. He'd been involved in a lot of the private meetings between Tan!Shallegh and his Core Power counterparts, and helped Tan!Shallegh and Morgan as well, but he still hadn't quite regarded himself as part of the command structure of the joint fleet.

But as he stepped into the massive conference room aboard *Va!Tola*, he realized he was the only civilian in the room. Everyone else in the room was an officer of one of the three fleets—and a senior one, at that.

The room was filled with Pincers and Fleet Commandants and Fleet Lords, flag officers of three different galactic powers. Rin didn't have the baseline to judge if *every* flag officer of the fleets was in the room—virtually or physically—but he suspected they were.

He was there as a member of Tan!Shallegh's staff—and he hoped that his rush down to where he had spotted Morgan wasn't *too* obvious or embarrassing.

There were at least fifty sentients physically present from the Imperial fleet, joined by at least four hundred people present by virtual holograms. While the conference room used screens and software to make it appear even larger than it was, it still felt cramped.

"Do you know what this is about?" he whispered to Morgan as he took the seat next to her.

"Not in detail," she admitted. "But the Wendira have been here for four cycles, and the combined fleet hasn't moved. I've been feeding analysis into a meeting with the three fleet commanders for that whole time, so I'm *hoping* they've decided on a course of action."

She gestured around them.

"Every flag officer is here, and every ship captain is watching," she told him. "People who aren't visibly in the conference can't ask questions, but they're listening and they'll see everything. I don't see why they would have pulled everyone in like this unless they had a plan to announce."

"But you don't know what that plan is?" Rin asked. He was surprised by that. As she said, she'd been providing analysis of the Infinite to the fleet commanders for days.

"Not that I can say," she murmured. "But even if I could, not enough to give a meaningful hint."

Rin nodded his acknowledgement. There were things they couldn't share with each other. That was the limitations of their jobs.

"Have you heard from Ki!Tana?" he asked quietly. "Or...anyone else?"

He wasn't entirely sure who their unnamed associates scattered across the galaxy were. He and Morgan had been recruited into the society for a specific task, and no one had given them contact tools. No decoder rings for them!

"Not a peep," Morgan admitted in a whisper. "I *think* she's probably the one who got anyone other than the Ren to sign on to this mess, but no one has ships heading our way yet."

He nodded, but further discussion was cut short by the arrival of three figures on the dais at the front of the conference room. It was just barely possible to tell that Tan!Shallegh was the only one of the three officers physically present aboard *Va!Tola*, with Ronoxosh and Tidirok virtually linked in from their own flagships.

"Thank you, everyone, for helping our staffs arrange this," Tan!Shallegh said by way of greeting. "I know that fleet commanders have a certain weight in such things, but everyone's cooperation is appreciated.

"For the non-Imperial portion of the audience, I am First Fleet Lord Tan!Shallegh, the commanding officer of the Grand Fleet of the A!Tol Imperium."

He gestured to Tidirok.

"I am Eleventh Voice of the Republic Tidirok," the Laian officer introduced himself, though he was probably the only one of the three known to *everyone* in the audience. "I command the Republic's First Defense Fleet."

"And I am Royal Commandant Ronoxosh," the Wendira finished. "I command the Eighth, Ninth, and Fifteenth Battle Hives of the Wendira Grand Hive."

He gestured at the other two officers.

"Together, we represent the joint command of our allied fleet, and it falls to us—and to all of you—to protect the Republic, the Hive and the rest of the galaxy from the Infinite."

The three sentients on the dais had the undivided attention of thousands of officers, Rin suspected, even if *he* was somewhat more interested in the cultural details of the three beings' uniforms.

Tan!Shallegh wore a black leather harness that exposed most of his skin but provided a place to mount insignia and an emergency vac-suit deployment system.

Ronoxosh and Tidirok, on the other hand, both wore what were effectively black tunics cut for their number of arms. While Ronoxosh was slightly smaller than the Laian officer, Rin suspected that the two could have traded uniforms and the Wendira's vestigial wings would have been the only problem.

"Our staffs have run hundreds of simulations about the Infinite's next moves, but we currently suffer from a lack of information and an extended deployment cycle," Tidirok announced. "It would take far too long to move the combined fleet to intercept any movement by the Infinite.

"We have established a list of most likely targets that will be distributed as part of a smaller briefing package for you to provide your officers," the Voice continued. "The critical point is that we will be moving the combined fleet forward to the edge of the Astoroko Nebula, the Trey-Four-Five-Nine System.

"Trey-Four-Five-Nine is on the Laian side of the Dead Zone, and we judge it is a central location among the potential target sites for the Infinite movements. It does not currently have any infrastructure, so we will be dependent for some time on the Republic fleet train, but the position will allow us to maneuver to intercept as quickly as possible."

Rin wasn't familiar with the Trey-459 System, but he heard Morgan inhale sharply at the name. He didn't really have a chance to ask her more as the briefing continued.

"Once in position at Trey-Four-Five-Nine, we will deploy roughly one-quarter of our escorts to expand the sensor screen across the Astoroko Nebula. We will also be coordinating with Ren and Wendira defensive forces to expand sensor networks on other sections of the nebula and maintain a linked network for rapid detection of Infinite movement."

Rin knew Morgan well enough to guess that her sudden stillness wasn't a good sign.

"However, we will be maintaining a full concentration of the capital ships of all three fleets in preparation for a major attack by the Infinite. As you will see in your briefing packets, we expect to face this enemy with a significant tonnage disadvantage but an overall firepower equivalency.

"We have grounds to believe that their larger bioforms will be lacking in long-range arsenals and we will be able to control the range of any major engagement to our favor. Based on those projections, the plan is to use the combined fleet as a central force that will move against and *crush* the next Infinite excursion from the Astoroko Nebula.

"Whatever their next move is, they will meet the massed forces of these fleets. The battle to come will not be easy," Tidirok warned. "The enemy does possess more longer-ranged firepower than we like, and estimates of their close-range weapons remain terrifying.

"But we *will* engage them, and we *will* be victorious. And then we will do the same to the expedition and the expedition after that. We will restore containment until such time as we have gathered sufficient allies to move against and neutralize the Infinite...for good."

RIN CAREFULLY FOLLOWED Morgan out of the conference and back to her office. He paused at her door, willing to give her her privacy if she needed it, but she gestured for him to enter. The door slid shut behind him and he heard a ping as the security system engaged.

"I'm guessing that wasn't what you expected," he said quietly.

"The analysis we sent in basically concluded that Trey-Four-Five-Nine and the rest of the Dead Zone systems were basically a lost cause," Morgan told him. "We couldn't detect or maneuver in such a way as to reliably prevent the Infinite from securing raw resources, so we needed to assess our vulnerabilities.

"That's factored into this plan in that they're positioned the fleet on the Laian border, but it still leaves us five cycles, at least, away from several of the systems where the Republic is most vulnerable."

She shook her head.

"I'm assuming both Tidirok and Ronoxosh have their own analysis teams assessing the Infinite threat and objectives," she told him. "I don't know what those teams are saying, but I think they're focusing on the raw-resource side of things."

"I don't follow?" Rin admitted.

"We keep thinking that the Infinite need more resources, because they're trapped in the Astoroko Nebula," Morgan said after a moment. "Except that the nebula itself is basically a gold mine of what they need. It's not dense or easily accessible, but there's more raw resources in the nebula than there are in *any* star system.

"But for us, or a force operating with a tech base familiar to us, those raw resources are all but useless, so we started with the assumption that they'd want to go after a system for raw resources. Except...if they're going to do that, Rin, they've already done it."

"So, what do you think they're going to do?"

"I don't know," she admitted. "If they don't need resources...they're either going for threat elimination or data. That means there's a decent chance they're going to come right at the combined fleet with every Category Six and Seven they can squeeze through a hyper portal."

"So, if we move closer, we make the combined fleet a target?" Rin asked. That seemed...unwise.

"We have to move closer," she admitted. "And I don't know what the right answer is, Rin, but I *do* know that we can't waste our time guarding dead rocks that might be useful for raw materials. There's too many of them out there.

"So, if we're going to sit the fleet somewhere, we should sit it somewhere that needs defending. If Tohrohsail was closer to the Nebula, for example, I'd say we were actually well positioned here.

"The Laian and Wendira analysis teams are thinking about how to hurt the Infinite...not about how the Infinite can hurt us," Morgan guessed. "Rin...I'm half-convinced they're just watching for us to bring a fleet in so that they know where the threat is.

"So they can squish it."

"What do we do?" Rin asked.

She sighed.

"Nothing. I follow orders," she told him. "I'll make my arguments to Tan!Shallegh again, but I'd guess I've already convinced him. We just needed to convince Ronoxosh and Tidirok, and we failed."

"So, we move forward, we get closer to the enemy and we see

what happens," Rin told her. "They'll see the same things you do in time, right?"

"I don't think the combined fleet can stop them," she whispered. "I think all we're doing is buying time, and if we screw it up, we buy less time—and the time *we* don't buy gets bought with inhabited star systems."

A chill ran down Rin's spine.

"We thought the sun eater was going to eat Kosha, colony and all," he murmured. "Are we looking at something like that?"

"We don't know how the Infinite will react to a civilian population, but they have fired on every single ship they have seen since leaving the Nebula," Morgan said quietly. "I am afraid, Rin. I'm afraid that if we get this wrong, we're going to lose an entire star system of innocents.

"The smallest bioform we've seen is eighty meters long," she reminded him. "*That* was one of the Servants. We haven't actually seen a Category One bioform from the Infinite yet. Do they even conceive of us as individuals or sentiences?

"Or will the population of whatever planet they capture simply qualify as available raw resources?"

"They might just...eat a civilian population?" he whispered.

"It's... It's more likely than not, but not certain," she told him. "We don't know enough about them. We don't know enough about how they dealt with the Alava."

"The Alava were terrified of them," Rin admitted. "They didn't even tell their subject races that the Infinite—the 'Enemy,' as they called them—*existed*. Something happened between the Alava and the Infinite that made their war to the death.

"If the Infinite were eating Alavan worlds, population and all... that could have been it."

"Because I needed more nightmares," Morgan whispered. "I don't *think* they're going to eat a civilian population...but I don't know."

She turned to look at the screen on her wall, which showed a map of the area around Tohrohsail and the Astoroko Nebula.

"I have to wonder if I think they'll leave civilians alone because I think a *civilized* people would," she murmured. "But then I look at that map—at a region where hundreds of stars and trillions of sentients were killed.

"It's hard to maintain hope for a civilized conflict when you're stationed on the edge of the Dead Zone."

CHAPTER TWENTY-NINE

TOHROHSAIL'S FORTRESSES AND DEFENSIVE FRIGATES FADED behind *Va!Tola* while Morgan watched in the operations center's holotank. The midsized defensive starships were the only mobile guardians remaining behind, looking small and fragile against the massive walls of metal moving outward toward agreed hyper-portal points.

It was hard to look at the fleet at a level where individual ships even registered. The FOC's hologram showed the fleets by squadron, and even *that* was overwhelming. Twenty ten-ship squadrons of Laian war-dreadnoughts. Fifty five-ship squadrons of Wendira star hives—and *two hundred* squadrons of the ten-megaton star shields. Twenty sixteen-ship squadrons of Imperial capital ships.

Almost two thousand capital ships and over four thousand escorts maneuvered away from the gas-giant fleet base. There was no way to assemble a coherent formation, so each fleet was moving in their own formation in a designated "lane" at least a million kilometers across.

"All right, team," Morgan said clearly, pulling the eyes of her team away from the holotank and back to her. "We now know what we have, for at least the next few five-cycles.

"We know where we're going and we know what we're watching for," she continued. "All of that falls on the regular Fleet Operations staff. Our job remains what it always was: analyze what we've seen of the Infinite's movements and project their next steps.

"They've been disturbingly silent for a while now. I want your ideas as to why."

Shotilik leaned her snout thoughtfully on top of her console.

"Because they're waiting to see what we do next?" she suggested. "They don't know how we're going to jump or how much firepower we have."

"And what if they have the full databases available aboard *Builder of Tomorrows?*" Morgan countered. "So, they know roughly what the strength of the Laian and Wendira Dead Zone fleets is. They know where the Laian bases are, potentially even know where the Wendira bases are. They know the Imperium is here, and they know about the alliances and security agreements."

"Would they understand them?" Ito asked softly. Morgan turned her attention to the Pibo woman. "We have to assume they have the databases, yes, but they have no context whatsoever," Ito pointed out. "They don't know who the players are, they don't know the races, the tech, the territory.

"Even the astrography has changed over fifty thousand years—the Dead Zone didn't exist then. They've worked out hyperdrives, but have they worked out how to read Laian hyper-density maps?"

"That would slow down their movement out of the nebula," Morgan conceded. "For worst-case planning, we need to operate on the assumption that they *do* know everything, but we also need to make a realistic estimate of what they're doing."

"My concern is: what happened to Swarm Bravo?" Shotilik asked. "We know a major force left the nebula but we haven't seen it since. Presumably, they were scouting and taking in realspace scans to validate the maps they had, but that doesn't explain where they went after that."

"They could have made it back in before we had a scouting fleet in position to see them, but it seems unlikely," Morgan agreed. "Where *could* they be?"

"Anywhere," Ito said instantly. "Anywhere in the Dead Zone, anyway, and well into Laian or Wendira space. If they have the hyper-density maps, they could be dozens to hundreds of light-years from the nebula by now.

"I just have no idea why they'd go that far without an objective."

"We don't know what objectives they have," Morgan said quietly. "What if they're looking for another cluster of the Infinite? If they have some idea of where the other Infinite were when their drives stopped...they could be trying to find reinforcements.

"If there were other Infinite out there, wouldn't we have seen them?" Took asked, the Yin turning to study the holotank with dark eyes. "The cluster in the Astoroko Nebula was uniquely concealed."

"If we had encountered them, we would know," Ito agreed. "But if they were in systems that were useless to us, that we only did long-range surveys of, we likely would write off sleeping Infinite as asteroids.

"We did that at quite close range in the Eye," Morgan warned. "When they aren't active, they don't *look* alive unless you know what you're looking for. Once they're awake, it's hard to miss because they're almost as warm as our spaceships, but they hibernate *cold*."

"So, there could be another entire fleet like the one in the Eye out there?" Shotilik said quietly. "I don't like those plains, Captain Casimir."

"I don't think we're looking at one of that scale, but there might be some more out there," Morgan said. "We don't know. We don't even know what we don't know. We *do* know that Swarm Bravo is out there somewhere and it hasn't pinged any sensors anywhere.

"It's not a standard hyperspace anomaly, so they could potentially have accidentally snuck past a lot of sensor outposts before the signatures were properly distributed, but *we don't know*."

She shook her head. She was starting to hate those three words.

A shiver ran through the floor and the team before anyone said anything more, the transition to hyperspace indescribable though thankfully short.

"We have analysis based on our vulnerabilities," Morgan said after the moment passed. "I think that's a good pattern to keep following. We have to focus on the main swarm in the Astoroko Nebula for now, though.

"What they have, what they can do. Right now, I'd guess part of their inactivity is a limitation on the number of hyper-portal ships they've created and how many missiles they have.

"That, to me, means that when they next move, it's going to be in overwhelming force," she warned her team. "If we're lucky, it will be somewhere the triple fleet can intercept. If we're not, they're going to take a force that makes Swarm Bravo look like a baby into Ren or Wendira space, and the political consequences will probably outlive us."

That got her some pained sounds of amusement.

"So, let's keep digging," she told them. "I know it feels like we're going over the same ground again and again, but that's what analysis means. Let me know if any of you need a damn towel."

Two of the junior noncoms, the group that was solely listening in on this conversation, were human.

Nobody else got the joke.

CHAPTER THIRTY

Morgan was on the flag deck when the answer to the question her team kept asking was finally answered.

Most flag decks were designed with a direct link to the flagship bridge, a video-screen wall that could make it look like the bridge was attached to the flag deck. It was rarely used for that—the level of distraction both ways often overwhelmed any value, so smaller, direct screens were used—but aboard *Va!Tola*, it had been commandeered for a different purpose.

The wallscreen on *Va!Tola* was linked to the same screen on *Storm Sentinel*'s flag deck, linking the two superbattleships' flag decks together into a single massive command center that *almost* sufficed for the task at hand.

From either of those flag decks, running the Grand Fleet alone was overwhelming. Trying to coordinate it with two other fleets, *in hyperspace* where most signals only traveled a single light-second, was an entire new nightmare.

They were managing it by a mix of relays and tricks like merging the flag decks of two capital ships into one virtual space.

"Someone pass an order to *Sentinel*'s bridge," !Pana said aloud, the A!Tol chief of staff surveying her dual domains from the Admiral's seat. "We need to pull them about five thousand kilometers closer in. The delay on the link is causing trouble."

In regular space, they'd link by hyperfold com. In hyperspace, that wasn't an option, and even twenty thousand kilometers was adding a measurable problem in the data transfers back and forth.

Morgan was working with Division Lord Etri, the neuter Pibo who ran Tan!Shallegh's operations team, on putting together a scenario throwing a simulated triple fleet—commanded by nine officers from the operations team and *Storm Sentinel*'s tactical department—against Morgan's team assessment of a Category Seven-X bioform.

Eighty-five thousand kilometers long, with shields, compressed-matter armor, missiles, and singularity cannons, Morgan figured the single Infinite behemoth had a decent chance against the entire massed allied force.

"*Storm Sentinel* Navigation confirms," someone from the other superbattleship reported. "We are adjusting course to bring them to fifteen thousand kilometers. We're swapping *Liara* into her old place in the formation."

Liara, if Morgan remembered correctly, was another *Galileo*-class superbattleship named for a Yin scientist.

Everything about the linked flag decks was going roughly as Morgan expected. It was calm and quiet—there was nothing on the long-range anomaly scanners, and they were only halfway through their nine-cycle voyage to the Trey-459 System. It was as quiet and calm as a wartime watch could be.

And then she saw the human communications officer—Staff Captain Guo Yin—leap back from her console as if struck, staring at the screen in front of her for several seconds of shocked silence.

Only a portion of the aliens on the two bridges could read human body language, but every human was looking at Captain Guo within moments—as were most of the aliens who followed her surprise.

"Division Lord," she finally addressed !Pana in a shaky voice. "We have an incoming Code Tsunami starcom transmission."

Code Tsunami meant one thing only: *Invasion imminent.*

"Summarize," !Pana ordered.

"Multiple Infinite bioforms have been confirmed entering the Tohrohsail System," Guo read out. "Estimate is over five hundred units and portals were still open when..."

She swallowed.

"Portals were still open when contact was lost with the Tohrohsail starcom," she reported. "It is unclear from the data what destroyed the starcom station, but the Infinite had been in-system for less than five minutes."

Both flag decks were deathly silent.

"I understand," !Pana finally said. "I will awaken the Fleet Lord. Share the message with the senior staff, but otherwise keep it to the flag deck until Lord Tan!Shallegh has made his decision."

There wasn't much point to that, Morgan knew. Every capital ship in all three fleets would have received the message. The Infinite had finally moved.

From the timing, Morgan guessed they hadn't figured out the Laian hyper-density maps—but they'd definitely worked out how to find the biggest fleet base near them and moved to neutralize the threat.

Only luck had prevented the Infinite from ambushing the triple fleet in their home anchorages!

"YOUR ASSESSMENT, STAFF CAPTAIN CASIMIR?" Tan!Shallegh asked moments after he'd taken his seat at the center of the bridge.

"Highest-likelihood scenario is that the force at Tohrohsail is Swarm Bravo, sir," she reported crisply. "If they were unable to read the Laian maps for hyperspace details and took a direct course to

Tohrohsail from engaging Korodaun, the attack would line up with the end of their expected arrival window."

Or they could have stopped, taken a massive quantity of sensor readings to send back to the Queen and then carried on and arrived closer to the middle of their window.

Either way, it was most likely Bravo, and Morgan now knew what had happened to that fleet.

"The good news is that Bravo is almost certainly short on missiles," she continued. "They were expecting, I would assume, to ambush the First Defense Fleet and engage at close range."

She shook her head.

"The need to defend the fleet base would limit our maneuvers, and they'd be able to pin the First Defense Fleet against the fleet base and wipe it out. It's a counter-force mission, sir, one that only failed because we decided to redeploy forward."

"And because they underestimated our strength," Tan!Shallegh said. "If they were expecting just the First Defense Fleet—or perhaps the Grand Fleet as well—they would not be expecting to meet the Wendira Battle Hives.

"We have more ships than they expect and more firepower." He snapped his beak harshly. "It is not solely my call, but I believe we will need to turn the fleets back. If they want a chance to eliminate the triple fleets, we will give it to them."

Morgan nodded.

"I *think*," she stressed, "that the combined fleets should be able to handle Swarm Bravo, so long as her missiles remain limited."

"That depends on how intelligent they are, Staff Captain," Tan!Shallegh reminded her. "Because Tohrohsail is a Laian fleet munitions depot as well as a repair base. Depending on whether they're smart enough to look for storage depots and to prevent the defenders destroying them, there are more missiles in that system than they fired at Korodaun."

"They're smart enough to find that," Morgan guessed with a grimace. "They're probably smarter than we are, but they often lack context for what we're doing. I suspect they can figure out a missile storage station."

"So do I," the Fleet Lord agreed. "I will speak with the fleet commanders. Casimir, reconvene with your team and analyze our data on the Tohrohsail System.

"I doubt they held, so I need to know what the Infinite are going to have to throw at us."

"Yes, sir."

"And remember that you will be asked one question I know you can't answer," he said grimly, "but you must have a guess for anyway: will the Infinite harm the civilian population of the system?"

Morgan nodded with a hard swallow.

"Fifty-two-point-six million Laians, Staff Captain," he continued. "Not all civilians, not by a coastline in a system hosting a fleet base, but still noncombatants. Your team needs to tell me if we're looking at a complete wipeout."

"What if we are, sir?" Morgan half-whispered.

"Then we need to consider whether it's worth it to retake Tohrohsail if we can't do so in time to save the people."

CHAPTER THIRTY-ONE

"I HAVE NO IDEA," RIN DUNST ADMITTED, LOOKING AROUND AT the analysis team Morgan had put together.

His lover was leaning against the holotank itself, silently lost in thought after repeating the Fleet Lord's question to Rin and her team.

"The Alava feared them," he told the team. "But we know very little about their interactions. We know they were around for long enough for a rogue faction based around adopting their biotech to take up residence out near Kosha, with a local security force that was using a Dyson swarm to power shipyards that surrounded an entire gas giant.

"Even the Alava didn't build such things quickly. We're talking at least decades, and some of the evidence we saw out there suggested they'd been out there for centuries, completely ignoring the central authority."

The team sat in quiet contemplation of a horrifying question.

"I can't help but think that if the Infinite had been exterminating every settlement they came across, the Alava would have been more unified in dealing with them," he admitted. "But the tone of some of what we *do* know suggests that a lot of the Alava thought the Infinite were just animals until later on.

"Then they were *the Enemy*, hated and feared in equal measure, the threat that led the Alava to break the universe."

"What happened in between?" Shotilik asked.

"We don't know," Rin said. "My guess? That rogue faction of Alava started experimenting on the Infinite and did *something* one step too far. I don't think the Alava meant to start a war—but I think the Infinite decided they needed to *finish* one.

"I'm scraping and connecting facts that might not be connected," he warned. "But I think the Infinite started a campaign of annihilation, wiping out planets and systems as they advanced on the main Alavan systems.

"But before that, they existed alongside the Alava for centuries. Measured and controlled as the Infinite campaign seems to have been, they still crossed hundreds of light-years in decades of fire and war," Rin concluded. "That doesn't line up with the rogue factions working on stolen Infinite biotech or anything similar.

"*Something* changed in the relationship between the Alava and the Infinite. There are, now that I've looked for them, reference to spacegoing beasts that might well be the Infinite—and they go back for a long damn time."

The Infinite as a force and a threat were a memory of the final years of the Alava, but there were records of similar creatures going back to some of the earliest records the Mesharom had copied down from their old masters.

"So, the Infinite didn't destroy every alien they encountered originally," Shotilik concluded. "And then they started wiping out the Alava whenever they came across them. I guess that only leaves one question, but it's not like we can answer that one, either."

"Do they regard us as the Alava they wiped out...or the people they basically ignored before that?" Took asked. "We cannot control the winds of their minds. But at least we can conclude that there is a *chance* they haven't burnt Tohrohsail to the bare rock."

"What kind of chance?" Ito asked, her voice strained even through the translator. "One in five? One in three?"

"One in three is what I'm going to tell the Fleet Lord," Morgan decided aloud, rising from the holotank, and turning around to look at them all.

"Thank you, Rin," she told him. "We needed that information. We don't know what they're doing now—we can only go on what they did before.

"And the fact that Swarm Bravo just hit Tohrohsail with everything they had. There's no way the forts and frigates held, people. We're three cycles out—and in three cycles, this ship and every one of her sisters engages the Infinite."

There was no way for them to send messages home or *anything* until they left hyperspace and could link into the hyperfold network. Even then, Rin understood that it would take longer than normal if the starcom station in Tohrohsail was gone.

"We don't know if they see us as successors to the Alava," he murmured. "But I suspect we'd really prefer it if they didn't."

CHAPTER THIRTY-TWO

MORGAN DIDN'T KNOW WHAT DISCUSSIONS HAD TAKEN PLACE IN the closed virtual conferences between the top levels of the fleet's command. She did know that less than half a cycle had passed between the combined fleet receiving the news of the attack on Tohrohsail and the entire force turning around.

"No contacts in hyperspace around the system," Etri announced from *Storm Sentinel's* flag bridge.

Every member of Tan!Shallegh's staff and their support teams were on duty at that moment. Morgan had the operations officer's console on *Va!Tola* linked to her analysis team in the FOC. If something happened to *Storm Sentinel*, her team would *become* the Fleet Operations team.

Until then, their job was to intake data and make assessments of the enemy.

"Shouldn't there be *something* in hyperspace?" !Pana asked, her skin shading darker.

"It's possible for space around Tohrohsail to be empty," the Pibo operations officer said slowly. "But statistically unlikely. For the entirety of the time the Grand Fleet was there, there was a near-continuous stream of supply transports flowing back and forth from the Republic."

"Then there are almost certainly Infinite sentinels in hyperspace," Tan!Shallegh declared. "I know they are not running interface drives, but we do not want to be surprised at close range by even smaller bioforms.

"Focus the fleet's sensors, Division Lord Etri," he ordered. "There has to be a way to detect them."

"Not unless they move, sir," Etri admitted. "We'll watch for them to twitch, but unless they move or activate an interface drive, they're invisible outside the visibility bubble."

"Both the Laians and Wendira have ships that can stealth in hyperspace," Morgan pointed out. "Maybe one of them can send scout ships forward to clear the zone around the system?"

She agreed with Tan!Shallegh's assessment. For the hyperspace around Tohrohsail to be as quiet as it was, the Infinite had been wiping out any ships coming through. That meant there *were* bioforms in hyperspace—and even a smaller bioform could cause a lot of havoc if they only discovered it at three hundred thousand kilometers!

"I will ask," Tan!Shallegh agreed. A privacy shield descended around the Fleet Lord a few moments later, leaving the rest of the flag deck teams to their duties.

Morgan's duties were mostly preparation at this point. Her team had given their best estimate of what they were facing in Tohrohsail and would actively update as the battle continued.

They were reasonably certain they were facing Swarm Bravo, which gave them some basic information. There were no shielded units but lots of missile-launcher-equipped bioforms. Seizure of the fleet depots in Tohrohsail meant that the Infinite had a *lot* of ammunition to play with, too. The estimates Morgan had received said there were at least twenty million missiles in the fleet base's storage facilities.

Swarm Bravo had a lot of long-range firepower to play with.

What they *didn't* have was hyperspace missiles or starfighters, which gave the combined fleet advantages from its diversity.

"Two squadrons of star intruders are moving forward to sweep the hyperspace-equivalent of the Tohrohsail System," Tan!Shallegh reported as his privacy shield lifted. "The rest of the fleet will hold position here, at one light-minute, while those carriers advance."

The star intruders had been humanity's first encounter with the Wendira—if not necessarily the Imperium's—when several of them had been used to attack a human colony in the Alpha Centauri Incident.

Stealthed carriers, smaller even than the star shields, let alone their star hive siblings, the star intruders were effectively unarmed other than their starfighters. Each carried a Grand Wing of two hundred and fifty-six of the unique-to-the-Wendira spacecraft, piloted by the short-lived Wendira Drone caste.

With only twenty A!Tol long-cycles to live, Wendira Drones' only hope for immortality was history. That urge had given the Wendira some of their greatest musicians and artists—and also provided them with a near-infinite supply of pilots willing to strap in for missions with an average fifty-four percent loss rate.

Morgan watched as the massive array of hyperspace anomalies marking the combined fleet came to a halt relative to their destination. It didn't look like anything kept moving, which meant the ten carriers already had their stealth systems engaged.

"Are we getting anything relayed back from them?" !Pana asked. "I'm not seeing com drones."

"That would risk the stealth," Etri suggested. "We'll see when they deploy their fighters. It's not like the intruders themselves can deal with the bioforms."

It only took a few minutes to cross the distance to the system, but it was almost ten before new anomalies appeared on the scanners. The star intruders had positioned themselves evenly across the area of hyperspace that corresponded to the Tohrohsail System and then launched their starfighters simultaneously.

Twenty-five hundred–plus tiny anomalies sparkled across the display as the fighters swept for enemy ships.

"What do we have on their current class?" Morgan murmured into her channel with her own team.

"*Scythe of Doom*-class," Took replied after a moment, the Yin woman probably looking up the data as she was answering the question. "Upgraded from the *Flying Sword of Fire* class we saw at the Centauri Incident. Modular weaponry: they can be fitted with either missiles, a plasma cannon or a hyperfold cannon. Capable of point-eight *c* under interface drive. Twenty-seven-hour endurance."

Morgan nodded silently, watching the fighters sweep across. Another anomaly appeared, then two—then six, as the bioform sentinels started maneuvering to engage the tiny scouts.

It turned out that half of this wave of fighters had been equipped with missiles. Six bioforms started moving, and ten thousand missiles appeared out of the darkness to storm in on them.

The other half of the *Scythes of Doom* were right behind the missiles, plasma cannons flashing. None of the bioforms even managed to initiate a portal before they vanished.

There was a pause on *Va!Tola*'s flag deck, then Tan!Shallegh snapped his beak.

"Grand Fleet will advance in concert with our allies," he ordered. "Prepare to transition to normal space."

THOUSANDS of individual hyper portals cast their own anomalies through the void of hyperspace, blending together in the sensor screens until it looked like one massive portal tens of thousands of kilometers across.

The three fleets didn't have enough synchronization to create a single portal like that, though Morgan knew it would be more efficient. That kind of planning, using a small number of hyper-capable ships to open a portal for an entire fleet, was essential to their enemy

—and normally a sign of an extremely well-trained and -practiced fleet.

The patchier method of individual portals still delivered the combined fleet to their destination, tens of billions of tons of warships taking shape in the outer extremes of a system that should have belonged to them.

Scanners strained to provide a clear picture of the star system, but Morgan only had eyes for two pieces of data.

First, the location of Swarm Bravo. The majority of the bioforms were where she'd expected. At least a thousand of the Infinite creatures were gathered around the Laian fleet base and the gas giant the fleet base fueled from. Presumably, they were still tearing through the wreckage of the command centers and storage depots for anything they could use.

The second piece of data was any evidence that the civilian population was still present—and Morgan exhaled an immense sigh of relief as stations and asteroid colonies began to ping up on the map in yellow—active neutrals. They had power, which meant they probably had air and heat—which meant they had *people.*

There was no way to hide major space installations, and Tohrohsail didn't have a habitable planet. Every one of the fifty-plus million people in the system lived aboard something immediately identifiable by even basic scanners.

And the vast majority of those facilities were intact. The updates continued to flow across Morgan's screen, and she noted that there *were* bioforms standing watch over the largest clusters of habitations, but those habitations were intact.

"No ships," Shotilik murmured. "All of the installations and stations outside the fleet base appear to be intact, but I'm not reading any shipping."

"Only about half of those colonies are self-sustaining, in any wind," Took argued. "There *has* to have been shipping for all of them to still be functioning, even after only eleven cycles."

"Took, keep your eyes on that," Morgan ordered. "See what you can identify of the intact noncombatant populations and what the Infinite appears to have made of them. Everyone else, focus on Swarm Bravo.

"If they've only got Category Twos and bigger, are they even *capable* of pulling the missiles from the depots?" she asked. "I'd love to be able to tell the Fleet Lord that the big guns don't have missiles."

"On it," Shotilik replied. "Tachyon scanners show they have detected us—on *their* tachyon scanners, I assume—and are organizing their herd to face the fleets."

The combined fleets had come out of hyperspace a long way from the gas-giant fleet base. At eight light-minutes, they were well outside the range of any weapons system the fleet had. The point had been to give them a chance to decide whether or not to embrace the engagement.

"Casimir?" Tan!Shallegh asked, his voice cutting through the flag deck with the ease of long practice. "Anything unexpected?"

"They appear to have left the stations and outposts outside the fleet base alone," Morgan told him. "We won't really be able to break down what that means until we can interview people afterward, beyond the fact that there *are* civilians here to rescue.

"The main force is at the fleet base, which supports the logic that they have some ability to extract supplies from the storage base and can be assumed to have full missile loads," she continued. "If the Laian inventories are right, we can expect them to have roughly twenty million missiles."

Which was about as many as the Laian First Defense Fleet had in their magazines. The next few hours were going to see incomprehensible numbers of weapons deployed.

"Understood. Let me know if *anything* sticks out, Staff Captain," Tan!Shallegh told her. "Assuming we're looking at your type-M units, we are assessing this as a winnable battle, even one in our favor."

"Based off what we saw of Swarm Bravo when they fought Korodaun and Tan!Stalla...I would agree with that assessment, sir,"

Morgan admitted. "But we have not yet fought the Infinite in regular space on a major scale.

"They *will* have more surprises."

"I know," the Fleet Lord agreed. "Keep your eyes open for them, Staff Captain, and I will hope you see the currents before they drag us under."

"Yes, sir," Morgan said, turning her attention back to her console. What else could she do?

———

"AND THERE IS the answer to that," Shotilik told her a minute later, relaying a long-distance visual from a probe to Morgan's console. The bioform in the video feed was...just tentacles. Enough so that even Morgan, who'd grown up around A!Tol, had a moment of atavistic horror at the sight.

"It's a Category One bioform that appears to be acting as a symbiotic life form to the bigger units," Shotilik told her. "We've now seen half a dozen of them go *into* Category Fours and just kind of get swallowed.

"But those tentacles are small enough and flexible enough to get into the Laians' storage depots. Not so sure about the computers, but I'm going to guess they worked out an answer for that quickly."

"Good catch, Commander," Morgan replied, suppressing a shiver as she watched the bioform detach itself from a Laian storage depot, dozens of missiles held in its tentacles. "That's disturbing."

"Yes. But those C-Ones are probably key to the Infinite's technological adaptation," Shotilik noted. "They're probably doing a lot of the work around building and installing the hardware they've adapted from the Laian systems.

"But on the other hand, if that's as small as they get, we don't need to worry about Marine-equivalent bioforms boarding our ships and taking over."

"Small mercies," Morgan muttered. "I'll tell the Fleet Lord. Anything else we need to be concerned about?"

"No. They look about what we expected," Shotilik said. "They've pulled the last of these manipulator bioforms back into themselves and are all but sorted out. I'd guess we'll see them accelerate toward the fleets in a minute or two."

"Understood. Thank you."

Morgan relayed that to Tan!Shallegh, who gave her an acknowledging tentacle gesture while his attention was focused on a conversation with the other two fleet commanders.

Finally, Tan!Shallegh returned his attention to the flag deck—just as the tachyon sensors showed that Swarm Bravo was finally moving out at its ridiculous acceleration.

"The combined fleets will advance to two light-minutes and initiate an engagement with hyperspace missiles and starfighters," he told the flag deck. "We will use the HSMs to target the largest bioforms while the starfighters sweep up the smaller units.

"Once we have expended fifty percent of the Grand Fleet's HSMs, we will advance to regular-missile range," he continued. "The expectation is that the enemy will attempt to force a plasma-range engagement.

"We believe that our hyperfold cannons have a longer range than the Infinite's plasma bursts...so we will permit them to close the range until we can unleash those cannons."

His beak snapped in determination.

"There are still fifty million Laians in this system. We *will* save them."

CHAPTER THIRTY-THREE

THE INFINITE MIGHT NOT HAVE INTERFACE DRIVES, BUT THEIR unknown reactionless propulsion was still disturbingly fast. With accelerations of a percent and a half of lightspeed per second, they didn't seem to max out at *all* below the impenetrable barrier of lightspeed.

The combined fleets, on the other hand, advanced at sixty percent of lightspeed with only a few seconds of acceleration. It was a matter of minutes for the two forces to close to the targeted two-light-minute range, and then the allies reversed course.

The Infinite would continue to close, but for the moment they were out of range—and two of the three fleets facing them had weapons that could cross the distance.

Each of the two hundred and fifty star hives brought by the Wendira Battle Hives carried over a thousand starfighters. Another two hundred star intruders each fielded just over two hundred and fifty apiece. Within moments of reaching the designated range, over three hundred thousand star fighters, each piloted by a sentient being determined to earn immortality, blazed into space.

And by the time the last starfighter was in space, the first salvo of hyperspace missiles was on its way. Designated "single-portal" missiles to distinguish them from the still-more-advanced weapons commanded by the Mesharom, the Imperium's hyperspace missiles were launched through self-contained portals concealed at the armored hearts of their warships.

They crossed two regular-space light-minutes in seconds and then activated the hyper emitters they carried, diving back into normal space with suicidal ferocity and detonating ten-gigaton anti-matter warheads as they found their targets.

When Morgan had fought the Infinite the first time, she'd refused to fire first. That decision haunted her now, but it also meant that the Infinite had no idea weapons like these even existed. They were confident that no weapon their enemies possessed could reach them at that range.

They were maneuvering enough to throw off long ballistic fire. They were *not* maneuvering enough to throw off missiles that arrived in seconds, guided by real-time tachyon targeting.

There were four Category Fives at the heart of the fleet, the largest units in the Infinite armada and the ones that they were *sure* carried singularity guns. Eight hundred–plus kilometers across, they dwarfed any warship the Imperium had ever seen.

So, Tan!Shallegh had sent the *entire* massed firepower of his fleet at one bioform. There was no point in counting the explosions. At least several hundred HSMs emerged inside their target, ten-gigaton warheads detonating in the flesh of their enemy.

Immense as the Category Five bioform was, it couldn't take that kind of damage. It never even had a chance to die. It was simply *gone*.

"Fleet targeting move to C-Five-Two," Tan!Shallegh said calmly. "Maintain fire concentration."

It might be overkill—but it was definitely *enough* kill, and when it came to a bioform eight hundred kilometers long, the last thing they could afford was to leave it intact after hurting it.

The Infinite were evading now, desperate maneuvers that threw off the Grand Fleet's targeting data. Their entire formation dissolved into chaos—but there was a beauty to the chaos, a pattern Morgan couldn't quite pick out but which told her that it *wasn't* chaos.

It was a planned evasive maneuver, just as well-thought and logical as the evasive maneuvers *Va!Tola* was engaged in. Like their maneuvers, it would look random to the outside but was coded to keep ships from colliding with each other.

The sheer volume of fire the Grand Fleet was throwing at a single target was enough to render the maneuvers pointless. A second Category Five died in an antimatter sun tens of thousands of kilometers wide.

And then the allied fleet discovered that the *inverse* of the logic that killed the Category Five was equally true. With enough targets in play, it didn't matter whether your fire could hit a specific target. It had a good chance of hitting *a* target.

Eight microsingularities punched through the allied formation like javelins thrown by angry gods. Traveling at eleven nines of light-speed—99.999999999% of c—and absorbing any tachyons that came near them, the black holes were impossible to see coming.

And impossible to stop.

One hit a Laian war-dreadnought, tearing a hole half a kilometer wide through the massive starship. Another clipped an Imperial battleship, delivering the same devastating damage to the bigger ship that a similar strike had inflicted on Morgan's *Defiance*.

Two Laian escort cruisers just...disappeared, torn to pieces and the wreckage dragged along with the mass of their killers. Another Wendira cruiser was almost missed, the singularity itself passing by but its gravity well tearing chunks out of the warship.

Even at this range, the combined fleets were simply too big a target. The microsingularities didn't have time to curve toward anything, but they didn't *need* direct hits. And near-hits were far too easy with thousands of ships gathered into a single formation.

Morgan grimaced—but the last Category Five died as she did so, and nothing smaller could host the singularity guns. They hoped.

Plasma and hyperfold cannon fire now filled the space around Swarm Bravo as the Wendira starfighters reached their targets. The range was still dropping, but the two fleets hadn't yet reached missile range of each other.

And if the Wendira Drones had their way, they never would. Morgan had never seen the deadly small craft in action, only heard stories from her mother and her honorary aunts and uncles.

Now she watched them tear into the Infinite. Formations designed to alternate squadrons to confuse enemy targeting had been adopted to alternate entire Grand Wings. The Infinite unleashed a full million-missile salvo at the small ships as they approached, but Wendira fighters were notoriously difficult targets—and that was for gunners who knew what they were facing.

The missiles took their toll, but it was far from enough to stop the hundreds of thousands of fighters swarming over the Infinite, hyperfold cannons and missiles of their own hammering down on bioform after bioform.

But their power generators could only handle so much sustained fire, and the starfighter strike finally passed beyond range of Swarm Bravo. They were...much reduced, Morgan judged. Three hundred thousand–plus starfighters had gone in.

If she was reading her numbers right, only two hundred thousand had come out.

They'd gutted the smaller bioforms in exchange. If there was a Category Two bioform left in the Swarm, *Va!Tola*'s scanners couldn't see it.

That just left the middle of the road. The Category Threes and Fours, ships ranging from two kilometers to a hundred long.

There were a hundred and fifty of them left, and Morgan was already running the math on their missile armament—because the math on their velocity was clear!

"MISSILE RANGE IN THIRTY SECONDS," !Pana announced calmly. "All defensive drones are deployed." She paused. "Are we clear of incoming singularity fire?"

"We should be," Morgan replied. "My team has numbers on the missiles on the remaining ships. We're estimating the Cat-Threes at an average of a thousand launchers and the Cat-Fours at five thousand. Total is four hundred thousand launchers on the Cat-Fours.

"Our scans and opticals suggest these guys carried the biggest chunk of their launchers."

The four Category Fives had carried almost a quarter-million launchers between them, with the remaining three hundred and fifty thousand launchers spreading over nine hundred Category Threes and Twos.

"Bucklers and shields will hold," Tan!Shallegh said calmly. "They have neither. This should be...short."

"We can hope," Morgan agreed. Her consoles were already running through the range estimates on a Category Four's plasma bursts, and she didn't like what she saw.

"Shotilik, confirm these numbers," she ordered.

The missile launches started. Both Swarm Bravo and the combined fleets fired simultaneously—and Morgan's team's analysis appeared to be perfect. Exact numbers were impossible, but roughly four hundred thousand missiles were heading toward them.

And the combined fleet sent a million missiles back. She had *never* seen firepower deployed on that scale before, and she'd been present for the Battle of Arjtal, where the Imperium had fielded its largest Grand Fleet prior to the one she was aboard now.

"Orders to the fleets," Tan!Shallegh said suddenly, clearly in coordination with the other two fleet commanders. "We will advance to maximum hyperfold-cannon range while sustaining full-rate missile fire."

Morgan swallowed and checked her console.

"I have the same numbers, Captain," her Rekiki subordinate told her. "So does Ito. The Cat-Fours' plasma bursts will sustain integrity to twenty light-seconds."

Six million kilometers. A million kilometers longer than the range of the hyperfold cannons carried by the allied fleet—and while the hyperfold cannons' shots were instantaneous and hence more accurate, the combined fleets were a *very* large target.

"Fleet Lord, we estimate that many of the larger units can engage us from beyond our hyperfold-cannon range," she told Tan!Shallegh. "We've been revising the numbers based on everything we've seen today."

"Understood," the Fleet Lord said levelly. "!Pana, Grand Fleet ships will increase evasive maneuvers. Etri, make sure our allies know."

The incoming missiles were melting away under the fire of the defensive drones, but the range was already dropping. Morgan was about to ask why they didn't change the plan—but the vectors gave her the answer.

It was already too late to adjust velocities. It would take six seconds to reverse the fleets' courses...and those six seconds would take them to the edge of six million kilometers, where Swarm Bravo's velocity advantage would bring them into range within moments anyway.

They'd run the numbers too late.

Morgan watched as the two forces hurtled together and plasma fire began to blink on the screens exactly as her team had predicted. The Category Threes were firing as well, but their plasma bursts lost containment before reaching the fleet.

The bigger bioforms' weapons didn't—and the organization of the combined fleet meant that their fire almost inevitably ended up focused on only one component of the allied force. In this case, the Wendira.

Star shields maneuvered to get out in front of the hives, protecting the under-armed carriers from the incoming fire with their own shields and hulls. For all of their mass and protection, they were facing blasts of star stuff easily the same size of the light capital ships.

Wendira ships died by the dozens.

"Hyperfold-cannon range," !Pana reported. "All ships engaging."

It was a blur now. No living mind could keep track of what happened over the following few seconds, but the targeting priorities were already programmed into the systems. Tens of thousands of hyperfold cannons worked over the biggest bioforms first, the blasts of energy skipping the intervening space to hammer into armored hide and internal flesh alike.

Plasma now flashed both ways, and proton beams added their coherent particles to the chaos, but the hyperfold cannons were the true close-range ship killer of the three fleets—and the Infinite bioforms were uniquely vulnerable to internal damage that bypassed their defenses.

The silence, when it came, was as sudden as an axe falling.

"All targets destroyed," !Pana reported.

"Stand down all beams and launchers," Tan!Shallegh ordered. "Stand by for maneuvering orders from the Laians. They'll probably want us somewhere specific."

The silence seemed to stretch into eternity, but the Fleet Lord was already turning to other officers.

"Etri, I want a report of our losses and damaged units within a twentieth-cycle," he ordered the operations officer. "Leezor"—he turned to the Anbrai logistics officer, also on *Storm Sentinel*—"I want an assessment of every ship's munitions status by then. We'll coordinate with our fleet train to replenish our HSMs as quickly as the waves allow."

They *shouldn't* be facing another fight soon, but they were still learning how this enemy thought and fought.

"Casimir, get your team digging into everything that just

happened," he ordered Morgan. "Link up with the Laians; they'll be interfacing with their civilians and getting reports on what happened during the occupation.

"For eleven cycles, the Infinite controlled this system. I want to know what the locals saw in them."

CHAPTER THIRTY-FOUR

Rᴜɴ ᴇɴᴛᴇʀᴇᴅ Tᴀɴ!Sʜᴀʟʟᴇɢʜ's ᴏꜰꜰɪᴄᴇ ʜᴇsɪᴛᴀɴᴛʟʏ.

"You called me, Fleet Lord?"

"Take a seat, Doctor," Tan!Shallegh ordered, gesturing Rin to a chair on the same side of the desk as him. "I have a conference with Ronoxosh, Oxtashah and Tidirok in a few moments, and I would like to get your perspective."

"I'm...not sure what perspective I can provide, my lord," Rin admitted, but he took the seat anyway. When the First Fleet Lord asked you for a favor, you gave it. It was hard to avoid.

"Like Captain Casimir, you have an understanding of this enemy that I think still eludes most of us," Tan!Shallegh told him. "You know their ancient enemy better than anyone else alive, except perhaps some Mesharom.

"Your knowledge is useful...but mostly, it gives me an excuse to include you in the meeting," the Fleet Lord said with a red flush of amusement. "I find your perspective, as neither a fleet officer nor a diplomat, surprisingly valuable."

"I am at your disposal until the Empress or the Institute give me new instructions," Rin admitted. "If you want me to sit silently in high-level meetings, I shall."

An incoming message icon lit up on the Fleet Lord's operating system, and further commentary was cut off by Tan!Shallegh tapping the icon, linking both of them into a conference.

There were more people in the virtual conference room that unfolded around them than Tan!Shallegh had suggested, but given Rin's own presence, he wasn't entirely surprised. The holographic illusion filled the Fleet Lord's office, giving the impression that ten sentients from five different species were sitting in a single space around Tan!Shallegh's desk.

The fifth species was a surprise. Rin tended to forget that both the Republic and the Grand Hive had secondary races, as they were both even more dominated by their founding species than the A!Tol Imperium was. But the figure standing behind Voice Tidirok resembled nothing so much as a two-meter-tall stalk of broccoli, with waving green prehensile fronds acting as both hair and hands—a Shondra, one of the few non-Laian races of the Republic.

Oxtashah was alone, but Ronoxosh was accompanied by two smaller but heavier-chitined Warrior-caste officers., bringing the total to ten.

"I must thank all of you," Tidirok began before anyone could say a word. "We recognize the losses incurred by your forces retaking a Republic system and liberating Republic citizens, and we can offer only our gratitude.

"The Infinite did less damage here than we feared, but that may not have lasted. Millions live thanks to your truth and honor. Thank you."

"What do we know of the Infinite occupation so far?" Tan!Shallegh asked.

"Not much," Tidirok admitted. He gestured with a pincer to the Shondra behind him. "Akata is the civilian intermediary for my fleet. They have been interacting with the civilians and learning what we can."

"Not much so far," Akata's translated voice admitted. "It will take time to recover sensor records and carry out interviews across an entire star system."

"For now, the refueling infrastructure is intact enough for us to begin replenishing the fleets," the Voice told them all. "The First Defense Fleet will be dependent on our fleet train for other needs, though. The depots here were thoroughly looted and destroyed."

Rin had seen images of the many-tentacled small bioforms used for that work. He doubted they'd left anything they weren't trying to extract intact in one piece.

"All of this is secondary," Ronoxosh said, the first thing any of the Wendira had said since the meeting has begun. "Secondary to the treachery the Laians inflicted upon my people."

"Treachery?" Tidirok demanded.

Rin was...surprised by how unsurprised he felt. One battle as allies, and the Wendira and Laians were *already* having troubles.

"One hundred and eleven thousand, two hundred and sixty-eight starfighters destroyed," one of Ronoxosh's unnamed Warrior companions listed off. "Six star hives lost. Twenty-seven star shields and sixty-three lesser escorts wrecked.

"Versus *total* losses for the Laian and A!Tol fleets of less than sixteen ships," the Warrior concluded. "The numbers alone lay bare your plot, *Voice*. We are to be used as drones, freely expended to protect your ships while weakening the Grand Hive."

The conference was silent for several seconds.

"My understanding is that losses in the fighter strike were lower than expected," Tidirok said quietly. "And all of our ships were on the same line, Commandant. Ronoxosh had complete tactical command of your ships. I did not order your fighter strike. Your ships were not positioned in front of ours.

"I regret your losses. Your presence here helped save this system, and I would be a poor ally if I did not honor your dead as my own today. I swear to you, we did nothing to make your ships a target."

"And yet the Infinite focused their fire upon us when the final clash was joined," the same Warrior officer said. "One must wonder, then, what drove them to target us. One must wonder, given how intact this system is, if the Infinite are truly as much your enemy as you claim."

"*Enough*," Oxtashah suddenly snapped, the Princess's voice cutting through with a tone that sent a shiver down *Rin*'s spine—and he wasn't biologically programmed to follow Wendira Royals.

The Warrior Fleet Commandant physically quailed and seemed to retract into himself.

"I do not believe there was treachery today, merely the tides of war," she said grimly. "But we can see, I think, the vulnerabilities we face in joint operations. While this alliance is utterly essential to us both, I fear that this combined fleet may prove to be a dangerous proposition.

"Nonetheless, I will consult with our Queens before any further action is taken," Oxtashah told them all. "There will be no more talk of treachery," she said flatly, glaring at the images of her subordinates. "But I *do* ask that an analysis be performed, to see if we can identify why the Wendira ships were targeted over all others."

"That analysis is already underway," Tan!Shallegh said calmly. "I have guesses, but we will freeze the water of guess to the ice of *data*."

"Thank you," Oxtashah said. "I think we should cut this meeting short before any of our people say something they may regret."

"One last thing, in that case," Tidirok interjected. Every eye drew to the Voice of the Republic. "I will need the names, Princess Oxtashah."

It took Rin a moment to realize what Tidirok was asking—but the two Wendira Warriors clearly picked it up instantly.

"The names, Voice?" Oxtashah asked, her voice slow and careful.

"Of your dead. All of them," Tidirok told her. "It is my understanding that your Drones fight so that they will be remembered. Regardless, I would have the name of every Wendira who died to save a Laian system.

"Whatever else happens between our peoples, I will see those recorded and a memorial built. They died for the Republic, not the Hive, and so the *Republic* will remember them.

"You have my word."

CHAPTER THIRTY-FIVE

MORGAN WATCHED THE FOOTAGE IN THE HOLOTANK WARILY. IT was a recording of the bridge of a Laian supply ship, a bridge that would normally hold at least seven people.

In the image she was watching, it held one. A large metallic-black Laian male, his carapace carefully patched over where age had grown his flesh past what his chitin could handle. She'd only seen Laians of that age a few times before, and she suspected the ship's pilot was on his last years.

"Course is locked in," he announced. "I'm transmitting everything. I don't know if this will work, Tosonak."

"If it doesn't, twenty thousand people are going to die," the person on the other side of the radio announced. "Night-Moon-Light Station doesn't have the fuel to maintain their power cores for more than twelve hours more.

"I still think you should send someone else. You have thirty captains willing to take this flight, sir."

"And every one of them younger," the pilot replied, going through controls with the kind of care that suggested rusty skills. "I may own the company, Tosonak, but I've lived my life. I won't send others to die for me when I'm more expendable."

"Bioform is heading your way, boss," Tosonak told the Laian—apparently a transport company CEO named Tosolor. The voice on the radio was a child of the CEO's group marriage.

"I see it. Transmitting the messages now."

Morgan couldn't see or hear the message Tosolor sent, but Shotilik was standing at her shoulder.

"From what I've seen, it's a mediocre translation into Alavan text of 'this is a mission of mercy, we are unarmed,'" the Rekiki told her. "I don't know how Tosolor managed to pull that off, but you'll see the effects."

The bioform grew larger on the freighter's scanners. It was only a Category Two, but that was more than enough to obliterate the three-hundred-meter in-system freighter Tosolor was piloting.

"That thing is more than close enough to kill me," the Laian muttered. Morgan wasn't sure if Tosonak could hear him, but he *had* been recording and sending everything his sensors saw. The recording *she* was watching was directly from the ship's internal cameras, though.

"Wait!" he said loudly. "I have a response? Tosonak, I'm forwarding you a message. I need to... Wait, it's in the Tongue?"

Someone had apparently run the translation software at higher levels than normal, Morgan realized. At this level, places like the Sahara Desert tended to be translated as "Desert Desert."

"Tosonak, I have a transmission from the bioform," the pilot declared. "It says... It says, 'Course and cargo?'"

"Then send them the suns-burnt manifest, Tosolor," the Laian on the radio begged. "Send them it now!"

It took the older pilot a minute to find the data according to Morgan's time stamps, while the bioform calmly matched velocity and repeated its request two more times.

"There," Tosolor finally declared. "Manifest sent." Apparently to make certain, he picked up a microphone and tapped it on.

"Um, I'm bound for Night-Moon-Light Station with helium-3 fuel, water and food supplies," he declared into the microphone. "They have less than twelve hours of fuel and three days of water and food."

Silence. Shotilik accelerated the playback and the time stamps said it was five minutes before anything changed.

There was no response. The bioform just veered away to hunt another ship.

"They're leaving," Tosolor said, his astonishment clear even without the translation. "Maintaining course for Night-Moon-Light Station. Tosonak—pass on the Alavan code and...and...*everything* to every suns-burnt shipper in the system.

"I think they'll let us keep the stations running. I...wouldn't try getting to the fleet base or leaving the system, but I think they'll let us make sure people can eat and breathe!"

The recording froze.

"Tosolor is a billionaire by Imperial standards and owns roughly twenty percent of the civilian shipping in the Tohrohsail System," Shotilik observed. "Tosonak is his declared heir. They were likely being more formal than usual, as the recording was to be distributed if their delivery was successful—as it was."

"So, the Infinite let the locals travel around the system unimpeded?" Morgan asked.

"Eventually," Shotilik said. "They wiped out everything that fired on them. No surprise there. Initially, they also fired at any vessel that maneuvered anywhere near them, and they were everywhere in the system.

"By the time they drew their forces more toward the fleet base, everyone in the system had gone to ground," the Rekiki noted. "The fact that the Infinite hadn't attacked—or even interacted with—any of the settlements that hadn't tried to fire on them was considered a good sign, but Tosolor was the only one crazy enough to try to make a supply run."

"To a station that was almost out of everything," Morgan said.

"Yeah. The station in question was due for its five-cycle resupply when the Infinite arrived. Their reserves were just about gone when Tosolor decided to risk himself to make the delivery."

"And the Infinite continued to allow deliveries after that?" she asked.

"Except for one half-cycle period after someone tried to make a run for hyperspace, yes," Took confirmed, the Yin looking through her own data. "Interestingly, they *told* the locals that. Omnidirectional transmission telling all ships to lock down and that any ship making for hyperspace would be destroyed."

She shook her head.

"It wasn't *great* Laian, but it was understandable to the locals. They weren't good at communicating, but they were capable of it."

"That's promising," Morgan replied. "Do we think they're likely to follow similar allowances for mercy missions and necessary supplies in other systems?"

"Probably, but..." Took and Shotilik exchanged looks.

"So long as we don't betray the trust," Morgan guessed. "Everything we've seen says they were relatively calm to the Alava, even, until something changed."

"While we have no confirmation that Swarm Bravo was in communication with the main body in the Astoroko Nebula...um..." Shotilik shook her head. "I would suspect that any abuse of their goodwill will result in a lot of long-term pain."

"So would I," Morgan agreed. "I'll include the recommendation against using that in our report in the strongest language possible."

"Whatever you're planning, find a way to make it even clearer," Took suggested. "If the Infinite had locked down all shipping in Tohrohsail, best guess is about a million people would have died before we liberated the system."

"There might come a time when we need it anyway," Morgan warned. "Rumor has it we're going to be stepping back from full tactical coordination to operating as separate fleets with operational and strategic coordination.

"It's not a good plan; it's just the one that stops our allies from thinking the other is backstabbing them."

"I'm glad that's the Fleet Lord's problem," Shotilik said drily. "And that I *just* have to work out what a brain the size of a planet thinks is appropriate war strategy."

CHAPTER THIRTY-SIX

"I DON'T KNOW *WHY* TAN!SHALLEGH WANTS ME IN THE meetings," Rin admitted, passing Morgan a glass of wine as he settled onto the couch in her quarters. She was still standing, pacing back and forth in the small space with the nervous energy of a caged tiger.

"I suspect we're well past the point where anything I know about the Alava or the Infinite is really going to have an impact," he continued. "That war is fifty thousand years dead and so are the Alava.

"We don't *know* what they did to turn the Infinite genocidal and we don't know how to avoid doing it ourselves. They already seem to have adopted a shoot on sight policy with us and everybody else."

"I suppose the Queen tried to talk to me originally, but that conversation didn't go for very long," Morgan told him. "I think the local shippers had more constructive conversations with the Infinite than I did—and theirs were basically just 'Please don't shoot me.'"

"I'm surprised that worked," Rin admitted. "It suggests that the Infinite are both more able to communicate with us now than they were when we took *Defiance* into the Nebula and, well, more... reasonable, I guess, than we've been anticipating."

"They're still pretty damn angry with us," his lover replied.

"Swarm Bravo didn't attempt to talk at all before they came out ready for a fight."

"They were here to eliminate the combined fleets, though, weren't they?" Rin asked. "Threat management, I guess."

"That's my team's guess, too. They're trying to identify and eliminate threats to their base in the nebula, but with the Wendira in play, they underestimated our forces here. So, we came out ahead...but I have no way to judge how material the loss of Swarm Bravo is to them.

"Eleven hundred bioforms seems like a lot, except we know they have at least five hundred Category Fives and Swarm Bravo had *four*. It's going to be a long, messy war—and that's assuming we get the reinforcements and allies to hold."

"It sounds like it, even if the Wendira and Laians are getting twitchy about working in the same systems," Rin told her. "Tidirok has apparently been promised another hundred war-dreadnoughts in the next sixty cycles."

"And we're getting the rest of the HSM-equipped Imperial ships in the same time frame," Morgan told him. "That's classified, but you're sitting in the damn meetings with Tan!Shallegh. You're as cleared for it as I am."

"And our associates?" he asked quietly.

"I'm assuming they're part of why the Ren have actually pulled together a battle fleet to cover the Coreward side of the Astoroko Nebula," Morgan said. "Apparently, they're up to thirty billion tons of capital ships watching their borders, which is reassuring."

"All right, so we've established everything is going as well as it can in this damn war, but we're still talking work while you pace back and forth, wearing a trail in the carpet," Rin told her. He took a sip of his wine.

"Everything is a mess, Rin," she said. "I feel like I need to do more, but fuck if I can see any answers. Give me a squadron of ships with Final Dragons and we could end this in an afternoon!"

"There's a reason the Empress hasn't sent any Final Dragon

starkillers out here," Rin reminded her. The smaller strategic weapons were a stolen design, one that even most Core Powers couldn't match.

The last thing the Imperium needed was for the galaxy to realize that the Final Dragon weapons existed—and Rin suspected that they'd need to lose a good chunk of the Laian Republic, allies or not, before A!Shall authorized deploying them.

"I know." She sighed, and finally took a seat next to him with a surprising suddenness. "And I'm not writing home, and everything I say and do is work. But what else am I supposed to do, Rin?"

"Breathe?" he suggested. "I know, I know, we're both worka-holics, and out here, there's nothing much to do but work. I'm trying to dig in to what we've got on the Infinite in the Alavan archives, but it's not much. I feel like I'm just looking at the same things over and over again."

"That's how I feel, looking at what we've got for data since the Infinite woke up," she said. She sighed and shook her head. "I don't know; rub my shoulders?"

Rin chuckled and gestured for her to sit on the ground in front of him.

"That seems like a good starting place."

THE NIGHT WENT ABOUT AS WELL after that as could be hoped, including the rest of the bottle of wine, and Rin woke up in Morgan's quarters the following morning. His communicator was chirping its usual alarm—as was Morgan's—but finding the handheld devices took longer than it should have.

That was partially because they were both wrapped up in the blankets and sheets and partially because they were both naked and Rin found Morgan's body rather distracting.

Finally, they were both sitting on the bed with their respective devices. Morgan favored the scroll-like device originally designed by the United Earth Space Force and updated with Imperial technology—two five-centimeter cylinders that pulled apart to unroll a thin-screen tablet.

Rin's communicator was smaller, a single five-centimeter cylinder that could set up holoprojected screens and keyboards. It could *also*, however, interface with his cybernetics and feed information to his retinas directly.

He couldn't control the data without using the holocontrols—the Imperium wasn't a fan of permanent neural interfaces, and his own study of how the Alava's interfaces had killed them didn't help—but he didn't need a screen.

"Strange," he and Morgan said simultaneously, then paused and looked at each other.

"You first," he told her.

"I have a brand-new appointment with Fleet Lord Tan!Shallegh in a twentieth-cycle, right when I'm supposed to go on duty," she told him. "There's a notation here, advising me that both Wendira and Laian officers will be present, but it's still listed as a private meeting."

"That is strange," he agreed. "Related to your analysis?"

"Probably, though gods know I've written enough reports that I don't know what they think I can tell them that isn't in the paperwork," Morgan said. "What's strange for you?"

"I have an invite to a private meeting with Princess Oxtashah," Rin said. "We've spoken in private a few times since the peace conference, but I didn't even know she was aboard *Va!Tola*."

Morgan checked something on her communicator.

"She's coming aboard now," she told Rin. "I might even guess that she's coming specifically to talk to you. That's *definitely* strange."

"And intimidating," Rin admitted. "That woman may not be one of their Queens, but she's a post-childbearing Royal caste of the highest bloodlines. She's *going* to be one of the Queens, sooner or later."

There were only ever thirty-two Queens, the oldest Wendira female Royal castes of eight specific bloodlines. Oxtashah was one of those lines—that was what gave her her authority—and was post-childbearing.

She had to be getting close to taking a crown herself—and she was coming aboard an Imperial superbattleship to talk to *him*?

"Well, I guess we should both start getting ready," he told Morgan. "I don't think we have much time to spare."

He still took a moment to ogle his lover, which got him a brilliant grin as she apparently turned to do the same. There was very little as good for a man's ego as a lover who thought he was worth looking at.

No matter how worried he was about what was coming next.

CHAPTER THIRTY-SEVEN

DESPITE THE NOTE ON THE APPOINTMENT THAT IT WOULD include Wendira and Laian officers, Tan!Shallegh was alone in his office with no video links. The A!Tol was looking at reports—the perennial task of any senior officer—and closed them down as she entered, gesturing her to a chair.

The drink machine in his desk was already disgorging her coffee, the office system clearly having done the digital equivalent of taking notes from the last time.

"Your staff made this appointment on quite short notice, sir," Morgan admitted. "What's going on?"

"It's complicated," Tan!Shallegh told her. She realized there were swirls of yellow across his skin, an unusual color for A!Tol. It was often interpreted as meaning the A!Tol was lying, but it was also associated with just feeling dirty.

What was going on?

"Did you know that I opposed both the development and then, later, the deployment, of the Final Dragon weapons?" the Fleet Lord asked.

"I did not, sir," Morgan admitted.

"Your stepmother earned her Duchy by destroying a rogue development program around similar stolen Mesharom weapons," Tan!Shallegh said quietly. "That's classified, though it may have been covered under the Final Dragon information you were given."

Morgan blinked and took a swallow of her coffee.

"It was not," she admitted slowly. "I was only aware of the official story, that she broke an organization attempting to reopen the war with the Kanzi."

"Which is also true," Tan!Shallegh said. "What we kept secret was that that organization had acquired and successfully reverse-engineered a Mesharom starkiller. Duchess Bond destroyed the organization and acquired their weapons.

"She destroyed those weapons in turn before surrendering herself to the Imperium," he summarized neatly. "I felt then that a concealable starkiller represented an unacceptable threat to the balance of power in the galaxy. That even the *Mesharom* had such a thing was and is still unknown to much of the galaxy.

"My opinion of miniature starkillers had not changed when we began the Final Dragon program," he told her. "But I am merely the *First* Fleet Lord, not the *only* Fleet Lord. And my Empress feared we would need a secret sword to protect ourselves as we drew closer to parity with the Core Powers."

"Hence *Defiance* and her sisters," Morgan said quietly. "Sir, this is background for...?"

"You were in the Astoroko Nebula with starkillers," Tan!Shallegh said grimly. "Our allies don't know that yet, but a plan is being discussed where it is relevant. You were at the Eye and the storm around it—the 'rosette,' I think your report called it. You looked at it with the eyes of an officer with starkillers to hand.

"In your opinion, would the use of starkillers on one or more of the blue giants of the rosette take out the Infinite in the Eye of the Astoroko Nebula?"

"Ah," Morgan breathed. "Yes," she confirmed. "That was our plan, in fact, before our Final Dragon weapons were destroyed.

"We estimated that one star wouldn't be a guaranteed kill on the target, but if we simultaneously detonated six—the number of starkillers we carried—it would probably be overkill."

She shrugged.

"We planned for overkill."

"I don't like it," Tan!Shallegh said grimly. "I don't like starkillers, and I am horrified by the thought of wiping out a sentient race, even the Infinite, who have been unhesitatingly aggressive so far."

"But?" she asked.

"There are three analysis teams, including yours, that have assessed the risk of the Infinite," he said quietly. "Yours has the most pessimistic conclusions, but the Wendira and Laians agree with you in principle.

"Our next encounter with the Infinite will almost certainly see them having more fully integrated and adapted the interface drive and interface-drive missile technology to their biology," Tan!Shallegh continued. "We faced less than one percent of their strength here in Tohrohsail, and, in clear waters, had they surprised us at anchor, we would have lost all three fleets."

Morgan was silent. She'd drawn the same conclusion but hadn't actually put it in her report. Arriving by surprise, the Infinite would have controlled the initial engagement positions and would have forced a plasma range engagement in short order.

It would have been a pyrrhic victory for whoever had won, but the odds would have been in the Infinite's favor...and the Infinite could lose Swarm Bravo more readily than the galaxy could lose the combined fleets in Tohrohsail.

"What is the plan, then, sir?" she asked.

One of the Fleet Lord's manipulators produced a small black box the size of Morgan's palm, seemingly from nowhere, and placed it in front of her.

"We have, with the assistance of our Laian allies, refitted four of our *Bellerophon*s to a new standard—designated *Bellerophon*-S—

including Laian-provided stealth fields," he told her as she stared at the insignia box.

"Thanks to the incorporation of some of our own tricks, that makes the *Bellerophon*-Ses the largest and most powerful stealth-capable units available," he continued. "We do not have stealth-equipped starkillers, but it turns out that both the Wendira and Laians *do*.

"The Wendira are redeploying their Battle Hives to secure their own border, falling back on a strategic coordination rather than tactical. The only coordinated mission going forward is one no one is going to be talking about."

Morgan was listening, but she also caved to curiosity and opened the insignia box.

Inside, resting on a layer of black fabric, was the crossed silver-spears insignia of an Imperial Division Lord. An officer who would command, say, four hypermodern battleships.

"Neither the Wendira nor the Laians were prepared to place their starkillers under the command of an officer from the other," Tan!Shallegh said drily. "They were both, fascinatingly, prepared to place ships and starkillers under *your* command, specifically."

"Me, sir?" Morgan asked.

"You saw the Queen yourself," he told her. "They believe—and I agree—that you have a heart-level understanding of this foe that none of us can match.

"The spears are technically temporary," he continued. "But so long as you manage to return from this mission, I believe I can make them freeze. Do you accept this tasking, Staff Captain Casimir?"

"You want me to command a mixed-race fleet, including two species that absolutely hate each other, and an unspecified number of starkiller weapons of mass destruction?" she clarified. "I presume I am to take said fleet into the Astoroko Nebula and trigger the simultaneous detonation of a significant portion of the rosette of stars around the Eye?"

"Correct and correct," Tan!Shallegh agreed. "I do not like this mission, Casimir. But I cannot argue against its necessity. The galaxy as we know it may well be at risk. The only way we can combine Laian and Wendira starkillers in one force is under your command.

"Will you accept the mission?"

"Yes," Morgan said quickly, before she could change her mind. What choice did she have? Without something drastic, the Infinite could easily end up *eating* the galaxy.

And this was definitely *something drastic*.

ONCE MORGAN HAD the new insignia pinned on the collar of her uniform, the formal meeting with their allies started. Royal Commandant Ronoxosh and Voice Tidirok appeared on separate screens, each of them looking first to Tan!Shallegh and then to Morgan.

And never, she noted, at each other. That might have been an effect of the conferencing software, but she suspected it was fundamentally accurate.

"Division Lord Casimir has accepted the mission and will command the special task group for us," Tan!Shallegh told the other two flag officers. "As previously discussed, the Imperium will deploy four modified stealth battleships under her command to provide the STG's heavy firepower.

"Have you come to a conclusion on what level of force each of your fleets will be able to contribute to the special task group?" he asked.

"We have four stealthed starkillers and will additionally commit four star intruders and ten escorts," Ronoxosh said immediately. "Thirty million tons of warships and the starkillers."

The ships Morgan had been told she was getting from Tan!Shallegh would total forty-six million tons, but the Imperium didn't have starkillers that fit the mission profile. It probably evened out, she reflected.

"The First Defense Fleet also has four stealth starkillers," Tidirok said after a moment. "We will also provide two squadrons of our stealthed attack cruisers."

The Laian seemed extremely pleased with himself for a moment.

"That is twenty cruisers and *eighty* million tons of warships," he noted.

Morgan managed not to chuckle aloud as Tidirok "outbid" his Wendira counterpart.

"And all the officers involved are aware that they will be under the command of an Imperial officer?" Tan!Shallegh asked. "The last thing the special task group will be able to afford is confusion over the flow of command. The Astoroko Nebula is unquestionably enemy territory."

"I have personally selected the Swords in command of the squadrons committed," Tidirok promised. "They have worked well with human Imperial officers in the past, and I have no doubts about their ability to continue doing so."

Ronoxosh's wings flickered slightly in aggravation—probably a recognition that he didn't have the ability to pick officers who'd served with Imperial officers at all, let alone ones who'd served with Morgan's species.

"The Sub-Commandants in question have been selected with extreme diligence," he finally said. "They will obey Division Lord Casimir's orders as if they came from the Queens themselves."

Morgan was already mentally assessing her force. It was escort-heavy—inevitable in a stealth force. Her four *Bellerophon*s would be the key weapon, HSM-equipped snipers she could hopefully use to eliminate potential sentinels before there was any risk of the STG being seen.

The Wendira star intruders weren't much larger than the Laian cruisers, but with four of them, she'd have a thousand fighters. *Replacing* fighters would be a problem, though, so she could only count on one full-power strike from the stealth carriers.

The twenty Laian attack cruisers would be more-reliable backup hitters, with the ten Wendira escorts serving as much to disguise the starkillers if they lost stealth as anything else. The standard form of the strategic weapons was much the same size as a Wendira escort or an Imperial destroyer.

"The mission is very simple," Tan!Shallegh reminded them all. "Which means that execution will be complicated. The special task group will endeavor to penetrate the Astoroko Nebula without being detected and reach the stars around the Eye of the Nebula.

"If possible, Casimir's force will preposition all eight starkillers for detonation via hyperfold transmission," he continued. "The simultaneous nova of eight stars should render a hyperspace escape by the Infinite impossible, trapping the Queen and the majority of her forces inside the Eye, to be destroyed by the nova blast waves.

"It is a brute-force and arguably immoral solution," Tan!Shallegh concluded. "But it *should* bring a swift end to this situation."

Morgan couldn't disagree with any part of Tan!Shallegh's assessment.

"I will want to meet with my new officers as soon as possible," she told all three fleet commanders. "Within the cycle, preferably, though I will need time to transfer aboard my flagship."

"It will be made to happen," Ronoxosh assured her.

"Your Swords of the Republic will be briefed of their mission within the next quarter-cycle and deploy to support your flagship shortly thereafter," Tidirok said.

"Good luck, Division Lord."

The two fleet commanders faded away and Morgan's attention returned to Tan!Shallegh.

"So, which ship will be my flagship?" she asked.

"I suggest *Odysseus*, but the choice is yours," Tan!Shallegh told her. "You will command *Odysseus*, *Agamemnon*, *Sirites* and *Tan!Loka*. *Odysseus* has a multiracial crew where *Agamemnon* is human-crewed."

Sirites and *Tan!Loka* were, Morgan guessed, Anbrai- and A!Tolcrewed respectively, given that they were named for mythical heroes of those races.

"*Odysseus* makes sense to me," she replied. "Captain Cathrine Koumans, correct?"

Morgan was at least passingly familiar with the name of every human Captain in the fleet, though she hadn't met Koumans.

"Yes," he confirmed. "All four Captains are aware of their assignment to the special task group but not of its mission. Briefing your officers and crew will fall on you.

"I took the liberty of having !Pana assemble a small staff to support you, as you won't have the time yourself," he continued. "I trust her judgment and believe you will be pleased."

"May I make a request?" Morgan asked.

"Of course."

"I want Bethany Rogers," Morgan told her boss. If she was going to take command of a new fleet with a new staff, she needed at least one person she knew she could rely on.

"*Staff Captain* Rogers is already designated as your chief of staff," Tan!Shallegh told her, with the red flush of an A!Tol chuckle. "She should be aboard *Odysseus* by the time you arrive."

"Thank you, sir," Morgan said. "In that case, I think I should be about it, shouldn't I?"

CHAPTER THIRTY-EIGHT

It turned out that Princess Oxtashah *did* have access to an office on the Imperial superbattleship. Rin had never met her in it before this appointment, but the space had clearly been set up for the Wendira to use on an ongoing basis.

The temperature, humidity...even the air mix was noticeably different from the rest of the ship when he walked in. The lights had been adjusted, and multiple pieces of Wendira-style furniture—modified to allow for wings and the sheer scale of a Wendira Royal—had been installed.

The Princess was alone when he entered, and waved him to a single human-styled seat. There was a bottle of water next to it that he guessed was probably lukewarm already, but he took the seat and studied Oxtashah.

She was fiddling with a device and laid it down as he looked at her. Rin wasn't an expert by any means, but he was *reasonably* sure it was a privacy generator that meant *Va!Tola*'s crew couldn't see what was going on.

"Dr. Dunst, I appreciate you meeting with me," she told him. "I understand that I have no real call on your time or expertise except through the alliance with your government—an alliance that is..."

"Struggling?" he suggested drily.

"No," she said. "Difficult, yes. But I do not believe the alliance itself is in danger, which is actually both promising and reassuring. The Infinite have done us a favor, even as they threaten destruction."

"A common enemy often brings together old foes," Rin agreed. "How may I assist you, Princess Oxtashah?"

"I have questions, Dr. Dunst, questions I know you know the answer to," she said calmly. "I do not know if you feel you *can* answer them, but I know you know the answers."

That was never reassuring. Rin tested the water carefully in lieu of answering. It wasn't as bad as he'd been afraid of—whoever had brought it in had probably been aware of both the temperature of the room and the timeline before it was going to be drunk. There was ice in the bottle still.

"Ask," he suggested. "I know many things I am not permitted to share even with my fellow Imperials, let alone the representatives of an ally who was recently an enemy."

She chittered her wings in amusement.

"The Taljzi Campaigns, Dr. Dunst," she said calmly. "A Mesharom battle fleet, dozens of war spheres, joined the Imperium to campaign against an enemy in possession of the technology of Those Who Came Before.

"And yet none of the reports that had spread from your Imperium, none of the stories of the battles and victories, even seared of facts as they are, even *mention* the war spheres," she noted. "A mighty fleet, one that outmassed and outgunned any Core Power, just...disappeared.

"What *happened*, Dr. Dunst?"

Rin swallowed an ice cube and coughed against the chill running down his throat. He *did* know the answer to what she was asking—it had been an Alavan artifact the Taljzi had turned against the Mesharom—but she was correct in her first guess.

He couldn't answer that question.

"I'm afraid I can't answer that," he said quietly. "Even if I knew..."

"You know," Oxtashah said calmly. "But you are bound by oath. I understand that. But there are rumors that have reached me about what happened. That an artifact of Those Who Came Before served as a deadly trap that destroyed the Mesharom, smashing their greatest fleet like it was a toy."

"I can't speak to those rumors," Rin said. "I'm not sure I can help you."

"Please, Dr. Dunst, I have more than merely a desire to push the boundaries of your oaths," Oxtashah told him. "In fact, I must ask if I may have your oath—and if you will honor a promise of secrecy to me as thoroughly as your promise to your Empress."

Rin hesitated. That was a dangerous promise to make.

"So long as it does not threaten the Imperium, I will keep secret what you ask me to keep secret," he finally said.

"More than sufficient, I think," Oxtashah said. For a moment, the office was silent, and Rin wondered what the hell was going on.

Then a hologram appeared in the air above them. The image was both familiar and unfamiliar, and he sucked in a breath of shocked surprise as he studied the hologram.

The star was a red giant, a grossly expanded former main-sequence star that had either begun to run low on fuel or been damaged by some failure of advanced technology. The presence of the outer layers of an Alavan Dyson Swarm suggested the latter, the orbiting plates blocking much of the view of the trapped star.

The star was wrong, and even the Swarm was slightly different from the one out near the Taljzi, but it was the same style of massive Alavan artifact that the Taljzi had turned on the Mesharom.

"Do you know what this is, Dr. Dunst?" Oxtashah asked.

"I think so," he said quietly.

"But you can't tell me, can you?" she said. She chittered in amusement again. "So, I will tell you. This is a stellar-energy-capture swarm built by Those Who Came Before, designed to send energy via a modification of their teleporter systems to facilities in several surrounding star systems."

Her wings flickered in a shrug.

"Fate, time and the Mesharom obliterated the facilities this swarm supported," she noted. "But somehow, they missed the swarm itself. My people discovered it while surveying the wreckage of the Dead Zone for fleet base locations after the War of Mistakes.

"We have studied it for centuries and we hesitate to do more than touch it," she admitted. "But I understand, from the rumors I have heard, that the Taljzi turned a stellar-capture swarm into some kind of superweapon and destroyed a Mesharom battle fleet.

"A weapon that could destroy thirty Mesharom war spheres could perhaps turn the tide against the Infinite, could it not?" she asked. "We do not know what was done to the swarm by Arjtal. We cannot duplicate it.

"But we *have* a stellar-capture swarm, Dr. Dunst, which leaves me with a question for you that I hope you *will* feel able to answer.

"Do you believe that you can duplicate the Taljzi weapon, given a swarm in this state of disrepair?"

Rin was silent for a while. He wasn't sure how much time—enough that he worried about how Oxtashah was going to take it—passed before he finally sighed and spread his hands.

"I *can* tell you that the weapon had many limitations," he said quietly. "I'm not sure it would be the game changer you seem to think it would be. I can also say that I don't have the skill to replicate what was done alone.

"But...it is possible that I could assemble a team from the Grand Fleet who might."

He was reasonably sure that Kelly Lawrence was somewhere on the fleet, for example. His former cyber-archaeologist friend had decided that joining Imperial Fleet Intelligence was a use for her skills that would put Marines between her and any more space pirates.

And Lawrence had been on the team that had disabled the Taljzi Dyson swarm.

"That would require me to reveal one of the deepest secrets of the Grand Hive to, at the very least, the team you assembled," Oxtashah said quietly.

"We would need to bring Tan!Shallegh in at a minimum," Rin told her. "That decision is yours. I will not betray your secrets, Princess Oxtashah, but to do what you want, we will need to bring in others."

"Thank you, Dr. Dunst," Oxtashah said. "I will consider my options. I appreciate your assistance and your honesty."

Rin, for his part, kept his gaze on the hologram of the Dyson swarm. The Alava had never thought small.

He had to wonder if that was related to how they'd convinced the Infinite that the entire Alavan species needed to die.

CHAPTER THIRTY-NINE

To a very real extent, Morgan had never bothered to unpack on *Va!Tola*. She'd never quite had time, and it appeared that had been the right call. She'd served as an analyst team lead for Tan!Shallegh for less than thirty cycles.

Once everything was packed away, she took a few minutes to sit on the bed and breathe. She still needed to meet with her team and let them know she was shipping out, but everything was running at maximum velocity.

Her ulterior motive proved out, though, as Rin knocked on the door before she gathered herself enough to leave.

"Come in," she told him.

Her boyfriend took in the neatly packed duffel on the bed and her posture with a calm expression, then his gaze focused on her collar.

"Division Lord, huh?" he asked. "Congratulations."

"It's temporary, theoretically, but they needed an Imperial officer both a Wendira and Laian detachment would listen to," she said. "I'm commanding a special joint mission—can't say much more than that, I don't think."

"But you're shipping out," he concluded, sitting down on the bed next to her and squeezing her hand. "And you had no warning, so there's nothing to blame you for, is there?"

Morgan chuckled. She hadn't been thinking about that, not really, but the worry had been there.

"Still good to hear that you don't blame me," she told him. "How was your meeting with the Wendira Princess?"

"Complicated," he murmured. "I... I can't talk about it. Not yet. Maybe not ever. I gave her my word."

That was strange, but Morgan knew she couldn't press him. She squeezed his hand back and leaned her head on his shoulder for a few precious moments.

"You have a thousand and one things to be doing, I'm sure," Rin told her. "I saw you weren't at your station, and thought I could steal some emotional support, but I don't want to get in the way."

"You only get in the way when you think it's the right thing to do?" Morgan asked, reflecting on the time he'd gone over her head to get himself attached to a mission as a civilian advisor. He'd been *right* —not least because they'd needed to keep some of her clearances and knowledge secret—but that hadn't made it less aggravating.

"Sometimes, that's what it takes," he agreed. "Professionally and personally, I'm supposed to have your back. Regardless of what you think about it at a given moment."

She sighed.

"Right now, you're probably right in sending me on my way," she admitted. "I just needed a moment to breathe and, well, hoped that you'd see I was off duty and check in."

"Well, here I am," Rin said with a grin. "And you've told me that you're leaving, which sucks, but I always knew what I was getting into, *Division Lord*."

"Be nice, *Doctor*," she countered with a smile of her own. "You think you'll survive on your own?"

"I did before; I will again. Tan!Shallegh appears to have adopted me," Rin told her. "I don't know if I'm being nearly as much use as I'd like, though. It's not like we're going to find a forgotten Alavan archaeology site with all of the answers about the Infinite."

"Would be nice, though," she admitted. "Feels like we don't have nearly enough answers."

And she was about to make sure they *never* got those answers. Obliterating the main core of the Infinite was unlikely to convince the survivors to sit down for informational interviews.

"Well, either way, it looks like you need to get to it," Rin told her. "Up and at them, Morgan. Space waits better than the tides did, but duty waits for no one."

"It waits a little," she replied, then kissed him fiercely. Coming up for air, she smiled at him. "But not much. I'll be back, Rin."

"Don't make promises you don't know you can keep, Morgan."

RIN'S words were echoing in Morgan's mind as she walked into *Va!Tola's* Fleet Operations Center. Her entire team was on duty, but the moment she walked in, everyone stopped and turned to look at her.

Shotilik was there a moment later, the big Noble-caste Rekiki saluting fist to chest.

"I see the news already made it," Morgan said drily—and then noticed that Shotilik had acquired a third gold pip on her insignia, marking her promotion to full Captain. "And that congratulations are in order, *Staff Captain* Shotilik."

"We were informed a hundredth-cycle ago," Shotilik confirmed. "I was informed...a hundredth-cycle before that? Along with the promotion."

"So, you're taking over, I hope?"

"Until the Fleet Lord finds someone better," the Rekiki said. "Or you come back. Whichever works."

"The only person I can think of who even *might* be better is going with me," Morgan told Shotilik with a chuckle. "So, you'll be keeping the job."

She stepped past the Rekiki and faced the rest of the team. She hadn't had a chance to get to know most of them as well as she'd have liked, but they were still her people.

"Everything about this team has been a rush," she told them. "So, I guess it's no surprise that my leaving is a rush. I'm transferring to the battleship *Odysseus* within the twentieth-cycle."

Her duffel was probably already on her shuttle, waiting for her to catch up.

"The entirety of three fleets is now armed with the knowledge and analysis this team has done," she continued. "Given the limited information and time available to us, we have done amazing things in projecting and analyzing this enemy.

"Our knowledge of them remains far from perfect, and refining that knowledge will continue to fall on you. That's why you are remaining a separate team, even as the data you've provided is absorbed by Fleet Operations.

"I would have liked to have had more time with you, but duty calls us all," she told them. "And I have faith in you and in Staff Captain Shotilik, that you will continue to provide the Grand Fleet and Fleet Lord Tan!Shallegh with the knowledge they need.

"Thank you."

"We'll do our job, sir," Shotilik promised quietly. "I'm getting the impression yours is going to be...fraught."

"Duty is duty," Morgan told her. "We do what we must."

She had to agree with Tan!Shallegh. The mission she'd been asked to take on was dirty business—but the other option was to risk everything.

CHAPTER FORTY

MORGAN'S SHUTTLE RAMP EXTENDED SMOOTHLY TO THE DECK, matching positions with a perfectly turned out double file of Tosumi Marines. The four-armed avians, distinctive in midnight-black ceremonial armor that offset the raucous colors of their feathers, held plasma rifles at port arms and formed a path across *Odysseus's* flight bay.

Two women were waiting at the far end of that path as Morgan traded salutes with the Marines and boarded her new flagship. One of them was the petite redheaded woman who'd stood at her right hand as she'd taken *Defiance* into one crisis after another, now promoted to *Captain* Bethany Rogers.

The other was a stranger to Morgan, a situation that couldn't be allowed to last. Captain Cathrine Koumans was the senior of her four captains—technically, in fact, she would have been about three years senior to *Captain* Morgan Casimir—and Morgan knew she would need to depend heavily on her Flag Captain.

Koumans was a tall and broad-shouldered woman, with a shaven scalp and heavyset features that returned Morgan's assessing gaze evenly.

"Welcome aboard *Odysseus*, Division Lord Casimir," she greeted Morgan. "I believe you know Staff Captain Rogers?"

"I do indeed," Morgan agreed, clasping hands with her new chief of staff. "The Fleet Lord apparently felt that I shouldn't be allowed out without my usual minder."

She then turned and took Koumans' firm handshake.

"And I know you by reputation, Captain Koumans," she told *Odysseus*'s commander. "But I don't believe we've served together at all."

"No, I was on the Coreward Kanzi frontier while you were dealing with their murderous cousins," Koumans confirmed. "We also serve who stand and wait, they say, but it goes against the grain nonetheless."

"Someone had to watch our backs," Morgan agreed. "Let's not forget that the Kanzi civil war started because some of their fleet commanders *did* try to backstab us."

That had not ended well for them, and the civil war had given the High Priestess and her chosen partner, High Warlord Shairon Cawl, the chance to rebuild the entire Theocracy. Morgan couldn't necessarily approve of dragging out the civil war the way Cawl and his mistress had done, but she could see the need.

Slavery was not a societal structure that died easily.

"My officers are swamped, preparing to ship out," Koumans said after a moment's silence. "Normally, I'd have my officers and your staff here to greet you, but most of your staff is still on their way and, well..."

"Your people have work to do that's far more important than stroking the new division commander's ego," Morgan said with a chuckle. "There will be time for everyone to get to know each other. This mission should be...straightforward enough, in some ways, but my understanding is that if we succeed, I get to keep the division."

The division in question was the 73-2-2—the Seventy-Three-Twenty-Two in the English-translated parlance of the fleet's officers.

The Second Division of the Second Echelon of the Seventy-Third Battle Squadron.

Of course, since the Houses of the Imperium were still arguing over trying to reduce the fleet strength back to the fifty battle squadrons it had been limited to when Earth had been conquered, Morgan was unsure how long the Seventy-Third Battle Squadron would exist.

On the other hand, the Infinite were a *great* argument in favor of keeping the fleet at seventy-five squadrons.

"Then we will have plenty of time, yes," Koumans agreed. "Shall I give you the tour, Division Lord?"

"Or should you, perhaps, be returning to helping your officers deal with that pile of work?" Morgan asked. "I can find my own way to the flag deck, Captain. I'm familiar enough with the basic *Bellerophon* design for that, and I know what our time pressure looks like."

Koumans had solid self-control, but Morgan still picked up the other woman's internal struggle over that. Tradition said the Captain showed the new flag officer around—but the plan was for the special task group to ship out in less than three cycles.

"I...would probably be better served helping my people, yes, sir," she conceded.

"Staff Captain Rogers and I will be on the flag deck if you need us," Morgan told her. "If you can break time free for yourself and your officers to dine with me this evening, that may work best for us all."

"I will make it happen, sir," Koumans replied.

The flag officer's *suggestions*, after all, carried the weight of orders from someone else.

ODYSSEUS'S FLAG deck was quiet when Rogers and Morgan entered. A standard task force information graphic hung in the middle of the holotank, currently showing data on the four battle-ships of the Seventy-Three-Twenty-Two.

The flag officer's seat was right next to the tank, with a clear space in front of it for Morgan to stand and study the tank—or pace in front of it, as she'd known some officers to do. Like the FOC aboard *Va!Tola* that she'd just given back, the flag deck had the space for a dozen officers and support staff. Consoles ringed the holotank and the Lord's seat, all facing toward the flag officer to allow ease of communication.

Morgan had seen the flag decks of a dozen different *Bellerophon*s of various different iterations. She'd served aboard the original *Bellerophon* at the start of the war with the Taljzi before the battle-ship's destruction.

But she had never before, in the seventeen years of her career, walked onto a flag deck that was *hers*. *Morgan Casimir* commanded this division and the task group that would be assembled around it over the next few days.

That didn't feel quite real.

"What's the division's status?" she asked Rogers as she approached the main hologram. There were no warning icons on the display, so that meant things were acceptable—but *acceptable* wasn't the same as *ready for a suicide mission*.

"All four ships are taking aboard last-minute supplies and muni-tions," Rogers told her. "First thing I ordered was a series of tests on the stealth systems. We don't want to bring them up fully while we're still around the combined fleets, but we want to know if we're going to have trouble."

"Any sign of it so far?" Morgan asked.

"They've passed power and stress testing so far," her chief of staff said. "We're not going to be able to test them for real until we're in quieter space, but my understanding is that they *should* function even better than the Laian systems they're based on."

Morgan chuckled.

"And how much *other* tech is built into the systems?" she asked. "I didn't think Laians could stealth anything over five megatons."

"Apparently, it's just really expensive to build," Rogers said. "That's a question for Koumans more than me right now. I'm not as caught up as I'd like to be."

"Who is?" Morgan asked. "I'm assuming we have both Taljzi and...Dragon tech built into the stealth system?"

"That's my understanding, but I haven't had a chance to review the reports yet," Rogers repeated.

Dragon tech was systems based on the Mesharom Archive: the data Morgan had retrieved from a wrecked war sphere along with the ship's crew. Officially, it had been done without the Mesharom's knowledge, and the Mesharom Conclave would probably be pissed if they found out the Imperium had it.

Unofficially, the commander of the ship had given them his access codes in exchange for the rescue of the survivors of the Mesharom fleet. Morgan suspected the blind eye the Mesharom were turning to the Imperium's recent tech programs was at least partially intentional.

She turned her attention back to the holograms, touching commands as she refamiliarized herself with the flag deck controls. Her training on the software was *years* old. In the normal course of events, a promotion to flag rank would have come with a refresher course on all of these systems—and probably some high-level academy training around tactics and strategy, too.

Right now, she was being given the command without any prep at all—and told to go blow up a nebula.

"Once we confirm who our Wendira and Laian officers are going to be, I want an all-captains meeting scheduled ASAP," Morgan told Rogers. "I'll meet the squadron commanders first, but we'll need to be moving on the main meeting as well."

"We have three cycles, Bethany," she said quietly. "That's when the Wendira are leaving, and our special task group is expected to use their departure as cover."

"Who are we hiding our mission from, sir?" Rogers asked. "I mean, it's not like the Infinite are watching us."

"That we know of," Morgan replied. "That we know of, Staff Captain."

Much of the secrecy, though, was that they were operating out of the middle of the Dead Zone, where a hundred stars had been murdered with the very weapons her task group was tasked to deploy.

Standing among the wreckage of dead stars, no one wanted to admit they'd ordered *more* stars killed.

CHAPTER FORTY-ONE

Somehow, Rin wasn't entirely surprised to be summoned to a meeting with Tan!Shallegh at the end of the ship's day-cycle. The Wendira were in possession of an asset of potentially immense value, but they didn't know what to do with it.

The Imperials *did*, but Rin would need a team and to call on expertise from people who weren't there. Hyperfold and starcom communications could quickly get him a full report on how the Taljzi-modified Dyson swarm was shut down—but he couldn't ask for it without a reason.

Oxtashah and Tan!Shallegh were the only people in the Fleet Lord's office when Rin arrived. The door slid shut behind him—and then a *second* set of security doors, ones he hadn't realized the space even had, slid shut over those.

"Take a seat, Dr. Dunst," Tan!Shallegh told him. "At Princess Oxtashah's request, this room is now sealed against any and all surveillance. No one, aboard *Va!Tola* or not, can hear or see anything going on in here."

The A!Tol leveled his eyes, always pitch-black, on Oxtashah as greens and blues—determination and curiosity—flickered across his skin.

"You have requested Dr. Dunst and absolute privacy, Princess Oxtashah," he noted. "This is, I must admit, a strange set of requests. I hope that you can make matters clear in short order."

"I can," she promised. She laid a portable holoprojector on Tan!Shallegh's desk, and the same image she'd shown Rin earlier appeared in the middle of the room. The Dyson swarm circled its star in quiet certainty, the multilayer creation shedding light that went surprisingly well with the art around the room.

"A stellar swarm," Tan!Shallegh noted. "Not, I am guessing, the one near Arjtal."

"No," Oxtashah agreed. "This one is in the Dead Zone, Fleet Lord Tan!Shallegh, some thirty light-years from the Astoroko Nebula. Lost to the records the Mesharom possessed, it remained intact as time and looters stripped the systems and facilities it fed power to.

"It is almost entirely inactive, and we have hesitated to do more than study it for the time we have been aware of its existence," she told them. "But my understanding is that the Taljzi converted a similar energy-capture swarm into a modified Alavan teleporter cannon and used it to destroy a Mesharom fleet."

"I do not have the authority to confirm or deny her suspicions, Fleet Lord," Rin said quietly. "I told her she would have to go to you."

"*If* such a thing were the case," Tan!Shallegh said calmly, "what do you think we can do?"

"I believe that your people disabled the Taljzi weapon," Oxtashah replied. "And in disabling it, I believe you learned enough to know how to turn *our* swarm into the same style of weapon—creating a deadly trap that we would be able to lure the next Infinite strike force into.

"A weapon that could eliminate a Mesharom battle fleet would easily turn the tide of battle against the Infinite, could it not?"

Tan!Shallegh was quiet for at least fifteen seconds, colors swirling across his skin as he considered the proposal.

"There was such a weapon," he finally confirmed. "I do not fully understand what the Taljzi did, but I am told it was a merger of modern and Precursor technology—if nothing else, the Alavan systems had to be taught to recognize an interface drive.

"It was a perversion of a system designed for in-flight refueling of Alavan ships," the Fleet Lord told her. "Given that the Alava had regular refueling facilities scattered across their entire territory, I do not know if that system will even exist on your stellar swarm."

"It seems worth the investigation," Oxtashah said calmly. "Any tool that could protect our people seems worth trying. Do you have the knowledge and personnel to make the attempt?"

"Dr. Dunst?" Tan!Shallegh asked.

"I've been going through the Grand Fleet personnel files since Princess Oxtashah raised the possibility with me," Rin told them. "There are eleven sentients in the Grand Fleet who worked on disabling the Taljzi system. I have identified thirty-six more with skills and knowledge that could potentially assist in the process of duplicating the effect...including myself."

He had never even seen that Dyson swarm in person.

"From my own previous information and the research I've done today, I believe that we should be able to establish relatively quickly whether or not the necessary subsystems exist in this particular Dyson swarm," he told them. "But we are talking about a system of stations that wraps around an entire star. *Relatively quickly* is still on the order of five-cycles, at least.

"Even if the subsystems do exist, they need to be operating and linked together," he continued. "That's dependent on pure random chance. We don't know enough about the pre-failure structure of the swarms to say anything else.

"Even if everything in the *swarm* is the way we need it, I understand that an interface drive was uniquely easy to target with the teleporter system. The Infinite's propulsive organs may not be as readily targetable—especially given that any fleet used as a lure to bring them to the system *will* be using interface drives.

"The range is limited to within the system of the swarm," Rin concluded. "If we manage to get the weapon online, it will require that lure—and we may not be able to easily protect those ships from our own trap."

"These are all possibilities that must be planned for," Oxtashah told him and Tan!Shallegh. "But I believe the necessary next step would be to deliver a team of Imperial specialists—those forty-seven individuals—to our facility in the Skiefail System to review the data we have?

"We have allowed very little information on the Skiefail stellar swarm to leave that system," she warned. "Your team would be transported there on my personal ship."

"Dr. Dunst?" Tan!Shallegh said.

"Fleet Lord?" Rin guessed what the A!Tol was going to ask.

"Are you prepared to organize and lead this mission?" Tan!Shallegh asked. "You will have clear access to any personnel or resources in the Grand Fleet, but you will need to assemble your team prior to the departure of the Wendira Battle Hives.

"We can easily conceal the departure of Princess Oxtashah's star hive with the rest of her people's fleet, but a later movement would be more obvious."

He glanced at Oxtashah.

"I assume," the Fleet Lord said calmly, "that you do not wish to bring the Laians in on this project."

"While relations are improving between our peoples, I do not feel that my Queens would accept them learning of this secret," the Princess replied. "I will share what I must with your people to make this come to pass, but I cannot include the Laians in this."

"I understand," Tan!Shallegh conceded. "But understand that I will take no action that threatens them."

"We will permit your people to disable the weapon as you leave, if you feel that is necessary," Oxtashah told him. "Though I must point out that, by its very nature, the system we have discussed is purely defensive."

"So it appears, always," the A!Tol agreed. "Please arrange transport for Dr. Dunst and his team to the swarm, Princess Oxtashah. I will authorize whatever assistance is needed to enable the swarm.

"But we will be keeping very close attention on its future fate, do you understand?"

"Of course, Fleet Lord," she said. "We all wish to see the Infinite defeated and our nations safe. This is merely another tool toward that goal."

———

RIN REMAINED after Oxtashah had left, waiting in silence for the Fleet Lord to speak first.

"I do not like sending a group of my people into the unknown like this," Tan!Shallegh finally said. "But I see the value. Is there anything you will need?"

"Mostly the people," Rin said after a moment's reflection. "If I can bring fifty people with me, I think we'll have the best chance we're likely to have. A direct encrypted link to certain people at the Institute and at Arjtal may speed things up as well."

"I will have the communications team set something up," Tan!Shallegh said. "You will be relaying through Wendira starcoms, however, which does limit our ability to maintain security."

"I *need* to talk to the people at Arjtal," Rin warned. "The people I can bring from the Grand Fleet are only half the answer. We *will* need the expertise of people who aren't here."

"What can be done will be done," the Fleet Lord told him. "But I must ask that you be *extremely* circumspect about what is shared on that channel, encrypted as it is."

"What can be done will be done," Rin echoed back at the A!Tol. "There's some equipment we could use as well. A mobile molycirc computer core that we can trust will be essential."

"Whatever you need," Tan!Shallegh reiterated. "I'd send a task force with you if I thought it would help."

"It won't," Rin said quietly. "The Wendira probably won't even tell us where Skiefail is if they can avoid it. The upside of that, I suppose, is that they're the ones who'll have to lure the Infinite there."

"Do you think you can make it work?"

Rin sighed.

"Without a lot more data, I can't even guess," he admitted. "*If* everything we need is intact and linked together, and *if* we can successfully duplicate the Taljzi's work, we're still looking at something that took *them* fifty long-cycles to prepare—and I doubt we'll have fifty *cycles*."

"Even if you succeed, that will likely cause problems unless you really can disable the weapon as you leave," Tan!Shallegh warned. "A weapon like this... Defensive or not, it changes the balance here between the Wendira and the Laians.

"And in a war like this, I would not expect to build a weapon without seeing it fired."

The A!Tol shivered.

"No one has yet created a functional duplicate of Alavan teleporter technology with modern systems," he noted. "Even the Taljzi just removed intact teleporters and used them in different locations. Their attempts to study the internal components failed—as have the Mesharom's, according to the data we have from them.

"You will be working with technology and software around the one great mystery of our Precursors. I believe Oxtashah is above the waters, but that does not mean no one will attempt to *keep* you after you have worked on that tech," he warned. "If it comes to that, I don't know if we will be able to retrieve you."

Rin swallowed. That was not a risk he had considered, but he nodded levelly.

"It should be a safe mission," he said. "Even with that. I don't think the Wendira want to start another war."

"When this is over, they may believe that we may not be able to prevent them detaining you," Tan!Shallegh said. "And...depending on how badly we get hurt before this is over, they may end up being right.

"You and your people deserve to know what you're walking into. It *should* be safe, but you are going into Wendira territory and beyond our reach."

"I understand, Fleet Lord," Rin promised. "And I'll make sure my recruits understand. I don't think it will be a problem."

He was reasonably sure everyone in the Grand Fleet was scared of the Infinite by now.

CHAPTER FORTY-TWO

The holographic image of an Infinite bioform dominated the conference as Morgan's new officers joined. Laians, Wendira, humans, A!Tol...all of the captains and flag officers were quieted by the sight of the massive Category Five creature.

"Welcome, everyone," Morgan told them, concealing a smile at the nervous silence. "I am Division Lord Morgan Casimir of the A!Tol Imperial Navy and the commander of this combined special task group."

She waited for that to sink in and to make sure no one was going to raise trouble, surveying her new officers. Two human captains, an A!Tol captain and an Anbrai captain made up her Imperial officers. The rest were about what she'd expected.

All nineteen of her Wendira captains were Warrior-caste Wendira. No Royals, no Drones—not even any Worker caste, though the ships' *crews* were only about fifty percent Warriors, from her understanding. A Warrior-caste Sub-Commandant named Irisha commanded the Wendira detachment.

On the other hand, only twenty of her twenty-four Laian Republic captains were actually Laian. The others were four different species, including a broccoli-like Shondra, a Lotis—a squat four-armed sentient she wasn't familiar with—a Zo—an ethereally thin and almost translucent biped with no visible eyes—and an Eerin —a heavily-furred hexapod.

They fell under the command of the Thirty-Eighth Sword of the Republic, a glitteringly black Laian female named Protan.

Everyone's attention was still focused on the bioform, and Morgan gestured toward it.

"This, officers, was one of the Category Five bioforms that attacked this system," she told them. "Eight hundred kilometers long, two hundred at her widest point, carrying an estimated eighty thousand missile launchers and capable of generating up to six independent plasma bursts powerful enough to overwhelm even a war-dreadnought—*and* of creating microsingularities propelled at eleven nines of lightspeed.

"Her ammunition and missile launchers were fortunately limited to what they could manufacture or steal of Laian munitions," she continued. "A Five-M-type unit, as we have designated this creature, is a cyborg mix of Infinite biotechnology and stolen Laian weapons systems.

"So far as we can tell, this particular creature was not capable of independent hyperspace travel and was limited to their standard reactionless drive, accelerating at one-point-five percent of lightspeed per second."

Morgan's recitation of the capabilities of their enemy was holding everyone's focus, even though they all *should* know this already.

"A Category Five-M Infinite bioform is capable of engaging an entire Laian war-dreadnought squadron, with escorts, with near certainty of victory," she concluded. "They are the most powerful bioforms we have yet encountered outside the Astoroko Nebula."

She tapped a command and the Five-M vanished...replaced with something *else*.

"*This*, officers, is a Category Six-A bioform," she told them as the sphere of hyper-compressed matter appeared amidst them. "The shell was an Alavan mothership, approximately eleven hundred kilometers in diameter and manufactured of hyper-compressed matter. Still far short of theoretical neutronium but significantly tougher than any known modern armor.

"So far as the scans we have from the nebula can tell, the entirety of the shell is filled with an Infinite bioform that has *consumed* the interior structure—crew, power cores, everything. She is capable of generating an unknown number of independent plasma pulses, as well as extending prehensile tentacles at *least* a hundred thousand kilometers with enough strength to crack compressed-matter armor.

"We also expect that by the time we encounter the Six-As again, they will have been retrofitted with some form of interface-missile armament." She smiled thinly. "We also believe it is highly likely that the Six-As, like the rest of the Category Sixes, possess microsingularity cannons.

"This bioform represents a single unit capable of threatening the entirety of the Laian First Defense Fleet. Our special task group would stand very little chance against it."

She wiped the close-up away and replaced it with the scans of the Eye of the Astoroko Nebula.

"The Eye is defended by forty-six Category Six-A bioforms, two hundred and twenty-two unarmored Category Six bioforms—all of whom are significantly *larger* than their armored cousins—and eight Category *Seven* creatures averaging *sixty thousand* kilometers in length."

Morgan paused again, making sure her people were following her, and then gave the holoprojector one last command.

The scan of the entire Eye vanished, replaced by the reconstructed video of the Queen rising out of the Eye's gas giant.

"All of it to defend this creature, which we believe to be the oldest of the Infinite and the likely progenitor of at least this cluster," Morgan told them all. "We have designated her Category Eight...and are mostly calling her the *Queen*."

She surveyed her officers.

"Now, does anyone in this room have suggestions as to how our three nations could engage and defeat the forces massed in the Eye of the Astoroko Nebula in conventional battle?" she asked quietly.

A deafening silence answered her.

"My understanding," Sub-Commander Irisha finally said, "was that we were not planning on doing so."

"We are not," Morgan agreed. "That is what this special task group exists to avoid. But it is not easy to stand amidst the ruined worlds of the Dead Zone and readily embrace the concept of murdering stars.

"We all must understand the risks we face in this operation *and* the reason why this operation has been contemplated," she told them. "We will need to infiltrate past whatever sentinels the Infinite have set throughout the nebula, recognizing that if we are detected and fail to eliminate the sentinels in time, we will face an utterly over-whelming force.

"Our objective is *these* stars," Morgan explained, pulling the zoom out to show the cluster of stars at the heart of the nebula. "Twelve relatively newborn blue giant stars form a gravitationally balanced structure around the not-yet-ignited dwarf at the heart of the Eye.

"This rosette of stars creates a massive realspace and hyperspace anomaly that interferes with hyper portals, hyperfold weapons and even our hyperspace missiles," she noted. "It forms the bars of the Infinite's prison, and we are going to implode that prison on them."

Eight of the stars, selected after careful calculation, flashed red.

"Targets Astoroko One through Eight," Morgan said calmly. "The plan is to preposition one stealthed starkiller at each of them. The STG will then withdraw at least one realspace light-year and send a hyperfold detonation code that should trigger simultaneous detonation of all eight stars."

A simulation started on the hologram, the stars rapidly expanding to fill the Eye with fire and radiation.

"There is a high likelihood, that my staff has estimated at seventy-five plus/minus ten percent, that the sequence will trigger sympathy novas in the other four stars," Morgan noted. "Whether or not those occur, we believe the gravitational effects of the novas will keep the Infinite contained in the rosette while the realspace effects wipe them out."

"Sounds straightforward enough," Protan observed. "Every ship in the group is stealthed. Even the Wendira shouldn't be able to screw this up."

Morgan had a hand up before Irisha could speak.

"Sword Protan, make one more prejudicial comment, and I will be asking Voice Tidirok for a new Laian squadron commander," she told the Laian calmly. "We *cannot* afford to be at each other's throats. If we fail, large portions of the Grand Hive and the Republic alike will be sacrificed to buy time for the galaxy to muster the forces necessary to overcome the Infinite.

"Am I understood?" she asked.

There was a long silence, and then Protan bowed her head.

"I offer my apologies, Sub-Commandant Irisha," she said, though the words didn't sound *entirely* sincere to Morgan. "For the good of the Republic, I will control my words in future."

Morgan turned her attention to Irisha, whose body language she couldn't read. After several seconds of silence, Irisha's vestigial wings snapped inward.

"I acknowledge your apology, Sword," he declared. "Let it fall."

"Good." Morgan gestured to the three-dimensional image of the Astoroko Nebula. "Now, we've talked about what we're *planning* to do, but that requires our stealth fields to be completely impermeable to the Infinite and our hyperfold communicators to be reliable enough to send the activation codes to starkillers in terminal mode."

While the command module of a starkiller was hyper-capable on its own, *no one* wanted to cut that timing any closer than they had to.

"What all of us are here to discuss and work out as a group is what we do when that perfect world fails to be our reality."

CHAPTER FORTY-THREE

"You want me to *WHAT?*" Kelly Lawrence demanded, the athletic computer specialist almost physically recoiling from Rin as he finished his initial explanation.

She took a deep breath and then rose from her chair in his borrowed office. He'd brought the privacy-field generator with him when he'd boarded the cruiser Lawrence served aboard, making certain no one on the ship would listen in on their conversation.

He let Lawrence pace the office for a good thirty seconds before he cleared his throat.

"We have access to an Alavan Dyson swarm," he repeated. "We're putting together a team of experts—people who either worked on the Taljzi one or have enough other background to be useful—to see if we can duplicate the Taljzi's trap."

Lawrence put her hands on her hips and turned back to him, probably consciously accentuating the uniform she wore—that of a Lesser Commander of the Imperial Navy.

"I am the senior intelligence officer for Division Lord Scheinberg," she pointed out. "Part of the command staff of an entire *squadron* of Imperial cruisers. And I took a job with Navy Intelligence because I decided that *serving in the Navy* was safer than poking around Alavan ruins.

"Now you want me to go back into the unquestionably *most* dangerous type of those ruins and try to duplicate the most insane thing anyone ever did with those ruins?"

"There will be fifty of us, Kelly," Rin told her. "We'll have the full support of the Wendira research team as well. It's not like I'm asking you to do it alone—and you went *into* the Taljzi swarm knowing you might have to leave on a bloody fusion rocket!"

"I was younger and dumber then," Lawrence replied. "And, frankly, the only man I was interested in in a hundred light-years was making the same trip, and I was twenty-five and horny."

"This is safer than that," he argued. "We're looking at an *inactive* system and seeing if we can turn it on. Even if we manage to turn it on, we'll know how to turn it off.

"But the possibility of trapping an entire Infinite swarm is really tempting, I have to say. We could save a lot of lives if we pull this off... and of the eleven people in the Grand Fleet who worked on that project, you were the most senior and the most involved in the actual weapon system."

"Yes," she conceded. "Which means I know how nuts the task you're talking about is. How's your Alavan code, Rin?"

"Better than it was," he told her. It was probably better than hers now. He'd been practicing the strange coding rules and symbology required to work with what little functional Alavan software existed.

"How's your Taljzi code?" she noted. "How do you feel about trying to duplicate the MacGyver kludge assembled by a team of people who, thanks to some seriously fucked-up cloning tech, effectively had two hundred and fifty years *each* of experience working on the system?"

"Given that we know what they did, and we know it worked, pretty good, actually," Rin said. "But I'll feel a lot better with you on the team."

Lawrence was still standing, glaring down at him.

"You want to fuck with a Dyson swarm and an industrial tele-porter," she pointed out. "Those are *both* technologies no one in the galaxy can duplicate."

"And us working on them will make us targets for a lot of people," Rin agreed calmly. "But if we don't get some kind of gamechanger in play, the odds of any of the three fleets we've been working with surviving the next long-cycle are tiny.

"We lost half a million people retaking Tohrohsail, Kelly. How bad do you think it will be if, say, the First Defense Fleet is shattered?"

"Bad," she said quietly. "Millions on the war-dreadnoughts alone."

"If we can take down the next swarm with a trap, we can save those lives."

The room was silent, Lawrence standing thoughtfully.

For at least a minute, neither of them said anything. Then she finally exhaled and nodded.

"You're insane, Rin Dunst," she told him. "I mean, I should have figured that out when I found out you had a *computer* implanted in your ass."

"*Somewhat* higher than that," Rin objected, but he was grinning at her as he spoke.

"All right. I'm in, I guess. I'm assuming there'll be formal orders?" she asked.

"Yeah. It's volunteer-only, so Tan!Shallegh wasn't issuing those until we'd confirmed people were in." He slid a chip across the desk to her. "That will cover everything you need. Everyone has to report aboard Oxtashah's ship within a cycle.

"We're starting to run short on time. Nobody is cleared to know about this mission. We haven't even told the Laians the Dyson swarm *exists*."

"This just gets better and better," Lawrence said with a resigned sigh. She picked up the chip and gave him a vague salute. "Into the shadows we go. Lead on, Professor."

CHAPTER FORTY-FOUR

DESPITE THEIR LOSSES, THE THREE WENDIRA BATTLE HIVES still assembled thousands of starships. Their separation from the other two fleets and movement toward the hyper limit was a sea change, looking more like a tidal effect on the main tactical display than a movement of individual ships.

And tucked away in one corner of that tidal effect were the forty-seven starships of Morgan's new command. If the Wendira movement had been on a smaller scale, she might even have worried that her non-Wendira ships would stick out.

With over a thousand *capital ships* alone, Morgan was utterly unconcerned about that. Her four battleships were easily within a margin of error of the mass of a star shield to a broad scan—and the fleet commanders would be actively discouraging narrow scans of the departing fleet for multiple reasons.

"Lead Wendira units are opening portals," Rogers announced. "STG ships maintaining courses and profiles as ordered. No problems."

Morgan nodded. There wasn't much to say at this point. Billions of tons of starships were vanishing into hyperspace, and her relatively tiny command would enter their portals in the final third of the formation.

"All ships confirmed ready for hyperspace and stealth," her chief of staff continued. "We have full tactical telemetry."

And *that* was part of why an Imperial officer was in command of the STG, Morgan knew. Right now, she knew more about the ships under her command than either side was willing to let their ancient enemies know.

Especially the starkillers.

"Portal in four minutes and counting," Captain Koumans' navigator reported.

"We have the course laid in for once we transit?" Morgan asked.

"Follow the Wendira for two tenth-cycles, activate the stealth field and run straight for the nebula," Rogers replied. "Charts say we should be between eight and ten cycles on the trip."

"Good, good." Morgan watched the display continue to flare with Cherenkov radiation pulses as hyper portals opened again and again. She still hated the mission. There were too many unknowns—they didn't even know enough about the Infinite for her to be okay with obliterating them—but she agreed with the logic.

Whatever ships got out of the nebula before she blew it to hell would still be a problem, but it seemed likely she'd take out most of the Category Sixes and larger. That would change the entire tone of the war.

"Portal in thirty seconds."

She'd taken the mission. There was only so much self-reflection she could do over its morality.

"Task group will transit as instructed," she ordered calmly.

THE GRAY VOID of hyperspace washed over Morgan's command as they ever-so-slowly drifted away from the Wendira fleet. Once the last of her ships were clear of the visibility sphere of the rest of the fleet, she breathed a small sigh of relief.

They were most vulnerable to someone asking weird questions while they were inside the distance where people could see them as more than a dot on an anomaly scanner.

And as for those hyperspace anomalies...

"Do we have solid communication links?" Morgan asked.

"Directed laser links established with all ships," her new communications officer, an A!Tol named Lo!ko, confirmed. "Should be solid through the stealth fields."

"Distance to the nearest Wendira ship?"

"Five hundred thousand kilometers and rising," Rogers reported. "What are you thinking?"

"We're not scheduled to go into stealth for another hundredth-cycle, but...pass the orders," Morgan said. "The sooner we go dark, the sooner we get to the Astoroko Nebula and the sooner we can end this nightmare."

"Understood. Updated orders being distributed," Lo!ko replied. "Standing by for your command."

"Let me know when all ships have confirmed receipt," Morgan ordered. "Let's not risk a lone trailer."

A few seconds passed by as messages flickered along beams of coherent light.

"All ships have warmed up their stealth generators and are waiting for your command," Rogers finally reported. "Timing sequencing will be tight—we have a full quarter-second delay on the farthest units.

"Set a shared time for execution of thirty seconds from my mark," Morgan replied. "Simultaneous execution.

"Lo!ko—stand by to transmit. The mark is...*now*."

"Time stamp recorded, orders transmitted," the A!Tol replied.

Seconds ticked away. There was no noticeable sensation when *Odysseus*'s stealth field activated, wrapping all of her signatures—

even the hyperspace anomaly signature—in a blanket of technological wizardry.

The main display was clear on the moment when everyone *else* activated their stealth fields. The entire task group vanished as one. The delay on seeing the farther units vanish was barely noticeable, but it still marked that the ships had *actually* stealthed simultaneously.

Over the course of the following seconds, the ships reappeared on *Odysseus*'s tactical plot as the laser links stabilized.

"Telemetry links holding with all units," Lo!ko reported. "Full communication maintained."

"Understood. Everyone has the course?" Morgan asked, confirming for the last time.

"Yes, sir."

"Then let's be about it."

CHAPTER FORTY-FIVE

The hardest thing to get used to aboard the Wendira ship was the gravity. Rin was used to adjusting to gravity swings and atmospheric difference, but they were usually relatively small. No species in the A!Tol Imperium breathed less than nineteen percent oxygen or came from a planet with a gravity of less than ninety percent of Earth's.

The actual standard atmosphere mix and gravity set for most multispecies space facilities in the Imperium was twenty-three percent oxygen and point-nine-seven gravities. Laian facilities were at slightly higher oxygen and gravity than Imperial ones.

The star hive *Zokalatan*—*Ambitious Sword*, in English—was set at twenty-one percent oxygen and point-eight gravities. The air was similar to the average on Earth, if denser and damply humid in near-exact contrast to the Laian ships Rin had visited, but the dramatically reduced gravity took getting used to.

"Dense atmosphere and low gravity," Lawrence observed as they watched one of their hosts actually fly across a drop that plunged deep into the ship. "I think I always assumed their wings were vestigial."

"Warriors' wings are," one of their companions noted. The Imperials had been given a set of rooms that looked out over the carrier's central launch tube, a twenty-meter-wide column that seemed to run the full height of the ship.

The speaker, Abraxis Mok, was a Tosumi doctor and physicist. He'd acted as medic on the expedition to the Dyson swarm near Arjtal while also working as part of the team itself—a dual role the four-armed avian had taken on a dozen expeditions before that and was taking on this mission.

"The Warriors make up for it with armor that gives them flight capabilities," Mok continued. "But Workers and Royals can both fly in their natural environment. Drones and Warriors, for whatever evolutionary reason, cannot. A trade for proportionally more-powerful muscles in general, I suspect."

"Any problems with our hosts?" Rin asked. Lawrence and Mok were the senior members of his team, as much as his team was standing on any kind of hierarchy. Everyone with Rin was either military or military-adjacent, but they were also all scientists.

"I'll admit I'd like to adjust the atmosphere mix in our quarters, but it sounds like that isn't possible," Mok told him. "My species finds this level of oxygen concentration...difficult."

"It's what humans are used to, but that doesn't make it fun for you," Rin agreed. "Have we asked?"

"I have, and they were not promising," the doctor told him. "I am not certain the crew is entirely clear on why we are even aboard, let alone how helpful they should be to us."

"I guarantee you, Abraxis, that the crew has *no* idea why we are aboard," Rin warned. "And we are not to change that. *Zokalatan* has not yet diverted from the main fleet, but I suspect we will see significant lockdown of external-sensor availability once we do.

"I doubt even the crew of Princess Oxtashah's personal ship know about our destination. That's going to cause some complications."

"How much of all of this are we keeping secret?" Lawrence asked.

"We have full authority to share everything we learn with the Imperial Institute and Tan!Shallegh," Rin told them. "The Imperium has been asked to keep this all classified, but we are not restricted in what we share with the people we have authorized on our side.

"In exchange for that, we have to try not to expose any unnecessary information to unbriefed Wendira. They are to control information procedures on their side," he concluded. "It's a fair deal, even if it means the people responsible for feeding and housing us have no idea what we're doing here."

"This was pitched to me as the most important mission of the war," Lawrence said with a chuckle. "Shame nobody told the chef that."

"What, you don't like unflavored universal protein with vitamin powder?" Abraxis Mok asked.

All three chuckled. UP was a gray tofu-like substance that had been chemically reduced to contain absolutely nothing that could threaten any species. It could provide a lot of the basic needs of almost every known species, with the remainder made up for by vitamin powders.

With work, it could even be made palatable. The Wendira were not bothering to put that work into the food they were providing their Imperial guests.

"I didn't think we'd need to include a cook on the mission," Rin admitted. "My mistake, it turns out. We'll survive."

"Some of us have lower caloric reserves than others," Lawrence complained, but there was no real heat to it.

"How long?" Mok asked.

"My understanding is about five cycles to the Skiefail System," Rin told them. "The Wendira have restricted almost all of their information on the Skiefail swarm to the system itself. Very little data has left Skiefail, so they can't give us information to prep.

"It's going to take us a couple of days just to internalize what is *known* before we can even start looking for the pieces we know we need." He shook his head. "I don't know how long we're looking at to get the weapon online, or if it will even be possible.

"All I know is that I doubt we'll be fast enough to be ready for the next swarm, and I'm worried about what that will mean."

"A lot of dead people nobody could save," Lawrence said quietly. "We'll work fast, Dr. Dunst. I have a damn good idea of what components I'm looking for. By the time we're done going through whatever they already have, I figure I'll be able to tell you if it's *impossible*."

"So, we can cut off before we waste too much time, at least," Rin concluded. "That won't make us many friends, but I suppose it's better than accidentally blowing up a Dyson swarm."

"Oh, don't worry; if we fuck up trying to turn this shit on, we probably won't have to worry about our reputation," Lawrence told him. "If we do it *right*, it's safe. If we do it *wrong*, we'll probably nova the star the swarm is anchored on."

"Oh." Rin stared out into the launch deck, watching another set of Wendira Workers flutter up toward the top of the ship.

"I'm not sure I realized that part," he admitted. "But... Well, it doesn't matter. We have work to do."

CHAPTER FORTY-SIX

THE GRAY VOID OF HYPERSPACE WASN'T NECESSARILY *DARK*, BUT the feeling of being isolated in a dark and lonely void was about the same for a ship in hyperspace and a ship in deep space. The grayness of hyperspace was brighter, but the chaos of its nature meant that even friends were invisible beyond a certain distance.

Morgan had spent a significant chunk of her adult life in hyperspace, and she, like most people, consciously turned her office lights just a *little* bit brighter when underway. She also found herself seeking out other people more as well.

It was a constant struggle against the unconscious awareness, in every sentient mind, that they just were *not* supposed to be there. That this place wasn't designed for them and only incredibly advanced technology had brought them there and kept them alive.

That brought her to a quiet dinner with Rogers, Koumans and Koumans' XO, an Indiri named Razh Tal. The damp red-furred amphibian was eating a different meal from the other three, but she seemed to be enjoying it.

Morgan had no idea what the pale green spheres Tal was eating *were*—if they were universal protein, someone had done a *lot* of work with them—but the classic steak-and-potatoes dish Koumans's steward had served up for the humans went down well.

"My compliments to your staff, Captain," Morgan told Koumans. "To turn frozen steak into something that good takes skill and practice."

"I'm honestly not sure my staff could handle *fresh* steak at this point," Koumans admitted. "I don't think *Odysseus* has been within twenty light-years of Earth. *Ever.*"

She raised a glass to Tal.

"She was built by the Indiri, not your father's yards. I'm surprised she was named for a human hero, given that."

"My people name ships from lists provided by the Navy," Tal noted, swallowing the last gelatinous green piece of her meal. "The *Bellerophon* class, for example, has a list of twenty heroes from each of the Imperium's races. Almost six hundred names—and that barely swims the surface of the pond of our aggregate mythologies."

"And the Indiri shipbuilders always like to keep things nice and stable," Morgan said. "We borrowed a lot of their best practices when we set up the Raging Waters of Friendship Yards—including naming ships based on the Navy's list rather than all after our own heroes."

She shrugged.

"I don't think that's *solely* responsible for lifting us to the third-largest shipbuilder in the Imperium, but it didn't hurt."

That ranking ignored, of course, that the rest of the top ten yards were either A!Tol or Indiri. Humanity had one *very* successful shipyard that had helped propel the Duchy of Terra to major economic prominence, but the Indiri had six across four star systems—and the A!Tol and the three Imperial Races had another twenty across more systems.

Even those five species combined only accounted for sixty percent of the Imperium's shipbuilding, but that still meant that roughly three percent of all Imperial warships were built in Sol.

Morgan's father had certainly not grown any *less* rich in the last thirty-plus years.

"I have to wonder, Casimir, why the daughter of the man who *owns* that yard is a military officer," Koumans said. "Unless that's...intrusive."

Morgan chuckled.

"The *plan* was...somewhat different," she noted. "But remember that my father is looking at another century to two centuries of healthy, active life managing his businesses. He owns fifty-five percent of a one-third stake in Raging Waters of Friendship—*I* don't own *anything*.

"I could have worked my way up in the company and taken over, but I also wanted to follow in the Duchess's footsteps." She shrugged. "I joined the Militia, got dragged into the Taljzi Campaign, and then when the Navy took over, they asked me to step across to provide my experience.

"A few long-cycles later and here we are." She gestured around them, taking in the warship and the task group it led. "And, well—like my father, I've got a few centuries left to run a full Navy career and go into business.

"If I can do good serving the Imperium now, it's worth it."

The stewards arrived to sweep away the dishes and leave behind glasses of wine—four of them, as Indiri processed Terran alcohol safely, if not necessarily in the same way as humans.

"House Tal is mostly shipbuilders," Razh Tal noted as the four women relaxed. "Joining the Navy isn't discouraged, but making a *career* of it is. Having military knowledge is handy when designing and building warships, but my House generally prefers to make money, not war.

"I joined for the experience toward my family's work and, well...I ended up in the right place at the right time and led an emergency rescue team that saved sixteen hundred lives on a civilian liner.

"After that, I decided I could do more good in an Imperial uniform than in an engineer's pond."

Rogers laughed.

"Yeah, I hear you there," she told the Indiri. "As one of the first kids born on the new colonies, there was a bit of pressure to 'show the flag' by signing up for the military, but none of us were really planning on staying.

"I never had *quite* so dramatic a sign that I was in the right place as saving a passenger ship!" She toasted Tal. "I found the service suited me, though, so here I am."

Morgan leaned back in her chair and half-toasted, half-saluted her chief of staff.

"And then you got saddled with me," she noted, carefully shifting the conversation so that Koumans *wouldn't* have to answer the implicit question if she didn't want to. *She* had access to the confidential portions of the woman's file, after all, and some people were more sensitive about certain things than others.

"I could have ended up with worse commanders," Rogers replied. "Captain, what brought you into the service?"

Morgan's attempt to get Koumans out of the question had clearly failed. Fortunately, the Captain didn't look particularly bothered. She shrugged.

"I was nineteen and dumb," she admitted. "My partner and I wanted a baby, and I didn't want to use a tube. So, I enlisted to get Imperial healthcare, which ran me to the front of the line for the womb-growth procedure."

Koumans shook her head with the half-bitter chuckle of old foolishness.

"Then, of course, I discovered that while I had been growing a womb and going through basic training at the same time, my partner had been fucking around and had got my best friend pregnant," she said. "So, when the offer to attend the Academy on A!To for officer's training instead of enlisting came up, I flipped him the bird and took it."

"I'm...not even sure how intensive that procedure *is*," Rogers said after a long moment. "But I can't imagine doing that *while* going through basic training is any fun."

"It is not," Koumans agreed genially. "My ex was an *asshole*. The Imperium is my family now, and I married the Navy. I'm busy enough here!"

"Aren't we all," Morgan murmured. "Aren't we all."

A dark pall descended over the meeting as they considered their mission.

"Honestly, sir. What *are* our chances?" Koumans finally asked.

"Fifty-fifty," Morgan admitted calmly. "We don't know for sure that we can actually stealth past the Infinite—that's why we brought four HSM-equipped battleships. The hope is that if stealth fails, we can snipe any Infinite before they can report in.

"But we *also* don't know what their FTL communications look like. They could be better than ours. They could be nonexistent. We don't know—so even the sniping plan is risky.

"The truth is," Morgan reminded them all, "that if we lose stealth, we are doomed. We have a small chance of being able to hide and sneak out carefully, but most likely, failure will end us all."

"My math says that so long as we blow at least a couple of the stars in the rosette, the effects will keep the Infinite contained for at least half a long-cycle," Rogers pointed out. "As long as we get in, we can make a difference."

"If it comes down to that, none of this fleet will be going home," Morgan said quietly. "I'll take that option if I have no choice—it's pretty obvious that even trading this entire fleet for only ninety cycles of time is entirely worth it—but I would very much prefer to bring everyone back.

"Imperial. Laian. Wendira." She shook her head. "Everybody lives, if I can make that happen."

"Except the Infinite," Koumans murmured. "I wish they'd talk to us."

"The only communication we've had with them is demands and

missiles," Morgan said. "They haven't exactly been making a warm and fuzzy impression on the Imperium."

The room was silent, and Morgan finished her wine with a sigh.

"In the end, our orders are clear. Our weaknesses are clear. Our strengths, thankfully, are clear. We know ourselves, though we don't really know our enemy. That's enough for fifty-fifty, so far as I read Sun Tzu."

And it had to be enough.

CHAPTER FORTY-SEVEN

The Skiefail System was disturbing in its emptiness.

Rin Dunst had lost count of the individual star systems he'd visited in his life. It was easy to become blasé about the sheer scale and size of a solar system when you traveled between six of them in any given year. Easy to forget that any given inhabited planet probably contained more cultural diversity than every city and spaceport he'd seen combined.

But he knew what a solar system *should* look like. There should be asteroids and planets and gas giants. The proportions and orders should vary based on a billion factors over the life of the star system, but those worlds and worldlets should *be* there.

In Skiefail, they were not.

As *Zokalatan* had approached her destination, additional equipment had been provided to the Imperial detachment—including a full holographic setup linked to the star hive's sensors.

Rin had beaten Lawrence to forbidding any connection of the sensors to their portable computer by about two and a half seconds. The molycirc core—a chandelier-esque structure of crystalline silicon two meters across and three high—was loaded with critical information for their work. Some of that information was probably unknown to the Wendira.

They weren't going to risk its corruption or theft, even to feed visual data on the swarm into it. All of that data would be recorded, placed on hard-data mediums, sanitized with handheld devices and only *then* connected to the portable core.

But for now, the sensor link was giving the team a gods'-eye view of the star system they were going to be working in for the next few five-cycles at least—and it was *empty*.

Every world, every asteroid, every *meteorite* had been scooped up by Alavan construction ships and fed into immense refineries. If Skiefail was anything like the Dyson swarm in Taljzi space, a significant portion of a *second* star system had been disassembled to provide raw materials as well.

The Alava had never thought small.

Eventually, even the nerve-wracking nature of the outer system's emptiness couldn't pull their attention away from the heart of the problem. Skiefail itself was a bloated wreck of a star, a yellow dwarf forced to twice its original size by failures of the Dyson swarm's systems.

"I make it about seven thousand intact stations," Mok observed. "That's, what, thirty percent survival?"

"Around there, assuming it's the same as the one we have Archive files on," Lawrence agreed.

Rin's subordinates didn't know the source of the Archive files on the Dyson swarms—but they did know that the Archive included a detailed diagram of an intact Alavan Dyson swarm. That was their baseline for all of this.

"That's slightly lower than the Taljzi swarm, right?" he asked. "That was thirty-five percent?"

"Yeah," Lawrence confirmed. "Ten thousand intact or partial platforms. What a goddamn mess that was. Only some of them actually matter, though," she reminded everyone. "The rest were glorified solar panels, supposed to feed power to the central transmitters by microwave beam."

"We care about the control center and the teleporters, right," Rin agreed.

He took control of a portion of the hologram, zooming in on a selection of the platforms. He stared at the space stations for several seconds and shook his head.

"Finding those in this is going to suck, isn't it?" he asked.

"I'm *hoping* that the Wendira have cataloged the existing platforms while they've studied it," Lawrence told him. "The primary matter-transfer control center should be one of the larger remaining stations—and the teleporters *are* visually distinct from the collectors.

"We need a control center, a *plasma* collector and a teleporter station," she concluded. "The teleporter stations are most likely to have self-vaporized at some point. The plasma collectors are mostly likely to have been eaten by the star's expansion...and the Archive diagram says there were only three control centers in the first place.

"So, when do we get access to their files again, Professor?" she asked Rin.

"Once we're on their support station. None of their data even goes aboard a ship that *could* leave Skiefail without the Queens' explicit sign-off."

"Paranoid. Great." Lawrence shook her head. "What was our guarantee that they'd let us *go* when we were done?"

"Nobody wants a three-way war, Kelly," Rin reassured her. "They don't want to fight the Infinite *and* the Imperium."

"Right. Even after we build them a superweapon," she said drily. "I'm sure everything will be fine."

"If nothing else, we're going to make sure we hold the key to that superweapon," Rin promised. "I think we're all on the same page on *that* point!"

TRANSFERRING all of their gear over to the Wendira base station was at least straightforward. Even the molycirc computer core had been designed for portability. It all packed up, and helpful Wendira Drones hauled it all onto the cargo shuttle put aside for them.

"It's weird," Lawrence murmured as the shuttle blasted clear of *Zokalatan*. "Anyone else get the impression that the crew doesn't even know where they are?"

"I'm actually certain they don't," Rin admitted. "From what Oxtashah told me, they're keeping this whole mission entirely under wraps. The pilot flying us is probably one of the few crew members to know what's going on."

"So weird," Lawrence repeated. "And nerves-inducing."

"Well, it's not *our* problem," Rin countered. "Eyes front, Commander Lawrence. Our objective awaits."

The swarm grew larger as the shuttle zipped toward it at half the speed of light. If they'd been able to look directly at the star, Rin suspected that the presence of the platforms would be easily visible to the naked eye now.

Of course, looking directly at a star was a *terrible* idea, and he was looking at a scanner screen instead.

"We're two minutes out," he told his people. "Looks like our destination is a parasite station attached to one of the bigger platforms." He paused. "Lawrence, does that platform look like what I think it is?"

The cyber-archaeologist was right at his shoulder a moment later, and he *heard* her sigh in relief.

"If you think that it's one of the matter-transfer control centers, you are correct," she told him. "That little baby controlled the transmission of twenty-eight percent of this star's power output to target systems within fifty light-years.

"The swarm had three of these platforms, each controlling four primary and four secondary teleporter stations. The stations aren't designed for independent control, so while we'll need to rig up systems to get the teleporters to work at *all*, we still need this girl to give them instructions."

"And I'm guessing her computers are as fucked as every other Alavan computer out there?" Rin asked.

"Yup. The Taljzi had interface modules that allowed the core Alavan operating system to link in to the computer cores they provided, basically rebooting the software on hybrid hardware," she told him. "That's going to be our first step, I suspect."

"There's no steps, Kelly," Rin reminded her. "We need to do this all as simultaneously as possible. A team on the computers, a team on the teleporter, a team on the plasma collector."

"Fuck. Let's leave the plasma collector, then," she said. "Unless we've got a lot more Wendira resources than I think."

"Is that...safe?" Rin asked.

"No," Lawrence told him bluntly. "We'll be sequencing two teleporters, one to pull matter in and one to throw matter out. Without the plasma collector to provide exact control of how much mass is in the pickup zone, we might overwhelm the containment system at the teleporter station."

"And vaporize everything we've done," Rin concluded. "But we *can* rig up the weapon without one?"

"We can. *Assuming* we find a teleporter station," she reminded him. "The control center is a win—but my *god*, do we still need to get lucky."

CHAPTER FORTY-EIGHT

In the being walking across the landing bay toward them, Rin Dunst saw the reason some people gave for the enduring war between the Wendira and the Laians. The stranger was an older Wendira, his head broader than the Warriors and Royals Rin had seen to date, with his wings folded around him in a shape that distinctly resembled the shell of a Laian.

There was no way the Worker-caste Wendira could be mistaken for a Laian or vice versa, but Rin had to admit the resemblance existed. It would have taken a *spectacular* degree of arrogance for that resemblance to have created a reason for a war...but people of all species could manage that.

"Dr. Rin Dunst, I was only just briefed on your team's arrival a few hours ago," the Worker told him excitedly, the translator defaulting to English units for non-Imperial time counting. "I am Castellash, the senior scientist and expedition leader here in Skiefail. I hear you have worked on a similar such facility before?"

Even the translation device was having trouble keeping up with the rapid-fire speech of the excited Wendira, and Rin found himself grinning.

"I haven't, Director Castellash," he told the Wendira. "But several of my team members have, and I am fully up to date on the work we did on the other swarm."

What he *hadn't* known before they'd started the trip to Skiefail, he knew now. Reviewing all of their documentation, down to the raw reports from individual technicians, would have taken more time than he had—but he'd had five days. He knew enough.

He hoped.

"Of course, of course." Castellash's wings flickered out for a moment, removing *any* resemblance to a Laian, before wrapping around him again. "We have done nothing except catalog and observe here, Dr. Dunst, for three hundred years. To potentially see some of these systems activated... That is incredible!"

"I need to see that catalog," Kelly Lawrence interrupted. "As soon as we can. Do you have a listing with images of all of the platforms?"

"Of course, of course, yes," Castellash told her. "Do you wish to see your quarters first—"

"I need to see that catalog *now*," Lawrence told him. "If certain facilities are not intact, this has been a long trip for nothing. The sooner I can confirm that one way or another, the better."

"Of course, of course!" the Wendira agreed. He waved a claw, and several shorter Drones crossed to them. "My staff will see your team to their quarters. If you and Dr..."

"*Commander*," Lawrence corrected. "Lesser Commander Lawrence, Imperial Naval Intelligence. Dr. Dunst and I will both look at this catalog."

Lawrence had been learning command voice in the Navy, Rin concluded. He wasn't going to complain too loudly, though.

"Agreed," he told Castellash. "There is no time for us to play games or dance around the point. Show our people their rooms, but the team leads need to get to work."

He waved Mok over, the Tosumi joining them with a carefully brisk pace.

"The Wendira have a catalog of the intact platforms," he told Mok. "We need to review it first."

"Agreed," Mok said. "Where are we going?"

"This way, please," Castellash told them. "We have prepared a working space for your team; it seems we shall get started."

CASTELLASH LED them to a space that would do quite handily for their needs. Large chunks of the Wendira space station were clearly prefabricated—and not in regular use. That had allowed them to take an external gallery and assemble fifty consoles and several laboratories' worth of equipment.

"You have full access to all of our files, data and analysis from here," the Wendira told them. "We were instructed to hold back nothing."

"What will we have at our disposal for spacecraft and other resources?" Rin asked, gesturing his team leads toward the computers.

"Everything we have," Castellash told them. "My entire expedition has been placed at your disposal, Dr. Dunst. We have eight shuttles and four larger sublight spacecraft but no hyper-capable craft.

"My understanding is that you are to have unlimited access to our hyperfold communication network as well," he added. "I am the only person on this station with that access normally, but I understand that you need to consult with support in the Imperium."

"Exactly," Rin told the Wendira. "There are key members of the team that worked on the other Dyson swarm that are not here but are available to answer questions. We have the best we could assemble from the resources on hand—but we were lucky to even have eleven people who'd worked on the project."

"Found the catalog," Lawrence announced. An image of a station appeared above the console she was working at. "Passing access to Mok."

"Set up a console for me as well," Rin ordered. "I know what we're looking for."

"How can I assist?" Castellash asked.

"Make sure we have that full access," Rin told the Wendira. "I could use an inventory of assets to help sort out what we have to work with—and any maps you have of the station this one is attached to.

"That control platform is one of our key pieces. We need to confirm that the systems we need are intact, but its existence is a good sign."

"What happens if what you're looking for is gone, Doctor?" Castellash asked, glancing worriedly at where Lawrence and Mok were already flipping through images of the various platforms.

"It depends on which piece, Director," Rin told him. "This facility is attached to one of our two critical components. If we can't find the plasma collectors but we do find teleporters, we can probably achieve our target, but it will be a more fragile system.

"If we don't find teleporters, even having the collectors and the controller won't do us any good."

"Then I hope we discovered the stations you need. I lost shell-brothers at Tohrohsail," Castellash admitted. "I fear for the Hive."

"I fear for the *galaxy*, Castellash," Rin told him. "So, if you'll excuse me, I'm going to see if we have the *right* ruined ancient space stations."

CHAPTER FORTY-NINE

"Anomalies detected at maximum range," Rogers reported. "Estimates put them just inside the Astoroko Nebula."

"Understood," Morgan replied, checking the main display. "What have we got?"

The holotank was showing the estimated position of the special task group—they weren't close enough to any stars to definitively locate themselves at that moment—as they approached the Astoroko Nebula in hyperspace.

"Looks like they've positioned bioforms along the perimeter of the nebula," Rogers told her. "We're picking up more as we approach. They look to be separated by about a realspace light-year."

"Even so, that's a lot of ships to be using as a defensive screen," Morgan noted. "Any sign of more major movement?"

"Not right now. We're only going to get eyes on a small portion of the nebula as we go in. Unless our timing is just right, we won't see any deployments," the chief of staff replied.

"I know. I can hope," Morgan said. "Let's adjust our course to cut right between their sentinels at maximum range. They *shouldn't* be able to see us through the stealth fields, but we have problems seeing them in hyperspace as it is."

"What about immobile scanner units?" Morgan's new operations officer, an Ivida named Ort, asked. "We can only detect them in hyperspace while they're moving."

"We can't do anything about them," Morgan admitted to him. "We'll keep our eyes peeled as we close, in case we see *something*, but so long as they're staying still, they're invisible to us.

"We have to plan with what we can see and hope that what we *can't* see is still far enough away that we're covered."

Against the Laian hyperspatial anomaly scanners the Infinite system was presumably based on, their stealth fields were good to sixty light-seconds in both realspace and hyperspace. That *should* be enough, but Morgan didn't know what tricks the Infinite might have added to their stolen sensor systems.

"If we adjust as specified, we'll add about four twentieth-cycles to our trip to the first star in the rosette," Rogers warned.

"I doubt this will be the last diversion from our planned course," Morgan replied. "Make the course change and watch for surprises.

"We are in the Infinite's territory now."

MORGAN CAUGHT herself holding her breath as the task group approached the Infinite's sensor perimeter. There wasn't anything *else* out there other than the scouts, not that they could *see*, at least.

But she was grimly certain that if those sentinels detected her ships, she and all her people were doomed. She'd flee any pursuit out of hyperspace, where she could engage with her entire arsenal, but that wouldn't be enough. Not against the immense numbers available to their enemy.

"Closest approach in forty seconds," Ort announced. "No change in profile on the sensor screen. No immobile units detected. Everything appears clear."

Seconds ticked by.

"New contact," Ort snapped. "*Big* contact. No...two contacts. Separate. Resolving now."

"In the tank, Commander," Morgan ordered.

A chunk of the big holodisplays shimmered, then resolved into the icons of unknown contacts. Two of them, close together but on different vectors.

"That's two swarms; confirm the vectors," Morgan said. She could see *something* to them, but she wanted confirmation.

"Labeling Charlie and Delta," Ort confirmed. "Swarm Charlie is on an exit vector from the nebula; she is heading out at sixty percent of lightspeed. Vector is...toward Wendira space."

"Wonderful," Morgan said grimly. "Rogers? Let's start plotting a point to drop out of hyperspace and phone home. Ort, confirm that line and get me one on Delta."

"Swarm Delta looks like a defensive force," the ops officer told her. "Their velocity is significantly lower, and they are actively accelerating on what looks like a circular course. They are orbiting the rosette at two hyperspace light-cycles."

"That'll be between one and three light-years, depending on where they are in the nebula, right?" Rogers asked.

"Yes, sir," Ort confirmed.

"If we're seeing Delta at this range, they're big," Morgan said quietly. They were still five light-cycles, over a week's travel for her ships, from the rosette.

"Charlie is much closer and was lined up with them for a few minutes, from our perspective," Ort told her. "That's why it looked like one contact. But...yeah. Estimated minimum mass for Swarm Delta is five *trillion* tons."

Morgan swallowed a silent whistle. That had to be multiple Category Sixes at least. Mass wasn't as clear an indicator of capability for the Infinite as it was for, say, Core Power ships, but it helped.

The entire Laian space navy massed about half a trillion tons, and that was about standard for a Core Power. Swarm Delta outmassed the entire musterable fleets of the three nations currently engaged with the Infinite by over three to one.

"Swarm Charlie is smaller, but still..." Ort was Ivida. His face didn't move, but he shook his head from side to side as he stared down at his screen. "Twenty percent uncertainty, but I make it around a trillion tons."

"We definitely need to drop out of hyperspace and send a message," Morgan decided. "It'll cost us a few more twentieth-cycles, but we need to give Delta a chance to move out of our way, anyway."

"How soon?" Rogers asked.

"Get us half a hyperspace light-cycle away from the sensor screen," Morgan ordered. "Then we'll bring the entire group out of hyperspace for a twentieth-cycle. Long enough to phone home, though not long enough to get replies.

"We do need to keep moving."

MORGAN CONSIDERED her audience carefully for several seconds as she stared at the recorder, then shrugged.

"Fleet Lord Tan!Shallegh, you will be receiving attached sensor data from all of my ships," she told the First Fleet Lord. "We have confirmed the presence of a screen of sensor sentinels in hyperspace through the edge of the Astoroko Nebula.

"Based off the dispersion and presence of those ships, I would judge that only stealth ships have any chance of penetrating the nebula undetected."

She had taken a risk by bringing her fleet out of hyperspace, but the allies needed to know Swarm Charlie was in motion.

"More immediately important is that we have detected a new swarm moving out into Wendira space, estimated at a mass of one trillion tons," she warned him. "It's hard to estimate even hull numbers, let alone types or classes, at the ranges we're scanning, so I can't say much more than that.

"Even so, that force represents an existential threat to our ally. I feel it was worth taking the risk of dropping out of hyperspace to send this message."

She drummed her fingers on the desk for a moment.

"We also now have a better idea of what the Queen has mustered to defend herself," she continued. "Swarm Delta represents a nodal defense force of some five trillion tons. I suspect there is more than one such force securing the core of the nebula, but so far, our stealth fields appear to be holding up to Infinite scans.

"I intend to proceed with my mission as previously instructed. I do not expect to be able to make long-distance hyperfold transmissions once we have entered the immediate area of the rosette.

"Calculations suggest a minimum thirty-six-hour realspace approach to be able to fire each starkiller, but the rosette prevents anything else." She shook her head. "Currently, the plan is to deploy the starkillers under automatic control at eighteen light-hours, but that may or may not survive contact with reality.

"We will not be able to complete our mission before Swarm Charlie engages the Wendira," she admitted. "It is...uncertain whether Swarm Delta and any other defense nodes will be materially impacted by the destruction of the rosette, so we may still be facing an utterly overwhelming threat if our mission succeeds.

"This will be my last transmission until we have exited the rosette," Morgan told her superior. "I will do all within my power to complete this mission and bring my people out alive. If we succeed, it should be relatively clearly visible to anomaly scanners at some distance.

"If we don't..." She sighed. "If we fail, you won't hear from us again, Fleet Lord. I hope to speak again in a few cycles.

"Gods speed you, Fleet Lord Tan!Shallegh."

CHAPTER FIFTY

GOING THROUGH SEVEN THOUSAND SPACE STATIONS' WORTH OF photos, three-dimensional models and energy profiles took Rin and his people over a day. Even dividing it into smaller and smaller chunks as more of their people came into the lab, it was still a slow, painstaking process.

In theory, identifying a solar-collector station was easy, and they didn't *care* about the solar-collector stations. In practice, even the Alava didn't manage exact duplication of their Dyson swarm units and every station was slightly different.

Add in that at least some of the "space stations" in the Dyson swarm were actually *ships*—both defensive and utility craft that had settled into stable orbits when their crews and engines had died—plus a dizzying array of additional support stations that existed in similar numbers to the control and teleporter stations, every station had to be examined in detail.

"All right," he finally said when the last reports cycled into his computer. "Everybody, we did it."

His team looked blearily back at him. He'd told people to take the rest they needed, which seemed to have resulted in no one actually taking *enough* rest—including him, if he was being honest.

"We've now gone through seven thousand, one hundred and thirty-four individual contacts," he told them all. "The Wendira did a fantastic job of cataloging all of this."

Castellash and several of his senior people had spent several hours reviewing the identification criteria Lawrence had put together, and then joined in. They looked even more wiped than the rest of his people, but the station director's wings fluttered in appreciation as Rin recognized their efforts.

"The good news is that we found an intact teleporter station," Rin noted. "Two of them, in fact, and three more damaged ones where we might be able to rig up the teleporters to work, at least.

"Bad news is that we haven't found a single plasma collector," he told them. "So, we're *going* to rig up those teleporters on the damaged stations if we can.

"Commander Lawrence, do you want to explain the problem?"

Lawrence stepped up to join Rin, then turned and faced the team sitting at their consoles.

"We don't even *begin* to understand the science—or even the hardware—of an Alavan teleporter system," she told them. "What we do understand is, roughly, how an Alavan teleporter with half its functions obliterated by the Fall *operates*.

"And the key point to that is that one end of the transfer is always going to physically be at the teleporter. The system the Taljzi rigged up pulled plasma from a collector station in low orbit of the star.

"What exactly that station was originally intended to do is unknown, but what it did for the purposes of this system was limit how much plasma was being pulled into the teleporter station. The Taljzi reinforced the receiver chamber and added their own containment fields, making it capable of handling the amount of plasma they were pulling from the collector station.

"A second teleporter unit then transferred that plasma to a destination fed to it by the control center," she noted. "That destination was being tracked in real time by a wonky gravity-hyperspace interface scanner, making the interface drive the easy target."

"From the review of the Taljzi documents, the Dyson swarm they encountered actually did this by *accident* several times," Rin told them. "They did have an emergency refueling system already set up that the Taljzi mostly just needed to get control over.

"Something about pinging that interface sensor made what was left of the swarm think it needed to refuel somebody." He shook his head. "The irony is that the Taljzi Dyson swarm was *more* dangerous because it was more intact.

"The Skiefail Swarm is less intact, and the computers on the control station appear to be completely offline. The Taljzi had to work out how to take control of a half-working computer and then repair and replicate an existing system.

"We have to actually bring the computer online, reestablish hardware links, bring both the teleporter and the interface scanner back online...and as Commander Lawrence said, the plasma collector controlled how much plasma the teleporter had to handle."

"Without that lower-level station, we are teleporting directly from the lower corona," Lawrence said calmly. "While we *should* be able to control the volume we're bringing in, we have less control over temperature and mass. There *will* be a small but recurring chance, with every single shot, that the plasma will destroy the teleporter.

"And that's *after* we've done all the work to make the damn thing fire in the first place."

The room of scientists and techs was silent, and Rin smiled thinly.

"Mok and Lawrence are leaving for the first teleporter station in thirty thousandth-cycles," he told them. "Thirty of you are going with them—Lawrence already knows who, and you should have a note on your communicators.

"The rest of you are going into the control station with me, where we are going to have a long talk with a dead computer about how nice it would be to live again."

He gestured around the lab.

"This will be our base station and our main operating center," he noted. "Once I've had a chance to look at the station computer, we're going to set up our molycirc core here and run some amazingly long cables.

"We've got a lot of work to do, and we don't know how much time to do it in. So, take your rest when you can—and let's get to it."

CHAPTER FIFTY-ONE

EVEN IF THE LIGHTS HAD STILL BEEN POWERED, THE ALAVA hadn't seen in quite the same wavelengths as humans. Rin wasn't sure the space station would ever have managed to *not* be a foreboding, ominous maze.

Thanks to the Wendira attaching their main expedition station to the control center—it *was* the largest intact space station—they had decent maps of the structure.

But they had been determined to take things very slow and very careful—and when dealing with a facility the size of a Dyson swarm, that meant things had been taking functionally forever. They'd mapped the station, but they hadn't even put up lights of their own.

Floating drones spread light out in front of Rin's team as a trio of Wendira Warriors led the way. He wasn't sure they needed the armed escort, but he wasn't arguing, either.

Even with the lights from the drones and the light mounted on his vac-suit's shoulders, the place was dark. There was no air, nothing. His suit provided air and faux gravity alike to make up for their absence.

"This way," he told the Warriors, calling them back to an intersection via the shared radio net. "There's an elevator shaft a hundred meters along this corridor. We need to go down fifteen levels."

"How do you know what you're looking for?" the lead Warrior asked. None of the soldiers had given their names.

"I know where the computers we're looking for were on another one of these stations," Rin told them. "And I'm familiar with Alavan architecture, *and* that is a level directory on the wall there."

He shone his light on the faded text. It was a massive chart attached to an illegible map.

"It says we're on level seventy-six and that the computer core is on level sixty-one," he told the Wendira. "Roughly the middle of the station. This entire facility existed to provide brains for the rest of the swarm."

Or, at least, for about a third of it. He'd be happy if he could get it to talk to a hundredth of the platforms it had once controlled.

He only needed it to talk to five, after all, and it had once controlled *thousands*.

"Direct as you will, Dr. Dunst," the Warrior told him, stepping out along the corridor he'd directed them to.

Just *getting* to the computers was going to be a nightmare. Then they'd need to hook up power—but at least if there was one thing they knew they could find on a *Dyson swarm*, it was power!

WHEN RIN STEPPED into the central computer core of the ruined Alavan station, the true scope of their task finally sank in. Up to that moment, it had all been theoretical and somewhat distant, easy to breezily assess the task versus the skills to hand.

But the central computer core was a cylindrical room sixty meters in diameter and sixty high. They entered onto a balcony that circled the top, and he stared out into that open expanse filled with fifty-meter-tall cylinders of ancient molecular circuitry.

All of that circuitry, every one of those computers, had been built under laws of physics that no longer applied. He knew that some of them *would* be able to work if he gave them power. They'd be missing chunks of their memory, processing power, *everything*.

This was a graveyard for a people whose arrogance had broken the universe. Their computers didn't work anymore. Their stations were ruins. Their dreams shattered. Nothing of the Alava remained but their ruins and their artifice.

And their enemies.

"All right," he said slowly. "It's a bit more intimidating in person, but we brought the gear we need to do the basic setup. The central spire is the best place to start, according to the notes we have from the Taljzi swarm."

He considered the whole situation, then grinned.

"Turn off your boots' gravity and just float on down," he told his team. He suited actions to words, keeping one hand on the railing as he stepped over and turned off the gravity field. With a solid push "down" from the railing, he started himself heading toward the bottom of the chamber.

Sixty meters of molycirc passed him as he descended, and he shivered. Even the largest molycirc cores produced by any modern power—*including* the Mesharom—couldn't exceed ten meters before the crystals had fundamental issues.

The core he'd brought was far less powerful than these computers had been—but on the other hand, they'd been built when the conductivity levels of a lot of materials had been very different. The key was finding bits they could bring online, linking them with the Taljzi-designed hybrid tech and then inserting their own Alavan code.

He touched down at the base of the central spire carefully, activating his boots at the last moment as he reached the floor. To his shock, there was a body there—a four-armed Alava, mummified by millennia of vacuum, had been in the process of opening a maintenance panel when their world had ceased to be.

"Sonders, give me a hand here," he instructed the first tech to touch down next to him. "Let's not be rude to the poor guy, but he can't help us today."

He and the tech carefully moved the Alava's body, shuffling him carefully into a corner before returning to the open maintenance panel.

One of the other techs had begun to set up the hybrid interface, and Rin fully opened the panel to look inside.

"Everything looks intact here," he murmured. "Just no power. I wonder what happened to that."

The equivalent in Taljzi-controlled space had never powered down, according to the records the Imperium had from the Taljzi. The control station had its own solar collectors and had still been receiving power transmission from several of the collector stations.

"We can run some power from batteries to make sure everything boots up," Sonders suggested. "That will give us an idea of what we need to link in while we go look at the solar collectors. Do as much in parallel as possible?"

"Not much choice on that one," Rin agreed. "We've got batteries?"

"Enough to run the core for a few hours if we need to," another tech confirmed.

"Let's not aim for that," Rin said. "We'll try to boot it up and run a self-diagnostic. That's all for today. I'll want to know more about the sensors and teleporters and power collectors before we seriously try to turn this on."

"Doesn't it have control as soon as we turn it on?" Sonders asked.

"No; if we trigger the self-diagnostic, it will lock itself out," Rin told the tech. "Plus, we're definitely not going to feed it enough power to do more than boot. Watch the amount of power we give it," he instructed, pulling up notes on a holographic panel above his vac-suit arm.

"We want to give it one-point-six-five megawatts," he concluded after skimming the report. "Nothing less will run it at all, so that should be barely maintenance-level power."

"All right."

The techs set to work, laying in cables and setting up batteries while Rin stepped back to survey the spire. Like Lawrence, most of his work would come once the hardware was online. He could direct people *to* the right hardware and could help recode the Alavan software once it was online, but he wasn't much use for this part.

"Lawrence, report," he instructed as he switched his radio to a longer-range network.

"We've made entry to Teleporter One," she told him. "No power, but our initial exterior survey suggests the receptors are intact. We can either bring a solar collector online or see what the Wendira have for power transmitters."

"We'll need to do the same here," he said. "Power systems are offline. The Taljzi swarm had power, didn't it?"

"When the furry buggers arrived, apparently," she agreed. Taljzi —like their Kanzi cousins—looked much like humans wrought in two-thirds scale, then covered in blue fur.

"They got luckier than we did," Rin said. "But, of course, we have all of their notes. Control-center computers are intact but offline. We're going to run a self-diagnostic to see if we can ID what parts aren't working and need hybridization."

"What does the interior of the teleporter station look like?"

"A morgue," Lawrence said grimly. "The Wendira have only physically been aboard *maybe* a tenth of the stations. They didn't make it to this one, so...bodies and skeletons. I'd say the place had a crew of about a thousand and none of them had any warning."

"Based off the sites I've examined, they just dropped dead where they were standing when the cybernetics shut down," he told her. "Welcome to why no modern cybernetic has any interface with the autonomous nervous system!"

"And you *still* have more than I want," Lawrence told him. "My opinion of your sanity on that matter, by the way, is *not* improved by moving the bodies of people whose implants killed them."

"Fair enough," Rin conceded. "Have you made it to the tele-porters yet?"

"Not yet, but so far, things look pretty intact. Based off the Taljzi swarm, either the teleporters were transmitting when the universe changed and instantly blew themselves up, or they were on standby and quietly shut down."

"Funny that they can still transmit, even now, if the ones that were transmitting died," Rin murmured.

"Well, it's one thing to run complex energy fields under a different set of physical laws," she noted. "It's an entirely *different* level of hell to try and *maintain* complex energy fields while the laws of physics are changing.

"I don't think the Alava designed for that possibility any more than we do!"

CHAPTER FIFTY-TWO

RIN RUBBED HIS EYES IN EXHAUSTION AND STARED AT THE CODE. It was a modification of the Taljzi code written for their swarm—and he wasn't entirely sure he even *understood* their code.

"You're sure about this scan data?" he asked Mok. The Tosumi was the only other person in the lab on the Wendira station. Everyone else was busy working on the hardware in the Alavan stations.

"As sure as I can be," Mok replied. "I went over all of the scan data we have from the Infinite, but we're not even entirely sure what the ice-cursed scanner is looking at. Something about the hyperspace interface, but we've never duplicated it."

"But you think the Infinite's reactionless drive *also* has a signature on the interface?" Rin said.

"Ninety percent," the astrophysicist doctor replied. "Maybe ninety-one. I think the actual physics behind their engine are closely related, but without a sample to test, I can't confirm it.

"The drinkable water of it all, though, is that the Infinite *will* ping the Alavan scanner. Just not as a ship—but then, the *interface drive* shouldn't properly register as a ship."

"But it does," Rin said quietly. "We *know* that because it was occasionally triggering on Taljzi ships long before they actively modified it into a proper weapon."

"I *think*—but this is just guessing—that the Infinite drive won't register as strongly and likely won't be classed as a ship without us doing something."

Rin snorted.

"That's what this code fixes," he told Mok, tapping the screen. "The Taljzi eventually added an identification database, basically, to the system, telling it that interface drives were ships. They weren't able to narrow it down to only target particular drives, but they convinced the computer that interface-drive ships needed fuel.

"And since the teleporter was grabbing coronal plasma rather than refined hydrogen, well..." Rin shrugged. "Even war spheres died. I've rewritten the code to include your estimate of what the reactionless drive looks like."

"Can we take interface drives out?" Mok asked. "We've only seen those on their missiles so far."

Rin grimaced.

"We *know* the sun eater developed a biological interface drive," he told the other scientist. "I have to assume that the Infinite have done the same by now. There are definite advantages to both systems, so...some of their fleet may well arrive on interface drive.

"Plus, looking at the signature we've included for the reactionless engine, I think that will ping for interface drives as well," he admitted. "When we turn this on, every friendly interface drive in the star system needs to turn *off* or they're going to die."

The lab was silent.

"Did you ever think you'd be doing this kind of work, Dr. Dunst?" Mok asked. "Assembling a weapon from xenoarchaeological artifacts?"

"No," Rin admitted. "I knew that the tech artifacts I recovered would be studied and attempts would be made to replicate them, but

I was never expecting to be involved in that side of things. I was a *field* archaeologist."

He stared at the code blankly for a moment, not seeing the symbols.

"Then we met the sun eater and I got dragged into a pile of overly classified bullshit," he said. "And here we are. I do what I can."

"I was recruited to *disable* a weapon like this," Mok said quietly. "As a doctor and an astrophysicist, I study people and stars. I was brought in to the Taljzi swarm to study the stellar effects of the thing.

"Assembling the weapon I once destroyed...feels wrong. And yet..."

"Any chance to save people," Rin said. "So, here we are."

He tapped the code on the screen.

"We're only a cycle or two away from being able to load this into the control center, though we're further from having the teleporters online," he told Mok. "I'm going to see if I can refine the code to give us a bit more direct control of the targeting, but my suspicion is that if the Taljzi couldn't manage it, we can't.

"They had hundreds of years of personal experience with their swarm. *I* just have their notes."

"Which I hope is enough," a familiar translated voice told him. Rin looked up in surprise to see Princess Oxtashah standing in the entrance to the lab, flanked by her Warrior bodyguards.

"It might be, Your Highness," Rin conceded. "I didn't expect to see you here."

"*Zokalatan* has remained here to act as a security force," she told him. "And to stay in the communications loop for the war. May we speak in private, Dr. Dunst?"

RIN LED Oxtashah to the office the Wendira had put aside for his use. Like the lab, it was a prefab space clearly unused before his team's arrival. Unlike the lab, he'd barely used it. All of his gear was in the lab he shared with the rest of the team, leaving the office without even chairs that were comfortable for humans.

Awkwardly perching on the desk, he looked at Oxtashah. Her wings were ever so slightly lifted from her carapace, seeming to twitch unconsciously every so often.

He didn't know Wendira body language...but he suspected she was terrified.

"How may I assist you, Princess Oxtashah?" he finally asked when she didn't speak.

"How soon will the weapon be ready?" she asked.

"Faster than I dared hope," he admitted. "Ten cycles. Maybe twelve. That will only be two teleporters, though. Given time, we think we can get up to five online. The odds say we won't get many shots from any given teleporter, so more is better."

He spread his hands.

"This won't be a sustainable weapon, Princess," Rin warned. "We don't have all the pieces that the Taljzi did, so we can't build as solid a system as they did. There's about a point-two percent chance every time one of the teleporters activates that it will pick up more plasma than we can contain—and the station will be destroyed."

"So. Five hundred shots," she whispered.

"Statistically," he agreed. "If we have two teleporters, we'll probably get a thousand shots—and the odds are that we'll get a one-shot kill on anything up to a Category Four. But..." He shook his head.

"There is a small but real chance that the guns will overload on their first shot. This is not a reliable trap, Princess."

"You may not have twelve cycles, Doctor," she warned him. "And it will need to be as reliable as you can make it. A new Infinite swarm has been detected, heading into Wendira space. Far stronger than the last; my people's Battle Hives are prepared to face it, but they likely lack the strength to overcome.

"The only option they may have is to lure them here."

Rin nodded slowly.

"So, we punch the bear in the nose and hope he follows," he said grimly. "How long *do* we have?"

"I do not know. My communications with the Battle Hives are over a cycle out of date," she admitted. "As of then, twenty-six hours ago, they had not yet relocated the swarm."

"Have you requested help from the Laians and A!Tol?" Rin asked.

"We cannot." She shook her head. "Ronoxosh's pride may have broken our Hive. By refusing to work together, we now cannot ask for aid without seeming weak."

"Which is more important? Seeming weak or *surviving*?" Rin said quietly.

"It is not my decision," Oxtashah told him. "The Royal Commandant will engage the swarm. He will lead them here. The weapon *must* be ready when he arrives."

Rin swallowed but nodded firmly.

"I will talk to my team," he told her. "We may need more assistance."

"The entirety of *Zokalatan*'s crew will be placed at your disposal," she replied firmly. "I have made this clear to my officers. Secrecy will no longer save our Hive. We cannot bring forward sufficient fleets fast enough to save our outer provinces.

"This weapon *must* work."

CHAPTER FIFTY-THREE

THE TELEPORTER STATION WAS A MAZE OF MYSTERY SYSTEMS, ancient black molycircs and other strange devices ticking away as they slowly powered up. White-painted hybrid systems were everywhere Rin looked as he walked through the platform, each of them with a name and purpose scrawled on them in black marker.

They had atmosphere aboard the working stations now, at least, though gravity was still provided by people's boots. Air was necessary for efficient work—but being able to move things in zero gee was often useful as well.

"Where's Commander Lawrence?" he asked the first person he met—a Worker-caste Wendira working on installing white-painted power cables into a mystery gray device that was shifting shape as Rin looked at it.

"The containment chamber," the Wendira replied, pointing a pincer without looking at him. "Keep toward the center of the station."

"Thank you," Rin said. The Wendira was clearly focused on his work, so Rin set off in the indicated direction.

There were more Wendira as he got closer to the center of the station. Some individuals, other teams. Most of the teams were a mix of Imperials, Workers and Drones—and they started to be everywhere as he reached his destination.

The containment chamber was the primary receiving and transmitting node for the teleporter that filled most of the space station. It was a hundred-meter-wide sphere, its interior forged of compressed matter.

White-painted force field generators were being installed all around the surface at ten-meter intervals, dozens of the devices being linked to massive power couplings as they attempted to build a system that could hold whatever they grabbed from the star.

"Lawrence," he called out when he saw the woman. "Where are we at?"

She looked up at him in clear exasperation, then waved him over.

"You know, you could call me on the radio or something," she told him. "You didn't need to take a shuttle all this way."

"I'm in charge of all of this, and I needed to see the station," he replied. "Plus, I needed to step away from code for a bit—*and* I want your opinion on the latest code sets."

Lawrence shook her head.

"Fine, fine," she said. "We're running against an unknown time limit to build a weapon of unknown but cosmic power, and you want to do site and code review. Sure!"

"Kelly," he said sharply. "Doing things quickly doesn't mean *rushing*. *Rushing* tends to result in things going slowly, doesn't it?"

She snorted.

"Fair. I could probably use a step back from containment-field calculations, anyway. Want the tour?"

"Please. Then we can talk code."

She waved her hand around.

"This is the containment chamber," she told him, repeating the obvious. "All calculations suggest it's oversized for what the teleporter can currently do. We're picking up a fifty-meter-diameter target, which gives us space to set up a stronger containment field."

"Were the Alava really transmitting plasma between star systems?" Rin asked.

"Yes and no." She snorted. "It's pretty clear plasma transmission was always intended to be shorter-ranged, but they were still sending plasma to other star systems. Mostly, though, they were sending straight-up electricity. Up to fifty light-years."

"I'd seen the records and projections, but that's still mind-blowing," he admitted. "Can we do that with this system?"

"Gods no," Lawrence told him. "Not a bloody chance. Too much of it required the universe to work in a completely different way. I'm not sure the electricity transfer could work at all anymore—but the *matter* transfer still does.

"Somehow."

"So, we pull coronal plasma in from the star to here, and then we flick it out again?" Rin asked. "It's here for, what, a millisecond?"

"Twenty-six," Lawrence told him. "Which is about twenty-four milliseconds longer than you want a twenty-five-meter-radius ball of solar plasma inside *anything*. This shit makes our fusion reactors look like campfires."

"The delta isn't *that* much larger," Rin argued. "I've seen the numbers."

"It's an order of magnitude. For whatever reason—and no, we can't adjust it—we're grabbing the plasma from the hottest part of the star. We're not sure why, but it's the only pickup that seems to work without the collector station.

"Good news? This setup is going to hit a lot harder than the Taljzi one did."

"Bad news, that point-two percent failure chance," Rin guessed.

"Exactly. Come on." She led him across the sphere and out into a corridor. "Along here are what little local controls we have. Honestly, it's basically nothing. These are communications receivers from the control station."

Stepping into the room next to the corridor, Rin noted that most of the original equipment was piled along one wall, replaced by white-painted Wendira transceivers.

"Of course, none of the Alavan coms still work," she said.

"I set up the other end," he reminded her gently. "We're using standard hyperfold transceivers. We've even managed to test the weird hyperspace interface scanner they have."

"And? I didn't see that report yet," Lawrence asked.

"Instantaneous to four light-hours, at least," he told her. "We didn't want to run the tests further out than that, because we only *have* one escort to send dancing around the star system." He grinned. "And doing it for as long as we did made Sub-Commandant Likox *really* uncomfortable."

Likox was *Zokalatan*'s captain. A senior Warrior, probably well past due for promotion, he'd been personally tasked with Princess Oxtashah's safety.

Rin found the man stuffy and paranoid, though he did understand where it was coming from.

"And the teleporter itself?" he asked. "Where is that?"

"You're standing in it," Lawrence told him. "The entire damn station. I'm sure we could narrow down how much of it we need to turn on, but the Taljzi decided never to risk it...and we can't really take risks, can we, sir?"

"No," he murmured. "Swarm Charlie was located again forty hours ago."

Which meant *he'd* heard about two hours ago. Hyperfold coms were faster than light, but *faster than light* did *not* mean *instantaneous*. Once the update reached a starcom, it reached its recipient within minutes, but getting a message to the starcoms took hours— roughly an hour per light-year.

"Fuck. Where?"

"Too close to the Shakol System," Rin told him. "The Battle Hives were scrambling, and it's entirely possible battle has already been joined."

The Shakol System was the main industrial node of the Wendira province closest to the Astoroko Nebula. That meant it was where the Wendira had concentrated their entire defense fleet. Once again, the Infinite appeared to have gone directly for the jugular.

Of course, the *jugular* in this case was two hundred–plus fully rearmed star hives.

"We should be receiving updates every nine twentieth-cycles— half a Wendira day—until...Well, until Swarm Charlie is here."

There was no one else in the communication relay chamber, which allowed Lawrence to curse fervently for several seconds.

"We're not ready, Rin," she admitted.

"You need to *be* ready," he told her. "Worst case? The Hives lead them straight here. Shakol is three cycles from Skiefail. They could be here in less than seventy-two hours."

"We need the system online in sixty."

Lawrence exhaled a sharp breath.

"Maybe," she said. "*Maybe.* This is a nightmare, Rin. What we're building. What it's supposed to face..."

"I know," he told her. "That's why I wanted you to look at the code I prepped. If I've done it right, I *think* we've created a mask that can conceal existing signatures. We may be able to hide the Wendira fleet's interface drives."

"You'd need a live hyperfold connection from the ship in question," Lawrence said instantly. "If the interface scanner is instantaneous..."

"I know," he agreed. "It's a manual brute-force solution—and you're the only person, even in this team, I trust to review my Alavan code."

"I'll take a look," she promised. "But then I need to get back to work if you want two teleporters in sixty hours."

CHAPTER FIFTY-FOUR

"And that makes three."

Morgan watched the force they were designating Swarm Delta-Three swim through hyperspace. Her entire task group was motionless, a full hyperspace light-cycle short of their destination, watching as the third of the Infinite's defensive flotillas orbited past.

"We're too damn close," she muttered. "Ort, what do you make their closest approach to the STG?"

"Just over three light-hours, Division Lord," the Ivida officer told her. "Path is the same as the first two. I estimate we'll be clear to proceed in a half-cycle."

Eleven hours and forty minutes. Another delay.

"Understood," Morgan conceded. "Pass the word to the task group. How long until we're in position for the first deployment after that?"

"Two cycles," Ort confirmed. "Two-point-five cycles until we exit hyperspace and can assess the situation at the first launch point."

The rosette was going to be a pain. Until they were on site, Morgan wasn't going to know if she needed to set timers or could use hyperfold detonation commands. If she had to set timers, she'd probably need to leave the starkiller crews behind.

"We'll need to watch the first launch all the way in, no matter what," she murmured to Rogers. "This is taking longer than I'd hoped."

"I wish we'd had a better scan of Swarm Charlie's vector," her chief of staff replied. "The report that they're at Shakol…"

Rogers shook her head. At least they could receive starcom messages in hyperspace, though they couldn't reply.

"We could pull this off, only to have the entire Grand Hive burnt down by the time we got out of here," she said.

"Right now, I'm concerned about the Delta swarms," Morgan admitted. "That's a *lot* of bioforms we can't be sure are going to get caught in the novas. And that's ignoring the fact that they're our biggest obstacle to completing our mission."

"Well, so far, this has been slow and painful…but we're still undetected," Rogers reminded her. "That's about as good as we could hope for, isn't it?"

"It is," Morgan agreed. "We might just be able to pull this off. The stealth fields are holding and we're almost there. We're so close it's painful to keep waiting, but we're almost there."

"And so far, no one has been lying doggo in our path, either," the chief of staff said. "We're blind to any Infinite in hyperspace that isn't moving, and that makes me nervous."

"Me too," Morgan said. "But despite everything the Infinite have done, they don't seem to have been ready for us to sneak in a fleet with stealth fields."

"Were there any on *Builder of Tomorrows?*" Rogers asked.

"We don't know. It's not like we got a nice, neat inventory for the mobile shipyard that officially didn't exist and was operated by a multiracial conspiracy to steal a wrecked Alavan fleet," Morgan noted. "I'd feel bad for what happened to them, but they found what they were after."

Rogers chuckled bitterly.

"And fucked everybody else."

"It's our job to unfuck it all," Morgan told her. "Go rest, Bethany. Almost half a cycle before we even bring the drives back online.

"We're going to be here for a while."

MORGAN WAS AWOKEN BY AN ALERT. Rolling out of bed with practiced ease, she hit a voice-only accept as she reached for a uniform.

"Casimir. What is it?" she snapped.

"Sir, we have an update from the Wendira," her com officer reported grimly. "It's...bad."

"There's not much we can do, Commander," she told the Yin. "Forward it to my quarters. I'll review and see if we need to change our plans."

"Yes, Division Lord," the junior officer confirmed.

By the time Morgan had her uniform on and the lights up in her cabin, the system on her desk was blinking with a received message. She told it to play, activating the holoprojector.

The image of a Wendira Warrior appeared above her desk, his wings drooping in exhaustion as he faced the recorder. It was not, she realized immediately, Ronoxosh. The officer had the insignia of a Fleet Commandant instead of a Royal Commandant like Ronoxosh.

"This is Fleet Commandant Icenar of the Ninth Battle Hive," the Warrior said crisply. "Royal Commandants Ronoxosh, Toramon, Kalrite, and Somar are all dead. The Shakol System has fallen to the Infinite.

"We have been forced to withdraw from the system in disarray. Our fighter strength has been reduced by over ninety percent, and we have lost over two hundred star hives and six hundred star shields."

Morgan exhaled as if she'd been punched in the gut. That was basically the entire fleet the Wendira had brought to Tohrohsail—and so far as she knew, the Wendira hadn't been significantly reinforced.

Icenar's flat report spoke of the deaths of millions of Wendira Warriors.

"We are falling back per the contingency plan, but we were badly outmatched by the enemy," he continued. "They are in possession of what appear to be biotech-derived interface-drive missiles equal to our own.

"Somehow, they knew where our anchorage was located and emerged within fifteen light-seconds of the position of the Fifteenth Battle Hive," he said. "There are no survivors of the Fifteenth. The Infinite have deployed hyperfold cannons in massive numbers with a range that exceeds ours by at least two light-seconds."

He paused.

"They have also demonstrated the use of what appears to be either hyperfold-transmitted or otherwise instantaneously relocated microsingularities. Our star hives are not armored against that kind of attack."

Morgan closed her eyes in horror. The singularity projectors had been the most terrifying of the Infinite's weapons—but she'd *also* feared that the Six-As had possessed Alavan teleporter weapons.

It seemed her fears hadn't been imaginative enough.

"I do not have direct control of all surviving units," Icenar admitted. "But I am in command of thirty star hives and two hundred star shields. We have escaped Infinite missile range, but a major component of the swarm is in pursuit of us. I hope to lure them into hyperspace after me, as per the contingency plan.

"We will enter hyperspace within a few minutes of this transmission and will reach the contingency system within seventy-two hours."

There was a long pause as Icenar stared blankly at the recorder. Finally, the recording froze and was replaced with another strange Wendira.

This was an *ancient* male Royal-caste Wendira, a massive creature with Royal Commandant's insignia who appeared to have lost his wings at some point in his youth.

"Fleet Commandant Icenar's report is being forwarded to all of our allies unedited," the Royal said. "We have been assembling a reinforcement fleet, but we did not expect Royal Commandant Ronoxosh's fleet to be completely destroyed.

"If the contingency plan works, Swarm Charlie should be removed as a strategic factor. If it does not—and I neither have certainty in the plan nor permission to share it—a major joint operation will be needed to eliminate the swarm and secure our worlds.

"I formally request that all of our allies provide forces to assist in neutralizing Swarm Charlie and resecuring the Shakol System."

That part of the message wasn't for her. Morgan closed it and stared blankly at the wall. There'd be technical downloads she needed to review, of course, but it looked like her mission had just increased in priority.

Singularity cannons were bad enough when their projectiles had to pass through space at lightspeed to reach their targets. *Teleported black holes?*

More than ever, it had become critical that Morgan's fleet remain undetected.

CHAPTER FIFTY-FIVE

"WELL, THAT'S THAT, ISN'T IT?" RIN TOLD A VIRTUAL conference of his senior people and Princess Oxtashah. "How long ago was the message transmitted?"

"Thirty-seven hours," Oxtashah told him. "We do not yet have Fleet Commandant Icenar or the Swarm on our long-range anomaly scanners. I have ordered Likox to send the escorts into hyperspace and maintain a watch there.

"That should give us a half-cycle or so of warning before the swarm arrives."

"Lawrence, Mok." Rin looked to his subordinates. "That means we'll probably see them in about twenty to twenty-five twentieth-cycles. We have fifteen tenth-cycles at most."

"Are you ready?" Oxtashah asked. "Can you destroy the Swarm?"

"The scanners and targeting software are ready," Rin said after a moment's consideration. "Or close enough, anyway. A few more link-ages and a couple more hours of code. Targeting will be ready, but..."

"But?" Lawrence asked.

"Our ability to protect friendly ships is poor," he admitted.

"We're going to be able to set up a link for *Zokalatan* and her escorts shortly that *should* protect them, but we can't do it for the fighters.

"I need an active hyperfold link to any ship we're protecting, and we can only shield a few. Maybe fifty?"

"The plan calls for the fleet to cut their interface drives on arrival in Skiefail," Oxtashah told him. "If we can allow a portion to maneuver under the shield of the weapon, that may change the odds."

"If the weapon is working," Rin said. He looked at the other two. "Lawrence?"

"We're there," she said. She looked exhausted, like she hadn't slept in days. "The first teleporter will be online in the next tenth-cycle. The second will be about a cycle after that, and we're *hoping* to have one of the partial stations online. We *may* have that done by the time the swarm arrives, but it's not likely."

"Two teleporters," Rin said grimly. "So, a thousand shots?"

"Roughly. We have to hope for one-shot kills, because I don't think the bastards will be bringing less than a thousand bioforms," Lawrence said grimly. "And I need to pull my people off the station before we initiate."

"Agreed," Rin said instantly. "The odds of losing the teleporter stations are too high for me to want to keep people aboard. We'd lose them all."

"Will it help if someone stays aboard?" Oxtashah asked.

"It might cut the odds of a failure by ten percent, get us another dozen or two shots," Lawrence admitted. "But I'm not going to ask my people to die for that."

"No. But I will ask for volunteers from the Drones," Oxtashah said grimly. "And we will remember their names for all eternity. That is always the deal."

"That..." Lawrence trailed off. "There are definitely people among your Drones who can do what we need. That just...goes against the grain."

"Your people live one way, Commander Lawrence," Oxtashah

told her. "*Mine* live our way. The only hope the Drones have for immortality is to be remembered. For this... For this, they would earn a thousand years if I had the power to give it to them.

"But all I can give those shortest-lived of our children is a promise that their sacrifice will be remembered—and if their sacrifice can save millions, they will make it gladly."

"If they volunteer," Rin insisted. He knew it was a feeble demand, but he had to make it.

"Of course," Oxtashah agreed. "We do not order our Drones to their deaths. Ever."

Rin exhaled a sigh and nodded.

"Then it seems we may actually be ready when the Infinite get here," he murmured. "Let's hope it is enough."

———

"JUST TO CONFIRM, there is nobody on those ships, correct?" Rin asked as his team settled in around him on the control station.

A Wendira holographic display had been hooked up to the Imperial molycirc core that was actually running everything. Hybrid interfaces designed by the Taljzi but manufactured aboard *Zokalatan* linked the upside-down chandelier of molecular circuitry to the ancient Alavan systems.

Only about a tenth of the Alavan computers were working, and Rin had no idea what proportion of the rest of the systems were online...except that it was enough. They had the scanners, they had the coms, they had the teleporters.

They'd done it. In theory, at least—which was what the two ships now positioned a light-hour from the Skiefail Swarm were meant to test.

"We have removed all of our personnel," Castellash confirmed. "Both transports are standing by to activate their interface drives by remote command."

Rin nodded and checked his own reports. He'd commandeered

Castellash's two largest sublight ships and had them fly out to a designated zone.

"Kelly, confirm the teleporter station is clear," he asked. They'd have a skeleton crew of thirty-two Drone volunteers on each station when the real fight started, but there was no point risking anyone for the test.

"Station is clear," Lawrence replied. "All systems show green from here. You have the button, Dr. Dunst."

"Confirm, I have control," Rin announced. He glanced around the room. They'd rigged up lights and systems at the heart of the Alavan station to make it more usable, but that somehow just made the black spires of the dead computers they *hadn't* been able to restore more intimidating.

A holographic image of Oxtashah watched from a communications console, and most of his team was scattered around the room, waiting for the word.

"Targeting system is online," he reported, entering the first commands. "Link to the teleporter is disabled. Neither ship is appearing. Boards are clear."

He waited a moment, double-checking everything.

"Director Castellash, have the ships bring up their drives," he ordered. "Let's confirm these sensors are working."

They'd calibrated them on live targets, but they still had time to test everything. The second and third potential teleporters were still being worked on, but he wasn't feeding those stations instructions—both the Alavan communicators and the new hyperfold setup had been physically disconnected, just in case.

"Drives are online," Castellash reported.

"And I see them," Rin replied as two icons appeared on his screen. The interface scanner operated in real time across a surprising range, picking up disruptions in the barrier between realspace and hyperspace.

"I have the feed from *Extana*," Rin continued. "Mapping the mask... Activating the mask."

One of the icons disappeared from his screen. If he'd done everything right, the Alavan computers now didn't know *Extana*, the larger of the two transports, existed. A mask had already been in place around *Zokalatan* and her escorts, though the ships were close enough to the swarm to probably be safe *and* had their drives offline.

"I am maintaining the mask. Drop both interface drives," he instructed.

The link from *Extana* changed as her sister ship disappeared from the scanner.

"Everything looks good. I have a mask on *Extana* that should pick up automatically when she raises her drive," Rin said grimly. "Time for the real test."

The room was silent as every gaze was focused on the hologram of the system.

"Commander Lawrence, complete the connection, please," he ordered.

New icons flashed up on his screen and the main hologram, turning a bright green to declare that systems were operational.

"All systems are green," she reported. "Containment fields online. Everything for the teleporter shows green."

"Scans are green, control interface is green," Rin concluded. He looked at the main display and the icons up there—the two transports, as their computers reported.

"No reaction to *Zokalatan* or the escorts," he reported. "Everything is quiet. Exactly as planned."

There was an audible sigh of relief. *Zokalatan's* interface drive was shut down, and she *shouldn't* have triggered the station's new defenses, even without the masking program. But the chance had been there, and that made this the most dangerous moment of bringing everything online.

"We now know that a mask over an inactive drive works *and* that an inactive drive is fine," Rin noted. He could theoretically stop masking *Zokalatan* and her escorts now, but why take the risk?

"Castellash." Rin paused as the Wendira looked at him, waiting for the order everyone knew was coming. "Bring up both transport drives, please."

Everything happened very quickly after that. An icon appeared on Rin's scanners, and the ancient Alavan processes kicked into play. Parts of the "in-flight refueling" system had been modified to create a weapon, but most of those had been convincing the control computer to accept an interface drive as a ship.

It detected a ship. It judged that it had not fueled that ship. It provided fuel. Icons flashed on the screens, reporting on the teleporter as it activated—and then the hyperfold com from the second ship cut off.

"Target identified and destroyed in...eleven seconds," Rin reported. "I am still receiving a feed from *Extana*. She is not showing as a contact on the scanners."

The room exploded in cheers. Both halves of the mission were complete: they'd built a superweapon *and* they'd found a way to protect their own ships from it.

As the cheers carried on, Rin met Lawrence's gaze. She looked grim and returned his regard calmly.

"What next?" she asked.

"We leave everything online and bring *Extana* in to the swarm," he told her. "That will take two hours. If the mask works for the entire flight in, we're good. Either way, we shut everything down when *Extana* is either here or gone.

"Then we wait."

CHAPTER FIFTY-SIX

"Anomaly scanners put the nearest contact at over a light-day," Ort reported on *Odysseus's* flag bridge. "We should be clear for a rapid-transition hyper portal."

"Isn't that going to be fun," Rogers murmured.

Morgan had to agree. It was *possible* to create a hyper portal, pass through and close the portal behind you in under a second. But the portal didn't have enough time to stabilize the way it normally did, which made the transition noticeably more uncomfortable.

"Needs must when the devil drives," Morgan murmured back to her XO. "Are all ships ready?" she asked more loudly.

"Checking in now," Ort confirmed. "Seventy-Three-Twenty-Two ships report ready." Pause. "Wendira ships report ready. Laian ships report ready."

The Ivida turned in his chair to look at Morgan.

"All special task group report ready for rapid hyperspace transition on your order," he reported.

Morgan considered the vague map for a few seconds. They could pick up the mass effect of the rosette clearly from there, rippling waves of anomalous readings on the scanners. They *should* be emerging between thirty-six and forty light-hours from their target star.

And they *should* be clear to do so. Nothing was on the anomaly scanners except those stars and the one element of Swarm Delta at over a hyperspace light-day.

But something made the back of her neck itch, and she was all too aware that she wouldn't see any vessels lying doggo in hyperspace. There was only so much delay she could take, though.

"STG will transit in sixty seconds from...*now,*" she ordered crisply.

There was no grand "leap into action." Her team had been planning for and expecting the order for days. Everything on her bridge was smoothly planned, and she hoped it was the same on the other ships of the special task group.

A timer was now on her main hologram, ticking down toward zero, and Morgan forced herself to keep breathing normally. She *hated* rapid transitions.

They weren't that bad, not really, but they were supposed to be avoidable, and she'd made too many of them in her career.

"Transition in ten seconds," *Odysseus's* navigator announced. "Nine. Eight. Seven. Six. Five. Four. Three. Two. One.

"*Transition.*"

The world tried to tear Morgan apart, and she grimaced as that one second seemed to take an hour to pass. Her muscles clenched and seized in rippling waves across her body, and she gasped in pain.

She was hardly the only one. Even as rapid transitions went, this was *bad.* She'd been through one worse, ever, and that had been *inside* the Eye of the Astoroko Nebula with damaged hyperspace emitters!

"Transition complete," Rogers reported, sounding short of breath. "All ships confirmed present. We are scanning... Range to target is one-point-six light-cycles."

Thirty-seven light-hours.

"Well in the zone," Morgan accepted aloud. "Full scans; I want to know what's out there, people."

Her team set to work, interfacing with the individual ships as they moved toward the star at half the speed of light.

"Stealth fields are holding across the task group; we remain invisible," Ort reported. "Hyperfold coms are...distorted but functional."

"Get a team on analyzing that," Morgan snapped. "If it will impact long-range hyperfold transmissions, we need to know that."

"Yes, sir," Ort confirmed. He paused. "We'll run the analysis, but it doesn't look good, sir."

"Then we'll deal with that," Morgan said calmly. "All ships will maintain course toward Target Astoroko One for now. We were always going all the way in for this one."

She checked. One of the Laian starkillers was designated for this deployment. In another universe, the blue giant they were approaching would have gone on to tear a chunk of the Astoroko Nebula away with it as it fell out of the rosette, eventually giving birth to a new star system.

In *this* universe, Morgan Casimir was going to kill it before it got to do that. That star system would die unborn to destroy the Imperium's enemies.

She was one of the few living sentient beings in the *galaxy* to have fired a starkiller, and she hated them more than anything else. But the nest of Infinite at the heart of the nebula was unfightable.

"No contacts, scanners are clean," Rogers reported. "There is nothing within several light-hours of us that our passives can pick up. Do we risk going active?"

Morgan had to stop and think for that one. Even pulsing their tachyon scanners would expose them to anyone out there, but at the same time...passives missed things. Just distance and moderate emissions control could hide a starship from the STG's passive sensors.

And that was for a *starship*, let alone a bioform that could have entirely different emissions profiles from what they were used to.

"Coordinate it," she said quietly. "Spread out ships for maximum heterodyning, and go active on *everything* for a one-second pulse. Radar, lidar, tachyons—the full array.

"I want to know the names of the local *dust*, clear?"

"Yes, sir!" Rogers replied crisply. "On it."

Morgan watched and waited. Without the limits of the hyper-space visibility bubble, her ships spread out into a rough disk half a million kilometers across in a few seconds, linked together by their FTL coms.

"Initiating synchronized active pulse...*now*."

The main hologram flashed gently as the tachyon pulse went out. Seconds passed as the FTL particles flashed across the dark void, leaving traces in the dark whenever they hit anything. Rocks. Dust. There shouldn't have been much out there.

And then the new icons started to appear on the screen. First just a handful as the tachyon pulse washed over what *could* have been a slowly forming asteroid belt...then dozens of icons as the pulse continued on.

"Contacts, multiple contacts!" Rogers snapped. "Contacts in full em-con at one hundred twenty light-seconds!"

FOR A MOMENT, everyone on the bridge froze in stunned shock. There was *no way* there was an ambush fleet waiting for them there. They'd been stealthed all along and none of the forces and sentinels they'd passed had reacted to them.

The only way the enemy could already be there was...

"They've been watching us all along," Morgan said flatly. "They detected us as soon as we came into the nebula and projected our course. *We've never been hidden.*"

"What do we do, sir?" Rogers asked.

"Can we resolve numbers and types from the pulse we already got?" she asked.

"Estimates only," Ort told her. "I make it sixty-six contacts, led by at least one Category Six...potentially a Six-A."

"Understood." Morgan looked at the hologram. "Assume Swarm Delta knew exactly where we were and re-vectored as soon as we transitioned. Can they position to cut off our retreat?"

There was a longer pause as the operations team ran their analysis.

"Yes, sir," Ort said quietly.

"Then we complete the mission," Morgan told her staff. "Bring up the tachyon sensors for long-range targeting. All Seventy-Three-Twenty-Two units will engage the Six with hyperspace missiles.

"Task group will commence a realspace run for Target Astoroko One," she continued. "Even one starkiller threatens the Queen. They may be prepared to negotiate—and if not, the deeper we are in the gravity well, the more damage we can do to Swarm Delta when they come after us."

Even as she laid one plan aloud, though, Morgan was assembling her real plan in the back of her mind.

There was a decent chance they could punch through the force in front of them and make a run into the rosette's gravity well. They'd be a nightmare for the Infinite to dig out of that—which had a chance of bringing *all* of Swarm Delta in to deal with them.

Swarm Delta's three components were fifteen trillion tons of warships, with hyperspace drives and probably missiles and potentially even hyperfold singularity guns. If she could lure them inside the hyperspace dead zone around Target Astoroko One and *then* detonate the star, well...

The special task group was already dead. If she could take *fifteen trillion tons* of Infinite bioforms with her and have a decent chance of hurting the Queen and the central nest, she was going to take it.

"Tachyon scans now running continuously," Ort reported. "Confirming numbers and identities now. Swarm Echo is sixty-five combat units, mostly Category Threes but led by a Six-A. Range is one-twenty-six light-seconds, but they are now accelerating toward us at the standard one-point-five percent of lightspeed per second."

"Initiate evasive maneuvers to hold the range. Do we have a solid target lock on the Six-A?" Morgan asked, surprised at how calm her tone was.

No, not even that. Surprised at how calm *she* was. She was dead. All of her people were dead. They didn't know it yet, but that was already written. If the Infinite had always known where her ships were, they were dead.

The only real question was why they hadn't *already* finished her people off.

"All *Bellerophon*s are locked on," Rogers confirmed.

"Synchronize firing systems," Morgan ordered. "Full time-on-target salvos. Fire when ready."

The main hologram was shifting now as they closed into battle mode. The map plot had shrunk in around the two forces, with new icons appearing across the bottom of the big projection as her ships began to feed live updates on all of their weapon systems.

The HSM launcher icons flickered as they fired, dozens of tiny portals opening inside Morgan's ships and the missiles charging through.

"That's confirmation that we can still fire HSMs in this mess," Rogers observed. "We didn't from *Defiance*, so I was wondering."

Morgan chuckled.

"Those portal generators are small enough and powerful to cut through almost any interference," she reminded her chief of staff. "We used them to send shuttles into a *planet's atmosphere* once."

Of course, none of those pilots had survived, but that had been because she'd sent them into the teeth of the Taljzi cloner's defenses. They'd achieved the mission—but none of those brave Marines had expected to come back.

Now it seemed that Morgan had the same kind of duty.

"Tachyon scans suggest multiple hits on the Six-A," Ort confirmed. "Target is still mobile."

"Target has Alavan armor," Morgan said drily. "I don't think even the HSM's warheads are going to do much without a direct hit or an internal emergence."

"Well, there are always fish in the water," Ort replied. "Second salvo away."

There's always a chance. At two light-minutes, the chance wasn't great, but it was there.

"Can we evade around them and maintain range?" Morgan asked as more hit icons appeared over the big bioform.

"Most likely," Rogers said. "I don't know if we'll keep it this open, but we should stay out of plasma ran..."

"What is *that*?" someone asked.

"Interface drives," Ort replied. "All units in Swarm Echo just brought up full-power interface drives at point-six-five *c*." He paused. "They're not scanning quite right, so I'm guessing they've done *something* odd, but those are definitely interface drives."

"Understood," Morgan confirmed. "There goes evading them. Can we keep the range open while staying inside the zone where Swarm Delta can't arrive on top of us?"

The closest Swarm Delta force was theoretically at least a day and a half away, but Morgan wasn't taking bets that there'd only been the swarms they could see out there.

"No," Rogers said grimly. "They have the interior position, sir, and now match us for velocity. And we have to assume they can match our vector changes now."

Morgan was running mental calculations and watching the screen as they spoke. More missiles were hammering their primary target, but the Six-A was huge. Even if they were scoring direct hits, it was a twelve-hundred-kilometer-diameter sphere wrapped in hyper-compressed armor.

It might take every HSM they had to seriously hurt the beast— and that was what she was planning on throwing at it.

"Hold the range open as long as we can without leaving the gravity zone," she ordered firmly. "If we can empty our HSMs into the big bastard before we let anyone into missile range, that would make me *very* happy, people."

New course lines and maneuverability spheres appeared on the hologram as the STG continued maneuvering.

"Wait...what was that?" Ort demanded as an icon flashed on the screen and disappeared. "Running analysis."

Morgan held her tongue. She could guess and she didn't like the answer.

"Teleported microsingularity, sir," the ops officer finally reported. "It's smaller than the ones they fired from the projector, and dissolved into Hawking radiation in under a second without new mass."

"But if one of those appears *inside* one of our ships..."

"That ship is in serious trouble," Morgan finished. "Increase evasive maneuvers across the fleet. They missed once. Let's *keep* them missing."

The range was slowly but surely dropping. The Infinite understood *exactly* what Morgan's limitations were—if she passed the invisible line in space where a hyper portal could be created, she was vulnerable to ambush.

She would also be able to escape—except that she no longer believed she was invisible to the Infinite. That rendered escape impossible. That left only the mission.

"*Drown you,*" Ort suddenly hissed. "Three internal emergences. I have detached armor plating and...and..."

"Blood," Morgan finished for the Ivida. "Blood on the scale of a creature that size, I'm guessing?"

"Fluid loss and flesh, yes, sir," Ort concluded. "Target remains mobile, but I think we just blew off a good chunk of her armor."

"Program the remaining missiles to go for the weak spot," Morgan ordered. "Time to regular IDM range?"

"Two minutes," Rogers replied. "Laying in targeting patterns now. Defensive drones deploying across the fleet." She paused. "Sub-Commandant Irisha is requesting a com channel, sir."

"Put him through," Morgan ordered.

The Wendira officer appeared in a hologram projected above the arm of her seat, putting him exactly at her eye level.

"Division Lord," he greeted her. "I request permission to deploy my fighters. We can reduce the enemy's smaller platforms before they are able to engage with missile fire. Respectfully, I am your expert on starfighter tactics, and I assess this as our best chance to influence this battle."

Morgan paused. Irisha was definitely correct that he knew starfighters far better than she did—she'd barely even considered them in her thoughts as she projected the battle in her head.

On the other hand, her five star intruders only had twelve hundred and eighty starfighters between them. The odds were that none of those starfighters would survive closing with sixty-four Category Three bioforms.

Something in Irisha's gaze told her he knew that. So did his Drones, who had almost certainly volunteered to a one to fly the strike.

"You are the expert," she conceded. She glanced at the screens. The range was still over one light-minute, but the need to stay inside the star's gravity well was limiting the STG's ability to keep the range open.

"Deploy your starfighters as you judge fit, Sub-Commandant," she told him quietly. "There will be later phases to this battle."

"Only if we survive this one, sir," Irisha said calmly. "Fighters will deploy immediately, targeting the Category Threes. I leave the Alavan sphere to you."

"Thanks," Morgan replied before the channel dropped.

"Rogers, Ort, deploy hyperfold-equipped drones to support the Wendira fighters," she ordered. "They don't have tachyon scanners, so we'll keep them updated as thoroughly as possible as they close."

She leaned back in her chair and studied her enemy through narrowed eyes.

"And, Ort?"

"Division Lord?"

"Kill that goddamn sphere."

"Working on it, sir."

The Six-A was now starting to take the threat seriously. Prior to the internal emergences, it had simply charged toward her ships at the head of its fleet, flinging microsingularities at her at long range. Its armor had shrugged off near and direct hits with ease, even the ten-gigaton warheads of the HSM missiles barely scratching the hull.

Now, however, a good chunk of that armor was missing and the beast was hurt. It was trying to dodge now—but it was also the only thing in the Infinite force that could reach Morgan's ships.

"Another singularity miss," Rogers reported. "That's one too far and one too short. I think we all know what comes next."

"I'm hoping for more misses," Morgan said with a forced chuckle. "Or for Ort to blow the damn thing to hell."

"Starfighters are out," her chief of staff told her. "They'll reach weapons range twenty seconds before everybody gets in missile range. They might do some good."

"They might die for nothing," Morgan replied. "But we need them."

"Shit!" Someone snapped. "Direct hit on *Tookoolale*. She's *gone*."

"Confirm that," Morgan barked. *Tookoolale* was one of the Laian starkillers. Her crew was small, only twenty-five, but the starkillers were still the point of this entire mission.

"Confirmed," Rogers reported a moment later. "Microsingularity emerged inside the starkiller power core and consumed sixty percent of the ship before evaporating. *Tookoolale*'s command pod was consumed as well.

"Her crew is gone."

"And so is a starkiller," Morgan replied. "Ort, *kill that sphere!*"

The operations officer didn't even bother to reply. He and four tactical officers were bending their every moment and thought toward that exact mission—and as Morgan snapped at him, he made a strange clicking sound.

"Hit," Ort reported. "I think a missile hit the breach. I have more fluid loss...and she is losing speed. More missiles are incoming."

"Hit!" Rogers snapped. "*Taxula* is gone. We're down another starkiller."

Taxula was one of the Wendira weapons, but it couldn't be coincidence that it was the STG's starkillers that were being hit. The Infinite knew *exactly* why Morgan was there.

And she realized that they were prepared to sacrifice the entirety of Swarm Echo to make sure she didn't have any starkillers left to fire.

CHAPTER FIFTY-SEVEN

Part of the planning assumptions around Morgan's mission—and the general strategic structure of the allies' response to the Infinite—had been that a lot of Swarm Bravo's intelligence had died with the swarm.

That theory started to fragment the moment the Wendira starfighters hit missile range of Swarm Echo. Irisha's fighters were veterans doing their work *perfectly*. Rapidly rotating formations, dispersed squadrons, seemingly chaotic maneuvers—everything that could make targeting them harder was being done.

But Echo was clearly expecting it. Missiles lashed out the moment the starfighters were in range, each of the Category Threes flinging at least a thousand missiles at the smaller ships. The patterns were broad wedges, covering as much space as possible until the missiles found a target.

"They've seen data on the starfighters," Morgan said quietly. "They shouldn't have. Only Bravo fought starfighters, and we wiped them out that day."

"That answers the question of whether Infinite have an FTL com, doesn't it?" Rogers replied. "Without relays, even hyperfold coms wouldn't have made it back to the Queen. They've some trick of their own."

"And today it won't save them," Morgan said. "Irisha's people are too good."

They weren't good enough to save *themselves*, but they were good enough that over half of the starfighters survived to reach hyperfold-cannon range of the Infinite fleet. Ten seconds after *that*, the fighter strike was over.

"All fighters confirmed lost," Rogers reported. "Estimate...fourteen Category Threes destroyed."

Fourteen ships bigger than Laian war-dreadnoughts, wiped out in exchange for thirteen hundred starfighters. It was probably a fair trade—the Drones who flew the starfighters would have called it a fair trade—but Morgan still hated it.

"Regular-missile range...*now*."

Rogers's report echoed in a suddenly quiet bridge.

"Engage as specified," Morgan ordered softly. Every one of her ships pulsed on the main display as they fired, hundreds of interface-drive missiles flashing onto the screen. She fired barely two thousand missiles.

The fifty remaining Category Threes and the half-wrecked-by-now Six-A fired *seventy* thousand back.

"Full defense screen deployed; all missiles targeted on the Six-A," Ort reported.

"I have the defense screen," Rogers reported. "All drones reported in, and I am interfaced with local control."

"Maybe we should have held the fighters for this," Morgan murmured. Sixty seconds of flight time was enough for her to regret her choices. Those thirteen hundred fighters would have been another twenty-six hundred hyperfold cannons to defend her fleet.

"We've got this, sir," Rogers replied. "We have shields. They don't."

"So far," Morgan muttered, but she kept that quiet. If Swarm Echo's bioforms had shields, she'd have seen them by now.

"Singularity hit," Rogers reported a moment later, shaking her head. "*Kozovan*, one of the Laian starkillers. She's gone."

They were now down three of eight starkillers, and Morgan could already guess the targeting path of the missile swarm.

"Pull the surviving starkillers back behind the rest of the task group," she ordered. "They've been targeting the starkillers as a priority so far. I doubt they've changed now we're in missile range."

The seconds were ticking away as the missiles crossed the void. Morgan's ships were running at an angle to the swarm, buying themselves time in each range bracket. They knew the Infinite had plasma cannons and hyperfold cannons—both had been thrown at the starfighters.

"Missiles hitting the perimeter," Rogers reported.

No one was giving details, but Morgan watched the cascade of red dots fall onto her fleet like a deadly rain...and disappear. There were multiple layers of defensive drones. Hyperfold-cannon-equipped drones were the farthest out and carried the longest-ranged weapons, lashing into the missiles while they were still millions of kilometers away.

The laser-equipped drones were next. They had the lowest kill rates of the three weapon systems in play but the second-longest range when backed by tachyon scanners. They took their own cut of the missiles—and then the survivors ran into the rapid-fire plasma cannons of the final internal screen, backed by the lasers, plasma guns and hyperfold cannons of the ships themselves.

The battered survivors lunged through, but their targeting was clearly confused. Thousands of missiles tried to pass *through* the fleet to engage the starkillers and were wiped out by guns firing from behind them.

Others took the targets in front of them, swarming onto the ships of the special task group—primarily the Wendira escorts.

Less than five hundred missiles hit *anything*—but over three hundred of them slammed into two Wendira fast escorts, ships that were designed to hide behind ten-megaton battleships.

"*Osofa* and *Kana* are down," Rogers reported grimly. "The escorts can't take that kind of firepower."

"And they're close enough in size to the starkillers to confuse the missiles," Morgan replied. "Fuck. How's that sphere looking, Ort?"

"We hit her, and we hit her hard," Ort replied. "She's dropped to point-four *c* and didn't fire in the latest missile salvo. She'd leaking fluid constantly, but she is still maneuvering after us."

"And firing singularities," Rogers reported grimly. "*Astarax* is gone. We're running out of starkillers, Division Lord."

"Keep focusing fire on that Six-A," Morgan told them. "Maintain the defensive screen, keep the starkillers back and clear them to maneuver independently. We can't shield them from the teleporter; we can only stop the missiles."

"Next wave is in the perimeter," Rogers reported.

The flag deck fell silent, people hoping not to distract the officers and techs buried deep in the dual process of saving them from the enemy's missiles—and killing the enemy before they launched again.

This time, none of the missiles were confused. All of them dove "down" and tried to dodge around Morgan's main body, driving to get at the starkillers she was protecting. She watched as Rogers turned drones and even sent the Laian cruisers diving toward the missiles at sixty percent of lightspeed to expand the defensive perimeter.

It wasn't enough. Missiles hammered into the starkillers, which were actually *tougher* than the escorts...but not tough enough.

The last singularity hit was as much insult to injury as anything else, and Morgan swallowed grimly as Swarm Echo completed their mission. All eight of the special task group's starkillers were gone.

"All starkillers lost," Rogers reported. "They... They mucked our targeting up pretty good there, sir."

"They've learned the game far better than I feared, Staff Captain," Morgan told her chief of staff quietly. "Now it's our turn."

"*Freeze in broken ice,*" Ort suddenly exclaimed. "We've got her. Chunks of armor breaking free; interface drive is offline. The Six-A is dead, I repeat, she is breaking up and *dead.*"

Morgan's attention turned back to her enemies. The big holo-gram showed exactly what Ort was saying—the last salvo of missiles had clearly managed to slip past the Infinite's defenses and hit the unarmored inside of the Category Six-A bioform.

Armor that could stand against a point-eight-five-c impactor coming from *outside* the hull was far less durable when hit from behind. Massive plates, the size of cities, spun off from the dying bioform as its drive signature cut to zero and massive sprays of fluid, easily visible from drones only a few million kilometers away, filled the void around the creature.

"Adjust your targeting," Morgan ordered coldly. "Take down the Threes."

It wasn't going to change anything, but it would buy her fleet *time*.

And maybe, eventually, Morgan would think of something to do with that time.

CHAPTER FIFTY-EIGHT

THE COMPUTER CENTER ON THE ANCIENT ALAVAN CONTROL station was starting to take on the look of a proper command-and-control facility. More holographic displays had been brought in and linked up to the molycirc core running everything—after Lawrence's teams had purged the Wendira hardware, of course.

There were Wendira scattered around in support positions, but it was Rin and his collection of scientists who were handling the various workstations. They had direct control of what the archaeologist suspected was the most powerful weapon in the known universe.

A quarter of his people were civilians who had been accompanying the Grand Fleet because of the unusual opportunity to interface with the Laians and survey their space. The rest were at least officers and navy technicians *as well* as scientists.

Still, it was an unusual assembly to be in control of a weapon, a crew that told the tale of how the Skiefail swarm had been converted into one.

"We are now in the time frame estimated for the arrival of the Battle Hives," Castellash told him. "Without contact, we cannot anticipate their exact arrival."

"I know," Rin agreed. While the messages they'd sent by hyper-fold would have been relayed to Fleet Commandant Icenar by star-com, the Wendira officer was unable to respond. They had to hope that the Battle Hives had received the message with its instructions.

Rin looked over the room, his dozens of scientists, the chandelier-esque Imperial computer core and the massive towers of black Alavan molecular circuitry that surrounded him.

"Commence system activation," he ordered, projecting his voice so everyone could hear him. He didn't spend nearly as much time teaching as the Imperial Institute of Archaeology might prefer, but he'd done enough to be able to make himself heard to a classroom.

Green lights flashed up on the holograms as the hyperfold links established and hybrid systems interrogated ancient hardware for readiness reports.

"Teleporter one is online."

"Teleporter two is online."

"Teleporter three is online." Lawrence reported the last activation herself, satisfaction in her voice. Teleporters one and two, after all, had been structurally intact and required only reprogramming and minor repairs.

Teleporter three had been struck by a meteorite at some point in the last fifty thousand years, and they hadn't even been sure they'd be able to bring it online. Lawrence had worked miracles there.

"All systems online," Rin reported aloud, for the recorders more than anything else. "Sensor board is clear. We have hyperfold links and active masking for all warships in the system."

"My vessel is prepared to sortie in defense of the swarm, if need-ed," Sub-Commandant Likox observed from one of the holograms. "Oxtashah has relocated to the expedition station."

Hopefully out of the line of fire of whatever came next, Rin reflected. Unfortunately, the expedition station was attached to the control station, and if the Infinite worked out what was going on, *that* was going to be their priority target.

"Scanners are clear except for masked signatures," he said aloud. "We are standing by for hyperfold links to create new signature masks."

Even if Icenar sent the links the moment his ships emerged from hyperspace, there wouldn't be time to mask them before the swarm fired. They needed the incoming Wendira ships to cut their drives the moment they entered the system and only bring them up *after* they were masked.

Not only would the teleporter destroy any Wendira ship that didn't cut its interface drive, that would expend one of their strictly limited number of shots. Rin would mourn the dead if there was a mistake—but they could easily end up mourning that wasted shot more.

"Now we wait," he told his team. "Please tell me someone brought coffee."

SEVENTEEN OF RIN'S fifty people were human, which meant there were actually *two* coffee machines that had made the migration to the control center. In total, there were seven devices that turned water into hot stimulants for various species.

He was on his fourth cup when the alarms finally blazed to life. Checking the time, he nodded silently to himself.

Hyperspace travel times were always a guess. There were currents and density changes and all sorts of things that affected how fast a ship traveled. Most were constant enough to be mapped and included in the projection, but none were *always* the same.

Generally, hyperspace was denser and ships moved faster as you drew closer to the core of the galaxy. There were always currents of denser space and patches of lighter space, no matter where you were, and all of these things had some random variation.

There was still an average "most expected" time, though, and

Fleet Commandant Icenar's survivors had arrived exactly in the middle of it.

"I have a lot of hyper portals," the Pibo tech watching the interface scanner told them. "Multiple ships passing through and cutting interface drives. Estimate...four hundred twenty contacts. Thirty are definitely star hives."

There was no range at which the hundred-megaton Wendira supercarriers wouldn't be clearly distinguishable from their escorts. Rin was no military expert, but that had always struck him as a bad idea.

"That's Icenar," he said aloud. "Stand by for incoming hyperfold links and prep the masks."

He wasn't sure he could mask four hundred–odd ships—but even the escorts would be detected and vaporized by the Skiefail Swarm.

"No additional contacts," the sensor tech reported. "Wendira fleet is drifting in-system at four hundred KPS. That won't get them to safety."

"No. They need to be invisible," Rin murmured. They weren't, and that meant they were going to lose more of Icenar's ships. There was nothing Rin could do to change that.

"We have a link with Icenar," Likox's hologram reported. "He's asking how many ships we can protect from the weapon."

"I don't know," Rin admitted. "In theory, all of them. In practice... I don't know."

There was a long pause.

"Even the escorts have three hundred souls aboard," Likox pointed out.

"I'd really prefer it if he didn't bring up his interface drives," Rin replied. "But I know what he's looking at. I need a live link to every ship so we can run the masking code. Do we have an ETA on the Infinite?"

"Three hundred forty seconds," the Wendira officer said grimly. "If Icenar's ships are still in easy range of where they hypered in..."

New links *finally* began to appear on Rin's dashboard, and his fingers flew across the console, linking the telemetry data he was receiving to the software that was scrubbing their existence from the Alavan sensor data.

"The hives are clear," Rin snapped. "I'm working my way down by order of mass—each ship should get a pingback when we've confirmed they're covered from the interface scanner."

"They need to watch that link. We *will* have enough warning to tell them if the mask fails, but only barely."

"Understood. Passing on the updates," Likox replied. "What happens now, Doctor Dunst?"

"We find out in five minutes if this was all for nothing," Rin told him. The star hives were now moving, blazing in-system at seventy percent of the speed of light. Unlike Imperial ships, Core Powers didn't really build an overload speed into their ships.

To push that far over their usual max of point-six *c* was dangerous, but Rin understood. The Infinite were likely to come out of hyperspace exactly where the Wendira had—and by now, everyone understood how bad an idea being within ten light-seconds of an Infinite Swarm was.

"Last of the star shields are now masked," his assistant told him. "Working on the escorts, but I think we're at the point where we're risking corruption of the overall sensor scan."

Rin exhaled and checked the clock.

"They can't get far enough to clear our targeting, can they?"

"No."

He turned to Likox.

"I'm sorry, Sub-Commandant," he told the Wendira. "We can't mask the escorts without risking our targeting of the Infinite. They're on their own."

"There are still fifty thousand people out there," Likox whispered, his wings snapping wide in an unconscious stress reaction.

"And if we're only a little lucky, we'll kill the bastards coming for them while they're still alive," Rin countered. "I don't like it any more than you do, Sub-Commandant. Quite possibly less. But we *have* to destroy Swarm Charlie—or two full Battle Hives died for *nothing*."

"Estimated emergence in sixty seconds," Lawrence barked. "Everything is online; containment is at full power. We're ready, Rin."

"We'd better be," Rin snapped, turning away from the link to the Wendira officer. "Because there are fifty thousand people out there who are going to die if we get this wrong."

That was just on the hundred and fifty–odd escorts still drifting near their emergence points, too. The *other* fifty-plus escorts, two hundred star shields and thirty star hives had over two *million* souls on board.

"Hyper portal! *Massive* hyper portal."

Everyone in the room turned to look at the main hologram as it spat out information on what they were looking at. The Infinite, it seemed, still weren't creating individual portals for their ships.

Instead, they had created a portal almost a hundred thousand kilometers in diameter, and the first ships through were a phalanx of twelve six-thousand-kilometer-long Category Six behemoths.

Rin's attention turned back to his own console as more bioforms flashed through the hyper portal, looking for a report that had to be there. It *had* to be...

There.

"Their drive has an interface signature," he snapped. They'd projected and analyzed and calculated and estimated—but the only copy of the strange Alavan scanner they had was the one he was using right now. They'd had no way to know for sure that their estimate of how the bioforms would look to the Alavan systems was right until that moment.

They were close enough, and Rin held his breath. Five seconds. Six. Seven. Ten. There was plasma in the containment chamber now and...

"Firing! All teleporters firing!" Lawrence's half-shouted report echoed through the command center. "Resequencing and firing again. Cycle time is three-point-four seconds.

"Station team, watch those containment fields!"

That was why there were Wendira Drones aboard the teleporter stations. They could watch the scanners tracking the plasma content coming in and adjust the shields in real time, far faster than even someone with a hyperfold command link.

"Did we get them?" Rin asked. "I need a report!"

"Escorts are reporting that the lead formation is *gone*," Likox's hologram proclaimed, his wings flickering in excitement. "Even the Category Sixes just...vaporized."

And more bioforms were pouring through the hyper portal. At least three hundred bioforms had entered the system, including another dozen Category Sixes—and every three and a half seconds, three more of them died.

"My god," Lawrence murmured. "What have we built?"

"What we set out to," Rin told her. "The ultimate trap. A mirror to the one that destroyed an entire Mesharom battle fleet."

The Infinite formation was chaos. They didn't even seem to know what was hitting them, and several units tried to dive back through the hyper portal, only to discover what the allies had known for a long time: given the energy levels involved, even a sustained portal was only one-way.

Then the portal vanished.

"Wait, are they all through?" Rin asked.

"Negative, anomaly scanners are still showing significant masses on the other side of the barrier," Likox told him. "They realized what was happening...but how? They can't have a starcom; they couldn't have transmitted back, could they?"

"At least one of the ships that made it through has emitters," Rin's aide barked. "Exit portal opening."

"And collapsing," Lawrence said grimly. "Not sure if that spiked their interface signature or what, but the teleporters just nailed the ship opening the portal."

"Of course it spikes their signature," Rin murmured. "My god. They can't run."

The Wendira escorts were still far too close to the Infinite, but with their drives down and death stalking the bioforms' ranks, the Infinite were ignoring them as they tried to run.

"According to the escorts' scanners, several dozen of the Infinite just flipped to an interface drive," Lawrence noted. "They're running...but they're just making themselves easier targets."

Rin forced himself to watch. If the Infinite had another drive system beyond their reactionless propulsion or their stolen interface drives, they didn't try it in time. Five and a half minutes after the wall of massive bioforms had entered the system, not a single bioform was left.

"Lawrence, status on the teleporters?" he asked softly.

"I'm...glad they ran," she said after a moment. "Three is done. Containment field nearly failed, and the on-board crew shut her down. No casualties, but the gun is out of commission. Probably permanently.

"One and Two are in better shape, but I'm not liking the insta-bility data I'm being forwarded." She shook her head. "It looks like we overestimated how many shots we were going to get, Rin. We fired a hundred and ten from each platform, and one is already gone and the other two are looking shaky.

"I don't think we'd have been able to handle another hundred bioforms," she concluded. "So, yeah. I am *very* glad they decided to run."

"What happens now?" Rin asked, glancing over at Likox.

"That's up to fleet command, I think," the Sub-Commandant suggested. "But if it were up to me...we'd go after what's left of Swarm Charlie with everything we have, Laians and Imperials included."

Rin exhaled a long sigh and tapped a series of commands, shutting down the interface scanner and, with it, the entire weapon.

"Your ships can all bring their drives back up," he told Likox. "I suspect the Skiefail swarm has done as much as it's going to for you. The Infinite aren't coming back to this system."

And neither, if Rin had any say in it, was he or any other Imperial!

CHAPTER FIFTY-NINE

"THAT MAKES THREE," ORT REPORTED, HIS VOICE SOFT AS another swarm emerged from a hyper portal. "I'm not sure this tactic is working."

"It's not and I never expected it to," Morgan admitted.

The special task group was running along the edge of the rosette at half the speed of light. The battle with the ambushing swarm had left them wounded and battered, missing half the Wendira escorts and one of the battleships along with the starkillers, but they were still there.

Unfortunately, the Infinite knew that. Three new forces—detachments from Swarm Delta, Morgan presumed—had now entered normal space at the edge of the impermeable zone around the rosette.

They were carrying out long, sweeping patrols that cut off any exit for Morgan's fleet, but something still didn't feel quite right.

"Why aren't they coming after us?" she asked aloud. She looked around at her staff, all present on the flag deck and all looking exhausted after thirty hours of running. "Any of the three detachments we've seen since Swarm Echo could have taken us out, but they're hovering at the edge of the impermeable zone, just...waiting."

"We did kick the shit out of Swarm Echo," Rogers suggested. "Maybe we're making them nervous?"

"We used up seventy percent of our HSMs and thirty percent of our sublight missiles doing that," Morgan pointed out. "Not to mention losing every one of our starfighters, five of the Wendira escorts, all eight starkillers and *Tan!Loka*. They have to know they hurt us."

"Or do they?" Ort asked suddenly, the operations officer suddenly sitting up straighter. "They know we're here. No question about that. They knew our original course, obviously. They can clearly pin down roughly what direction we're going...but what if they can't actually *see* us through the stealth fields?"

Morgan looked at the operations officer and blinked.

"Walk me through it," she ordered.

New shaded zones appeared on the map in front of the operations officer, then duplicated themselves on the main display at Morgan's order.

"Let's say they've got a one-light-thousandth-cycle error radius on detecting us through the stealth field," Ort suggested. "Eighty-four light-seconds. So, a *fifty-million-kilometer*-diameter zone we could be in."

A shaded zone appeared around their course, marking that error radius.

"So, they don't know where we *are*, but they can tell what course we're following," the ops officer continued. "If they can detect us at that eighty-four light-seconds, those patrols will make sure we can't escape without being detected and engaged—but if they come in *after* us, they can't guarantee the same."

"Okay, I see it," Morgan told the Ivida. "Except that an eighty-four light-second variance on their detection of us would *not* have let them put Swarm Echo directly in our path the way they did.

"They had our target and our emergence point estimated to within ten light-seconds, maybe less," she continued. "There's no way they'd have a different scan error now unless..."

She trailed off as it struck her. She turned to look at the red-highlighted shapes on a different screen, one that listed their losses, and swallowed a curse.

"A starkiller is an Alavan star drive," she announced.

Everyone on the flag deck looked at her in confused surprise.

"Sir?" Rogers asked.

"The first starkillers were created when the Mesharom attempted to duplicate their masters' jump drive," Morgan told them. "Not something we really publicize, because we're not supposed to know that much about the starkillers' origins.

"But they are, mechanically and materially, an Alavan jump drive. Which means if there is one goddamn thing in the entire *fucking* universe that the Infinite could detect, no matter what we did, it's a goddamn starkiller."

The miniature versions, the Final Dragon weapons she'd carried on *Defiance*, might be safe. But the regular destroyer-sized weapons were straight-up, barely modified Alavan star drives. The Infinite knew their old enemy better than anyone else still living.

"They saw right through our stealth fields because eight of our ships, the weapons that were the entire purpose of our mission, were basically brilliant beacons to their scanners," Morgan concluded.

"And now the starkillers are *gone*, they can't see us nearly as well."

"I don't like the price, but that might be handy, since we've already paid it," Rogers said grimly. "What do we do?"

Morgan looked at the three red splotches on the display and sighed.

"I wish I had coms with the rest of the galaxy," she admitted. They weren't even *receiving* messages. The distorting effect of this many stars in close conjunction was blocking starcom reception as well as hyperfold transmission.

"We don't even know what happened with Swarm Charlie, and we can't tell anyone that our mission is a bust," she continued. "All we can do is save ourselves, realizing that everyone is going to think we're dead."

"That sounds like you have a plan, sir," Rogers pointed out.

"It does, doesn't it?" Morgan murmured, studying the display and its shaded error zone around their trip—and the overlay marking the chaos that the rosette was inflicting on hyperspace scanners.

"We're at the narrowest part of the impermeable zone created between realspace and hyperspace by the rosette," she said. "It's thirty light-cycles across here—larger inside the stars than outside, constructive interference being what it is.

"The rosette's radiation and gravity patterns also screw with real-space sensors, though not as badly, and will augment the stealth fields' effects."

The rosette was also a full light-year across. Tiny in the grand scheme of things, especially for a formation of a dozen blue stars, but immense by any practical standard.

"We go inside the rosette," Morgan decided aloud. "We use it to reinforce our stealth fields and we run dark at a random angle. For...a hundred cycles, at least.

"Even the Infinite can't blockade every possible exit from the Eye of the Astoroko Nebula," she said. "So, we go deep and we run long. If we're in the impermeable zone and hiding behind stars for a hundred cycles, that's a fifty-to-sixty-light-cycle-radius zone we can emerge in.

"Everyone outside is going to think we're dead," she repeated. "But we have the supplies for it. Hell, we have the supplies to do it and run all the way back to the Imperium if things *really* go to shit in those hundred days."

"I don't...hate it," Rogers said. "Koumans? Your thoughts."

The battleship's Captain looked as exhausted as the flag staff.

"I'm not sure any of us are thinking clearly, but it makes sense," she conceded. "If nothing else, we dramatically expand the error radius of their scans and force them to either commit more ships or spread them more thinly.

"And if they spread them thin enough, we might be able to punch out and make a run for it."

"It pretty much doesn't matter what we do; we're going to have to fight our way out," Morgan told them. "But the more we confuse them, the less forces they have directly in position, and the more likely we are to make it through."

"It makes sense to me," Koumans said. "And it's your call, Division Lord."

That sent a chill down Morgan's spine, and she looked at the map and the icons of her fleet. Even with her losses, there were still thirty ships under her command. The better part of forty thousand people.

"Our mission has already failed," Morgan noted. "The only task left to me is to extract as much of my command intact as possible. This is the best choice we've got. Ort—work with the navigators, get the course set.

"Once we're closer to the stars, we'll stand down to status three and send most of the crews to sleep," she continued. "We all need rest, or this is going to get worse fast."

CHAPTER SIXTY

Morgan hadn't planned on sleeping for twelve hours, but that was how long her communicator said she'd been asleep when she finally woke up. A quick check of the ship's status told her that they hadn't quite made it to the theoretical line that marked the "surface" of the rosette, but also that nothing was pursuing them.

She took the time to properly shower and re-braid her hair before putting on her uniform and returning to the flag deck. The short ritual made her feel both cleaner and more human.

Everything she could do to sharpen her mind was important now. It would be another thirty hours, in her judgment, before they were entirely safe from detection. They wouldn't—they *couldn't*—be at battle stations for all of that time, but that was the time where quick decisions might still be needed.

Only a portion of her staff was on duty when she stepped onto the bridge, exactly as it should have been. Ort was the senior officer on duty, rising as she entered and gesturing for her to join him.

"I'm glad you're here, Division Lord," he greeted her. I didn't want to wake you, but there's something strange going on."

"Good strange or bad strange?" Morgan asked, standing beside the Ivida's chair and looking at the man's screens—currently showing a series of visual reports from *Odysseus*'s Fleet Operations Center.

"Strange strange, I think," Ort said after a moment's thought. "Take a look. This is Delta-Six, the third pursuit swarm to come into regular space after us, and their course over the last six hours."

Morgan noticed the time stamps first.

"This is nearly real-time," she noted. "How?"

"This is our vulnerable period, so I took the initiative to lay a series of drones behind us," Ort told her. "The farthest drones can't hyperfold-transmit to *us*, but they can transmit to the drones along the chain. As we pass through the rosette, it will become impossible to sustain even that, but it gives us eyes close to the enemy now...and I think it may have just proven its worth."

"Well done; show me the course data," Morgan said.

Delta-Six's course was much what it had been before initially, a series of carefully calculated curves that limited the STG's ability to escape without detection. And then, suddenly, the Swarm's course sharpened into a straight line.

Morgan checked the vector and raised an eyebrow.

"Have they entered hyperspace yet?" The course was straight away from the rosette, likely making certain they'd cleared the impermeable zone where entering hyperspace would be impossible.

"Not yet, but that's my read of their course as well," Ort told her. "It'll be another hour before I have data on Delta-Five and Delta-Four, but...if they've both broken off pursuit as well, something's going on."

"Something happened we don't know about," Morgan agreed. "The Queen can't afford to tie up a thousand bioforms hunting for us. But..." Morgan shook her head. "The Infinite have more units than we can count, don't they? They don't even have any of the big ones in the pursuit swarms; they're just Threes and Fours."

Just ships between one and one hundred kilometers in length. Dealing with the Infinite was completely throwing off her sense of scale.

"My guess would be that somebody *else* just hit the edge of the nebula and they're redeploying to secure their perimeter," Ort told her. "Or...they're worried someone's going to."

"If Swarm Charlie just got its ass kicked, they might be worried about their perimeter," Morgan agreed. "But they've got a lot of resources. In their place, Charlie would have had to be completely wrecked before I started redeploying the people hunting the guys *in* my territory.

"That sounds like the Wendira may have surprised them?" Ort asked.

"Have the group hold position here," Morgan ordered. "We'll wait for the data update on Delta-Four and Delta-Five.

"If all three Delta groups have entered hyperspace, we don't need to hide inside the rosette. If there's no one hunting us, I'll take the risk of making an outright run for it!"

TWO HOURS LATER, Morgan had woken up her flag staff and everyone was gathered around her in a briefing room—including Irisha and Protan, attending by hologram.

"All three of the pursuit swarms broke off two and a half hours ago," she told them. "Simultaneously, so far as we can tell, which says they have some kind of FTL com that works in this mess.

"Most importantly, though, that means we are no longer being blockaded. I am inclined to take the task group and make an immediate run for open space," she said. "I wanted to check in with everyone before we make quite so drastic a change in plans."

"I prefer it to spending a hundred cycles running in the dark," Irisha replied. "But my people are no longer truly capable of contributing to a fight. My star intruders have only defensive weapons left, and all of my remaining escorts are damaged."

"My cruisers are undamaged," Protan said. "We can make the

run, and we can position ourselves to protect what remains of the Wendira fleet."

Her holographic gaze focused on her people's ancient enemy. "Your people have borne the brunt of this mission, Sub-Commandant, but I believe my people can keep them safe for the way home."

Morgan was actually touched. Fighting on the same side seemed to be doing a *lot* of good for the Wendira and the Laians. It gave her hope.

"We are not sure how well our stealth fields work against the Infinite in hyperspace," Ort warned. "This is a risk."

"It will always be a risk," Morgan replied. "It is possible, even, that this is a trap. They could easily have recognized what we were doing and created what appeared to be a tempting opportunity to escape.

"We're going to watch our anomaly scanners with extreme care as we get close to our portal point," she told them. "*Hopefully*, we should see any ambush before we transit into hyperspace.

"But I think we have to take the risk. A hundred cycles in here will leave the families of all of our people thinking they are dead. A hundred cycles of running and hiding will damage the mental and physical health of our crews.

"If we have the opportunity to break out, I feel we have to take it," she concluded. "But...I am still prepared to accept arguments as to why we shouldn't."

The briefing room was quiet and she looked around. There were half a dozen species in the room. A dozen in her task group. They mostly had different cultures—the A!Tol and the Imperial Races were a special case—and different assessments of risk and courage.

All of them returned her gaze.

"I think we have to try, sir," Bethany Rogers finally said, speaking for all of them. "We owe it to our people to get them to safety—and we owe it to the people we left outside the nebula to report on our mission.

"It's a risk, but we're all soldiers. We made our choices when we swore our oaths and put on our uniforms. Our duty is out there, Division Lord Casimir, and I think we need to go find it."

"Unanimous, then?" Morgan asked her officers with a small smile. "I wasn't quite expecting that, but I was hoping for it.

"Talk to your departments; put together your operations plans. We're still probably going to have to punch through a picket, though we may be able to dodge around everybody. Plan for a running fight, people.

"But plan for getting us all out of here."

CHAPTER SIXTY-ONE

There had been no Infinite bioforms visible on their scanners, even through the daisy-chained probes, for a full cycle—over twenty-three hours—when Morgan finally ordered her people to make a run for it.

"We watch the starcom receivers closely as we move," she ordered as the ships came back up to their full speed. "We're still cycles away from picking up a signal, but the sooner we have an update on the outside world, the better."

"If they pulled all their units back, Swarm Charlie probably got smashed up pretty well," Rogers estimated. "But I'd love confirmation of that."

"We won't get it until we're at least a realspace light-year from the rosette," Morgan said. "But I want to *know*, not guess."

"They could still have the entirety of Swarm Delta sitting just on the other side of the hyperspace barrier," her chief of staff warned.

"I know," Morgan agreed. "And we're going to be ready to turn and run at any sign of trouble. We've got a full watch on every anomaly scanner in the task group. We'll know if it's an ambush."

"Will we know before it's too late?" Rogers asked.

Morgan glanced around the flag deck to make sure no one was close enough to overhear their half-whispered conversation.

"Forty-sixty," she admitted. "But we owe it to our people to try to make it out of this mess. The sooner we're in open space, the happier I'll be. If I never see this nebula again, it will be too soon."

"It has certainly made an impression, hasn't it?" Rogers agreed. "We're over thirty hours from being able to enter hyperspace, sir. Standard watches and schedules?"

"Until the final hour," Morgan confirmed. "Once we're close enough that they can come out of hyperspace *inside* our weapons' range, I want everyone at battle stations until we've made the transition."

"At least we're not running in blind."

"We are very much running blind," Morgan confessed. "But we're never *not* going to be running blind, Bethany. It's this or three goddamn *months* in this place, and I am so, *so* done with this nebula and this goddamn necklace of stars."

Rogers chuckled softly.

"I don't think anyone in the STG is going to argue with you there," she admitted. "I'm down for the run, sir; you already knew that."

"Everyone is," Morgan said. Not many people *wouldn't* be down for trying to escape being trapped by the enemy. It was her job, as Division Lord and task group commander, to judge whether running was the right call.

She was...eighty-ish percent sure she'd made the right call.

DESPITE HER OWN orders to make sure that everyone got enough rest, Morgan ended up having to take medication to sleep around hour twenty-four.

She returned to the bridge, once again having taken the time to shower, braid her hair and even do her makeup. She made sure to *look* her best as she led forty thousand people to an unknown fate she was unquestionably responsible for.

"Anything on the anomaly scanners?" was the first thing she asked.

"Nothing," Ort replied. "Of course, we're still a light-hour from the edge of the impermeability zone. It *looks* like their singularity teleporters have around the same three-light-thousandth-cycle range as our hyperspace missiles, so it's not until we're in that area that we're in danger."

And then they'd detect anything that had been in place since at least five minutes before. If it was a trap...they'd see it coming, but Morgan wasn't sure they'd see it coming in time.

"Take the group to battle stations," she ordered. "We're in the final stretch of the realspace run. Full stealth-field checks on every ship."

With other ships to hand, that involved dropping the com links temporarily and doing everything they could to find the ship without knowing where it was. At the range of the task group's formation, the stealth fields *were* defeatable, but it still allowed them to assess if the systems were working as expected.

"On it," Ort agreed.

There were no lights and alarms on the flag deck to denote battle stations, but Morgan could hear the faint echo of the alarm echoing through the rest of the ship.

Her staff and their teams filed in over the next minute—fast enough to tell her that everyone had been anticipating the call to battle stations. Within ninety seconds, every station on the flag deck was full, and she had a virtual link up to the battleship's bridge.

"All ships have checked in," Ort reported. "Laian cruisers are assuming escort positions around the Wendira ships."

If nothing else came of this mission, that sight offered Morgan hope for the future. The Laian warships had formed a defensive sphere around the star intruders and escorts, interlacing the defensive drones from both fleets and positioning the Republic ships to take any hits aimed at the Hive vessels.

Enemies all too recently, today the Laians were positioning themselves to defend the more-vulnerable Wendira ships.

"All ships in formation," Rogers told Morgan, a few moments after the chief of staff took her own seat. "All stealth fields have passed the testing sequences. We are as good to go as we're going to be."

"Thank you," Morgan said calmly, leaning back in her chair. A single command brought a timer onto the main display, counting down the thousandth-cycles until they could enter hyperspace—and a second timer, on the screens of her own seat, counting down the minutes.

"TWO HUNDREDTH-CYCLES TO PORTAL," Ort announced.

Twenty-eight minutes. Too long for Morgan to hold her breath. Too short for her to not feel completely on edge along with every other member of the task group.

"Anomaly scanners are still clear?" she asked.

"So far," the Ivida confirmed.

Fourteen light-minutes. They weren't quite into the danger zone, but they were close enough that they should, in theory, be able to see an ambushing force. The problem was that the anomaly scanner was lightspeed-limited in realspace.

It was entirely possible that something was a realspace light-day or more away and would still be in position by the time they reached the edge of the impermeable zone. On the other hand, they weren't already there.

That gave Morgan at least some hope.

She checked the reports coming in from her task group. Everything was showing green except for munitions stocks and the escorts. There was no way to replenish their missiles there, or to repair the battered escorts that had borne the brunt of the missiles that hadn't found starkillers.

If they had to fight, it would be over quickly one way or another.

"Wait," Ort suddenly snapped. "Anomaly contacts! Multiple anomaly contacts!"

Morgan's attention jerked to the main screen as their destination zone suddenly acquired purple-red contacts. The contacts were moving fast—it was hard to tell what their hyperspace velocity was, but their pseudovelocity was massive multiples of *c*.

"*Portal opening.*"

One moment, everything had been quiet.

The next, the largest hyperspace portal Morgan had ever seen tore through the barrier between realspace and hyperspace. A full light-second across, it overwhelmed their anomaly scanners into useless static—and the waves of Cherenkov radiation pulsing out from it rendered half of their other sensors blind.

"Sensors are blinded," Ort announced. "Passive visuals are down. Infrared is down. Radar is overwhelmed. Tachyon scanners are still live; I have contacts coming through the portal."

"ID them now!" Morgan ordered.

"I make them Category Seven," Rogers said, her voice suddenly flat and utterly toneless. "I repeat, multiple Category Seven contacts. Estimate at least five, possibly six."

"We've only seen eight of the bastards in *total*," Morgan replied. "What the *hell*?"

She could see the same reports, the reports that had broken Rogers' hope for escape. The massive, eighty-thousand-kilometer-long forms of the Category Sevens stood out starkly on the anomaly scanners.

There were other bioforms there too, at least fifty Sixes and Fives, but the Sevens dwarfed everything else into insignificance.

And then the entire portal pulsed again as a new contact came through, the one that had required the portal to be that large and whose presence overwhelmed the Category Sevens as thoroughly as they'd overwhelmed everything else.

"I have a Category *Eight* contact," Ort announced uselessly, staring at his screens as the portal closed and the Infinite Queen was suddenly fully visible to every scanner Morgan's fleet possessed.

CHAPTER SIXTY-TWO

THIS TIME, THERE WAS NO GAS GIANT TO CONCEAL THE FULL extent of the Queen's leviathan bulk. She was the same roughly spermatoid shape as her lesser siblings, but she dwarfed even the already-immense Category Sevens.

Forty thousand kilometers across at her widest point and almost two hundred thousand kilometers long, the behemoth exceeded anything mobile Morgan had ever seen except the sun eater. *That* had been an Alava-modified Infinite that had consumed multiple entire suns over the last fifty years.

The Queen was larger than worlds. Larger than *gas giants*, though not as large as the immense super-Jovian near-star she'd slumbered in. Nothing that large had any right to move at all, but the Queen moved.

And moved *quickly*.

"I'm reading interface-drive signatures on *all* of them," Ort reported quietly. "The Queen is moving at point-seven *c*."

"Bring us about," Morgan ordered desperately. "Get us away from them. *Now*."

She suspected the Infinite were still having problems localizing her fleet. So, they'd brought enough ships that it didn't matter.

"Sir..."

It took Morgan a moment to place the officer speaking. Her communications officer hadn't been a critical part of their mission for a while, with the only communications being inside the task force.

"What is it?" she asked the Catach officer.

"We are receiving a transmission from the Queen," the carapaced mammal said quietly.

"Sanitize and play," Morgan ordered. "Everybody else, keep us running. Take us to full speed."

She'd communicated with the Queen before—but that had ended badly. She didn't see any reason why this would change.

There were twenty light-minutes between them and the Infinite were gaining at twenty percent. Her orders would cut that to ten, but full speed reduced the effectiveness of their stealth.

The Wendira and Laian units could get up to point-six-five c, but the Imperial ships couldn't do that without going to sprint mode—and sprint mode could only be pushed for about ten hours.

"Playing the message," Litcha reported.

The voice wasn't the booming overwhelm of poorly translated and modulated voice transmission that the Queen had used before— or that the sun eater had adopted. It was a calmer voice now, speaking in Laian instead of Alava.

"Your NestBurner escorts are gone. Tell us, TinyLife, are you still slaves?"

Morgan looked at Litcha.

"Commander? Is that it?" she asked.

"Yes, sir," the Catach confirmed. Much of the young alien's face was invisible, their armor plating having unconsciously compressed around their snout and eyes in a defensive mode.

"We are not slaves," Morgan murmured. "What do they think is going on?"

"You said..." Rogers trailed off.

"Rogers?"

"You said the starkillers were Alavan star drives," her chief of staff said slowly.

"Yeah. Almost exact duplicates for the standard unit," Morgan agreed.

"The Infinite might have thought they *were* Alavan ships," Rogers pointed out. "That would explain why they targeted them first, almost as well as them knowing what the starkillers were."

Morgan exhaled a breath.

"Well, that's an interesting disaster, isn't it?" she murmured. "Do we play along to see what she says...or tell the truth?"

"We can't outrun them, sir," Rogers told her. "They've got us pinned against the rosette, and I don't think we can make it far enough for the stealth fields to hide us."

Morgan considered the message and stared at the massive bioforms hunting her fleet. She could lie...and maybe squeeze her fleet out.

But this was the first time any warship had received communications from the Infinite since she'd fled from them in *Defiance*. Truth might buy them something more important than one fleet.

Truth might buy them *peace*.

"Radio transmission, I assume?" she asked Litcha.

"Yes, sir.

"Then we'll send one back. Translate into Laian for them."

"Yes, sir," the Catach confirmed.

"We were never slaves," Morgan said into the recorder. "The Nest Burners are long, *long* dead."

She considered adding more, then shrugged.

"Send it."

The transmission time was dropping rapidly, but the Infinite were still almost twenty light-minutes away. Every ten minutes that passed took away another light-minute of that safety, but it still took four minutes for Morgan to get a response.

"Message received, sir," Litcha reported.

"Play it."

"The NestBurners could not die," the Queen's voice insisted. "They were un-destroyable. You serve them as all who came before you did."

Morgan sighed again, considering what she could do.

"Time to HSM range?" she asked softly.

"Seventy thousandth-cycles," Ort reported quietly. "They are at one-light-hundredth-cycle."

Morgan nodded and looked at her staff.

"I figure we talk," she told them. "We try to convince her of the truth and see if maybe, just maybe, we can talk her down."

"The odds are not in your favor, sir," Rogers pointed out.

"Oh, the odds are *fucked*," Morgan agreed bluntly. "But it's the only chance I see."

She gestured for Litcha to record and leaned into the microphone.

"I am Division Lord Morgan Casimir of the A!Tol Imperial Navy," she told the Infinite firmly. "I am not and have never been a slave. The Nest Burners, the Alava, destroyed themselves fifty thousand years ago.

"We serve no one. We defend ourselves against you and the war you bring to us."

She ended the recording and considered whether that was the right tack to take for several seconds.

In the end, she shook her head. It was what her stepmother would have done.

"Send it," she ordered.

The response would be faster now. They were sliding closer and closer to the extreme range at which they could fire—and Morgan had few illusions. There were hundreds of bioforms pursuing her, including some of the largest she'd ever seen.

When their singularity teleporters came into range of her fleet, they were all going to die.

"We have a response, sir," Litcha said quietly. "Playing."

"TinyLife in DeadFlesh are ever slaves and ever bound. And you say this is no more?" The Queen's voice was curious more than angry. "If not NestBurners, what did we destroy? Why do you fight?"

Every eye on *Odysseus*'s flag bridge was on Morgan as she breathed and thought.

"Range?" she asked.

"Nine light-thousandth-cycles."

"All right. All non-Imperial ships will go to maximum velocity at eight light-thousandth-cycles," Morgan ordered calmly. "The battleships will go to full sprint at seven light-thousandth-cycles."

She shook her head.

"I don't like leaving the Wendira and Laians behind, but what else can we do?" she asked rhetorically. "We buy time."

Her task group began to separate on her screen as the Core Power ships pulled ahead by five percent of lightspeed.

"And the Queen?" Rogers asked.

"We keep talking," Morgan replied. "Litcha, get ready to transmit."

Everyone turned to their tasks and Morgan marshaled her thoughts, trying to find not just the words that would save her fleet... but potentially the words that could end the war.

The Queen hadn't spoken to anyone *else*, after all.

"We came here with weapons of great power," Morgan finally said. "We came here to destroy you and your nest, to save our children and our nests from the war you have brought to us.

"We did not choose this lightly, but your attacks upon our worlds left us no choice. We did not wish this war, but we will destroy you to protect our own."

She gestured for Litcha to send the message before she could rethink it, and caught herself holding her breath as the lightspeed lag passed.

"Battleships are activating sprint mode," Rogers told her. "We are now holding the range at seven light-thousandth-cycles." The Staff Captain paused. "Do you think this is the right track to take, sir?"

"I don't know," Morgan confessed. "But I feel like lies might save *us*...but the truth might save everyone."

They passed the twenty-minute mark and Morgan *did* hold her breath. No response came. Silence.

"Sir," Ort said slowly. "The Infinite...they've cut their velocity to point-six-five. They've matched vee and course with the Wendira-Laian formation and are holding the range at seven light-thousandth-cycles."

"What?" Morgan asked. "That makes no..."

"Incoming message."

Litcha didn't even ask. They played the message instantly.

"We... The Infinite *know* you, TinyLife DivisionLordMorgan-Casimir," the Queen said. "You were the first to find us. When we were desperate. When we were mad. And you spoke then as you speak now.

"Those who came after you did not speak. They unleashed fire upon the Infinite. Only fire has passed between the Infinite and those we believed were NestBurnerSlaves since.

"And NestBurner weapons have been turned upon us, and you bore death into our very nests. We know you, TinyLife DivisionLord-MorganCasimir, but no other TinyLife has attempted speech except the afraid."

"Oh, good, they remember me," Morgan said faintly. "Which Alavan weapon did we turn on them?"

"I don't know," Rogers admitted. "But that might fit with our original assumption that Swarm Charlie had been badly defeated. They might well have been relocating her and the Cat-Sevens when we started looking like a handy contained sample for a discussion."

"Fuck." Morgan looked at the main display. The Queen was holding position at seven light-thousandth-cycles—basically ten light-minutes from the closest of Morgan's ships. The Infinite were clearly waiting for *something*. "Would you believe me if I told you that the people who shot at you were rogues, given that I don't think we've tried to talk to them since?"

"To be fair, they shot first when they met Tan!Stalla," Rogers pointed out. "Everybody has been *real* trigger-happy. Facing the unknown does that."

"Fuck," Morgan repeated. "And yet...she's waiting because she wants to hear what we have to say."

"Yep. All on you, Division Lord. Did your stepmother teach you how to handle impossible negotiations with overwhelming force?"

"Yeah. *Have a trump card*," Morgan replied. "I don't have one. All I have is the truth."

"Then make that your trump card, sir," Rogers suggested. "Because so far...it's working."

Morgan inhaled and nodded.

"Right. Litcha, record, please."

She leaned into the microphone again.

"We met here, you and I," she told the Infinite. "Among the ring of stars that trapped you for fifty thousand years. I offered peace and you fired on my ship. Those who came after were hunters, renegades like the ship I destroyed inside that same ring of stars."

That she'd fought and destroyed a conspirator cruiser in the Eye before realizing the Infinite were there should help, she hoped.

"They came for the Nest Burner ships you destroyed fifty thousand years ago," she told the Infinite. "To turn those ships upon our nests and betray their kin. As I suspect you know some Nest Burners did.

"I offered you peace once, and you unleashed fire upon me. When our ships met yours again, you unleashed fire once more without a word of warning. This is all the Infinite's doing, and everything we have done has been to defend *our* nests."

Morgan paused, breathing in as she reached for the right words.

"Is there another way?"

The message left, winging its way across ten light-minutes of the void as Morgan refused to even *dare* hope that the answer could be what she needed.

"Sir, we're receiving a data transmission," Litcha said. "Laian format and protocol. I'm sanitizing, but it will take a moment."

"No audio?" Morgan asked.

"Not yet."

"Show me the data once it's ready."

That took a full two minutes, eventually resolving in a Laian-style tactical plot that Litcha was able to project into the middle of the flag deck. The iconography was...wonky, but Morgan could make out that she was looking at an Infinite force—she guessed Swarm Charlie—entering a hyper portal.

"Fascinating; they're getting live updates from realspace," Rogers noted. "Relayed from the ships that have already gone through. We have problems doing that."

"Why are they showing us this?" Morgan asked—and then the bioforms started disappearing. *Big* bioforms. Just vanishing in balls of...starstuff.

"My god," she whispered. "Did they give us data on the rest of the system?"

"Some, sir," Litcha confirmed. "Showing now."

It confirmed what Morgan suspected.

"We duplicated the Taljzi Dyson swarm weapon," Morgan said. "My god, they must have pulled Rin and dozens of others into that."

"And they gutted Swarm Charlie with a weapon that was unquestionably Alavan in origin," Rogers concluded. "Damn."

"Audio transmission coming in now, sir," Litcha reported.

"This is the work of your TinyLife," the Queen told Morgan. "NestBurner weapons. We have seen these. We have seen these tear apart worlds and murder nests. This is what your TinyLife have wrought.

"And now fleets of your kin swarm toward this nest. They believe they have an advantage, but there is not enough DeadFlesh in these stars to challenge a Nest of the Infinite. But."

There was a long pause, and Morgan thought the message had ended.

"We have searched the stars," the Queen resumed again. "We have searched the light of untold suns and rocks and nebulae, and not one scrap of our kindred remains. We do not know what horror the NestBurners unleashed, but the Infinite are no more.

"But we remain and we will not die."

Morgan was silent, considering the Queen's position.

"Rogers," she murmured. "Do we know enough about the Alavan special project to say if the rosette might have shielded the Eye from some of its effects?"

"No," her chief of staff said with a bitter chuckle. "Literally all we know is that they broke the laws of physics and rewrote the conductivity potential of seventy-plus percent of inorganic material in the galaxy."

"But it would make sense, wouldn't it?" Morgan said. "If the rosette delayed some of the impact of the change, the Infinite inside the Eye of the Astoroko Nebula might have adapted without even realizing it.

"But the Infinite outside would have died with their enemies. Potentially, the Alavan modifications to the cloner and the Great Mother saved them, but the rest of the Infinite didn't have those. These are literally all that is left of their species."

"And if they're going to eat suns and worlds, I'm not sure that's a bad thing, sir," her chief of staff told her.

"Except they're not," Morgan noted. "They held Tohrohsail for days and harmed no one who didn't fight them. They allowed humanitarian cargo missions; they...acted like reasonable occupiers who happened to be giant organic starships."

"What are you thinking, sir?" Rogers asked.

"I think we have a chance to do the goddamn impossible," Division Lord Morgan Casimir told her subordinate. "I think we have a chance to end a war that never should have happened and save a species that is utterly unique in the galaxy."

CHAPTER SIXTY-THREE

Hundreds of massive biological starships charged through deep space, filling Morgan's sensors with a slow pulse of radiation and heat she could only describe as a heartbeat. Her thirty surviving starships fled before them at the same speed, keeping exactly ten light-minutes between the two fleets as Morgan considered what she wanted to say.

Her gaze and attention were inevitably drawn to the image of the Infinite Queen, and she studied the being she was talking to more closely than she ever had before. They had hyperfold-equipped drones surprisingly close in now, and the true visual of the Queen was awe-inspiring.

The bioform was a pale red color, with blue and purple stripes the width of continents running along her length. It was clear where missile launchers and new systems had been mounted on her hide as cyborg installations—and it was *also* clear, with actual visual data, where old hardtech systems had been stripped away, leaving scars the size of starships.

Those weren't her only scars, either. Massive gouges, at least one the depth of a medium-size *planet*, had been blasted into the Queen's flesh over the millennia. The wounds were closed over now, but the dents and scars remained.

For all of her massive bulk, parts of the Queen were surprisingly delicate. Flaps and tentacles were scattered across her surface, serving purposes Morgan could barely begin to guess—though at least one was definitely concealing a group of infant Infinite bioforms; she saw one of the creatures poke its head out before a muscular flap irresistibly herded it back inside its mother's flesh.

Morgan marshaled her thoughts as the situation remained frozen, and then finally activated the recorder.

"We do not wish to end you," she told the Infinite. "And I do not believe you wish to end *us*. We are both afraid. Afraid of what we don't understand, afraid of a clear and present threat. Our rogues attacked you, but you attacked us.

"You struck our fleets and our bases, seeking to defend yourself, and so we destroyed and trapped your swarms in turn. If we play this out, we will destroy each other for nothing.

"You do not *need* our worlds or stars," she guessed. "Any system, even ones useless to us, can feed the Infinite. We can share this galaxy and learn from each other.

"But to do that, the fighting has to stop. There can be another way."

How Morgan was going to pull that off, she didn't know yet, but she kept speaking and the answer fell out of her mouth, almost as much a surprise to her as anyone else.

"If the Infinite withdraw to this nebula and promise to *negotiate* for access to systems and resources, I can convince the fleets that are coming to stand down," she promised. "We can...reset our interactions.

"We can try again, from the presumption of peace. We *can* end this war."

The Infinite possessed abilities even the Mesharom didn't understand. The Queen herself had likely seen thousands of years of history prior to the Alavan Fall. They could learn so much from the Infinite, and yet they were so close to destroying each other.

"Do you think she'll buy it?" Rogers asked.

"I think she stopped outside weapons range because she was waiting for something like this," Morgan told the other woman. "I think the Queen *wants* peace. I think she wants to talk to us, to learn about the galaxy where she has found herself.

"But above all else, I think the Queen wants to preserve the Infinite—and these are all that are left."

Twenty minutes. For twenty minutes, Morgan waited. She managed not to get up and pace, concealing her nervousness and her fear from her staff. If she'd guessed wrong, the Infinite would destroy her task group.

Then they'd probably destroy the combined fleet and overrun large chunks of the Wendira and Laian nations. They'd clearly come a long way in upgrading their bioforms with hyperdrives and missiles. Not much was going to stop them now.

"Incoming message," Litcha finally reported.

"TinyLife DivisionLordMorganCasimir, you speak hope, but your promises require faith and trust. You ask the Infinite to risk everything."

Morgan bit her lip.

"But the Infinite betrayed *your* faith once. We will extend ours in repayment now."

"All Infinite ships have ceased their pursuit," Ort suddenly exclaimed. "They're holding position."

"You have our permission to exit this nebula, TinyLife DivisionLordMorganCasimir," the Queen told her. "Your DeadFlesh may go with you. We will speak with your leaders...so long as *you* accompany them into this nebula.

"Any DeadFlesh that enters the Nebula without you will be destroyed. We will negotiate for peace, DivisionLordMorganCasimir, but we place our trust only in you.

"That must be enough for hope."

CHAPTER SIXTY-FOUR

EMERGING FROM HYPERSPACE INTO A SECTION OF SPACE THAT *wasn't* a nebula was a relief. Morgan could hear multiple members of her flag staff making assorted signs of relief.

"Ort, confirm the coordinates," Morgan ordered, burying her own desire to audibly sigh.

They'd stopped at one point inside the Astoroko Nebula, still under the guns of a Category Seven, to check in with Tohrohsail. Every fleet in the region was supposedly headed *here*, to combine into a single hammer for a spoiling attack on the Nebula.

From what Fleet Lord !Loka had told her, no one was expecting the attack to seize control of the nebula or defeat the Infinite, but it was intended to finish off Swarm Charlie before it could be reinforced.

But there was no one here.

"We are in the right place," Ort replied. "Hyperspace was...cooperative. We are about half a cycle ahead of our expectations." He paused. "The Ren *should* be here, but they had the farthest to come.

"The Wendira shouldn't be here yet. The Imperials and Laians *could* be here, but even normal hyperspace densities would have seen them arriving when we originally expected to," the ops officer told her.

"So, we wait," Morgan replied. "Everyone should be receiving a starcom message asking them to rendezvous with us before launching the attack anyway."

But there was no way for anyone to tell *her* that. She hadn't even been able to respond to Fleet Lord !Loka's answer to her message.

"I'll be in my office," she told her staff. "Notify me the moment we have any contacts."

She'd spent a good chunk of the trip there preparing messages to send to various people scattered through the Imperium—and a few Wendira and Laians, too.

Morgan wasn't entirely okay with the fact that she'd been recruited to a secret society, but she'd be *damned* if she wasn't going to pull that lever to try to make peace.

And her stepmother made for a hell of a lever all on her own.

"I BELIEVE the Queen when she says it was paranoia," Morgan told the recorder. She wasn't being as careful in her wording as she might have otherwise been. *This* message was for her parents. She might be asking them to bring their political artillery into the field for her, but they were still her parents.

"We've spent this entire fight acting to neutralize a threat we saw to the galaxy—and the Infinite have spent all this time acting to neutralize a threat they saw to their very existence. Our conspirators managed to burn any chance of a peaceful second contact."

Morgan sighed.

"I'm pretty sure some of those bastards are still alive," she noted. "The financiers and politicians behind that push for war so they could steal an Alavan fleet... If I find out who any of them are, they'd better watch their step in dark alleys.

"The Infinite bear their responsibility for what has happened.

There are millions of dead people, and the Infinite killed them," Morgan said. "But the bastards who panicked and shot at them bear some of the blood guilt too.

"I think...I believe...that I will be able to convince Tan!Shallegh and Voice Tidirok of the chance for peace," Morgan continued. "But I can't be certain. I've also sent a formal report to A!Shall, but..."

She sighed and shook her head.

"The Infinite are unique, Mom, Dad," she told them. "I have seen nothing like them before and I don't think I ever will again. Even the lobotomized version of their biotech the Alava had created in the cloner and the Great Mother was a pale shadow.

"I think we can work with them. I think they can do incredible things for us—and we can make it possible for them to live again. My best guess is that the Queen is a *hundred thousand years old*. Even if she spent half of that trapped in a stellar box, just think of what she has seen and what she knows.

"We need to talk to them. I need you to convince the Imperium of that."

She swallowed.

"You know I don't like asking for political favors," she told them. "I know damn well being your kid has helped propel my career even when it shouldn't have, but I've never *asked* for you to use your influence on my behalf.

"Today I am. If A!Shall and the Houses of Imperium decide that we need to try for peace, that's one of three powers in play already on my side. I *know* you have a voice there, out of proportion with anything a regular Duchy has.

"Please. Help me end this war before it's too late."

"DIVISION LORD, we have hyper portals opening." Ort's voice echoed around Morgan's plain office.

"Understood," she acknowledged, looking at the list of messages she'd put together. With a sigh, she sent them off to the hyperfold communicator.

It would take about twenty hours for the messages to reach a starcom. After that, their recipients would have them in minutes. Responses would reach her shortly after that—if anyone decided *to* respond.

"Any idea who we're looking at?" Morgan asked as she shut down her office system and rose.

Her office was one door away from the flag deck, allowing Ort to answer her question directly instead of via the intercom.

"I don't recognize the ships, so I'm guessing the Ren," he told her. "On the main display."

Information was populating around the icons of the new ships as they emerged into realspace. The lead units were mace-shaped capital ships, with four large "flanges" emerging from a cylindrical central hull—a central hull that was just over five kilometers long.

"Estimate lead units at one hundred twenty megatons," Ort noted. "Three types of escorts, weighing in at thirty, ten and four megatons."

"Those are Ren dreadnoughts, all right," Morgan agreed. The Ren had a similar escort breakdown to the Imperium as well, though the masses for a given type were *very* different with thirty-megaton "cruisers," ten-megaton "destroyers" and four-megaton escorts.

"Primary armament is a spinal heavy hyperspace projectile cannon for the dreadnoughts," she continued, reciting from memory. "Estimated range, one light-minute with an instantaneous delivery time."

She grimaced.

"That stuck in my memory," she admitted. "Don't remember much of the rest."

"Similar to the Laians," Ort said after a moment's hesitation. "Mix of hyperfold cannons and point-eight-five interface-drive missiles, with proton beams for short-range backup.

"If anyone knows how their hyperspace cannon works, they haven't duplicated it."

"I prefer HSMs," Morgan agreed. "Hail them and welcome them to the rendezvous point. Triple-check your files for proper etiquette. We don't have a lot of contact with the Ren."

As she understood, the Laians had helped the A!Tol Imperium set up an embassy with the Ren in the last few years, but contact was still limited.

"We'll be courteous, but I'm waiting on the First Fleet Lord before I talk to anyone in detail," Morgan concluded.

Even if the Ren had brought a hundred dreadnoughts, each easily capable of obliterating her fleet.

THE WENDIRA WERE NEXT, arriving roughly an hour after the Ren. Morgan had seen the reports, but it was still something of a shock to watch a fleet that should have been two hundred and fifty star hives and thousands of escorts arrive as thirty star hives and four hundred escorts.

The second surprise was Rin contacting her from Oxtashah's ship within minutes of the Battle Hive arriving.

She quickly returned to her office to take the hyperfold call, looking her lover's hologram up and down for signs that he was okay.

"What are you doing on a Wendira ship?" she asked. She paused. "It was their Dyson swarm, wasn't it?"

He paused in surprise.

"How did you know about that?" he replied. "All we've really told anyone is that the Wendira smashed Swarm Charlie and took heavy losses doing it."

"The Infinite showed me their data on it, as part of their argument that we were all Alavan slaves," Morgan said drily. "I figured you were involved. Are you okay?"

"I turned an entire star system into a single gun," Rin pointed out. "That's a bit against my normal ethos, but...yeah. I'm fine. Caught up on my sleep on our way here."

Then he caught up with what she'd said.

"Wait, the *Infinite* showed you their data on Skiefail?" he demanded. "You *talked to them?*"

"I did," she confirmed. "It was an interesting discussion in a lot of ways, and it ended with them letting us go." She shook her head. "We went in with starkillers, but even realizing that, they let us go."

Rin shook his head.

"I would...give a lot to have been in on that conversation," he admitted.

"They're prepared to consider peace, Rin," she told him. "I won't say this has *all* been a bunch of misunderstandings—it sure as hell hasn't been—but both we and they have been responding to perceived threats.

"If we can stop and talk out what we actually need, I think we can end this without any more bloodshed. And, well." She smiled. "There are dozens, if not more, of the Infinite who coexisted with the Alava.

"I don't think their perspective on the Alava will be detailed or even accurate, but an outside perspective on them could be fascinating for you."

"You have *no* idea," Rin said with a chuckle. "My god, there will be people building their entire careers on talking to the Infinite—*just* about the Alava.

"Tell me everything, love. If you can, that is?"

"You know Oxtashah better than I do now, I suspect," Morgan reminded him. "I may need you to help convince her to talk."

CHAPTER SIXTY-FIVE

By any reasonable logic, convincing the hundred-thousand-year-old living starship protecting her nest that peace was possible should have been the harder and more intimidating conversation.

But as Morgan watched the last Imperial ships join the immense globular formation made up of four nations' fleets, she was nervous. Everyone had agreed to let her speak, and the virtual conferencing gear in her office was calmly running self-checks around her.

Talking to the Queen, she'd only faced one set of misconceptions and one set of priorities. She doubted that the Infinite were *immune* to a desire for vengeance, but their position was brittle in many ways.

They were powerful and numerous, but Morgan suspected that even she had overestimated how quickly the Infinite could replenish their numbers. They had modified and upgraded themselves with stunning speed, but she suspected they hadn't birthed very many *new* bioforms in the months since the first encounter.

If the Infinite nest was destroyed, they were gone. There were no more of them left. Once broken, the Queen and her children were broken forever—where even if the entire four-nation combined fleet gathered around *Odysseus* was wiped out, another fleet could be assembled in a long-cycle at most.

A soft chirp from her computers told her that the conference software was ready. With a sigh and a hard swallow, Morgan put her game face on and activated the conference. An illusory space overtook her office, replacing the completely unadorned space with a stylized A!Tol military meeting room.

She was, as she'd expected, the first one there. The other four people she was meeting were fleet commanders and diplomats. They'd join the conference *exactly* on time.

Tan!Shallegh was the first, the A!Tol's holographic form materializing a full thousandth-cycle before the designated start time. His black eyes focused immediately on Morgan, and a flush of red pleasure flickered across his skin.

"It is good to see you alive, Division Lord Casimir," he told her. "I feared I was sending you to your death."

"So did I," Morgan admitted. "But we thought it needed to be done. Now...we may have another option, sir."

"So I understand," he said. "I will wait for you to brief us all. Better to only swim these waters once, I think."

His tentacles fluttered in an amused shrug.

"I've already heard from Duchess Bond and Empress A!Shall," he noted. "Even without their words, I trust your judgment, Division Lord. I will listen."

"Thank you, sir," she said softly.

Another figure flickered into existence around the table before they could say more, a vast, unfamiliar shape. No one would ever accuse a Ren of being small—and Morgan suspected the virtual conferencing software was shrinking Strike Master Koh-Stan to fit in the illusory space.

Koh-Stan was an eight-limbed behemoth, four meters long with a segmented armored body that would allow them to lift *any* of their legs to act as a tool-using arm. Each limb had its own set of eyes and its own mouth, creating a rather disturbing creature to human eyes—

an impression not helped by Koh-Stan themselves being a hot pink color with black stripes.

The chlorophyll equivalent on the Ren homeworld had *much* to answer for.

"Strike Master," Tan!Shallegh greeted the Ren fleet commander. "It is a pleasure to speak with you once more."

"Indeed," a rumbling, interlaced chorus of eight voices replied. "I look forward to Division Lord Casimir's briefing. If nothing else, more intelligence on our enemy is always valuable."

"I appreciate your open-mindedness, Strike Master," Morgan told them.

Any further conversation was interrupted by the arrival of the virtual forms of Voice Tidirok and Princess Oxtashah, and Morgan concealed a hard inhalation as she faced the quartet of beings who would decide whether anyone would speak to the Infinite before they went in shooting.

"Voice Tidirok, Princess Oxtashah," she greeted the two aliens she knew. "I appreciate all four of you making time for this. I understand that it is not really the position of a junior flag officer to have made some of the promises and suggestions I made, but I was the sentient there, speaking to the Infinite."

"An impressive qualification all on its own, Division Lord," Tidirok told her. "The Infinite have not spoken to anyone *else*, after all. Only issued orders to civilians, at most."

"I regard their *actions* as speech enough," Oxtashah observed. "But I am prepared to listen, Division Lord. Speak."

"Agreed," Tan!Shallegh said. "You have asked for this meeting, Casimir. We are prepared to listen to what you have learned. So speak."

Morgan nodded, swallowing as she looked down at the notes she'd written.

"As you all know, I was sent into the Astoroko Nebula to deliver a set of starkillers and hopefully destroy the Infinite nest there," she reminded them. "That mission failed in short order, I'm afraid.

"We forgot that our starkillers are derived from an attempt to duplicate the Alavan star drive," she told them. From the way Koh-Stan rippled, the Ren officer might not have even *known* that—but there was no point in concealing ancient history.

"Because of that, we doomed our own use of stealth fields," she said calmly. "The Infinite are clearly able to detect the Alavan star drive technology through any concealment we have available.

"However, they believed that meant we were being escorted by a squadron of Alavan ships," Morgan noted. "So, when they ambushed us, they targeted the starkillers first and destroyed them all. This focus allowed my task group to prevail in our first encounter with them, but we were all too aware of the overall strength of the Infinite.

"We evaded further contact as best as we could, but they were attempting to trap us. Eventually, however, the news of Swarm Charlie's defeat clearly reached the nebula, and those forces were redeployed."

She shook her head.

"This was also a trap," she admitted. "The Queen wished to contain a small force of our ships to interrogate them. My belief that we had a somewhat clear escape allowed her to succeed in this mission.

"Without the ability to escape the force of Category Seven bioforms the Queen had brought with her, I didn't see much alternative to responding to her queries," Morgan concluded.

"The Queen was under the impression that we, like the Mesharom and other species that shared space travel with the Alava, were Alavan slaves. She called them the 'Nest Burners,' which does suggest *why* the Alava and the Infinite were trying to exterminate each other before the Fall.

"While it took some doing to convince her that we *weren't* slaves and had been defending ourselves against *her* actions, she also brought up that on her second encounter with us, we'd opened fire without communicating."

Morgan grimaced.

"That encounter was with the conspirators who tried to start a war between the Wendira and the Laians, sirs," she told them. "They quite accidentally succeeded in starting a war after all—between the Infinite and *everyone*.

"Fortunately, the Infinite somehow recognized *me* as the person they'd first encountered...and recognized that they started shooting at me after I'd offered to communicate."

Morgan remembered those panicked moments all too vividly— especially the one where she'd ordered dozens of her crew killed to eject a failing antimatter core and allow her engineers to fix her hyper emitters.

That nightmare would not fade from her mind anytime soon, therapy or no therapy.

"Despite everything that has come between us, the Infinite recognize that they fired first," Morgan said quietly. "So, the Queen was prepared to make an offer. She will keep her bioforms inside the Astoroko Nebula for a time and is willing to talk. To negotiate a peace, and terms on which the Infinite could perhaps become valued neighbors.

"Do not forget that these beings lived alongside the Alava," Morgan said. "They have concepts and science and knowledge we have never even touched upon. They have communications that can leave hyperspace. A reactionless drive unlike anything we've seen, with its own advantages over the interface drive.

"They have sensors and mining systems and technology unimaginable to us," she told the officers. She didn't even mention that the Taljzi cloner had been based on Infinite biotech. She wasn't sure that could be duplicated without other parts of Alavan tech—or that duplicating it was remotely moral.

"They don't need the systems we live in and could, in fact, provide us with entirely new ways to access the resources of systems we've regarded as worthless. There are no resources we *need* to conflict over.

"The entire war has been over fear—their fear of dying out and our fear of the unknown. We need to step away from that fear," Morgan told the officers she needed to convince. "We need to look at the Infinite not with the eyes of yesterday and what we have lost but with the eyes of tomorrow and what we can gain."

She exhaled a long breath as she ran out of steam.

"I know all of you have orders that justify moving immediately against the Infinite," she said. "So, it falls to you to decide to wait. To wait for more information. To wait for confirmation that our governments *will* negotiate.

"Their only requirement has been that I accompany our first delegation," Morgan concluded. "I feel...I hope...that the chance of the future is worth the risk."

She laid her hands on her desk and waited.

The virtual conference was silent for a few seconds, then Tan!Shallegh snapped his beak in laughter.

"Of course, my colleagues, while we have swum the deep waters of hyperspace, my Division Lord has issued her report to the Imperium," he noted. "My Empress and the Houses are united as one: the Imperium wishes to speak with the Infinite.

"We will not abandon our allies or our sworn oaths, and we will stand with you all to defend your worlds, but we feel that an attempt must be made at peace."

Koh-Stan shifted, a rippling motion of eight shoulders and faces that sent atavistic shivers through Morgan's brain.

"We Ren have not yet lost blood or iron against the Infinite," they noted. "We will follow the desire of the Laians and the Wendira in this; it is our oaths to them that bring us here."

Morgan wasn't sure exactly how this conference was going to break down. Did everybody get a vote? In that case, the Imperium had just voted for peace and the Ren had recused themselves.

"I am the *Voice* of the Republic," Tidirok finally said after a few seconds of silence. "There is a reason that my juniors are the Swords and Spears and Pincers of the Republic, but that our most senior officers are our *Voices*. We do not speak only orders, and we are charged to *speak* before we kill.

"I will consult with my Parliament, but while I do not believe we must always choose peace, I *do* believe that we must always choose to talk before we choose war."

Every eye went to Oxtashah, and Morgan was suddenly grimly sure that unanimity was required.

"Two hundred star hives," the Princess said softly. "Over six hundred star shields and over twelve hundred escorts. Plus the losses in Tohrohsail and in the attempt to blockade them. Twenty million Wendira and Laian dead.

"Do we forget them? Do we allow their deaths to be for *nothing*?"

"We have killed sentients who have been the Infinite's brothers and leaders for fifty thousand years," Morgan said quietly. "The Queen has lost children who have been at her right hand for longer than *any* of our *civilizations* have existed, but she offers a chance at peace.

"Please, Princess Oxtashah. We cannot bring back the dead. But we can build a future where no one joins them."

The conference was silent, and Morgan focused her gaze on the Wendira Royal...and realized that Oxtashah had probably lost more than a cousin at Shokal. She was a Royal—and that meant she'd laid somewhere in the region of *twenty thousand* eggs before her career as a diplomat had begun.

Oxtashah had almost certainly lost children at Shokal, and while the Wendira Royals didn't have the same attachment to their children as other races with smaller families, there *was* a connection there.

"Like you, Princess, the Queen is mother to thousands," Morgan half-whispered. "She has seen hundreds of them die in this war and wants to save all that remain. Will you send more of *your* children to their death to kill hers?"

The silence that followed stretched tight. Morgan could feel the tension in the room as she watched the Wendira Princess...until suddenly, Oxtashah's wings snapped backward in a violent unconscious gesture.

"No," she finally answered Morgan's question. "I will not send more children to their deaths. The eyes of the past versus the eyes of tomorrow, as you say."

"Humans call it the 'sunk-cost fallacy,'" Morgan told her. "Continuing on a course of action because of what we've already spent and lost, rather than assessing whether it's worth spending more.

"It's as true for lost friends and shed blood as it is for money."

"So it is," Oxtashah agreed. "Very well, Morgan Casimir. I will travel to the Astoroko Nebula with you and we will make peace with this ancient leviathan."

She gestured around the room.

"I think it is within *all* of our power to end this war for our people," she declared. "So, I suggest we take one ship, with the five of us, into the heart of the hive."

The Wendira's multifaceted eyes now bore into Morgan's gaze—and Morgan's soul.

"I trust your Dr. Dunst," she told her. "And I know he would follow you into hell, Division Lord Casimir. So, lead on into that hell.

"I believe that *you* believe we will find peace there."

CHAPTER SIXTY-SIX

RIN DUNST HAD NOT BEEN ON EARTH IN OVER TEN YEARS. EVEN before that, he'd been born and spent almost his entire life in the northern hemisphere. That Hong Kong was covered in Christmas decorations in the middle of what was *clearly* summer was...disconcerting.

It wasn't the main source of his discomfort, though. When he'd landed at the spaceport, he'd been met by a very earnest human Imperial Marine with a summer suit in exactly his size. The young man had turned out to be his permanent escort and was driving the car as they headed into a district of luxury residential towers.

Slowly. Hong Kong traffic hadn't improved over the centuries.

"Lance, who exactly assigned you to me?" he asked the soldier. "I wasn't expecting an escort."

"Sir, you're a Category One asset," the Marine pointed out. "You are *supposed* to have a permanent detail, but according to the brief I received, the Institute and the Marines haven't sorted that out yet."

"Huh." Rin stared out the window at the streets of Hong Kong. Even though—or perhaps *because*—it was Christmas Eve, the city was busy. Sidewalks were full of people, only about three-quarters of them *human*, cheerfully yelling and making their way around.

"We'll have you to your appointment in no time, sir," the Marine told Rin. "I'm coordinating with the Division Lord's detail."

"I supposed Morgan *would* have one of those," Rin admitted.

"Most flag officers do, sir," the noncom said. "And, of course, Division Lord Casimir is currently the center of everyone's attention. She *did* end a war."

Rin chuckled.

"Even if she thinks everyone else involved should get the credit," he murmured. "Typical."

"I can't speak to that, sir," the Marine said. "We *should* be at the Tower already, but, well..." He gestured out the front window at the barely moving traffic.

"I imagine everyone else is being equally delayed," Rin told the other man. A twinge of discomfort ran through him as he considered who the rest of said *everyone else* was.

"Captain Antonova's detail reports that she and Mrs. Antonova are equally delayed," the noncom confirmed. "Division Lord Casimir is on site. Speaking with her sisters, I believe."

The thought of meeting Morgan Casimir's sisters did *not* help with Rin's comfort. He'd traded a few messages with the twins, Leah and Carol Bond, but he hadn't encountered Morgan's younger sisters.

The twins had a reputation in scholarly and political circles. Both held PhDs—Leah in political science, Carol in economics—from top-tier Imperial universities. Leah was the heir to the Duchy of Terra, and Carol was rarely far away from her sister.

Combined, they were their mother's hatchet women—and multiple planetary leaders had ended up bruised and confused after assuming the pair of mid-twenties blondes were innocent, naïve or inexperienced.

"All of the Bonds are on site, according to the Militia details," Rin's escort told him. "That should make this easier, yes?"

Rin snorted.

"Not what I want to hear when meeting my girlfriend's parents for the first time," he told the Marine. "How many *other* people is the Duchess's detail coordinating arrivals for?"

The driver chuckled.

"Including Captain Antonova and her wife, seven," he noted. "And from the rumors that swirl around, *Megan* Bond is single, so I can't even math it."

Rin snorted. Somehow, the realization that he wasn't going to be part of the *only* polycule at Christmas Eve dinner was reassuring.

RIN BEAT Victoria and Shelly Antonova to Pegasus Tower—known for thirty years now as the residence of the family of the Duchess of Terra, who had been slowly taking over more and more floors over those years—by about five minutes.

Morgan saw him enter the marble-clad lobby from across the room and immediately abandoned the pair of taller platinum-blonde women she'd been speaking with. The gazes of a dozen guards followed the Division Lord across the lobby as she jogged over to embrace him.

"Damn, it's good to see you," she told him. "Been too long."

"*I* didn't get called back to the Houses to give briefings on Infinite psychology and the likelihood they'd keep the peace," he pointed out.

"No, you just spent a full long-cycle interrogating a brain the size of a planet about their worst enemies," his lover told him—and then kissed him *thoroughly* to keep him from responding. "Anything interesting in that?"

"A lot," he admitted. "Their perspective on *everything* is fascinating. The Infinite are going to make for intriguing partners."

"Yeah, we're talking about recruiting Cat-One bioforms to act as sentient shipboard communicators," Morgan told him. "We'll need to trust them a lot more than we do yet before we go that far, but it's on the Navy's mind."

"I'm glad you got people to talk to them," Rin said. "We'd have lost so much if we'd destroyed them. Or they'd destroyed us, but that seems more obvious."

"They could easily have killed either or both of us," she agreed. "But...we're home now. We made peace."

"Doesn't seem to have hurt you," Rin murmured. "No extra medals, though."

"Making peace generally doesn't get you medals," Morgan said. "Just warm, fuzzy feelings and a lot of attention that should have gone to others."

"Sir, Captain Antonova's car is arriving," a Marine interrupted.

"Good. We're still waiting on Carol's boyfriends, but I think I can take my cluster upstairs once the Antonovas are here," Morgan told the guard.

"Is this as complicated and messy as it feels?" Rin asked.

"Naw," Morgan told him. "This is just family...made a *bit* messier by bodyguards."

Yet another tall blonde woman entered through the front lobby, with a short and heavyset dark-haired woman in tow. Two Duchy of Terra Militia security officers accompanied Victoria and Shelly Antonova as they entered.

Rin allowed Morgan to drag him over to the other half of their polycule, standing slightly to one side as Morgan and Victoria kissed. They were delighted to see each other, which certainly helped smooth over his momentary confusion.

He'd accepted the polygamous relationship long before, but it was still strange to be there with his girlfriend's girlfriend—*and* said girlfriend's wife.

He offered a hand to Shelly Antonova.

"Rin Dunst," he introduced himself. "Imperial Institute of Archaeology."

"Shelly Antonova," the other woman replied. "I've read a couple of your papers, Dr. Dunst. Adjacent to my area of expertise but still valuable."

"Oh?" he asked. "You're an academic?"

"Xenopsychologist," Mrs. Antonova told him. "I work with the integration of multispecies populations, like the Laian Exiles in the Australian Outback. Some of your archaeological work on historic and prehistoric multispecies sites has been fascinatingly useful."

Their conversation was interrupted by a clearly coordinated attack, as Morgan wrapped an arm around Rin and Victoria wrapped an arm around Shelly—with the two of them keeping an arm around each other as well.

"I'm not honestly sure why I'm here," Shelly Antonova admitted quietly. "This isn't quite..."

"Because you are family," Morgan told her. "And Mom insisted. We're celebrating Christmas and family. Everyone needs to be here."

"Five kids and what, eight partners?" Rin asked.

"Yeah, Carol has two boyfriends, and Alexis has a matching boy-girl set of Marines," Morgan concluded with a grin. "So, we bring everyone together and we have Christmas."

"Seems appropriate," Rin told them all with a chuckle as Morgan directed them toward the elevator. "Christmas is a good time to celebrate peace, isn't it?"

AUTHOR'S NOTE

And that makes nine.

Nine novels of the Duchy of Terra, pretty much exactly half-and-half Annette and Morgan, all things considered. (Or, I don't know, forty-five, forty-five, ten, with the ten being everybody else?)

And nine makes a wrap. There are always stories and possibilities inherent in every setting, and I'll never say never, but this is the end of the Bonds' stories in this universe.

I'm glad you stuck with me and Annette and Morgan all this way!

If you're looking for more books of a similar ilk, with aliens and politics and starships, I humbly suggest checking out the Peacekeepers of Sol series that I started in 2019. Three books are out already, and more are coming.

You can find my full catalog at www.glynnstewart.com, where I'm confident that if you've made it this far, you'll find more work you can enjoy!

Happy reading!

—Glynn Stewart

JOIN THE MAILING LIST

Love Glynn Stewart's books? Join the mailing list at

GLYNNSTEWART.COM/MAILING-LIST/

to know as soon as new books are released, special announcements, and a chance to win free paperbacks.

ABOUT THE AUTHOR

Glynn Stewart is the author of *Starship's Mage*, a bestselling science fiction and fantasy series where faster-than-light travel is possible– but only because of magic. His other works include science fiction series *Duchy of Terra, Castle Federation* and *Exile,* as well as the urban fantasy series *ONSET* and *Changeling Blood.*

Writing managed to liberate Glynn from a bleak future as an accountant. With his personality and hope for a high-tech future intact, he lives in Kitchener, Ontario with his partner, their cats, and an unstoppable writing habit.

VISIT GLYNNSTEWART.COM FOR NEW RELEASE UPDATES

CREDITS

The following people were involved in making this book:
  Copyeditor: Richard Shealy
  Proofreader: M Parker Editing
  Cover art: Tom Edwards
  Faolan's Pen Publishing team: Jack, Kate, and Robin.

 facebook.com/glynnstewartauthor

OTHER BOOKS
BY GLYNN STEWART

For release announcements join the
mailing list or visit **GlynnStewart.com**

STARSHIP'S MAGE
Starship's Mage
Hand of Mars
Voice of Mars
Alien Arcana
Judgment of Mars
UnArcana Stars
Sword of Mars
Mountain of Mars
The Service of Mars
A Darker Magic
Mage-Commander (upcoming)

Starship's Mage: Red Falcon
Interstellar Mage
Mage-Provocateur
Agents of Mars

Pulsar Race: A Starship's Mage Universe Novella

DUCHY OF TERRA
The Terran Privateer
Duchess of Terra
Terra and Imperium
Darkness Beyond
Shield of Terra
Imperium Defiant
Relics of Eternity
Shadows of the Fall
Eyes of Tomorrow

SCATTERED STARS
Scattered Stars: Conviction
Conviction
Deception
Equilibrium
Fortitude (upcoming)

PEACEKEEPERS OF SOL
Raven's Peace
The Peacekeeper Initiative
Raven's Course
Drifter's Folly (upcoming)

EXILE
Exile
Refuge
Crusade
Ashen Stars: An Exile Novella

CASTLE FEDERATION
Space Carrier Avalon
Stellar Fox
Battle Group Avalon
Q-Ship Chameleon
Rimward Stars
Operation Medusa
A Question of Faith: A Castle Federation Novella

SCIENCE FICTION STAND ALONE NOVELLA
Excalibur Lost

VIGILANTE
(WITH TERRY MIXON)
Heart of Vengeance
Oath of Vengeance

Bound By Stars: A Vigilante Series
(With Terry Mixon)
Bound By Law
Bound by Honor
Bound by Blood

TEER AND KARD
Wardtown
Blood Ward

CHANGELING BLOOD
Changeling's Fealty
Hunter's Oath
Noble's Honor
Fae, Flames & Fedoras: A Changeling Blood Novella

ONSET
ONSET: To Serve and Protect
ONSET: My Enemy's Enemy
ONSET: Blood of the Innocent
ONSET: Stay of Execution
Murder by Magic: An ONSET Novella

FANTASY STAND ALONE NOVELS
Children of Prophecy
City in the Sky

Made in the USA
Middletown, DE
16 May 2021